Higher Math

HIGHER MATH

$$= \neq = \neq = \neq = \neq = \neq = \neq = \neq = \neq = \neq = \neq = \neq = \neq =$$

THE BOOK MOOSE MINNION
NEVER WROTE

*A Novel
by Jennifer Ball*

EDITORS:
Jennifer M. V. Ball
Nardi Carnell
Joan Carsley
Dr. K. L. Louwitsky, Ph.D.
H. Mertice Welsch

ff Faber and Faber

BOSTON • LONDON

First published in the United States by Faber and Faber, Inc., 50 Cross Street, Winchester, MA 01890.

Library of Congress Cataloging-in-Publication Data
Ball, Jennifer.
    Higher Math : the book Moose Minnion never wrote : a novel / by Jennifer Ball.
        p. cm.
    ISBN 0–571–12933–1 (cloth) : $19.95
    I. Title.
PS3552.A4548H54 1990
813'.54—dc20   91–18822
                                                                                  CIP

This is a work of fiction. All characters are products of the author's imagination. The author's use of names of actual persons, living or dead, is incidental to the purposes of the plot and is not intended to change the fictional nature of the work.

Cover design by Mary Maurer

Printed in the United States of America

To my extremely tolerant husband
and my exceptionally hungry pig.

Foreword

She so wanted to write this book. Sadly, it must now be presented *preposthumously*. Though not yet deceased, Marissa "Moose" Minnion lies on her death bed in the Corinthian wing of Pasadena's Huntington Hospital (coincidentally her birthplace). It was just over a year ago that Moose fell into anaphylactic shock after suffering an allergic reaction to Brazil nuts. (She was sensitive to anything South American.) While eating a Chinese chicken salad in a fashionable Westwood, California, restaurant, she lapsed into a coma and has remained in this somnolent state ever since, preserved on a life-support system.

We present her book to you as she would have wanted it, with whimsy and with charm. This is an embodiment of a life well lived, a celluloid documentary guised as a novel. Her observations are not glib, facile bits of sensationalism; rather, they are hauntingly truthful accounts of one who let nothing go undocumented. Most will believe her to be a piece of fiction, but we guarantee her to be (have been) most real. Her tale is derived from diaries, journals, scraps of writing found in her sewing box, jottings on napkins, remnants of letters, entries on her computer, and, primarily, theories and reflections garnered from a multitude of notebooks, which she kept in the style of her heroine, Harriet M. Welsch from Louise Fitzhugh's book, *Harriet the Spy*.

To retain the integrity of her writing we have left it as she wrote it, spelling errors, random chronology, and all. However, we have also included many footnotes—initialed due to some discrepancy among ourselves as to what is fact and what fiction. Much of our research and interpretation differs and we've chosen to preserve it all in order to explain to the reader particular references to her life, acquaintances, "in" jokes, and philosophies. We tried to keep our comments to a minimum, however, letting the work speak for itself.

We hope you find Moose adroit, amusing, baffling, challenging, compelling, fun, glib, "*joie de vivre*-esque," punny, quixotic, rum (as in the English meaning), sincere, twisted, visceral, and zeugmatic.[1]

We do.

The Editors

Jennifer M. V. Ball
Nardi Carnell
Joan Carsley
Dr. K. L. Louwitsky, Ph.D.
H. Mertice Welsch

---

1. She enriched our lives and our bread. (She worked a while for Wonder.) JMVB

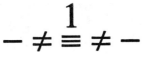

From the desk of Jennifer M. V. Ball:

I met Moose in college. More people called her Marissa then. Moose was a name she acquired from a boyfriend. He thought that when she flared her nostrils that's what she most resembled. She maintained that she never flared her nostrils, that it was a conspiracy fanned by her friends to make her think she did. Moose once told me that another romantic interest allowed that her nose looked like a two-car garage. She shared unusual relationships with men.

Compiling Moose's work has been difficult because many of her thoughts deserve a page of their own. Almost every sentence she wrote has a density of meaning, the poetic quality found in word conservation. Her ideas need to be surrounded by white space, framed by the perimeters of the page so that the mind can digest them without gluttony. These are not Twinkies in the world of fast food thought, but, instead, one forkful of charred lobster at a Maine fish fry, a melting spoonful of almond tortoni savored by candlelight in a N'Orleans bordello. One desires to indulge, but slowly, languorously; to indulge with no thought but the taste of the words upon the tongue, luxuriating in the "happy synapses" they create in one's brain. Her work demands that you put aside such pedestrian thoughts as:

"What's for dinner?"
"Did I turn the iron off when I left the house?"
"Is Bakersfield to the right or left of Fresno?"

Drift a moment before you begin. Set your mind to "Receptive." Pause. Breathe deeply. Commence.

I think of life in phrases, fragments, bits of egg shell: off-white and slightly salty. Life as ocean spray or gold doubloons—scarce, precious, and not easily counterfeited. I know not what I say, I just say it. Life sans plot, meaning, or the correct time. Life as art. Life as artifice. Life as Art Carney.

Moose Minnion
Santorini, Greece
May 14, 1984

Montana

The best thing about Montana is this place in Idaho.

This place in Idaho where the eve before New Year's Eve I tried to forget that every major relationship of mine always ends in torment (my own) and that generally I have to travel long distances to find this out.

In such a state of despondence I was easily persuaded by two strangers of varying degree to hike a mile in the snow on a moonlit night to these somewhat legendary hot springs. One of the strangers I'd known for three weeks and now thought of as a friend. I'd met her because I wanted to go to this after-Christmas party in Montana. It was 1979 and I still didn't own a car—an oddity in Los Angeles. I relied on public transportation and the kindness of strangers. There on the UCLA ride board was a person looking for a rider to Missoula, Montana, during the Christmas season. I'd been sick and was in my grandmother's nightgown making bread dough sculpture when she came over. She found me odd, but Prudence liked odd. She invited me to a party she was having a week later and there I remember meeting an English guy with one eye who was very rude to me. I think he was flirting.

On our way to Montana we stopped by my family's house for Christmas and my mother, mother that she is, made sure that Pru had several presents to keep her occupied so that she wouldn't feel unloved. (My mother was a great believer in love.)

The morning we left my parents' house we saw a double rainbow. My only other sighting of a double rainbow had been the summer before in Montana. It was a time in my life when I took these things as signs of something.

We went in Isadora. (Her car. Prudence named her car. That kind of thing reads "girl" all over it.) We talked, as two will do on long car rides: Overeaters Anonymous, anorexia nervosa, crazy mothers. She told me that she once spent three months in a mental hospital with anorexia and painted. I told her my mother once pointed a gun at me. We felt very close by the time we got to Montana.

Prudence was traveling north to meet a love interest. I was going for the same reason, but tried to pretend instead that I was going for the party. One travels long distances not solely for large gatherings, but for something more intangible. I have always gone out on a limb for love. A dangerous, romantic, disappointing way to live.

We met Prudence's disappointment first. He was nervous. I find men always want you to come visit and then as soon as you arrive they get cold feet, frigid and perfunctory, the fact that you came devaluing your appeal to them.

He lived in a basement apartment that would have been charmingly impoverished had there been two of you and one of you an artist. However, he lived alone and worked in a bookstore. All the requisites of living in a hovel were there: a hot plate, toilet paper hung on a coat hanger, windows smeared over with paint the color of mud, odd little holes in the floorboards which you knew didn't get there from someone's razor-sharp high heels, and a shower that smelled faintly of sulfur and prune juice. It reminded me of my grandmother's house.

Kendall (that was his name) was largely thin, gangling, and rangy, appearing the socialist bohemian. I think he tried to make Marxist statements, but I'm not completely sure, having read little Marx. Perhaps I've added the Communist twist to his personality in retrospect. It went well with his physique.

I remember that while we were in a Mexican restaurant he told us he was having a flashback from LSD. Did he mention something about elephants? I forget. I thought at the time that his flashback seemed fairly mild, from all I had heard about them. Having since experienced LSD myself, I now realize that one has the feeling of flashbacks but not really the flashbacks themselves: fleeting moments of a remembrance of glitter, the ground sparkling with jewels, spiderwebs, neo-Romantic typefaces; suddenly something before you turns into something else; you rub your eyes and peer again. It's ghost flashbacks that the average person recalls, rather than anything so harrowing as reexperiencing the LSD. Kendall's flashbacks were, I think, more of a way to draw attention to himself as they didn't appear to hamper his progress on the rest of Prudence's chimichanga.

I left Pru with this lanky, bolshevikish intellectual and went to stay with Husk, a curly-haired, six-foot-plus, hefty Montana-grown trumpet player. (He'd gotten the name "Husk" because he was big and shaggy like a Husky.) I had met Husk in Bigfork summer stock the previous year. He was in the orchestra, I was an actress. It was the summer that I played blackface. (They couldn't get any black actors to come to Montana because of the "Three Black Rule" and they'd already purchased the rights to *Showboat*.)[1] Husk called me "Sticky Biscuits" because I was always making biscuits in the show. He would

---

1. Moose always joked that Montana had a "Three Black Rule" which specified that black families had to live in border towns. This was because when black tourists drove through Montana, the border families would have to temporarily move into another state, so the number of blacks remaining in Montana would never exceed three. JMVB

call me this loudly, and then purposefully laugh through his nose when he did. I was the kind of girl that was charmed by this sort of behavior.

As the end of the summer approached, we knew it was also the end of our romance, but we were still friends. It's the kind of situation where you hope the other wants to keep in touch, but pride prevents you from saying as much. As time passed, I found that I missed Husk. I wrote him in November and he wrote back, inviting me up for the after-Christmas party.

I had arranged to meet him at the restaurant where he worked making Caesar salads at people's tables. Prudence dropped me off and I felt slightly panicked at seeing her and Isadora drive away. Something told me that things wouldn't be the same. When I walked into the restaurant, Husk seemed fairly unexcited to see me. Rude even. I was hurt; I wondered when I would ever learn. I considered going back to stay with Prudence and Kendall, but I'm proud. I didn't want anyone to know that I'd come all this way and for no better reason than love.

Husk and I were to drive up to Bigfork (where the party was to be held) the next day. I don't now remember where I stayed the night, if it was a single bed, if we ate dinner, what we said. It's all gone. Sometimes I feel so sad for memories irretrievable. A sign of age, I suppose. Of your body weeding out destructive or unproductive thoughts. Of housecleaning, packaging, removing pain to one's innermost regions, regions cordoned off, obscured, hung with tapestries so that you would never know that what lay behind them was an opening to your sorriest self. It's a brave thing for a body to do. It means well. But those thoughts don't go away. They are there; they are radioactive. A probe could find them. Even a simple sniff of what was served for lunch in grade school could locate them. And returning to my old haunts can cause an avalanche of memories to tumble down, paralyzing me. So I must get to them first. I pull them out one by one, relive the pain in small doses, like drinking hemlock to make you immune to your enemies. But often one's only enemy is one's alacrity to love. How do you immunize yourself to that?

My method is to build up resistance by jarring the memories loose, confining them to this page, but I fear that what falls out is hypothesis or conjecture. I can see Montana before me, but the events I remember seem scripted. The four summers I spent there run together like a bad watercolor. I can only recall the huge expanse of Lake Flathead, the wooded, winding drive around the lake past Yellow Bay, Blue Bay—the whole stretch of road concatenating distant memories of boyfriends, water-skiing, and too many varicolored drinks (my cousin drank several lethal blue ones called "Windex" and threw up all night).

There was the dirt road that ran by the river where we (the actors of the Bigfork Playhouse) would run daily, the healthiest time of our lives. Nature made us want to live up to its expectations . . . and fornicate in the most unlikely and beautiful spots: on a flat rock overlooking (though we never looked) Flathead at four in the morning as it lightly rained, on a blanket in a copse by a quiet brook, *in* the quiet brook.

These times were not with Husk. Husk and I only made love in the lean-to that ran adjacent to Ian's trailer. (Ian and Husk were best friends then. They baited gophers together to make extra cash. They wore shirts that read "Master Baiters.") Love with Husk was not unpleasant, but I know more about love now, both in its ephemeral sense and in the nitty-grittyness of intercourse. What we did was the closest stand-in to love that we had, as myth is a stand-in for hard science in cultures advanced enough to want to explain phenomena, but primitive enough not to know how to go about it. We didn't know how to go about love. We tried not to be hurtful because we liked each other a lot. We had a lot of fun because our primary interest was laughing. But real life often gets in the way of fun. Husk had another girlfriend two hours away in Missoula the summer that he and I spent together in Bigfork. He confessed to me that she was less fun than I. She was too serious, wanting to dictate his lifestyle. She never laughed at his jokes. Men are raised more blithely than women. I wonder what exactly it is that society does to women, because a lot of women are not much fun. They are controlling, afraid of having no control; they are *mothering* and *smothering* —no coincidence there. But it's a two-way street. There's something in many men that makes women want to control them. There's something in many men that wants to be controlled.

I didn't want to control Husk, but I wanted to be able to count on him. I wanted, as we drove toward Bigfork in his car the color of military green, the car that always had to be parked facing downhill in order to get it to start, for him not to drink a six-pack and drive erratically and talk viciously about people who had been our friends. Some sort of control was needed, but I didn't want to control him; I wanted him to control himself.

As Husk whipped around curves toward Bigfork, he noncommittally asked me how things were going. Impulsively I told him that I was going to marry an Iranian. I knew better than to tell him, but when something is on my mind, out it comes. I never keep my own secrets. Husk asked, grimacing, "Why are you going to marry an Iranian?" He took another swig of beer and turned a corner while I held tightly to the dashboard.

I explained to him fully about Hamid's uncle being killed, about Hamid going back to Iran and being thrown in jail for several months, about my father's relationship to Hamid (he was my father's teaching assistant and spent holidays with our family). I explained about marriage not meaning that much to me and that saving lives seemed a loftier consideration than worrying about the taint of divorce. (I wasn't going to remain married to Hamid; it was only to prevent him from being deported.)

There was a pause in the car. I waited.

Husk asked again as if I had said nothing, "*So* . . . why are you going to marry an Iranian?"

Fortunately, I didn't actually have to marry Hamid. Had I done so, I would have discovered the futility of such grandiose gestures. I am more selfish now. And when it comes down to it, such sacrifices are often hinged upon the sacrificee's whims. Hamid seemingly desired convenience more than his life – or perhaps his life was never really in jeopardy. My conditions for marrying were that he move to L.A. so that I could continue going to school. He wanted to stay in Sacramento where he was finishing college and was in line for a government job. Sacramento was just too close to my parents' house. Sacramento would have been death for me. It is too provincial, too boring. There's no beach in Sacramento.

Hamid ended up finding another woman (a student of my father's) to marry. She married him for the more traditional reasons. I even went to the wedding with my sister and cousin: "formidable womanhood incarnate." We are all good looking when we want to be, and Theresa and Darlene are five-nine and five-ten respectively. I think the bride felt a little overwhelmed, especially because she knew that Hamid and I had had an earlier arrangement. She was too conventional to understand the reasons.

Theresa, Darlene, and I actually came too late for the wedding but made the reception; it was held in the garage – or rather that's where all the food was: a sumptuous spread of luncheon meats (Oscar Mayer bologna, cotto salami, pimento loaf), the ubiquitous potato salad, heat-and-serve rolls, and the most delightful thing all day came in the form of a rotund woman who, poised in her bridesmaid dress upon the Westinghouse dryer, ladled out Chef-Boy-R-Dee ravioli to the unfortunate guests forced to squeeze by her in order to get out into the fresh air. (The garage had a bit of a doggy smell.)

I thank God that I never married Hamid. It would have been an exceedingly cute decision turned ugly. At the immigration office we would have had to lie about our brand of toothpaste. It would have been an unfunny version of "The Newlywed Game" and "The Newlywed Game" isn't funny.

I wish I had known the outcome then, that Christmas, as we barreled our way toward Bigfork. I wish I could have told Husk that I never actually married

Hamid. In my youthful innocence, in my misunderstanding of the male ego, I didn't think it would bother Husk, seeing as how we had no intention of marrying. But a sexual relationship, no matter if only for the summer, no matter how lighthearted, does something to both men and women. There are ties, if very loose and somewhat illusory. I find that men are often the more sappy about old flames, the more romantic, the more bruised. I see a correlation between this attraction and the time span of radioactive materials: the Half-Life Theory of Romance. Men are more affected by romance because they fight it for so long. They pretend they aren't in love, or even in any fraction of love, because they are taught to be tough and impenetrable. Women, however, can get involved very quickly and, when it is all over, can disinvolve themselves just as rapidly. We cry and then we continue. Men deny involvement until, WHAMO, suddenly they are INVOLVED. When a relationship is over, the man, having finally let down his guard, having finally admitted that he is, in fact, in love, is now at a loss for what to do with himself. If the relationship was for x amount of time, after $2x$ the male (we'll call him A) will still think of the female (B) fifty percent of the time. Four x reduces A's thoughts to twenty-five percent of the time. And no matter how much time passes, A will always have wistful thoughts of B hanging around the back of his mind. A male friend admitted once that when you get a lot of drunk men together they all commiserate over old girlfriends – the ones who dumped them. Men are easily nostalgic. But if they could have all those old girlfriends back, they'd lose them all over again.

I believe there is a logical reason behind this difference between men and women. Women have many changes occurring in their bodies. Changes which alter weight, appetite, mood, and temperament. Though you might fight such changes at first, ultimately you realize that you are going to be different people at different times. You adjust. Women live life adjusting. They may not do it quietly; indeed, I believe women are so very verbal because it is a way of monitoring those changes, of reconciling inner reality with outer reality. And they may not necessarily do it easily, which is why women are such effective manipulators. They adjust, but with vengeance. Powerlessness in some creates cleverness. Seemingly passive women can be the most powerful manipulators because they are so very subtle. No one expects it of them.

Men, on the other hand, deal more simply. They've proven their cleverness in all the sciences and math and things which follow patterns, but human relationships tend to throw them. Even Freud, brilliant though he was, didn't realize that women weren't so interested in having their own penises, they merely wanted to borrow them. Freud thought women longed to be men, but women only long to *live* like them.

And so Husk, not in love with me but feeling those elusive bonds, knowing that he did care about me but not able to give that care a place or a name, turned tough and bold. Mocking and strident, he told jokes that had no relationship to our conversation, though occasionally taunting me about how foreigners smell. And I, unused to people caring about me, didn't realize that somehow I'd hurt him, didn't realize that in all his parodies, in his Irish spoofs of "manly men," that he sometimes spoofed himself; that he was, perhaps, in his most manly moments, more vulnerable than I.

I wonder if he knows now that I never married Hamid. I ache to go back in time – a compassionate person now, no doubt due to more years and less energy – and tell him. Perhaps it would have eased his mind. Perhaps he would have laughed. Perhaps he wouldn't have poured the beer on the cop.

It was the tequila. I'm pretty sure. The tequila, and possibly my impending marriage. I think the tequila more the culprit, however, because it usually is. One time during the previous summer, we went to a big out-of-doors party with a band; the kind of rustic, dancing party they have in Montana where everyone gets and uses terms like "shit-faced." Husk drank so much tequila that night that we had to stop on the way home so he could throw up in front of the fire department. He had been somewhat abusive at the party, but after relieving himself he became quite docile. In a book it would be evident that this was foreshadowing. Sadly, in life you never know that these events are significant, that you will be called upon to reevaluate their portent.

I was reevaluating a lot of things as we pulled into Bigfork, driving down the two streets which encompass the downtown area of this thriving metropolis of five hundred. The fact that the town has five bars, one per every hundred people, was a point I liked to bring up when talking about Montana. It demonstrated that their priorities were, if unhealthy, not without conviction. One can't cast aspersions until one has given a winter of one's life in Montana.

Husk drove us out to Ian's mobile home. It overlooked an orchard. There was very little snow, but enough to make the apple trees look fairylike. Land, with a faint dusting of powder, spread out in all directions. Montana is a place you long to live forever in – until you live there in the winter, and then you long to get out, if just to have an income. Oh, the lucky few who have real jobs there – not jobs that last the summer and require only that you sing on key and dance a little, but jobs that can support you, monetarily and emotionally, jobs that make enough money so that you can fly somewhere warm after Christmas.

Ian had a job in Montana. He taught mentally retarded children. These children came from Bigfork and the surrounding area. To my mind, an area as sparsely populated as northwestern Montana that can still justify the hiring of several persons trained in the teaching of the mentally retarded suggests a high percentage of inbreeding. But at least it gave Ian a job.

Husk had lived all of the previous summer in Ian's trailer. I had lived half of it there. The lean-to where Husk and I slept was occasionally cold in the summer, but nothing like it was now. When I awoke the next morning Husk was still asleep, so I ran from the bed to the trailer mentally willing that Ian had already made wild huckleberry sourdough pancakes for breakfast. When I'm low it seems that food is my compensation. Sometimes the only way I can get up in the morning is to search in my mind for that one sweet thing in the kitchen that will get me out of bed. I think of breakfast as life's apology for morning. And alcohol covers the rest of the day.

There was a female clarinet player in summer stock who lived with her family on a small farm near Bigfork. Husk and I went to the farm once and picked corn and onions and potatoes and zucchini and wild raspberries, and later had a raspberry daiquiri party where I danced on the stove. I think Cotton was the one who made the daiquiris. Cotton was a great cook. She was going to write a cookbook, she told me that winter. I don't know that she ever did. It was going to have recipes like: Who's Afraid of Virginia Ham? Waiting for Goulash . . . that kind of thing. Cotton was the costumer for the Bigfork Summer Theater and had been for years. As actors we all had to put in time sewing costumes and building sets. In the costume shop conversation often ran from theology (the summer we had two ex-priests in the company) to edible underwear. I remember telling the ex-priests that I didn't actually believe there was a God, I believed in the Fairies—a kind of corporate God. They found this rather funny.

See, I figure that a God composed of several entities could go a long way in explaining why God appears to be so bumbling, as any decision-making team has the potential of being. Certainly basic good is accomplished, but with a fair amount of wars, race riots, slavery, and fine Egyptian women being entombed just because their royal husbands had short lifelines. And then there's the Slaughter of the Innocents—you know, where all these parents devised a way to lessen the number of mouths to feed by sending their children on a religious pilgrimage. Of course brutal marauders descended upon all these children going to see God. And I suppose the children even saw God. (Life humors itself by being ironic.) I suspect the parents were also aware that if marauders were out there trailing the kids they'd be less likely to wreak havoc at home. People have a way of justifying their decisions by purporting to act upon another's behalf.

{ *18* }

I choose to call this rather inept corporate-God-entity "the Fairies" because it strikes me as a much friendlier name. I like to believe in the Fairies as opposed to a solitary God because, theoretically, if one of them didn't like you, there's still a host of others. With God, it's all or nothing. If He's got it in for you there's no appealing to a higher power. Plus there's the fact that everyone's praying to God, and no one's praying to the Fairies. I'd rather pray to someone who's going to listen, even if they don't exist. As T. Rex[2] says, "The minor deities always are the better bet. Like Avis, they try harder." Every way you look at it, it makes sense. I figure as long as one is going to believe in myths, base one's decisions on faith, and generally run one's life on something no one has ever succeeded in proving, then why not make it fun? If you are going to pick a Supreme Being, pick one with a magic wand and a filmy dress. And if these Supreme Beings prove ineffectual in solving your problems, as they probably will, chalk it up to tests of one's merit rather than their incompetence. Even if it isn't true, it's certainly a more positive way to look at it. One doesn't like to feel one is worshiping second-rate deities even if one is.

Little incidents happen in my life which make me think that second-rate deities are all we deserve. Our usual inability to recognize good fortune precludes our benefiting from a really competent god. A while ago I saw this derelict searching in coin returns for change. He was at one end of a long row of newspaper machines. There were at least thirty of them lined up in front of a Safeway. He was shabbily dressed and obviously out of his mind. My heart leaped inside my chest as it is wont to do around my period, causing me to be sentimental about all sorts of things, especially those Pacific Bell commercials where some loved one calls another. I am a magnet for emotions at these times. Like iron filings they collect on me, especially around my eyes, causing me to weep. I have a soft spot for bag people, for children lost in the toy department, for sickly plants that the caterpillars have succeeded in devouring despite my unrestrained use of insecticide. And so, in this weakened and delusional state, I grabbed a handful of change at the bottom of my purse, stuck it in the coin return of a Coke machine which sat midway along this row, and then watched from a distance as the derelict drunkenly weaved from one machine to another, shaking them, cursing them, and singing mad songs to them. He went from the newspaper machines to the Bucking Bronco machine (where children get a taste of the Old West for a quarter a minute); he hit ten machines in a row with no success, and as I watched him approach My Coke Machine, my granter of good fortune, I felt like God watching as one of His wayward was about to be re-

---

2. *Another* one of Miss Minnion's summer stock boyfriends. (I think the name Moose is stupid.) NC

{ *19* }

warded. And purely on a godlike whim was I rewarding him. It had little to do with him. (It had more to do with my PMS.) Indeed, perhaps good fortune has more to do with how the gods feel than with how we behave.

Then, as I watched, he inexplicably veered across the sidewalk, completely missing the Coke machine and my dollar's worth of change, and immediately swerved right back again, cursing, shaking, and yelling at the *L.A. Times* machine that was *right next* to the Coke machine.

I stared in disbelief. I felt like crying. But I laughed. Sadly. And thought, yes, that's what it is to be a god: you put it all out there for them and, screaming, yelling, and cursing, in their ignorance they pass it by. You can't help but feel that fate is even more powerful than God.

I often thought about both fate and God in Montana. Give someone enough alcohol and let them fall asleep under the heavens and those types of thoughts come unbidden. It's the Big Sky. It's the Northern Lights. Montana is a setting for a religious experience, if one believes in religious experiences. The only religious experience that Ian, Husk, and I shared was that one night we were all set to go alter a billboard Ian had seen that read "God Answers." Our plan was to add the words, "Call 1–800–THE–LORD." We thought this hysterically funny. So we got some beers and some paint and went out to find the billboard. Ian had seen it on the way up to Kalispell. Well, we drove up and down the road to Kalispell several times but we never found that billboard. Husk and I had to leave the next week because the summer was over. Shortly after we had left, sure enough, Ian miraculously saw the billboard again. He still had the paint, but decided it was less funny than he had thought. The disappearance and reappearance of the message was just too coincidental for him.

One night earlier in the summer, as we were driving somewhere, Husk and Ian began to argue with each other about Pete Rose's apparent lack of self-confidence. Finally Ian yelled, "Do you want to cha-cha?!"

"Hell, yeah, I'll cha-cha!" Husk retorted.

Ian whipped the car into the dirt at the side of the road. Anxiously, I watched them both throw open their doors, run to the front of the car, and begin to dance cheek-to-cheek.

But it was winter now. And all of us had grown a little more serious in the interim. I thought of that night as I sat on the porch in my down jacket and long pants, and finished my huckleberry pancakes.

Husk and Ian came out of the trailer, steam pouring out of their mouths when they talked.

"You look like trains," I said.

"You look like a gopher," Husk returned. Then Ian and Husk did a take to each other.

"GET HER!" they yelled. (They were reliving their gopher-baiting days.) I ran to Ian's car laughing and got in. (You could park *his* car uphill and it would still start.) They got in too and started tickling me until I squealed to their satisfaction. We drove around all day, the three of us, listening to Manhattan Transfer and laughing about stupid things. I was pleased. I mistakenly thought we'd managed to recapture the summer.

The party that night, the one that I'd come to Montana for, was held in the theater, now closed for the winter. We got there late. I was so overwhelmed at seeing old friends that I didn't notice Husk and Ian leave.

A while later, Cotton came up and asked me where they had gone even as I formed the question in my own mind. She guessed that they'd gone to Sam's, a bar up the street. We went out of the front doors of the theater onto Electric Avenue (no doubt so named because it was the first street in town to have electricity).

And here I get confused as to what happened next. I find, during moments like this, that you try hard to remember things just exactly as they occurred, but there are often so many thoughts fighting for your attention that everything kind of blurs together, dreamlike: the cold, the snow, the Mountain Lake Tavern across the street where the summer before the WoPigs had suspended all the guys' underwear – dyed fuchsia – from the roof. (The company that summer split into "WoPigs" – a portmanteau of "woman" and "Miss Piggy," I believe – and "the Commandos" – male members of the company who wore a lot of camouflage. It was a very polarized summer. One of the Commandos couldn't figure out how we'd gotten the underwear all the way up there and asked, "Who helped you with that?" As my only WoPig act of the summer was to climb the roof of the Mountain Lake Tavern, I was a bit snotty with him.)

I started to look from the Mountain Lake up the street to Sam's, but my eyes never got that far because they managed to brush past the patrol car just in time to see Husk's curly blond head departing in it. And then Ian's voice came to me, slightly delayed by the cold, or maybe because my ears weren't ready to accept what appeared to be true: "That was your only choice, sir. No, I don't blame you at all . . . I know," his voice cracked in his enthusiasm as he spoke to the remaining officer, "I saw him pull off your tie."

Ian had to retain decorous behavior in order to remain a teacher in this small-town, smaller tolerance, backwoods county. Ian had a way of talking that sounded like a cartoon character. His voice modulated up and down and then clipped the ends of his sentences. I could tell he was trying his best to keep this to a minimum in case it was taken for insolence.

Cotton and I ran up as soon as the other patrol car left.

"What happened?" we both asked, Cotton in amazement, I in resignation.

"Owe-wah . . . " Ian stretched his words along with his neck as he rubbed his hand up and down his Adam's apple. "Husk just had a little too much tequila. He was walking down the street with a beer and Officer Beecher saw him. Officer Beecher asked him kindly to pour his beer out. And Husk, somewhat indiscriminately, poured it on Officer Beecher's head. And then Husk proceeded to call Officer Beecher a 'wrinkled-up old fucker' and pull off his tie." Ian paused. "*That's* when they maced him." Ian smiled without humor.

"I imagine that the 'old fucker' part didn't bother the cop near as much as the 'wrinkled-up' part," Ian added, nodding.

I thought it a moot point and wondered instead where I was going to stay the night as Husk and I had planned on driving back to Missoula.

Everyone began pouring out of the theater to find out what had happened. I hung back, hesitant to take part in the excitement because I felt so alone and I wanted to run the full gamut of my depression. I felt irritation with Husk. I wanted him to be the person that he had been last summer. Instead he was an angry, malicious individual. We all make mistakes, but I felt dragged down by his mistake and realized that my mistake was in believing I was *only* coming up for a party. My stakes were higher than I had let myself know, and now the price was more than I wanted to pay. I wanted to be home. I wanted to stop falling in love with people who let me down.

Ian, seeing that I was upset and knowing that Husk and I had planned on leaving, immediately told me that I could stay with him. At Ian's trailer we called the Kalispell sheriff. We found out that Husk had a woman judge. Bad news, Ian implied with an exhale of air as he hung up the phone. They wouldn't let us post bail (he had to sleep in jail—the judge thought it consciousness-raising), but we called the courthouse the next day and found out that they'd finally set bail. A collection had been taken the night before, so Ian and I drove to Kalispell to pick Husk up. I was quiet because I was angry. Husk knew it and tried to make jokes. He told me he thought this was all my fault because I was marrying an Iranian.

Ian, looking horrified, mouthed silently, "You're marrying an Iranian?"

"It's just to keep him in the country," I shook my head disgustedly. "Don't make this out to be my fault," I said pointedly.

Husk and I drove back to Missoula that night. I remember nothing of that ride either. I think we fought when we got to his apartment. I was tired of feeling unwanted, like I was imposing on him. Cotton had offered to let me stay with her. She was at her sister's and there was tons of room. I needed the comfort of Cotton. She was such a mom. Practical, sarcastic, great quiche. I went to stay with her, but I still felt unloved. I remember finding an opened can of Betty Crocker frosting in her sister's kitchen and eating it on the sly. Fingerful by fingerful. Capping the plastic top back on after smoothing it over with a knife.

"That's it. That's the last. I'm not going to have any more," I ordered myself, that is until half an hour later when my distaste for myself, for being stranded in Montana, for loving too many and too wrongly, led me back to the pantry and to the unwanted, processed, sugary taste of canned milk chocolate frosting.

And then Pru called. Husk had given her Cotton's number.

"Kendall knows of some hot springs that we should go to. They're either in Montana or just outside. He says he'll remember when he gets there," she laughed nervously. "We thought you might like to come."

My only thought was that I had to get away from the frosting.

We drove for almost two hours in pitch-black night, the scant snow marking nothing useful in our desire to see the road. When we stopped there were no signs, no cars, just a slight indentation at the left side of the road.

"Are you sure this is it?" I asked.

Kendall coughed. "I've been here once before, but it was summer. This looks like the place. I'll know soon enough."

We took the necessary supplies from the car: pot, wine, matches, towels, brownies. We began to walk. There was a trail. The moon was rising. Mystery hung in the air. Suddenly I felt a wave of peace rush over me. My life may have frustrations; I may get tied up in knots about what to do next with my days, my weeks (I haven't enough plans to include years and none of my calendars go past the current season); I may feel my life too arbitrary for me to exert a concerted force. But sometimes that's good. Sometimes that brings me to Montana (or the state next to it) on a moonlit night, to a wooded path with newfound friends, to a sudden clearing in the forest where the trickling of water can be heard, enveloping steam wafting through the pine trees, a magical, beautiful, enviable place that can never be described in a way to do it justice because who really wants to just read about hot pools in the snow? It's the sort of thing that can only be experienced naked, semi-inebriated, at night, with candles peeping out at intervals among the crevices of the surrounding rock.

Some people came and joined us. They smiled and "nuded up." We shared what we had; they did the same. The moon finally burst out over the trees, lighting the whole narrow valley, gilding the freezing river that ran mere feet from our baths. The newcomers told us that the thing to do was to get into the river and then run back into the pools. (There were three pools of differing temperatures, spilling water from one to the next like a plastic backyard waterfall.) I said, "Can't you get a heart attack that way?" They smiled and ran to the river. I tried to try it. I got in for less than a second, my feet and legs numbing instantly; cupping water with my hands, I flung it like a dervish as I dashed back to warmth and sanity. Pru and I smiled at one another. It's nice to meet good friends. She's now married to a man with wild hair and they write software in places like Thailand and Framingham, Massachusetts. I rarely see them.

The pinnacle of the evening, the zenith, the crowning touch, the night's orgiastic moment came with the sound of a flute—no, too woody to be a flute—perhaps a recorder, a piped instrument, a pan flute such as a satyr might play, haunting and lyrical, thinly rising on the night air. We looked up, expecting to see the music swirling toward us, a colored light, a mysterious smoke acting in an unsmokelike way. Winding around our bodies warmly, silkily, drawing us in further with the promise of more beautiful and rejuvenative waters, magical creatures, sexual encounters of an indescribable tempo.

I think of these things to remind me that I do like my life even if the tempo is now quite describable, even if I've traded in boyfriends who pour beer on policemen for a house in the suburbs with a sprinkler system, even if my once chronic depression (my usual motive for writing) has evolved into the barest suggestion of dilettantism—rather than relief, I now write for enjoyment.

Oh, I'm lying.

I still write to sate some sort of desperation. Some sort of immutable ache that forces me to bare myself on this computer. Better that than having sex with other people's husbands.

I still believe in magic, myth, love . . . it's just more theoretical now. I believe it when I write about it, when I vicariously relive my past. My life is happier now but very predictable. More charities call. Less of my time is spent skinny-dipping. I go to fewer parties, but now they're mostly catered. And I haven't been to snow-laden hot springs in years.

It's a conscious decision to grow up. But not one that I'm aware of having made. Only when reminiscing do I realize that something has changed.

Now, when I remember my past, former hurts make me laugh and former lovers hover in my brain, enticing me to call them.

Fortunately, their phone numbers are unknown to me.

2

$$- \neq \equiv \neq -$$

Lovers, former or otherwise, inspired the bulk of Moose's writings. She wrote as a tribute to them, and as a talisman against them. Having been raised in that in-between generation when women no longer stayed at home but still continued to graduate with liberal arts educations, Moose tended to focus on men. Love gave her an impetus; it gave her a goal. And the lack of love made her write, no matter where she was. With the crudest of implements, she would record her frustrations in painstaking prose.

The following was found with her college theater history notes, dated 1981:

I've been working on the story of my life since I was ten years old. It was easier then, not so much had happened. Of course I had to make more things up. Now even the things that are true sound like I made them up. Truth is not only stranger than fiction, it lasts longer.

I've been working on the story of my life since I was ten because I'm extremely vain and even if no one publishes it I'll force my children to read it.

And not only have I been working on the story of my life, but all my other personalities have been working on the stories of their lives as well. Which would be okay, except that they keep stealing my material.

But I'm in charge of our "collective consciousness" now (that sounds familiar, I must have stolen that from the personality writing the one-woman show[1]) and I'm writing because my third major relationship has just dissolved and I realize that there must be, for me, a higher level of self-actualization than cooking wok food and getting stoned every night. I actually thought it was theater and I actually *do still think* it is theater, but my theater and not others'. My life is theater and that's where I want it to remain. I don't want to have to drive there. I want to feel unusual emotions, challenge archaic mating structures, smoke a hookah, throw Greek plates, swim with mermaids, visit Delphi, argue philosophies, dare to live.

I sound like a dreamer, don't I? You're saying to yourself, "What's this kid

---

1. She stole this from Carl Jung. KLL

want? Disneyland?" Or as my mother would say (circa 1968), "You can't have fun-time all the time."[2]

To ensure that her life was theater, Moose wore blue velvet dresses from thrift shops, her grandmother's 1930s attire (she claimed that most of her wardrobe came from dead people), and no underwear. She raised ants, hung a portrait of Mona Lisa in the freezer, sent potatoes through the mail, and took pictures of her mannequin in the bathtub, all to enliven her days. But—as she wrote in 1982, still working on the story of her life:

It's the hours I have to contend with. My days, in retrospect, seem dynamic, scintillating, humorous, varied, and, above all, progressing toward a goal as-of-yet indiscernible but still there in the literary miasma. I know it. I trust. It's just that hour by hour I die. Slowly. Unaided by drugs. And so I write to remind myself of my wealth of experience even if I am poor in fame and major appliances.

It is this socialistic aspect of writing that appeals to me. You don't have to purchase expensive recording equipment, you don't need a piano or any musical talent whatsoever, you don't even need a clean piece of paper. You don't have to go anywhere particular, no one yells obscenities at you while you do it,[3] and most times, if you drink a little while you write, you generally enjoy it more. But, best of all, it's cheaper than therapy. Not only is it cheaper, it's more entertaining. I can vicariously relive my mad existence. Besides, I like documentation. Why do it if you're not going to document it? Because in the act of documentation you come to understand, for example, why you have slept with men over sixty. (That's the therapy part.) Philosophies are born. Compassion occurs. Your pain is elevated. You've made life art.

Remember:

Life can be art if you just lower your standards.
(I tried to remember this the whole time I lived in Chicago.)

Moose preferred to document life because sometimes it was the only way she could handle living it. If she recorded her pain then it was removed

---

2. Other famous quotes of my mother's:
"Fourth down from your longest and strongest."
"I never said life was fair."
"Halden! Just where do you think the trailer park is?" (This was a trick question.) (MM)
3. Marissa "Moose" Minnion had several short stints as a stand-up comedienne. JC

to a nether world, a world she could read about but no longer be affe(
by. Of course, it didn't always work. But it did often enough. And she found
when writing that so much of her tortured passion was eaten up by finding
the perfect word, the consummate phrase, the *bon mot*, that she did, in fact,
feel better afterward. Even if people disappointed her (and they always did),
she could describe her disappointment in such lurid technicolor that it became somehow jeweled, somehow beautiful.

It was this disappointment, this diffident animosity toward mankind that
created the premise of her book. She called it *Higher Math*, not to scare people off, but because in the book she attempted to figure out the most effective way to peaceably coexist with people while disliking most of them
intensely. This attempt took the form of equations. Simple equations. Simple because they were so logical. Obvious even, in the way that gravity is
obvious once you fall down.

Essentially what I've derived are practical equations which represent psychological truths in the way that mathematical equations represent physical
phenomena. To, in effect, codify human relationships.

"How horrible!" you say.

"Not so," I calmly reply. "Rather a tool, just as the pen with which I am writing this book is a tool, not intrinsically good or bad. The outcome depends upon
the user. With a screwdriver one can stab someone or fix a refrigerator." (The
outcome also depending upon whether or not one lives in New York.)

But best I should give you an example.

The Duration of Toleration Ratio

The Duration of Toleration Ratio says that the time that you spend with
someone should never exceed the time that you can stand them for.

Let X = person in question

$$\frac{\text{Duration of patience with X}}{\text{Duration of time with X}} = \text{Enjoyment of X}$$

With this ratio you can achieve the optimum amount of time with someone
while it's still pleasant to be with them and yet not go over that fine line when
a perfectly nice lunch, for example, suddenly becomes COMPLETE HELL!
Conversely, you can also estimate when someone is wearing a bit thin from
your conversation and leave so that you may still return at a later date. (The
antiquated expression for this used to be, "Don't wear out your welcome," how-

ever, they never gave you a method for figuring when your welcome was worn.) Face it, anyone's wonderful if you only see them twice a year, say for holidays. I know this from personal experience with my own relatives. In fact, I figure the only reason that people have strong family ties is because they have no friends.

Moose's relatives certainly helped to lead her to this theory. She records a conversation which took place in 1975 while she was visiting her cousins in Wyoming.

"Well, you know," Aunt Mamie said, just as soon as the waitress took our pizza order, "after I kicked Olive[4] out—mind you, it was because she never did *anything* besides watch TV till four *in the a.m.* —she never flushed the toilet, never picked up her clothes, never did *one iota of work*," Aunt Mamie's head bobbed on every word for emphasis, "she did the unthinkable and moved to an apartment building. Lord knows they must have been desperate for renters because Olive *is* strange. How she got that way, *I do not know,* but even when you feel sorry for her, she makes you sorrier you ever did. Well, eventually the apartment manager got wise to Olive and ordered her to move out. A course, I went over to help her move and the apartment was *knee-deep in filth.* She had two or three cats and *never let them out.* She didn't even give them a litter box. It stunk to high heaven! What I haven't done for my brother. I had enough kids of my own to raise."[5]

After this tirade my aunt tried to get the waitress's attention for more beer. That not succeeding, she tossed her beer mug about six feet across the room. Fortunately the restaurant was carpeted. The waitress came up and spied the beer mug.

"How did that get there?"

Snickering, my aunt answered, "Well . . . I guess it just fell." Her daughters laughed. I looked out the window.

Aunt Mamie asked the waitress for another beer.

"I'm sorry, but it appears that you've had enough already," the waitress said, punishing her.

"Whaddaya talking about? I've only had one beer."

"Ma'am, I'm sorry, but we aren't allowed to sell beer to customers who appear drunk."

"She's not drunk. She's always like this," laughed my cousin Lurelle.

---

4. One of MM's cousins, Aunt Mamie's niece. HMW
5. MM's Aunt Mamie had five. HMW

"Well, I'll have to insist that you give the car keys to someone else before I bring you another beer." They argued a bit more and Aunt Mamie finally pulled out her car keys and threw them on the table.

"There!" she yelled.

"Fine," the waitress said primly.

After the waitress left to get the beer, Aunt Mamie immediately put the car keys back into her purse.

"Mom, tell Marissa about Olive thinking that that girl was the devil."

"Oh, God!" Aunt Mamie was getting revved up. "Well, soon after this, Olive went on a YWCA camping trip. Sometime during the trip Olive started wearing a paper cross around her neck."

"She thought that this girl on the bus was the devil and was trying to kill her!!" Lurelle chimed in.

"Who's telling this story?" Aunt Mamie demanded.

The waitress brought more beer.

"Why thank you, honey," Aunt Mamie sugarily smiled.

The girls snickered.

"Who knows, maybe the girl really said she was the devil. Olive makes me want to tell her I'm the devil just to get her to flush the toilet," Aunt Mamie laughed.

"It was so gross!" my cousin Darlene shrieked. "You never wanted to go into the bathroom after Olive. I'd always try to get Selina to go in there. I'd fool her and say that Mom already flushed the toilet." Selina was the baby of the family.

"You guys are always picking on me . . . " Selina whined.

"Anyway," Aunt Mamie paused for attention, "they had to cancel the whole camping trip for everyone and come back because Olive was hysterical."

There was another pause as Aunt Mamie took a slug of beer.

"So thhhheeeeen," Aunt Mamie drew out, "we were helping her get settled in a new apartment—"

"With a cat box this time!" Lurelle hooted.

"—because God knows what country Flo and Jack[6] were in . . . Arabia, I think. Fred[7] and I had to help Olive buy groceries. She couldn't even do that by herself. We took her to the store and bought groceries for her and when we were getting the sacks out of the car she went berserk. She thought we were trying to kill her!"

---

6. Olive's parents. HMW
7. Mamie's husband. HMW

"She thought Mom was the devil," Darlene explained.

"I've thought that!" Lurelle laughed until Darlene elbowed her.

"She just kept yelling and yelling that we were trying to kill her—after we just bought her forty dollars' worth of groceries! I mean, if we were trying to kill her I would have bought things *I* like to eat! Anyway, she's yelling at us and leaning over into the car trunk to get the groceries and Fred yells, 'Okay, Olive, just put your head a little lower,' and then he pretends like he's going to close the trunk on her neck."

Moose obviously recorded this conversation as a commentary on the differences of humanity. Olive was a diagnosed paranoid schizophrenic. Moose's uncle Fred worked in a manufacturing plant. Blue collar workers and candidates for mental hospitals are not generally a good combination. It was this dichotomy that contributed to Moose's derivation of the Duration of Toleration Ratio, though later bouts of romantic disillusionment (specifically a painful "Love Connection" date) would account for its eventual form.

The Duration of Toleration Ratio occurred to me in bits and pieces, mostly after experiencing painful romantic attachments. I've discovered that men are attracted to me, but often the very thing they are attracted to ultimately drives them away. Men like me despite themselves. I'm too uncontrollable, too strong. They think I don't take things seriously enough. I have a drive to accomplish something which seems to war with their drive to accomplish something. But still I possess a trait that gets under their skin (and I haven't got any diseases so it couldn't be that).

One boyfriend (T. Rex), in the middle of a restaurant in Montana, told me to "SHUT UP!" when all I was talking about, in my spacey but sincere way, was teaching babies calculus. He thought I was being stupid or putting him on or not being logical. He wanted rhyme and reason but I don't live in rhyme and reason. Indeed, my family had a shortage of both. Their long suit (bridge analogy) was illogical didacticism (they were both teachers and loved to expound, often about subjects they didn't completely understand). See, my father taught economics and my mother taught psychology so I lived much of my life in theory.

It is because of the theoretical nature of my thoughts that I feel a book is the only way to go. I have an abundance of theories and, really, what else can I do with them? I would hate for them to simply go to Thought Heaven, the repository of unrecorded thoughts.

Selections I Have Personally Saved From Thought Heaven

Concerning religion:

I think it likely that the Virgin Mary got pregnant from a hot tub.

When I think of death warmed over I think of TV dinner death with heaven as mashed potatoes.

Just because God says that there is a meaning to life doesn't mean I have to take His word for it.

Concerning art:

Degas was the Harvey Edwards of his day.

Concerning boyfriends:

There's knowing you can do better—and doing better.

The thing about chivalry is that it makes it easy to know who goes out the door first.

Concerning law and order:

Have you ever noticed how much police cars look like saddle shoes?

Concerning science:

If one gets tan and then loses weight, will one get darker as all the tan squeezes together? (Possible solution for fair-skinned people.)

I have never been able to tell the difference between dogwood and quaking aspen, which leads me to suspect that they are actually the same tree and this has confused biologists for years.

Everyone's got their pet theories and most of them are wrong. (That's mine.)

Concerning fashion:

I, like the blind, wear others' taste in clothes.[8]

Concerning friction:

One should never censor oneself; others are so willing to do it for you.

Concerning math:

I think I'm unique, but then I would: reflexive property.

---

8. Moose wore a lot of other people's clothes and this fact figures in much of her work. JMVB

Concerning wishes:

If you get three wishes and wish yourself dead with the first wish, I wonder who would get the other two wishes. Since I thought of it first, can I have them?

Concerning family:

You can never go home again . . . but then, who really wants to?

I get notions such as Thought Heaven because my mind treats ideas like interchangeable parts. I used to call it Thought Gestalt: the taking of two older and somewhat obvious thoughts, combining them, and yielding a thought which is novel and more than what the two thoughts were worth separately. (Housewives understand this better than the rest of us as it is the whole basis of culinary arts: Dinner is greater than the sum of ground beef and a skillet. And I should know—in my house we ate gourmet Hamburger Helper. They were called Grand Tour Dinners and you were supposed to think that you were touring Europe through your mouth—a perfect example of what I'm talking about. Who in the world would have thought to add Europe to a dish like macaroni and cheese?)

Teaching babies calculus is such an engineered thought. I get a lot of flak for this theory. People don't understand that I often think something just because *it is an interesting thought to think.* It is irrelevant whether it is practical, viable, logical, inexpensive, or could conceivably ever happen in anyone's lifetime. I am a theorist. Theorists theorize. Not really a profession that one chooses for oneself, rather it descends upon one.

What's so wrong with teaching babies advanced mathematics? Perhaps it is the unsettling juxtaposition of the two parts, babies and calculus, that causes people to flinch. The combination of something as soft, sweet, wet, and innocent as babies with something as cold, calculating, and starkly intellectual as calculus, coupled with the fact that most people understand babies and have no grasp whatsoever of calculus. In actual fact, people have no grasp whatsoever of babies either.

I propose that we teach babies calculus because they haven't learned to say "No" yet. Consider: From ages zero to five a baby learns, percentage-wise, more than it will ever learn for the rest of its life. How could one simple thing like calculus faze babies any more than breathing? If parents slip it in quickly the babies'll never even know that they weren't supposed to learn it until after high school. And if they do find out, it'll be too late to be pissed off.

Math is something that requires energy to learn. Why do it later in life when you're tired? Babies have a lot of time. They are still fresh, still smooth-brained, still in wonder. They are formatted but not yet written on (computer analogy). Calculus'll give babies an attitude, something to rebel against in their cribs. After all, it's the rambunctious ones who are the world's thinkers.[9]

And as one of the world's thinkers (not to imply that I have a monopoly on it), I choose for my metaphor: math. Because really . . . math gets a bad rap. Everyone wonders, once you can balance your checkbook, how much more do you need? Nobody ever explains what purpose math serves, that it is merely a way to represent reality. Now, I'm not saying that I am good at math or that I understand many equations, but I like the concept of math. I like that it's composed of numbers and that you can count on it. I like its stability. I realize that I'm on dangerous ground. Do I really know enough about math to sum it up (as it were)? Was a semester of calculus in my junior year (that I only got a B in) enough to give me rein to spew on about it as if it were my closest friend? We'll see . . .

A Short History of Math

Al-jabr: Arabic for "algebra," meaning "to bring together."

In the sixteenth century they hoarded solutions to quadratic equations the way that present-day computer programmers hoard programs.

When I waitressed for the Omelette Parlor in Santa Monica I had to use the cash register. Whenever I made change I would make it up to hours instead of dollars, meaning that I would make the difference equal 60 instead of 100. Say something cost 43 cents. I would give the customer 17 cents back instead of 57. I had to explain this to one man whom I short-changed.

"Oh, I'm sorry; I keep doing that," I apologized. "I keep thinking in terms of time instead of money." (I was obviously thrilled to be waitressing.)

See, I attribute this quirk to the fact that I was Sumerian in a previous life and they used base 60. (That was the history part.)

A Few Mathematical Facts

The first derivative is the rate of change of a mathematical function. The second

---

9. Marissa "Moose" Minnion was a lively child who used to play wildly with the pots and pans, and who, at the age of three, while inspecting someone's coffee cup, spilled hot coffee all over herself. An event she still remembers. JC

(When she could remember.) NC

derivative is the rate of the rate of change. (Don't worry, this'll probably never be on "Wheel of Fortune.")

Mathematical elegance is "directly proportional to the number of ideas you can see in it and inversely proportional to the effort it takes to see them."[10]

The gravitational attraction between two masses results in those masses distorting or bending ordinary Euclidean space nearby.[11]

A Few Personal Theories

Math is just the logical representation of natural phenomena ignoring the infinite excesses. Which is not to say that math does not exist, but that it exists to make things workable, putting formidable concepts into manageable packages. In a similar way, knowledge keeps me safe and manageable as I chip away at my ignorance. If I can be constantly learning I am most happy. It is my protection, my force field, my room where no one can touch me.

Math is reducing things to their basic premise: the universe as yielded by an equation.[12] Putting things in measurable terms, palatable, manipulable terms. And it works. I find this eerie in a way. That a truth really appears to exist. That math does represent, and often predict, reality.

You can see that though I talk a lot about math, it's conceptual math, metamath, not the real thing. I make funny equations (though this doesn't mean that they aren't true as well) and hope that the purists don't scoff. If I can't understand their math, I make my own. And though it isn't as rigorous as calculus, to me it succeeds in being math because it attempts to depict relationships symbolically, ignoring the infinite excesses. Getting as close to life as one can with numbers. That's as much as can be done. All of life is calculus—it is only approximating as we strive toward infinity.

And besides, anyone could have written this book. I just did it first.

---

10. *Math,* written by David Bergamini and the editors of Time-Life Books, © 1969 Time-Life Books. (MM)
11. This is more specific than it need be. One mass will do. The warping of space is the result of gravity and will happen with any mass; the larger the mass, the more significant the warpage. HMW
12. A unified field theory has not yet been discovered. HMW

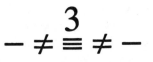

3

Perhaps anyone could have written *Higher Math*, but the fact is they didn't. Though conceivably one could argue that neither did Moose Minnion, seeing as how she is now oblivious to its final form. But then, one would be small and petty-minded were one to do so.

The book as she left it, though missing several chapter segues, was close enough to completion for us to surmise its order. We believe the next intended chapter covered more of Moose's family, a fitting passage to unveil the polymorphous complexity of Marissa "Moose" Minnion.

A Shortish History of My Family

My father bought a player piano for $300 when I was ten. It didn't work very well—no doubt why it was only $300. With it came all these old piano rolls: "Nearer My God to Thee," "Sunrise Serenade," "Stompin' at the Savoy." And then there was "Basin Street Blues." I loved "Basin Street Blues" and would play it for hours. It was good exercise because you had to pump the pedals to make music. My brother used to put the tempo on real fast and race through the song. (This was indicative of his future style with automobiles.)

Since the piano didn't work very well my father took it apart and replaced the tubing and generally puttered around. My father's really good at fixing things even though he teaches economics. I don't know if he's good at fixing things because everything in our house falls apart or if everything falls apart because he fixes it. He fixes my mother too; she falls apart a lot.

My mother teaches psychology.

I figure psychologists are nuts. I mean why would you go into that field unless you wanted to better understand yourself? You have to be slightly crazed to know that crazy even exists. Most people live fairly mundane lives. Nice, but tame. Most psychologists live mundane lives that they've thought about, scrutinized, turned inside out, taken apart, and put back together. Some do this well and some don't. But either way, no matter how many times you take it apart, it's still mundane. It's when they realize that, that they go crazy. And yet I truly do believe in psychology—I just don't want any psychologists for friends. They're always saying things like, "Considering the tools from your childhood, you've done quite well for yourself." Or perhaps I've met all the wrong psychologists. My mother, for example. And yet, my mother has some wonderful qualities . . . I'll get to them later. My grandmother had wonderful qualities too. She used to give me a penny to sing "God Bless America" when I was six. That is, when she could find a penny. My grandmother's handbag was always chock full of newspaper clippings, used Kleenex, bones for the dog, silver dollars, rubber bands, and Milk of Magnesia. Her house was like that too—a pigsty.

My grandmother taught home economics.

Our family is infested with insanity. It's a competition between my mother's side and my father's to see who demonstrates the most demented behavior. Right now it's neck-and-neck. My father's side is silently perverse, but I think my mother's side will win just on the basis of my grandmother. Who else do you know that buys a forklift because it's on sale? Okay, so it was only $4,000 (which is pretty cheap for a forklift). She got it in Sacramento, right off of I-5 if you're interested. She also bought a 1500-gallon gas tank that was eventually going to be buried in the ground. It never got there. It just lay in her yard like a beached whale, nestled there among the piles of trash and rusted-out refrigerators. She bought it during the gas shortage because she was afraid she wouldn't have enough gas to run the tractor should they ever start up the orchard again.

When I think about my grandmother I make an involuntary move to go call her because I realize I haven't talked to her in a long, long time, and then I remember that she no longer has access to a phone. As a very second choice I think back to our family visits. Driving to my grandmother's house is one of those memories that stretch out long and distant in my mind. I can feel it, I can hold the memory in my hands, but the words to describe it are barren and thin. The words make my memories seem simple in the retelling—nouns instead of paragraphs, scanty details instead of the whole complex picture—as simple as driving down the road to Grandma's house, but driving down the road to Grandma's house was never simple. Even as a child, the excitement I felt versus the dirt made me confused, made me irritable, made me fight with my brother. And when I got older, and going to Grandma's was an ordeal, we had to pretend to be excited for my younger sister's sake. I begrudged her her ignorance. She still felt that tingle, that surge of recognition as we drove down the last stretch of dusty road, the familiarity of seeing the sickly twin palms in the distance, the beat-up old cars and remnants of antiquated farm equipment strewn around the house. Theresa would start yelling, "Queenie, Queenie," as the diseased old coon hound with a huge growth on her shoulder came out wheezing and barking when we drove up the lane. History would repeat itself. The same things were always said on the way to Grandma's. We felt the same and fought the same way. My mother would get very crabby and say, "Look at this mess," as buggy parts and automobile carcasses hid in the long grass beneath untended almond trees. In centuries to come it would be an archaeologist's dream come true, but in this century only the rats called it heaven.

"Well, there's Graham Crackers!" my father would exclaim with contrived excitement as we turned in the dirt driveway. ("Graham Crackers" was the name my sister at the age of seven had christened Grandma, seemingly unaware, as children are, of how brilliantly the name fit.) And there indeed was Graham Crackers: washerwoman dress, disheveled hair with a scarf quickly pinned on, often a toothless smile (depending upon whether she'd had time to put in her teeth). She, like the White Queen, was in a perpetual state of frumpiness. Fat and petulant from too much Neapolitan ice cream (I'd seen her eat a half-gallon at one sitting), she waddled more than walked, some giant child's roly-poly toy that would never fall over no matter how it was dropped. ("Weebles wobble but they won't fall down.") She was the perfect character to live in a house as appallingly filthy as "the Ranch."

Though it might have been a ranch at one time, the name was now vastly superior to the place. To us kids, however, it was mysterious and wonderful for the first half-hour as we raced through the house to see all the "dessert parts," those things which were the reward for having driven so far in a hot car. There was a telephone that you cranked with a bell that rang and you talked through a mouthpiece just like on "Andy Griffith"—except no one answered because it hadn't worked for years. Upstairs, where there were empty, odd-shaped rooms filled with old pictures, fallen bedsteads, and the scent of rats, there were these two mysterious doors: one that went to a weird little walk-in closet that they never let us walk into because of spiders and one that would take you right out onto the roof and straight off the house. (The thought of this terrified me and I would never even go near this door in case I couldn't stop my legs.) There were closets full of old Navy uniforms up there that swayed with the souls of departed sailors. And from the upstairs window you could see where Grandpa had kept a pile of trash to feed the worms.

The Ranch seemed big to us kids, but apparently it was not big enough for Grandma because she kept building on rooms to house all the things she bought at Gemco. The Ranch was like a very dirty Winchester Mystery House. (The Winchester Mystery House is a house in San Jose that was owned by the heir to the Winchester rifle fortune. Some psychic told the heir that, because of all the people killed with her family's invention, she was doomed to die unless she continued building on to her house. So the resultant architecture is a hodgepodge of styles and designs: stairways leading nowhere, doors opening onto blank walls or two-story drops, gingerbread molding tucked away in obscure corners, stained glass placed where no light can shine through; a mish-mash, higgledy-piggledy, topsy-turvy, bad dream of a house, evolving as if the house itself had a genetic disorder. And, despite her efforts, the heir still died. No wonder psychics get a bad name.)

My grandmother, on the other hand, didn't build because she was afraid to pass on to the next life; she built because she was afraid to pass up a sale. She needed room to house everything she bought at half price. Having been through the Depression, she found merchandise at half price too enticing to pass up. And because she was so used to being poor, she could throw nothing away. She saved every tin can, every scrap of Kleenex, every used envelope, every old newspaper. Newspapers were an important commodity to her. Absolutely everything was covered by newspapers: the bathroom floors, the furniture, the food on the dining room table, even the bed she slept in. She considered newspaper protective material.

When there was a sale in town, which was at least once a week, she would stock up, buying things like five jars of mayonnaise even though she didn't like mayonnaise. Consequently, the Ranch became so full of stuff that you could literally only walk on trails through the house. One time my father put down a sack of cookies and we didn't find them until a year later. That is the truth.

Grandma had breakfast cereals that you couldn't even buy anymore. The cereal was so old that not only were there insects in it, but they and their ancestors had eaten up all the cereal and then died. She had rugs covered with throw rugs covered with old newspapers. She had closets upon closets of brand new dresses, each a different variation on a lavender floral motif, yet she would only wear a ratty bathrobe and slippers because she didn't want to get the dresses dirty.

On the south porch of the Ranch (that hadn't seen a sponge or mop since World War II) sat two Victrolas in mint condition with records like "Oakie Boogie" by Jack Gutherie and the Oklahomans, and "America the Beautiful" sung by a smug young Frank Sinatra. There were boxes of pastels from Grandma's artistic days, a case of Louisiana Hot Sauce from her regional cooking days, years of *National Geographic*s bundled up next to a pot-bellied stove, plus guns and cans of open dog food and dusty old needlepoint rocking chairs haphazardly topped with shredded dust covers. There were delicate porcelain figurines of cherub-cheeked children which had somehow managed to survive unbroken due to the fact that they were completely forgotten and had been for decades; there were floral arrangements from my grandfather's funeral, shotgun shells from his deer-hunting parties, several battered antlers that never made it over the fireplace, and, of course, the odd car fender. Grandma would scream if you went out there, slightly embarrassed at the mess, slightly worried that you'd steal something. She never had to worry about burglars, though. In order to find something to steal they'd have to clean it off first to figure out what it was.

Within the first few minutes of getting to Grandma's house the excitement of seeing her wore off. We would get permission to look around and, after we ran upstairs several times and Graham Crackers yelled at us to stop, we would go out on the south porch which was where we weren't supposed to go and she would yell at us again and then say to Mom, "Sis, can't you make those kids behave?" Then we would be forced to sit in one spot and, when the adults weren't paying attention, could only pinch each other for entertainment. Anyway, by this time we were in definite need of a bath. Even hugging Grandma left you none too clean. We had to wear thongs whenever we took a shower there. The shower was out on the west porch in no-man's land. The west porch was piled with a creepier kind of trash than the south porch. It was dirtier and stuck out at you as if to grab you. You wanted to stay there as short a time as you could in case some of the trash decided it would rather be with you. The old ringer washing machine was where we placed our clothes while we showered because it was the only thing halfway clean. Grandma still used it because many years before, in a drunken stupor, Grandpa had thrown her brand-new washing machine down the well. He was always throwing something somewhere.[1] The shower smelled rancid from years of use and had chips of paint peeling off the walls and clumps of dog hair floating down the drain along with the soap. If you touched the walls with your body you lost a year off your life. (That was the rule.) And once out, you dried off quickly with towels that you didn't look at too closely for fear of seeing peculiar stains that would later hang around your imagination demanding that you figure out what they were and were they gross.

My mother would tell us never to eat anything that we found at the Ranch until we showed it to her first. This got to be a running joke with my father and when he would ask Grandma how old something was and she would irritably say that she bought it yesterday, he would say, "Yesterday what year?"

---

1. When Moose was two, her parents brought her to visit her grandparents for the Christmas season. During the visit, Moose's grandfather threw away the Christmas tree (before Christmas) because an angel had been placed on the top and he wouldn't have "no goddamn religious symbols in his house." Moose and her parents went home early. JMVB

My grandmother lived poor, but only out of habit, not out of necessity. She owned seven houses in various states of decline, each of which was attempting to return to the earth in its own special way: one by spiders, one by rot, and one by a renter who left his bodily waste in the kitchen sink. Graham Crackers only spent her minor fortune every now and then on thirty-three cans of half-priced dog food or forklifts, so when I was fourteen, her current lawyer (she'd used every lawyer in town and was now on her second time around) convinced her that she should start giving some of her money to her children in order to lessen the inheritance tax. She decided to take us on a cruise to the Caribbean.

The cruise was more fun for us than for Grandma. She started taking Dramamine several days before we even left California. Mom told Grandma to wait and see if she got seasick first, but Grandma wasn't used to taking other people's advice, especially her daughter's. She took so much Dramamine that she slept the first five days of the cruise, and the cruise was only seven days long. Curiously, Grandma would always wake up for breakfast and dinner. On the sixth day my poor mother, who always feels guilt when she shouldn't, thought of a way to get my grandmother outside so she could at least enjoy the last two days of the trip. Pretending to go to the dining room with Graham Crackers, my mother pushed the elevator button for the deck. The elevator opened up and my mother said, "Whoops, wrong floor. Well as long as we're here, let's see the outside." Grudgingly Graham Crackers went, complaining all the way, but when she realized how beautiful it was (and how many more choices of food they had outside) she stayed.

My grandmother and food were inseparable companions. She was raised on a farm and learned that you never let food go to waste. When Graham Crackers would take us to breakfast at Denny's, she would always force us to pass her our plates when we were through, and she would scrape off onto the day's newspaper whatever we hadn't finished: half-eaten pancakes, the parsley garnish, runny eggs, and all. She would then add more syrup and wrap up the day's haul so that she could take it home to Queenie. It wasn't clear that Queenie ever expressed a desire for these leavings. It wasn't clear that Queenie ever got them because when grandma died, we found ten years' worth of moldy pancakes on the back-seat floors of several cars (she had nine). We could tell how long they'd been there by the dates on the newspapers. It was more important to her to not let food go to waste then simply to not waste it. She was raised poor and couldn't seem to remember that she was quite wealthy now. When circumstances change, if one isn't flexible, one continues to repeat patterns inappropriate for the new situation.

There was an interesting experiment done where they took some kittens and raised them in an environment where they were only allowed to see horizontal lines. Consequently, when these kittens were placed in a normal environment, they couldn't perceive anything that was vertical. They could jump onto a chair seat with no trouble, but they would continually run into the chair legs. That was my grandmother—continually running into chair legs.[2] As a child in a deprived environment, she learned to eat everything. Later, when she had money, she didn't realize that she could stop eating everything, stop saving every scrap, because it just wasn't necessary anymore. In effect, she suffered twice. She always said, "You can't teach an old dog new tricks," but she never knew that the old dog she was talking about was herself.

This cruise caused her excruciating pain because there was so much food she couldn't possibly eat it all. And believe me, she tried. You could, if you wanted, eat every moment of every single day. They had banana French toast and strawberry waffles for breakfast, a hearty soup at ten, a barbecue at noon, afternoon tea replete with scones and jam cakes, and huge six-course meals for dinner, always with a flaming dessert; one day they had "make your own sundaes" which amounted to an incredible assortment of sweets and ice cream and multicolored candy sprinkles. And then if you hadn't yet gotten your fill, you could go to the midnight buffet where you got a second chance at all the things you missed during the day. After stuffing your face one last time, you'd go back to your room and find waiting at your door a large bowl of oranges, bananas, apples, and chocolate bars.

My grandmother, sister, and I roomed together so there was an orange, apple, banana, and chocolate bar apiece. The only things that got eaten were the chocolate bars. (Who has room for fruit when there are so many sweets?) This left three pieces of fruit times three guests or nine pieces of fruit "going to waste" (in the words of my grandmother) at our door. She decided to pack them and bring them home to Queenie.

Nine pieces of fruit a day multiplied by a seven-day cruise in a tropical climate equals sixty-three pretty moldy pieces of fruit, which is exactly how many the customs official saw lying there beside Graham Crackers' ratty bathrobe when he opened her luggage. Interestingly enough, they don't let you take moldy fruit into the U.S. This was news to Grandma.

"Young man!" (The customs official was at least fifty.) "These here are my grandchildren and I've just taken them on a week's cruise to the Caribbean because they've never been to the Caribbean before—" (she was going for the

---

2. I know of many related studies (Weisel and Hubel, 1963; Hubel and Weisel, 1970; Hirsch and Spinelli, 1970; and Rauschecker and Singer, 1981), but none of them mentions chair legs. KLL

sympathy vote) "and now you're trying to tell me that I have no right to property that I have paid for with my very own money?!"

"Yew caannn't take ratten food into the U.S." He appeared to be familiar with this kind of request.

Grandma became most indignant, saying that she had paid for this fruit and that they'd better refund the cost of her trip. When they weren't forthcoming with money, Grandma peeled a banana and started eating it concurrently with a somewhat bruised apple which she took vicious bites out of. I could see that my parents were ready to have her committed, but somehow they got her quieted down and out of the customs official's hair. (I think my dad told her we'd take her to SmorgaBob's, which was her favorite place because it's All-You-Can-Eat.)

I knew it wasn't so much the principle of the thing that bothered her, it was that her sole motivation in life was to get a little bit more than she paid for, come out slightly ahead on the deal, buy two for one even if she'd never use the one. I have a little of the same in me and though rationally I fight it, I don't always win.

I didn't understand Grandma any more than the rest, I just accepted her. We had an interesting relationship. Often we would talk philosophy while she pulled my toes. (I love having my toes pulled.) She'd scratch and scratch my back in that big, old, lumpy, unmade bed of hers that smelled of Ben-Gay and chewing tobacco and we'd discuss everything from Democrats and the afterlife to falling in love and frontal nudity. (A male in a flesh-colored leotard posing as a statue on television prompted her to ask me, "Who'd want to see an old man's privates anyway?" I figured she would know.)

Grandma would retell old stories about how she used to work as a waitress at Richardson Springs up at Lake Tahoe and some millionaire used to tip her silver dollars. "He once asked to marry me," she recollected somewhat smugly, thinking that she should get points for this even though her life had turned out messy and dirty.

I try to envision her as the lively girl I see in an old picture I have. Two men are hugging her in front of a Model-T and they're all laughing. She appears thin and impetuous, free from her father's dictatorial control. Unfortunately, as is often the way of women, she married the very image of her dictatorial father and was forever trying to reconcile the fact that her "Mr. Right" was a very mean person. She told me that Grandpa made her sit in the back seat of the car on her wedding day while one of his buddies sat in the front. I pause, just thinking about the portent of this, how crushing it must have felt to realize that this was just the wedding day and there was still a whole marriage ahead. She was used to mean men, however, and thought it appropriately virile. The story she *always* used to tell was about her dog that sucked the hen's eggs. (I believe they puncture the egg with their canine tooth and then suck out the insides.) Once a dog learns how to suck eggs you can't retrain the dog, you have to shoot it. This being the case, her father made her tie up her dog when she was five years old and watch while he shot it. On a farm too much knowledge can be a bad thing. Especially for a dog. This incident was her major grievance in life and I can still hear my mother belabor the fact that my grandmother cared much more for that dead dog than she ever cared for her only daughter. (Much later in Chicago, hearing this story and knowing my family's penchant for expressions, my boyfriend T. Rex coined the phrase, "If they suck 'em you gotta shoot 'em.") My grandmother never forgot that dog and used it as the reason her life had turned out so poorly. One's life is a long time. If you hold onto life's wrongs savagely (as proof that life did you a bad turn) you can't help but be resentful because such wrongs will happen. The odds are for it.

My family is the kind that holds resentment close at hand, coddling it, feeding it. My grandmother hated her life, my mother, hers, and I occasionally am no different. I pout often. It's habit. Learned behavior. Finally, to yank myself out of despair, I admonish myself with sentiments like, "Look, you could have been born a slave." When I languish at the thought of my poverty, my obscurity, my lack of a microwave (I stupidly asked for a toaster oven on my bridal registry; don't ever make that mistake), I remind myself that everyone's had it rough. Ask anyone, they'll tell you. On a suffering scale of one to ten, everyone thinks they're a ten. They think they've had the hardest possible life that can be imagined. They don't compare themselves to the Jews during World War II or to Captain Ahab or Mama Cass.

Because I often don't get what I want in life, I have had to develop a philosophy to deal with disappointment; I have had to find a way to cushion myself to pain in much the same way that an oyster cushions itself to sand by forming a pearl. I force myself to step back a moment from life and remember that this is it. Forget heaven, hell—they may never come along. This is all there is.

It is at these moments that I wonder what is life and how did I qualify? I think life is the real reward for living. It's the prize and the consolation prize in one; it's door number one, two, and three; it's everything that Carol Merrill is now showing; it's all three bachelors *and* the Amana Radar Range . . .

Perhaps it'll be better if I explain it mathematically.

The Oyster Equation

$$(\text{Oyster} + \text{Sand})\text{Time} = \text{Pearl}^2$$

To be read: "An oyster plus sand multiplied by time equals a pearl squared."

You say, okay, I can see that somewhat. An oyster gets a piece of sand inside its shell and after a period of time creates a pearl. But why a pearl squared? I say a pearl squared because we are to oysters as a plane is to a line. Our ability to reason, to reflect, puts us into another dimension. To an oyster a pearl is just a means of protecting itself—purely functional. An oyster (I assume) has no reverence for the pearl other than simple mollusk gratitude for no longer being poked in the side. But in our dimension we have elevated this pearl, held it in awe, equated it with perfection, given it much more meaning than the oyster ever intended.

Okay, I see that, so what?

So, the pearl is no longer just a pearl; it has a duality, beauty, complexity—an accident of consciousness.

We can take this same equation, only now applying it to human beings instead of oysters.

$$(\text{Intelligence} + \text{Irritation})\text{Time} = \text{Knowledge}^2$$

To be read: "Intelligence plus irritation multiplied by time equals knowledge squared."

This is a little more farfetched to you. Intelligence plus irritation just makes me devious, you say. But deviousness is a kind of knowledge, albeit negatively bent. "Learn from your experiences," as the old adage goes. Experience blankets our vulnerable side. The most memorable experiences are formed by those things which we feel we should have avoided. Going to junior high dances and feeling a wallflower teaches one to avoid dancing in the future. Or, in my case, it taught me to ask the boys to dance because someone had to. (I was very forward for a girl.)

Frustration, the human variety of irritation, yields knowledge because your mind is forced to consider things that would not occur to you in a more blissful environment. The convolutions on one's brain grow more dense with the thrust of thought. A euphoric existence yields space between space; a frustrated one fills some of that space with substance, making both space and substance more distinguishable.

If the oyster had conscious thought like we do, it could have chosen to live with the pain or pushed the sand out of its shell instead of making a pearl. Now of course an oyster really doesn't have these options, but even if it did, making a pearl is infinitely preferable because it corrects an unpleasant situation. Living with discomfort is acquiescence of a negative nature. It's what makes a person kick his dog after the boss finds fault with him. Pushing the sand out is generally a nonexistent choice; it is suggestive of altering reality to suit you and this isn't likely. To create a pearl, however, is a gift of common sense. It is the taking of a bad set of circumstances and righting it. It is exerting an energy conducive to life, to beauty. In the case of the oyster, nature chose creativity over passivity.

Okay, I see all that, you say. But why knowledge squared? Who's above us to perceive our gems as we perceive the oyster's?

It doesn't take someone being above us, it takes us rising from our meager third dimension and being awed by time, by the fourth dimension, by the incredibility that we have experiences at all, awed by the fact that we even exist and are aware that we exist, and humbled by the fact that our existence is so very short-lived. If we can rise above our human dimension and allow ourselves to realize the gift of our existence, then knowledge serves the same dual role as did the pearl. Knowledge is beauty of a thoughtful nature. We take our intelligence and we take our experiences and we form philosophies. Perhaps it would be better to write it thus:

$$(\text{Intelligence} + \text{Irritation})\text{Time}$$
$$= \text{Knowledge}^2$$
$$= \text{Creativity}$$

Creativity is the elevation of knowledge, of experience. It is acknowledging how life is and depicting it as it could be. It is the ultimate of all joys. (How unfortunate for God that He only did it for six days.) Creativity is birth, is taking mere thought and giving it form, making it tangible, letting it breathe. Creativity is the result of thinking about something so intensely that you will it into existence. And ultimately creativity is the thing that people value most, for we are most lenient with those who create. Inevitably they know something the rest of us don't.

All well and good, you say, unmoved by my sophistries, but if knowledge squared equals creativity, then what the hell does a pearl squared equal?

And, tiring of your banal questions, I say flippantly, "Jewelry."

4

$$-\neq\equiv\neq-$$

A Psychoanalytical Perspective

from Dr. Kirsten L. Louwitsky, Ph.D.

Marissa was cognizant of the various manifestations of mental illness, growing up as she did around a plethora of aberrant behavior which distinguished itself as resultant symptomatic phenomena derived from various psychoses, neuroses, and personality disorders. These disorders included schizophrenia; severe paranoia; melancholia; obsessive-compulsive, passive-aggressive, and manic-depressive behavior; hysteria; alcoholism; and deafness (of no organic basis).[1] A good percentage of her relatives displayed one or more of these disorders and two were even institutionalized for short periods of time, though these two, interestingly enough, did not display any more severe symptoms than those who were not.

Marissa recognized an occasional instability in herself which worried her greatly, yet this instability caused her to believe in the artistic truth of her work. She saw creativity as "just this side of schizophrenia, but I'm never sure which side 'this side' is." Having grown up in a volatile family, with a mother who seemed (as far as we can discern from Marissa's account) to demonstrate signs of a personality split along with manic-depressive tendencies, Marissa feared for her own sanity. Uncertain whether mental disorder was genetic or environmental—and feeling it was most likely both—she lived a purgatorial existence waiting for the "claw of insanity to grapple with [her] brain." And it seems it did, for she committed herself twice to a mental institution while living in Chicago.

She records severe depressions that started while she attended UCLA. It was there that she also became aware of her personality splitting into five different identities, identities that were totally conscious of each other. "Ghost personalities," she called them, "personalities that have died and

---

1. Some cite the loud, querulous nature of her family as the origin of the deafness, but I see no clear cause and effect here (i.e., whether deafness stemmed from the yelling or the yelling was necessitated by the deafness). Though I would concur that the family most certainly contributed to deafness in others. KLL

now return to haunt me." She hypothesized that these personalities had existed when she was a child, but then died off due to, she suggests, forgetfulness on her part. "We were moving, school was starting . . . personalities require time to cultivate. If you become disinterested, so do they." She appears glib and is, but there is always an element of desperate truth in her work.

Much later her estimation of these "ghost personalities" changed:

I can see now it is the emotions that return to haunt you. They are the personalities that have seemingly died and lie hastily buried. Yet when even a minor rumbling beneath one's carefully erected facade occurs, when one's well-constructed personna [sic] is jarred, suddenly one's conception of life shifts, creating cracks in one's illusions. Then these dormant but very much alive emotions resurrect themselves and take on form. They become the people you know you aren't but suspect you could have been. They are worse than Dracula—a stake through their hearts does no good. They must be exorcised by a more modern day priest: one's therapist.

It was her therapist in Los Angeles who eventually helped Marissa reconstruct her mental faculties and fine-tune the personality she recognized as the one most incorporating of all the personalities. But before she achieved this functional level of living, able to survive while seeing her therapist once or twice a week, she went through what she termed "a hellish existence," admitting herself to Chicago's John Salinas Hospital for the Mentally Ill in 1981.

During this first visit to the hospital her writing took on a scarred, harsh tone. She wrote a great deal about her grandmother, not surprisingly as her grandmother was one of the two relatives to have spent a short time in a mental hospital, committing herself after finding out that her husband (Marissa's grandfather) was having an affair. During this period her grandmother had electroshock therapy and while recovering made several stuffed monkeys out of socks, something she denied doing to the end. Marissa also experienced electroshock therapy and, like her grandmother, suffered occasional lapses of memory (though she never made any monkeys).

The electroshock therapy had a profound effect on Marissa. As a result of its anesthetizing and amnesic nature, she suddenly found herself fighting to regain memory, writing all she could to force her mind into action. Her art overshadowed what she referred to as her "trivial excursions into mental illness." She could no longer afford to be insane if it got in the way of her ability to create.

While in the hospital, Marissa kept a journal. Her first entries after the therapy demonstrate her worst fears of forgetfulness and artistic mediocrity:

Nov. 12, 1981
I feel deprogrammed; my mind was accidentally erased. I carry no information.

I'm sure I could keep in touch with a lower frequency quite easily. I mean it's good to get hurt, but after a point you just don't learn that much more, you only gather scar tissue.

Where are my monkeys?[2]

A few weeks later she regained a little more coherence and her observations seem more artistically pleasing.

1:40 a.m. – My Traditional State – Nov. 17, 1981
And now we've learned to lobotomize our minds ourselves. We choose drugs to pacify our tortured natures. Unenraging us. Softening, cushioning, diffusing. Our lives become theater, our exchanges, cinematic. We watch ourselves and smile, indulgently.

I know too well about torture. I create the best myself.

She often wrote in terse sentences, cryptic, unabashed prose couplets. These were perceptions gained unobtrusively as she "watched life out of the corners of [her] eyes."[3] She often felt that her best writing was the result of discovering what she had tucked behind those corners.

November, 23, 1981
I keep losing my purpose. I'm sure I had one once. I woke up but forgot why.

On sodomy: I've fucked enough dogs without fucking dogs.

I am no one special. And besides that, my hair is dirty.[4]

I have two fears, really: one of not having enough friends and one of having too many.

---

2. During her hospitalization, Marissa often confused herself with her grandmother and was sure that she had sewn some monkeys. KLL
3. Moose Minnion Diaries, Vol. XXVI. JMVB
4. Apparently the conditions in the hospital were far from immaculate. KLL

I've got to go survive today so I can survive tomorrow. Rather a prospect which brings one up short. Perhaps life just isn't to be enjoyed after all.

She was only in the mental hospital for two weeks the first time, leaving, she says, because it didn't help her lose weight. "I only went to stop eating," she joked later. "Really, that is my main motivation in life. Frustration and despair is good until the point that it impairs my life and I find it extremely awkward to live. I want to enlarge my choices beyond 'Eat or die.' "

So she returned to her home in Chicago where she lived with her boyfriend, Rex ("T. Rex") Butarsky, a graduate student in theater, and tried to cope—succeeding, but only just. Marissa returned to her secretarial job at a radio station, hating every moment of it, but trying to make the best of it.

It was after leaving the mental hospital that her writing took on its darkest tone. She was apparently still not well. Without the comparative haven of the hospital, having to deal with the outside world proved almost too much. She continually tried to kill herself but never had the right utensils. She tried to slash her wrists, first with a letter opener and then with a paper cutter. Fortunately for us, clerical work does not provide the necessary tools for ending one's life.

Nov. 24, 1981

I know I'm not of enough consequence to be really crazy. But in thinking I'm crazy I've created my consequence.

Dec. 1, 1981

I come not to the meaninglessness of life, but the meaninglessness of my life among all these well-meaning lives.

People don't ever understand: I like to be troubled—it has a nice look. I wouldn't go so far as to say that I enjoy depression because that would imply that one wasn't getting the full benefit of being depressed. Rather I "miserate" with depression. (That's "commiserate" from within, without the benefit of sharing another's problems; rather you must share your own with yourself. To miserate acknowledges pain but perceives it as emotional art. One feels exquisite sadness.) Remember, depression can be happiness of a very somber nature.

Though Marissa certainly had a predisposition for mental breakdown, one wonders what it was about Chicago that catapulted her mind into a transcendental wasteland. Los Angeles, at first glance, would seem to be the more likely candidate for driving one over the edge, yet Los Angeles provides much more diversity in life-style, mentality, and personal cleanliness. Who would really notice in Los Angeles if one were losing one's sanity? No, Chicago is the much more disciplined of the two environments. It is more controlled, more dictatorial as to what is and isn't acceptable behavior; it is a city that has requirements for mental etiquette.

We are fortunate that in order to cope with the gradual awareness that insanity was eclipsing her mind, Marissa wrote lengthy and copious notes about her life in Chicago. These greatly help us to ascertain just what it was that crumbled her already fragile mental health. The first obvious sign of this deterioration is her use of the pronoun "she" when referring to herself in most of her writing at this time. It begins slipping in subtly, not all at once. It first appears in a letter to a friend in Pennsylvania. She writes: "She felt curiously unhappy, displeased at twenty-three. Uncertain of her anxiety, but anxious all the same." The rest of the letter then continues in the first person. But this displacement began recurring to a greater and greater degree. Finally she reached a point where her emotionally battered "I" was constantly protected by the clinically narrative third person singular.

Dec. 4, 1981

It was a time in their life when they stole things. Petty things. Baubles, primarily. Trinkets in the world of crime. A wine glass here and there, an ashtray, a stapler. Anything that would fit easily into a large purse. Coffee and postage from work, shaving cream and Tampax from her health club, a pair of gym shorts. He stole envelopes from the Goodman Theater. And casaba melons. They didn't rationalize, they just stole. It helped provide the extravagances, the delicacies of life: an occasional pound of hamburger, roasted cashews, chocolate cheesecake, even—

No, that isn't true. They didn't steal because they were poor. Being poor was novel. They stole because they were bored. It provided a thrill in the mundanity [sic] of a bleak Chicago winter. They stole because it was so cold. Stealing somehow made them warmer, got their blood coursing. She tended to be colder than he was so she stole more. Some days it was the only real joy she had.

The health club she belonged to overcharged so she let it supply her with an assortment of sundry items (toiletries, a couple of leotards—one a Christmas present for her sister). She felt that if she were generous with her ill-gotten gains then it was almost as if the world stole right along with her. Stealing gave her motivation for the day. She'd exercise before work, steal a little, and then be ready for the monotony of a clerical existence. But even the joy of stealing began to pall. You can only swipe so many wine glasses before the cost of the wine begins to offset the price of the glass. She'd do it during happy hour, taking her dinner from the free hors d'oeuvres (stealing of an acceptable nature), but she began to feel alcoholic. She loved to sit in the corner, sip white wine, and read Sam Shepard. It seemed so tortured. However, novelty done with any regularity becomes commonplace. Tedious, even. One tires of living up to one's capricious view of oneself.

She typed. He studied. It wasn't awful, but it wasn't life. Life as they both thought life should be. She dreamed of Greece. He dreamed of Growtowski.[5] They both dreamed of leaving Chicago. One might suppose they hadn't given it a chance, but they didn't care. As far as they were concerned it didn't deserve a chance. They found Chicago desolate and the weather heartbreaking. It was only natural—they were from California and came to Chicago the winter it broke all the records.[6] Eighty degrees below zero some days, due to the wind. "Wind chill" was the expression, and people from Chicago loved to use it. They loved their weather. They loved to personalize it and act as if it had made a decisive choice about whether or not to snow. Weather was something they could discuss for hours.

Winter makes Chicagoans feel stalwart, as if civilization hadn't developed so completely that it couldn't be halted by the elements. It was a rather silly rationalization for snow, she felt. She thought the natives intelligent peasant stock—ruddy complexions, that sort of thing. Good-hearted but not terribly bright. Mostly she was amazed that one of them, exceptionally eccentric and very wealthy, hadn't finally gotten sick to death of the snow and encased all of the city with a large dome. But they would have never allowed it. Chicagoans needed the snow because it gave them an excuse to drink.

Living her life through musicals, she equated Chicago with *Camelot* and thought it only snowed at night . . . or so she joked. Her co-workers thought her a crazy Californian and mistook her teasing for truth. Her humor was often misinterpreted as vacuousness. She attempted to make life art. She pretended Chicago was the Antarctic and the subway the last vestige of civilization. Or that she was Hodel in *Fiddler on the Roof,* ready to board the train to her loved one in Siberia. (In this case she often sang.) She dreamed of hot Montana nights, of skinny-dipping, of her wild youth. And she often cried. She always often cried. He thought, and somewhat hoped, that it was her period. Something biological. He didn't want it to be him. And it wasn't. Solely.

---

5. Jerzy Growtowski, director of the famous Polish Laboratory Theater, was also known for the book *Towards a Poor Theatre*, which was a collection of essays by and about him. HMW
6. I thought it broke all the records every winter. NC

They lived in a basement. Oh, not the kind of basement that's a wine cellar or is filled with black widows and old tires, but the kind they have in the Midwest and don't have on the West Coast. It was under the stairs and had a little Alice-in-Wonderland doorway. (It didn't, but she always told people it did; it somehow made life more fun.) Inside was the furniture that he had bought for seventy dollars and it showed. The bathroom they papered over with programs of plays that they went to (most always for free), snapshots of them clowning in Montana summer stock, résumé pictures of him that he had yet to write "Tyrannosaurus Rex" on like he promised, pictures from *Life* magazine and *National Geographic,* postcards from Jamaica from friends who were living a very different life than they. It was the kind of bathroom that you find in California bars where the men's says "Women's" and the women's "Men's" with tiny little arrows pointing to the other so that the unsuspecting will use the wrong one and be embarrassed.

The kitchen had a large pink acetate poster depicting Alice and the Caterpillar which she had found on sale in a Kalispell head shop. He didn't like it much but let her put it up in the kitchen.

The dining room was where they did everything as it was the only warm place in the apartment. That's where the heater was. A large oak table took up most of the floor space and it was around this table that they ate, wrote his papers, and debated the stark compositions of Edward Hopper, the philosophy of Giraudoux's *Madwoman of Chaillot,* the cutting edge of Sam Shepard's prose, and anything else that provoked their joint combative reactions.

All one can really say about their bedroom is that it was cold.

She worked for a radio station. She had to lie to get the job. She hadn't even known that she could type until she typed one of his papers for class. On the typing test for the job she typed eighty words a minute. At parties when she had everyone's attention (which was always, as she had the volume to get it and the outlandish stories to keep it), she attributed this feat to having had piano lessons as a child. Or to the fact that she'd had four cups of coffee that day and really had to pee. Secretly she knew it was due to her complete competence at everything. She knew she was brilliant. Or at least close enough to deserve the title.

At times she hated being a secretary, at times she loved it, but only when she could write and draw and mail things free (they never had enough for her to do), all while being paid. Correspondence affords the only freedom in a clerical environment. Her job was a means. It did nothing for her soul. It was survival but it wasn't surviving. At times she felt closer to death than ever before. Instead she cried. Tears were as close to death as she dared to get.

One begins to see here the driving factors that loosened Marissa's hold on reality: her comment about the cold bedroom, her sociopathic thievery and its consequent justification, her attempts to remove herself from the stark environment by first pretending (and later believing) that she was a character in a musical. Theater, always her first love, provided her with a release, but unfortunately this release soon proved too compelling. When they found her on the outskirts of Cicero, blue-tinged from the cold, madly insisting that she was going to Siberia and loudly singing "Far From the Home I Love," she realized, after regaining her precarious lucidity, that the only thing to be done was to return to the hospital in hopes that they could cure her.

"Cure" is hopeful word in terms of today's mental hospitals; "maintain" is a more realistic one. Funding is the primary problem, but also more time is needed to discover appropriate treatments as we are still, in many ways, medieval in our approach to mental illness. Not so medieval in our day-to-day treatment of the patients, nor in categorizing their particular disorders, but medieval in determining the causes of their maladies and, more importantly, how to treat them. There are many detractors who perceive psychology as an imaginative science. It is an unfortunate view, especially after one studies the work of a person like Marissa Minnion.

You cannot help but empathize with her mental wanderings as she searched for an understanding of her confusion and unhappiness with life. Had she received more effective help while in the hospital, perhaps she would still be with us today. Asthma and allergies are psychophysiological disorders brought on by stress and neuroses. We don't know what led up to the events that took her to the unfortunate ordering and subsequent consumption of the Chinese chicken salad, but I believe that there will be a time in the future when we will know how to predict these circumstances, enabling us to preserve the lives of many more artistically and neurotically inclined creators so that they won't be forced to create out of a fear that their creation is what keeps them balanced between life and death. Yet it is this balance, this fragile precipice over the depths of insanity, which is accountable for most creative endeavors. How do we make our artists functional and yet still inspired? Marissa termed creativity "that bastard of schizophrenia and rational thought." Her own creativity greatly puzzled her. She questioned. She probed. She worried about insanity and the fact that Kurt Vonnegut's son was schizophrenic. She knew that her creativity stemmed from too much feeling. Before she returned to the hospital for the second time, she agonized daily.

{ 53 }

Dec. 11, 1981

Dear Fairies (for they have been my saviors more often than God):

I plead for a reprieve. There must be more. I know that there must be more to life than this.

I must believe in my mind that I will someday live in Greece. That I will get there. I might not be happy there, but at least then I've found out one more thing about me. If I were in Greece I could write eloquent stories about simple lives.

Here I can only write what's in the forefront of my mind. Who wants to hear about how much I hate Chicago?

Oh, I want to be clever. Truly clever. Not apocryphally clever. Making up untruths that untwine after the turn of the page.

I won't survive many more of these days.

I need a drink.

Extensive use of alcohol and drugs precipitated her distancing of herself into third person and her eventual return to the mental hospital. She strove to preserve every facet of her Chicago life-style in her writing as if this would preserve her mind. Record-keeping was a way she could remember who she was. She referred to it as "documentation."

Dec. 13, 1981

Documentation was big with them. They took many pictures. He helped her buy a camera and sold her his lens and case for the gas and the electric bill. One of them got the better deal, but they never knew which of them it was. Before she came he took pictures of himself sitting with his fedora and beer. They drank a lot of beer. They tried not to, resorting in moments of desperation to Nyquil and also shots of rum bought at Christmas, originally for eggnog. They never got around to buying the eggnog.

They were indolent, arrogant, and constantly hungry. They drank too much and tried to stop, only going to parties where they knew there would be lots of food and pot. Of these parties she commented, "I will primarily remember Chicago as a place where people really know how to dress an apartment."[7] She admitted to despising Chicago, despising the Midwestern mentality, despising the weather, and despising herself for her deception. Because it wasn't the Midwest she despised, but something a bit closer to

---

7. Here she is so overtaken by her documentational style that the one personality quotes another. Previously she had written, "I'm quotable, just not quoted." Apparently, she saw fit to rectify the situation. KLL

home. Something that reminded her of her. But she allowed herself the deceit. It and stealing were the only solace she had.

Perhaps if one of the things that Marissa valued most had not been withheld she wouldn't have felt the need to readmit herself to the mental institution, this time for two months. But sex, that last vestige of being one's most honest self, was denied her. Suddenly her boyfriend had no interest, no inclination to be physically close. We are uncertain as to why.

Marissa met Rex Butarsky in Montana summer stock, a situation conducive to romance. Marissa had just graduated from UCLA in theater and, as is common with those who major in theater, had no clear idea of where to go next. Chicago was offered her (Rex was going there to get a master's in theatrical directing) and she saw no reason to decline. So she broke up with her Los Angeles boyfriend via the phone and, in a haze of newly found passion, went. But apparently youthful passion had no resistance to the bitter reality of an unfamiliar Chicago. The sex that had been so good during the summer became infrequent with the crush of winter. The realization of this fact confused her more than any other one factor in her stultifying Chicago experience.

Dec. 17, 1981

The thing that threw her so much at first was the lack of sex. And by sex she didn't mean, if you'll pardon the expression, merely "insertion," but rather the emotional quality: sex as a theatrical release, the physicality of unspoken comfort, knowing that someone still loves you. To be deprived after having been sated for so long might even constitute a shock to the system. Perhaps he didn't realize its importance to her. Oh, but how could he not? She tried to present her plight in amusing ways, offering to type his papers for sex or hinting that Christmas was approaching. No one should face such degradation. She felt that one time in four months would be approaching grounds for divorce, had they been married. But, not being married, they had no legitimate reason to obtain a divorce. Oddly enough, this kept them together.

She didn't seek gratification elsewhere because she felt too fat to be of interest to anyone. Besides which, she was convinced it wouldn't have been any good anyway for it was not insertion she sought. It was love.

T. Rex barely had enough love for himself and he held to it like a miser. A sorry sort of condition, because love and money only have meaning when they are exchanged. To hoard them is to render them useless.

She understood why he feared intimacy. He'd had an equally crazy childhood. But in her desperation she faced her flaws. His desperation denied them.

Without love Marissa turned directly to food. Realizing that sex would be a long time in coming, she chose the next available gratification. This gratification did allow her to return to the use of the word "I" as a representative of herself.

Dec. 29, 1981

Life has become futile again. Without meaning. It happened sometime between dinner last night and no breakfast this morning. Life lost its handholds. Those things which give it a thickness, a substance. I pretend I don't know why, but I do. One simple reason: food. When I eat shit there is an almost immediate and exact correlation to how I feel.

I am the books I've read,
The food I eat;
My thoughts are provoked by
The shoes on my feet.

Rex made cookies, little thin things that stuck to the waxed paper, with no eggs but lots of pecans. I, with my imagined hunger, ate them, waxed paper and all. No wonder I feel like this—I've got all these wood particles in my stomach.

I try to plan projects for the evening to prevent me from eating, but it does no good. Food gives me a purpose: I know I'm here to eat. I have sunk to the lowest level of survival. It's instinctive.

I try to get to the root of the problem. Why does eating give me solace? Where in my life did eating become a substitute for goals? I think it is goals and not love (the stock substitute for food, the generic answer) that eating replaces.[8] I think my situation is more unique, but then I would. It is always during dinner that I lose my goals, my reason to be, though I do continue to write, which would imply a goal of sorts. But no, I know myself too well. Writing excuses everything. If I can wring any prose out at all while I eat, then God knows I'd better eat. If there is a smidgin of creativity to be had for a pound of food, then suffer I will through those sixteen ounces. And this, the result?

I *love* potato salad.

---

8. I disagree. KLL

If I'm living a complete life I don't need to eat an incomplete food. (Said on contemplating catsup.)

T. Rex's theory: Bread is merely a vehicle to transfer the contents of a sandwich to one's mouth. (Rationalizing the purchase of yucky white bread.)

Don't ever confuse salt with sugar or else people will think you can't cook.

One of life's handholds is the recipe for Mock Apple Pie on the back of the Ritz Cracker box. Life charms me in its simple consistencies. And now you can even make furniture with Ritz Crackers.[9]

January 2, 1982

But I, fortunately, am not making quite so much corn bread these days. (We have, in weak moments, made butterscotch pudding corn bread—mixing the butterscotch pudding mix with the corn bread mix—as these were the most exciting things to eat in the whole apartment.)

Ah, the vagarious cravings of the poor. The vulgar combinations of condiments (tomato paste and water when we lacked catsup), the cadged Sweet 'N' Low, the nefarious concoctions. What our life lacked in variety we made up for in consumption. T. Rex's Surprise Moose Meat Loaf with a Quasi-Quiche Crust that we never sent in to a recipe contest.[10] We didn't eat particularly unusual things, just enormous quantities. And we split a six-pack many nights, or 750 milliliters of cheap wine, thus coloring the next day with a dismal air and causing us to drown our sorrows in an endless cycle. And pot. Thank God for pot. The all-encompassing drug that swirls about the brain cells, massaging them into complacency, pulling up a chair and making itself at home. True, it doesn't always work. Sometimes it just makes you dizzy or tired or dull. But more often than not it gives me that soft-focus, impressionistic filter that I so need. It's a nice ritual. It makes me laugh. I hover somewhere above reality but close enough to hold onto fragments of thought, hilarity, and my name—all else seems irrelevant.

I think I'd look at Chicago differently if the one thing I came for still existed. Do I love Rex? I listen to that Dan Fogelberg song about him meeting his lover

---

9. I guess life just lost one of its handholds (whatever that means) because none of us has found a Ritz Cracker box with a Mock Apple Pie recipe. However, when we wrote to Nabisco, they did send us the recipe. Although it really makes me wonder: who'd want to make pie out of crackers anyway? Apples aren't actually that difficult to find. I guess Miss Minnion thought if you can make apple pie out of crackers, you can certainly make an armchair, which she did. NC

10. We found the recipe for this, but it was so disgusting when we tried it that we almost puked. I figured you'd do the same and then sue us, so I burned the recipe. NC

in a grocery store and I start to cry. I love to be nostalgic. I know that is to be us. And here I am at a bar, not looking but looking.[11] I can't remember what it's like to be alone. I've gone from relationship to relationship. I think I'm scared. So I get drunk. It's not drinking alone if you do it in a bar. I came to this Victorian Bar. The ambiance isn't good. I'll drink fast then leave. I feel restless. Loose. Tight. Unresolved. Confused. Visigothish. I am feeling the pangs of a creative individual in an uncreative world. Moral turpitude. (It needed saying. I don't know what it means.) All I can do is write. I don't necessarily write because it helps. I write because nothing else occurs to me. I notice that I write in inverse proportion to the amount of sex I'm having. I needn't say more. Only a poem.

Sated. Ancient History.
Romans, Greeks,
   Mesopotamians . . .
I too should build coliseums with my free frustrated time.
Pinnacles, arches,
   Doric columns
with Legos.

   I yield to a modern age, and celibacy.

On January 3, 1982, Marissa readmitted herself to John Salinas and, after three months of continuous hospital therapy, she finally felt ready to return to urban life. One of the first entries in her notebooks strikes me as very youthful. She was starting afresh.

April 4, 1982
   The snow soft-petaled in waves. It's softness so literary it made me write this. I feel delirious. Perhaps it's the snow. Snow to a Californian has an obvious ephemeral appeal. Lightheadedly it drifts onto the El tracks as I lightheadedly travel to work . . . Ah, Chicago . . .

Unfortunately, after just a few weeks of urban life, her distaste for Chicago had returned.

Apr. 28, 1982
   Cities make me childlike, in awe, craning to see tall buildings. I like this aspect of Chicago. But then I must go to work and grow up. I must deal with the attendant pettiness of office workers. The watchfulness. The lack of trust.

---

11. For men. KLL

The mediocrity (*their* mediocrity) that infiltrates my mind. I become a void. I have no input. So I must create my world around me. I read a book a day. I read to become a part of another world. I don't read especially good books. I read romance, feeling a lack in my own life. The quickest way to kill romance is to have a relationship. It's not Rex's fault or mine. It's this all-pervading gloom. The drear of Chicago. Frozen emotions. Perhaps to thaw this summer. Oh, this will be a good summer, I just know. I am so ready to enjoy my life again.

And just what is it that I do in Chicago, you ask, that makes me hate it so much? Sixty-seven percent of my days I get up at six a.m., do typical morning things—eat, shit, dress, make lunch, make ugly faces in the mirror to make my own look better, kiss Rex several times and call him names like "Babushka," "Boo-Boo," "Moo-Moo," "Moosekeeper." Finally leaving about quarter to seven, though my digital always says 6:59 (it being exactly fourteen minutes fast), I walk, amid the slush, debris, and dog waste now thawing from the deep-freeze of a Chicago winter, to the El.

Riding the Chicago subway is not unlike a rather competitive game of musical chairs. I find the El (stands for "Elevated Train") somewhat akin to Disneyland's Mule Train ride. It's rickety and old, and lights flash off and on creating simulated lightning effects. It stops, stamps, jolts, and starts; passengers sway and tumble. Even the El men have characters reminiscent of railroad men. They shout out in Northeastern adenoidal twangs, "Fu-u-u-u-ullerton next, Fu-u-ullerton. This is the Ravenswood A-a-ay Train. Step aside for the out-going passengers. Step aside." One time there was even a public service announcement concerning the presence of a pickpocket on board. I think it was because it was Tuesday. Tuesday is always Pickpocket Day. Thursday is Lesbian Fondling and Saturday is Hood Day. The other days are somewhat open-ended. Sunday, being a day of rest, finds only the restless riding the subways.

Invariably the Ravenswood, the train I must take, has just left so I wait in the cold, or worse, the warming of the days. (Worse because I am bundled tightly for the cold and, as a result, sweat profusely.) The El comes. I board. My day is won or lost depending on whether I get a seat. Then I lose myself in someone else's imagination: Roald Dahl's, Victoria Holt's, Evelyn Waugh's, or more often someone much more obscure. Sometimes I look out the dirt-encrusted windows at the buildings flashing past. The nonexistent countryside. Thinking this soon will be but a memory. Urging this life to pass away by encouraging my nostalgia. Giving my Chicago existence the soft-focus treatment. Hearing the "music under."[12] Waiting for the credits. Anything to give me dis-

---

12. Film expression for music under dialogue. JC

tance, perspective, equip me to cope. I philosophize about the "El condition." The morning observance of quiet. The lethargic faces, the working masses, the sameness, the very things which cause me to revolt. I have a quickness of breath, a clenching of fists feeling. My skin itches with imagined infections. That overwhelming "gotta dance" sensation hits me when I can no longer take the pallidness of everyone and their seeking to smother me in their own tedium.

I become one of the masses. I am herded along with them, therefore I must be one of them. We aren't herded by sheep dogs or shepherds or anything as blatantly literal as that, still we are driven. Every morning at 7:45, I, among millions of others, see below my feet those same worn stairs of the subway, travel through underground holes in the bellies of mechanical worms, think dismal thoughts, and stare with the Blank Stare of Stupidity at another's coat, a bit of string in their mustache, the scuff marks on their shoes, anywhere but their eyes. While invading another's body space it is taboo to look in the eyes. That's more invasion than one can handle. We have, in a sense, adopted Japanese traditions. The Japanese, because they must live in such close quarters with paper-thin walls, have learned to "un-listen," to close their ears and minds to the lives of others. It is a necessity and the only way privacy can exist. On the subways we Americans have adopted this same technique, though perhaps not as well. We only have to do it for short durations; the necessity isn't as strong.

Every morning it is a hushed silence, almost a religious observance. Perhaps this is how religious observances start. Going to work is indispensable; it is one's livelihood. It becomes ritual. Ritual is habit which has been elevated. Soon something that will not change and cannot change comes to be revered in order to prevent it from changing. Rituals become the strongest when everything else is crumbling down around one. It is the last handhold one has.

Smoking, drugs, food—they too can be rituals. For some, they have replaced religion. It's not religion which grants serenity, it's ritual, habit, pattern, repetition. Brushing one's teeth for some. Ritual is consistency raised to an art.

Rituals allow one to "un-think," to go through the motions. They allow one's mind freedom while the body complies. And while my body complies, I consider Time—Time as a flask or a vessel, a container of our existence. I am aware of the relative unimportance of our days, years, even centuries. Someone will discuss what was on television last night and immediately I feel as if they were discussing Shakespeare's most recent work. It is an involuntary reaction; I am struck by the fact that all of life seems anachronistic. I feel we should be more civilized, more aware of ourselves as history. So soon we will be recorded in books, kept in libraries, and studied by future schoolchildren.

And, lost in such thoughts, knowing I was born a philosopher but am living the life of a file clerk, I suddenly notice that I've missed my stop so I fly off the train at Merchandise Mart and board the Evanston Express to Randolph and Wabash. Buffeted, I de-El, walk the wooden planking that is suspended over Wabash, down the stairs, along the pavement, and think typical walking thoughts. I peer in at the old ladies sloppily eating porridge at the 99¢ breakfast place, the place whose windows are smeared with posters done in tempera watercolors. (The ladies, too, are smeared.) I laugh at what I imagine to be their single-mindedness of life. I cross the street always on a red light, seemingly a Chicago law, and walk downward to the section I call the Streets of London. These are found underneath Michigan Avenue and are dingy, smelly, and dripping wet, with cobblestones pushing aside the asphalt that has been slovenly thrown on top of them. (You can generally tell when cities get cute by the cobblestones on the road. These cobblestones, however, weren't a recent innovation.) Trucks roar by; few people walk. I imagine that I am Nancy in *Oliver Twist* or the Little Matchgirl; that I am being chased, that I have come to meet my lover or blackmailer or fate down there in the slimy depths.

I then run up the stairs to freedom and boredom and find myself at Wacker and Michigan and go to One Illinois Center, revolve the revolving door, lean against the elevator wall as it takes me to the thirtieth floor, de-elevator, climb the stairs to the Chicago Health Club, sign my name, climb the stairs to the women's locker room, de-clothe, examine my fat in the mirror, weigh myself if I think I'll like the total, and take as much time as possible before I try to remove the total that I don't like. Finally I go and jog-stretch-legs up-legs down -touch toes-bend-strain-lift-sigh-more-more-dream about Greece-fifty jumping jacks-seventy-five jumping jacks-eighty jumping jacks-DONE. Twenty minutes and it's ah . . . take a shower, decide what to steal today—sometimes a leotard, maybe just toilet paper, probably a handful of tampons, occasionally a pair of jogging shorts for Theresa (always the philanthropist), shaving cream for Rex when they had it (I guess too many people stole it), several keys and key locks, anything to pick up my day and make it worthwhile.[13]

Finally, hair dried, body lotioned, legs exhausted, I reverse the above procedure and find myself crossing once more against the red, then down Michigan Avenue I go, singing songs to myself about how I hate Chicago, looking people in the eye until they see me looking, pretending I'm a tourist,

---

13. Apparently her stays in the mental hospital proved not to deter her much from theft. KLL

pretending I'm six, pretending I'm someone quite famous. I go through the *Sun Times* building and look at the big newspaper presses and think that Chicago, for being known as the Journalism Capital of the U.S., has some pretty lousy newspapers, but then, who am I to think? They do have nice wallpaper and their machinery is impressive. Outside that building, into another, outside that, and into my own as I feel the monotony setting in with every step I take. The elevator climbs to the sixteenth floor, which takes forever as we invariably stop at every floor except the thirteenth, there being no thirteenth to stop at. (I find, in a culture that prides itself on sophistication, the latest advances in technology, and level-headed thinking, the practice of refraining from numbering a floor thirteen due to superstitions that date back to all those old wives and their tales appallingly antiquated.) Down the hall of WCFL-AM 1000 I go, trying to avoid saying the monosyllabic "Hai" (a "Hi" muted on the long "i" sound, deadened as to be a dark "a" with a diphthong of "i"), into a large room of little cubicles, then into a small room of little cubicles, into a functional orange chair, and, peering at a complementary garish orange wall, I commence typing.

But to be honest I have little to type. I have little to do. Why am I so discontented? I provide my own entertainment, but I am still in prison. My mind can escape, but how far can a mind go without a body? Oh, true, many go much farther than mine. I haven't their talent.

So here I sit. Sometimes I have coffee. Sometimes I don't. I fix my hair. If I'm here early enough I xerox greeting cards that I have drawn. They have a wonderful Xerox copier here and nice paper. I also use colored, pseudo-linen stationery that I bought for $4.50 a pound at Marshall Fields. Or if I want to feel really productive, I xerox stage manager stuff that Rex will use this summer. The Xerox copier makes my day. Again I feel thrilled to be getting away with something. For of course, they don't know all the things that I have xeroxed, all the paper that I have used, or, for that matter, all the little articles that I have absentmindedly placed in my bookbag: the incidental pens, the postage, the two bottles of wine that had been sitting underneath my desk in a box for months. (It was awful wine, no doubt why no one else took it.) I took WCFL T-shirts and mailed them all away (using their postage) as Christmas presents, WCFL posters, rulers, and bumper stickers.

I venture to say that they wouldn't even care that I've taken these humorously trivial items as I am convinced that this station is a tax write-off for Amway products. I just can't believe that an organization run as effectively and as diabolically as Amway would own a radio station run as haphazardly as this one unless it all fit into the scheme of things, much the way that homosexuality fits into nature's scheme for birth control. However, the peons of the station, those secretaries who would be quick to tell me that I cannot xerox what I want, cannot use their paper, cannot take lunch at two p.m., cannot sleep in the bathroom, those secretaries would be affronted if I were to say that this station exists for the sole purpose of losing money. They would feel it degrades their job. Their effort exists for the reverse of the capitalist system, all the while supporting that very system through the conniving of businessmen who know the weak links and can manipulate them. I surmise this situation through a variety of facts:

1) The head DJ got a $1000 phone put in his car, theoretically so that he could "call in the news." According to my sources,[14] he has never done so and never intended to do so. He awakens right before his afternoon shift, starts drinking as soon as he is finished, and spends relatively little time in his car – which is probably best for both the news and the driving public.

2) We have parties every week with a modest gourmet spread and lots of wine and champagne. Everyone always drinks during lunch. How else could you discuss business if you didn't drink? No one would take you seriously. The older businessmen, who have been working in radio for years, come back to the office at about three, their noses red, their breath sweetened and heavy, and they joke around with me, trying to say sexual things to embarrass me. It blows them away when I remain unruffled. I play shy, quiet, and bookish here and let out little if any of my crazed, exotic, unclad personality. See, I told them that I majored in English. If you say that you majored in theater no one hires you.

And

3) Working in the sales department I have the opportunity to occasionally do the cash reports of the week's expenses and income. If those few weeks are any indication of their finances, they don't make nearly enough for all their revelry.[15]

Ah, but I tire of this. I cringe against the methodicalness of my present life so let me not encourage it here.

---

14. Her "sources" were one: the head secretary who had been there only a little longer than she. HMW
15. As corroborative evidence, MM and fifteen others were fired during the month of May, 1982. HMW

I am certain I am going bald.

So what else do I do in Chicago? After a morning of generally less than an hour of actual office work, I watch the minutes flip by on my digital radio/alarm till I allow myself to go get my portion of homemade, flavored, powdered-milk yogurt from the communal refrigerator in the lunchroom, a room that always smells of someone's day-old Spaghetti-o's. God forbid I should eat in there. It's haunted by the ghost of one too many tuna fish sandwiches. I find it repulsive and not conducive to digestion.

The other day I made the mistake of glancing at the switchboard receptionist's book as I was exiting with my lunch. I wanted to see if she was still reading *Rich Is Best,* which is the book she'd been in the middle of when I started working here – before Christmas. I figure she read about a page a day (a little faster than her comprehension). As it turns out, she was reading another book (finally) and mistook my prying eyes for actual curiosity, which of course spurred her to recite in glorious technicolor the plot of the book, which had something to do with Bolsheviks, mistaken identity, a countess, the requisite romantic involvement of the countess with the Bolsheviks, and a few other equally surprising plot twists. As this new book looked to be about 150 pages long and she was roughly on page thirty, it appeared that either quite a lot had transpired or else the publishers did the reader the great service of detailing the plot on the book jacket just in case one had a problem following the story. Now whenever I see her she tells me, in some regional Chicago twang that reminds me of a gangster's moll, that she's written the title of the book down for me in case I want to read it. This will teach me to be nosy in the future. I keep my lunch in my desk now in an attempt to avoid her in case she recommends another book.

After lunch is the absolute worst. I've discovered that hell isn't something that happens when you die; hell occurs between two and five p.m. every day. And the devil is the fat secretary who eats Fritos corn chips and then talks about everyone's sex life while breathing heavily in your face.

Throughout the whole day I live to escape. First, in the morning I live for lunch. Periodically I tantalize myself with escapes to the bathroom or to get some soda. Then after lunch I live for five o'clock, just for the freedom of not having to look at a nauseatingly orange wall, not having to listen to insipid secretaries discussing their trousseaux or how expensive their apartments are or the multitude of other insignificant issues they fill their bits and pieces of stolen moments with. I race out of the elevator, free. Board the subway with other such free people. I get home. The climax of my day is dinner. And once I'm home I'm miserable. I'm bored. I'd rather be at work. Oh, I love Rex, but we've been with each other so much. We need other input. And the few friends that we have here, who aren't really friends, are not worth calling up to do anything with. I start feeling as if I have no friends, as if I've never really had a good time, as if I've only ever been and ever will be fat. Life is encapsulated. I have no existence but the present one. I don't remember what I ever did with my life before.

Wait, I remember! I lived in California. It all floods back to me. (Why does one equate the retrieval of memory with natural disasters?) I have never missed any place as much as I miss California. California is my home. Me and Scarlett: we crave the land. Home. I never really knew I had one. Oh, I'm getting maudlin. Just get me out of Chicago!

5
$$- \neq \equiv \neq -$$

Traffic

Moving to L.A. for the third time[1] in my life had an inauspicious beginning. Fifteen miles above Ventura on the Golden State Freeway I had a blowout on my left rear tire and totally lost control of the car. I careened over three lanes of traffic and came within five inches of going over a bridge. I was in hysterics but unhurt and the car undented. I then got out of the car in the middle of the freeway and tried to push it off the road so no one would hit it. Fortunately a man stopped, seeing me in the throes of fastidiousness—I later realized that it really isn't necessary to risk one's life in order to clean up our public highways—and drove me to the nearest gas station. (He had on a name tag. I instinctively trust someone who wears a name tag in their everyday life. It just doesn't signify antisocial behavior.) Within forty-five minutes I was back on the road, shaken, but not ready to turn back. It would take more than car problems to deter me from L.A.

During those forty-five minutes I tearfully concluded that I was returning to L.A. because I'd given up on men and I might as well be famous. I'd left T. Rex three months previously in Montana where we were both acting in summer stock. Chicago had scarred us and we incorrectly felt the need to blame each other.

We left Chicago together. T. Rex's entire directing class had quit in disgust at the master's program and there was nothing keeping us there—no friends, no jobs, no beach.[2]

I left T. Rex partly because sex between us was a distant memory, partly because I wasn't as combative a debater as he was, and partly because T. Rex's family was even more troubled than mine and our kids would certainly suffer from such tainted genes. I remember T. Rex's sister, Tania. She'd been going to law school but somehow ended up as a Playboy Bunny in Chicago. (All the

---

1. We believe the year this chapter was written to be 1987, but Moose's third move to L.A. occurred in 1982. JMVB
2. Large bodies of salt water appear to play a significant role in the maintenance of Marissa's mental health. KLL

stories surrounding her made about that much sense, but you could never determine where exactly the truth lay – kind of like talking to a schizophrenic: the thoughts they express have some relationship to the real world, but you'd never manage to recognize the real world from their thoughts.) Tania didn't like me much. Probably because I breathed. She invited me and my friend Tuesday to Christmas dinner once at her apartment in L.A. (This was after T. Rex and I broke up – the only reason that she would have invited me.) The day before Christmas she uninvited us because (as she explained on the phone) "my boyfriend was just in a car accident and he can't wear any clothes." T. Rex, later apologizing profusely when he found out why Tuesday and I never showed up, convinced me to come over to her apartment for New Year's Eve. We were all sitting at the dinner table talking when Tania suddenly appeared behind me with a hand stamp such as a post office might use. Before I knew what she was doing, she'd stamped "Cancelled" on my forehead.

T. Rex had not had an easy life. His mother died when he was young and his father married an English woman who, after seventeen years in the U.S., had still not lost her accent. T. Rex's dad and the English stepmother also invited us to dinner one night. This was when we were still together. T. Rex probably could have warned me of what it would be like, but either out of fear that I wouldn't go, or fear that he wouldn't, he merely predicted that we would eat some kind of runny vegetable dish.

We were told to arrive between six and 6:30 p.m. It was 6:30 when we got there. Geraldine (the stepmother) immediately hugged me as I walked onto their back patio and simply wouldn't let go.

"Ooohh," she sighed. "I'm sooooo sorry." She burped. "We couldn't wait any longer I'm afraid."

I finally removed myself from her grasp, wondering where that odor of fermentation was coming from.

"We had to start eating," she said simply.

I was confused. T. Rex looked at his feet and his father, a neurosurgeon ("Of course he's nuts," Tania had told me, "You'd be too if you had to look at blood and pus all day long"), sheepishly said, "There's food left. We weren't sure if you were still coming."

"Why?" I bluntly asked. "What time is it?"

"Shix-thirty-shix," Geraldine cried.

I looked at T. Rex and rolled my eyes, implying, "You didn't prepare me for this!"

So, while they sat and watched us, we quickly ate on their patio: some sort of appalling egg souffle served in a clear pyrex dish, probably made from a recipe on the back of a Bisquick box, cooked vegetables that had long since lost any nutritive value, and wine (but of course).

Geraldine went to bed within ten minutes of our arrival. Her husband the neurosurgeon visibly relaxed, as did we all. How naive we were. We began talking about this and that. For some reason we began making jokes about Galt, a nearby town.

"You can all just go to Galt!!" Geraldine screamed, suddenly appearing on the other side of the sliding glass door, her blouse undone, her bra tilted, her hair in disarray.

"Go, go, GO!!!" she yelled.

I'd had enough. "Let's go," I said to T. Rex.

The neurosurgeon said, weakly, "Maybe it's best."

Geraldine cried to Rex, "Remember when you used to sell heroin? *I remember.* You thought you had me fooled. You had your *father* fooled. Not me!" (Her voice modulated up and down in excitement and drunkenness.)

Rex had casually warned me that she might bring this story up because she always did. She accused him of selling heroin because he always came home late from high school. T. Rex had shaken his head resignedly when he told me about Geraldine's accusations. "They didn't even know that the reason I always came home late was because I was directing *Godspell.* They never even came to see it." He shrugged his shoulders.

As Geraldine screamed at us to leave, she locked the sliding glass door. "And don't you come back. You find some other place to sleep tonight!" She was referring to her husband.

"Dad," T. Rex said, "I think she locked you out."

The neurosurgeon smiled shyly as if he had gotten away with something and began tossing a ring of keys up and down. Obviously he felt as if he had won this round.

T. Rex was a good guy, but when so much of his energy was devoted to rationalizing his family's behavior and trying to make himself feel better about it, he didn't have much energy left for a relationship. We passed through each other's lives and disentangled easily, amicably. The older generation doesn't much understand this kind of involvement. We live in a faster, more well-traveled time. Live with someone before you marry because why invest energy on a passing whim? Just to legitimize sex? Marrying T. Rex would have been a mistake, not because he wasn't a nice guy, but because we didn't know enough about ourselves to be able to recognize what we wanted in another person. We knew each other like two kindred spirits on the subway might. I can fall in love in a moment by a look, a smile, by anything that lasts an instant and needs no proof, requires that no laundry be done together or shopping or yard work; it's easy to become enamored with the barest of interaction. Our lives are freeways of movement, of maneuvering here, avoiding that guy there. It's easy to evoke passion, and is that wrong? The smartest of us realize passion's transience, the rest of us take a little more time, a few more marriages or live-in boyfriends.

A place like L.A., ruled as it is by the automobile, sets the metaphor for our lives. It lazes distendedly with miles of products for every facet of our automobiles' happiness: sun roofs, vinyl tops, sheepskin seat covers, classic and custom interiors, pinstriping, body repairs, white sidewalls – not to mention all the products that actually contribute to the car running. We can choose for our cars any variety of accessories and, so spoiled, we also wish that variety for ourselves.

I myself owned an Audi that, due to several accessories and a wonderful exterior, looked beautiful and ran like shit, certainly a metaphor for my life. I got to know the inside of my car intimately as it left pieces of itself alongside the road. I even went to bed with my Armenian mechanic, telling myself that I wasn't doing this *just* to lower the estimate on my car, but knowing full well that I was. Brutal, but true. And still it cost me $1200! In a state where mobility is important, this kind of automotive harlotry is not only known, but generally accepted with a nod and an admitted, "I've been to bed with *my* mechanic. He was German."

Growing up in California, I've always taken cars for granted. My family alone, at one point in the history of our being a family, owned a Ford station wagon, an Audi, a Volvo, a camper, and a Triumph in various states of repair. (My brother was always getting the accelerator to work but forgetting the importance of the brakes, an oversight which resulted in the Triumph coasting its way into someone's driveway on New Year's Eve, straight into their VW, which was jacked up on blocks and which – due to the conservation of momentum – was then launched straight into their bedroom where they were sleeping. My brother apologized.)

Cars are an easy-to-come-by commodity in California, not that they all run . . . In fact, there is a car sitting in my driveway right now that has to be towed away. It was working fine until I went to check the oil. I thought that I'd pulled the water dipstick by accident, but you know . . . there's no dipstick for the water.

"Head's busted," my brother wheezily chuckled when I told him. Oh, well. Someone just gave me this car. Like I said, they're easy to come by.

We Californians all grow up with an instinctual desire to get behind the wheel, an impatient longing for that golden birthday when we turn sixteen.

Getting one's driver's license is a symbol in California, a ritual not unlike losing one's virginity or lying on an anthill or circumcision. It is freedom, maturity, power. For some, driving is an acquired taste, like mango chutney or Scotch. If you grow up near public transportation, you aren't conditioned to yearn to drive; you aren't given red fire engines to pedal down the sidewalk. Or if you are, you never translate them into red Camaros and heavy petting.

A friend of mine from New York asked me if it's scary to drive on the freeways in L.A. (She was moving to Pasadena.) I told her to spray paint the inside of her car and she'd feel right at home.[3] I also explained to her that it was very important that she give a lot of thought to where she rented an apartment because the quality of life in L.A. is determined by whether you drive with or against the traffic when going to work.

The ability to drive is a finesse, a gift. I never realized this until I rode with a girl from Pennsylvania whose strongest automotive memory was when her friend fell asleep at the wheel and had a head-on collision with another car. Driving consequently terrified her. As I sat in the passenger seat four cars honked at her in a fifteen-minute period because every time she changed lanes she forgot that the rest of her car had to change with her.

I also had a roommate from Arizona who was rear-ended three times due to her hesitance in pulling into an intersection when the light was green. However, this is understandable because she was a simp. The last time I spoke to her she told me that she wasn't a nun but the next best thing to it.

Hmm.

I'm a lot like a nun when I drive in that I often refer to God. I will admit, I pride myself on being a good but accelerated driver. I can't abide people who drive the speed limit. I take a few chances, honk at imbeciles, dodge in and around stupid people. However, when I drove in England, all of this changed. There, *I* was the stupid person. You wouldn't think that a simple thing like reversing the side that you drive on could make such a difference. Everything else is basically the same. But it's like breaking your dominant arm and having to write for a while with your submissive and pitiful hand. Suddenly you feel a loss of spirit. Your personality changes. You even find yourself slow to speak at parties.

I went to England with Sam.[4] He had to go to Chemist Camp in Cambridge. (They called it something a little more highfalutin, but basically all it was was camp—they lived in dorms, they ate bad food, what else is that *but* camp?) First

---

3. The subways of New York are thusly decorated. JMVB
4. MM's husband, a medicinal chemist. They went to England in 1987. HMW

the airlines lost our luggage. In one of our suitcases was the alarm clock. Consequently we overslept. The car rental place was already closed when we called them. So we had to go to Heathrow and rent a much more expensive car. This turned out actually to be a good thing because the more expensive car had bendable side mirrors. It was my fault, really. I was yelling at Sam to park. I didn't mean immediately, however. That's L.A. conditioning for you. Whenever I see a space I have this urge to take it. What we saved in damage to the VW bus more than made up for the price of a car with bendable side mirrors.

Okay, so we hit three cars in a week. Fortunately, they don't sue in England like they do here. The owner of the Saab was very nice and even wanted to date me, but I told him that I don't date people I've just run into.

The Volvo was a more complicated matter. I had left Sam off in Cambridge. I was lonely. I went to the Cotswolds expecting quiet, quaint little villages and, not having been to England in July before, was overwhelmed by the scads of roving geriatric tourists. It seems that crowds make one more lonely. Give me an isolated pasture, a few cows, some sheep, and I don't mind my solitude. I revel in it. Especially if I have just a little weed. (I smuggled some over, artistically embedded in tampons. I wish you could have seen my handiwork. Something about tampons impresses me. I want to make them into party gifts or hang them from a Christmas tree . . . they've already got a string.) But hordes of tourists buying Burton-on-the-Water jam and Stow-on-the-Wold tartan muffs fill me with rage. I can't explain it. I yearned to escape. I yearned for peace. I yearned for a bath, specifically.

I went to the bed and breakfast I had reserved. It wasn't quite what I expected. My guidebook praised its "tiny drinking lounge . . . with a large bow window commanding a view of the river and village green." I saw a dingy hotel lobby with a window seat cluttered with antique soldiers and other bric-a-brac effectively obscuring any view other than that of the tourists who periodically peered in at the guests. However, I could have handled this. I could have handled it because all I wanted was to get stoned and take a nice long bath. After running the water for ten minutes I realized that I really didn't want to take a long bath because there was no hot water. No one had mentioned that there was no hot water. There were no signs. There were no warnings. This is the kind of thing that makes one say disparaging things about England. (Sam told my BBC friend Colin, "You know . . . they don't have enough toilets in England." Sam *was* the Ugly American.)

Resigning myself to a cold bath because I was filthy, I grimaced and took it. Later, during tea, still numb and sullen, I wrote the following:

It's England, it's wet. And I've just taken a cold bath. (No wonder the English never bathed for so many centuries . . . Now I understand the book *Shogun*!) Angrily (but politely) I asked the person at the reception desk why there was no hot water. She explained that they don't turn the hot water on until 5:00 p.m. I asked if this was usual.

She said, "Well, saves money on the gas you know, mum." (She didn't really say "mum.")

I said that this wasn't usual at any of the bed and breakfasts I'd stayed at previously.

"Well, this isn't a bed and breakfast you see. It's a hotel, mum." (My guidebook had said it was a B & B. Sam later told me that we should burn this book so that it would have at least one useful moment in its life.)

I asked if it was unusual for the guests to want a hot bath after their travels. She returned to an inversion of her previous statement about the cost of gas and I could see that we were in a bounded loop of conversation and no other thought would be permitted to enter. So I resolved in my mind that I would write them a letter stating exactly why I was only paying ten pounds of the seventeen owed. My complaints, apart from the cold bath, were: 1) there was no light bulb over the mirror (which made putting on my makeup somewhat strenuous), 2) when I arrived it took three rings at the reception desk before anyone appeared, and 3) the tea shop down the lane asked for money up front. (I won't put number three in my letter, but I will let it make me resentful toward them.)

Sam didn't really understand when I told him about hitting the Volvo. "Oh, so you hit the car because you were running out on your bill?"

"Not exactly," I said defensively. "It was early in the morning when I left and I forgot I was in England."

See, it happened when I went into reverse. Reverse is the most dangerous gear in any language. I heard a scrunch and saw bits of plastic fly out in a disconcerting manner. Nothing happened to the other car. At least it didn't appear so. It had those wonderful rubber bumpers. (The owners will probably never know they were hit, I rationalized to myself as I continued to pull out of the parking lot.) I thought, "Is this a hit-and-run? Will I be pursued through England all because of a lousy seven pounds?" (That's $11.90 to you and me.)[5] Then I decided that if I was barred entry to Great Britain for a hit-and-run it

---

5. Circa 1987. HMW

would be okay because even when they do have hot water it comes out of travel trailer showers.

Once I was a safe distance from the hotel I quickly scanned the rental policy and (thankfully) we weren't responsible for any damage or acts of God. (I think my driving was an act of God.) At this point I wanted to go immediately back to Cambridge, park the car, and continue my holiday on foot. I was past worrying about hitting other cars, I just didn't want to kill anybody.

As I drove I thought about the fact that the only country which drives on the left is England.[6] How did it ever start? My friend Colin said that he thought it was from the placement of the heart and that in chivalrous times knights would pass each other on the side furthest from the heart. Impressed with this reasoning, I asked, "Did you come up with that yourself?" Somewhat sheepishly he answered, "Not exactly." But later I thought, France had knights – why didn't they think of this? (Which may be indicative of France's dealings with tourists as well.)

I think that England would have made more sense had it been on the other side of the equator. This is how you would expect people to drive whose water winds the other way down the drain. No wonder Lewis Carroll wrote *Alice Through the Looking-Glass*: He was very confused by having to drive on the wrong side of the road.

Everything in England is based on this reversal. Hot and cold faucets are switched. (When I remembered this at the hotel, I immediately went back and made sure that I wasn't confusing the cold for hot, knowing that the help would have a laugh for days at the American who took a cold bath because she didn't turn on the proper tap. I wasn't.)

Salt and pepper shakers are opposite. Salt trickles out of one hole, pepper spews out of many. (I mentioned at a communal breakfast in England that everything is based upon their driving and a woman laughed, proving that something funny isn't necessarily untrue.) You would think, in a country obviously concerned about sodium intake (evidenced by the fact that salt is allowed only one puny hole to sift from), that their breakfast meats wouldn't be so ungodly salty. Let's face it – everyone says it – England has the worst food in the world. The only place you can get a decent meal in England is at an Indian restaurant. We went with Colin to this new "American" restaurant that he'd just found and was extremely excited about. He ordered nachos. They were smothered in lettuce and stewed tomatoes. (The English have an incomprehen-

---

6. Other countries driving on left: Australia, Japan, and British-colonized countries in Southern Africa. HMW

sible love affair with stewed tomatoes, especially for breakfast, and especially with French toast.)

"I've never seen nachos with lettuce before," I said innocently.

"Well that's how we make them here," Colin said a little snappishly.

I suppose it makes sense that a country which would serve nachos with lettuce, and French toast with stewed tomatoes, would not be much daunted by driving on the opposite side of the road from the rest of the world.

After motoring in Great Britain, I came to realize that driving is a kind of etiquette, not unlike drinking tea or throwing parties. Every region may participate, but styles vary greatly. In L.A., for example, it is expected, as the light turns from green to yellow, that at least three cars will turn left. Everyone knows this. No one honks. No one gets a ticket. In Chicago if you try this, the immediate cacophony of horns and rude remarks will certainly make you think twice before turning left on the next block. Do not think that the benefits of driving on the West Coast are greater than those in the Midwest, however, because in Chicago it is perfectly permissible to park in the *middle* of the street, turn on your hazard lights, and go in and eat dinner.

I view driving as the same game wherever you go, only boys' rules instead of girls' or rugby instead of football. George Carlin did a whole bit about football and how it is actually the re-creation of feudal England and rests entirely on the territorial imperative and the taking of land. Funny, but true.

I wonder what game some future culture will play that is a derivative of driving in the way that football is a derivative of feudal conquests. (I figure the automobile is at least as important in this culture as amassing land was in medieval England.) Call it "Traffic." It already is a board game. The graphics are all there: stoplights, freeway signs, left turn lanes, pedestrian paths, bikeways. Even poetry for a short time entered the world of the automobile in the form of electronic freeway signs which offered helpful tidbits for the weary traveler: "Save gas, don't pass," "Drinking is a crash diet," "Hiway workers—give 'em a brake," "Don't be a jerk—bike to work."[7] Who says the government doesn't support the arts?

Driving has truly become a literary endeavor now that the L.A. phenomenon of "personality plates" has swept the freeways. Personality plates are those personalized license plates which read "KTSBENZ" on someone's Mercedes, or "BUNNY" on a VW Rabbit. These plates are found on every third car in Los Angeles, and can you better understand now why freeway violence occurs?

---

7. The California Department of Transportation has no record of "Don't be a jerk, bike to work."
HMW

Chains of vowel-less but still decipherable words align themselves across the lanes. We seek anything to cure the monotony of traffic. "GNN TNC" (gin and tonic), "AF4DZK" (aphrodisiac), "6ULDVNT" (sexual deviant), "ENNUI," and "XLNDYX" are the better ones I've seen.[8] Someday I want one that says "LSN1DLN" (Alice in Wonderland), or perhaps I'll move to France and buy a license plate that reads "±ETRE" (you figure it out).[9]

You can imagine that a certain frustration might mount if you are stuck in traffic behind a license plate that, for the life of you, you simply can't figure out. And wouldn't that taunting plate so offend your eyes that you would want to lash out? Wouldn't you resent the competitive society that barrages you with intellectual games against your will? That foists another's simple-minded banalities on you when you least need them? Personality plates *do* express personality in that they subject you to knowing more about the owner of that car than you would care to. They advertise the driver's stupidity. Personal license plates are the commercials of the freeway. And worst of all, you can't turn them off . . . even if you *do* shoot the owner.

I'm waiting for the day when I see a whole sentence spelled out in front of me. I know that it will be some other galaxy finally finding a suitable method of communication with earthly life. Is, in fact, this visual shorthand, this letter conservation a trend of the future? Will we soon have Evelyn Wood Speed Speech? Will language itself become vowel-less, reduced to a series of guttural consonant sounds spoken quickly in passing? Oddly enough, with their economy of letters, computers and car license plates already speak the same language. Our machines will be communicating with other galaxies before we will. And they probably won't even let us in on it. (I already know that there are telephones that call up my phone and talk to it when I'm not at home.)

Only in L.A. could a license plate be said to have personality. Sam scoffs at the name "personality plates." "They'd like to think they have a personality," he says disgustedly, referring to the automobile owners who have twenty-five dollars to waste on them. Personalized license plates are only one of many panaceas for the masses. It's no wonder they have to rev up big sporty cars in the driveway or install a phony cellular phone antenna or have "ITS HIS" on their license plates: that's how they know they have personalities.

Our car is our wardrobe, our makeup, it contributes to our sex life, and is an almost clear statement of our tax status. Our car is the means of our survival

---

8. I can't decide if "XLNDYX" is "Excellent Dykes" or "Extra Large in Dicks." (MM)
9. As the license plate alphabet does not include + or −, moving to France would not have helped. JMVB

and one that doesn't run not only hampers one's ability to earn a living, it also alienates the neighbors. But I hate them anyway.

Cars with varying degrees of ambulatory ability were well known to Moose. More than once she had to "clothes hanger" a muffler to the chassis in order to make it all the way home without losing the tail pipe. A fire under the hood had to be put out with an old sleeping bag that was stuffed in the back of her parents' station wagon. The isolation one feels while watching cars whizzing past as one stands beside the road with an inoperable model was not unfamiliar to Moose and occasionally caused her to be incautious when coming to the aid of others. This good Samaritanism led to an unfortunate incident which later made its way into Moose's stand-up comedy act. It was a somewhat callow monologue, performed during the early eighties at the Los Angeles Comedy Store's Pot Luck Night (a night when anyone can get up and perform).

I have theories about everything. I have a lot of theories about L.A. In fact I just ran into this girl that I hadn't seen for thirteen years—she'd just moved here—and I have a theory that if you lose someone you'll find them in L.A. I mean eventually everyone moves here. And then they get robbed and then they go away again. L.A. is just an intercontinental bus stop. Or I like to think of it as one big dryer where all these mismatched socks come together to breed. And then they all do theater. I mean face it, everybody moves here to do theater. I moved here three times to do theater and was robbed each time. Okay, that's not quite true; the first time I moved here I was born here. There's really not enough cash in it to warrant robbing babies. But the second time I moved here I was robbed looking for a UCLA theater arts party on the beach. See, I helped these two guys jump start their car. I didn't know you don't do that. I should explain, I grew up in Davis—Northern California. It's a lot like Oz. Everyone bicycles there, it's very artsy-craftsy, people live in little solar homes on Bilbo Baggins Lane and still vote for McGovern. So I wasn't at all suspicious when these guys said, "Don't worry, we have jumper cables." They didn't. We had to take the battery out of my car, put it in their car, put it back in my car. And while they're doing this I'm going, "Oh, I was so nervous, but now I'm really glad that I helped you guys. People just don't help people enough these days." One guy even offered me ten dollars and I said, "Oh, I didn't do this for money."

Okay, so they wanted to thank me by taking me out for a drink so I said, "Give me your number and I'll call you," but I guess that pissed the other guy off because he got in the passenger's side of my car, pulled a gun on me, and demanded all my money. Well, I'd been to the Renaissance Faire that day and only had thirteen dollars. But I had this car, an Audi, which looks like a Mercedes in the dark, so he thought I was holding out on him. Meanwhile, the guy who offered me the ten dollars, which *obviously* I should have taken, comes up, sees his friend with the gun, and says, "Hey man, don't do this to her, she just helped us jump start our car," and they proceed to have an argument *over my lap* about whether they should rob me or not! After a couple of minutes the good guy gives up and the bad guy gets tough and orders me down to the beach. By now I figure it's probably not to play volleyball and I decide it would be safer getting in a head-on collision. Right then two cars pass, honking at me because my door is obstructing traffic. I honk back thinking maybe they'll come back and pick a fight. Then I started acting crazy (which is pretty easy for me to do). The guy with the gun gets nervous and takes my gear shift and puts it into neutral. I put it back in first. He reaches over and switches off my ignition. I turn it back on. He reaches out to close his door – I floor the car and he falls out . . . Okay, he still had my thirteen dollars, but I figure I'll write it off my taxes as charity.

So I'm driving along calling myself all sorts of obscene names because I'm so incredibly witless. I end up at my drug-addict neighbor's apartment. She's taken three Quaaludes, fixes me two Kahlua and Creams, we hide all her drugs, and wait for the police to come, but they take so long to get there that I get really allergic to her hyperactive Irish setter and have go to my own apartment so I can breathe. When the police finally arrive they are immediately suspicious – why am I in the wrong apartment? As they start telling me what a simpleton I am to be out on the beach, alone, at night, I look over and see all my pot plants on the window ledge, so I tell them how very right they are and I will certainly be more thoughtful in the future so as not to waste their valuable time.

A week later I go to look at police pictures. As I pull up to the police station the axle falls off my transmission and the car just dies. Has to be towed away.[10]

My parents gave me that car as a high school graduation present. And I have a theory about that too: never look a gift Audi under the hood . . .   especially if you got it from your relatives.

Because the first two cars Moose owned were given to her by her parents, she spent much of her time taking the bus. Taking the bus in L.A. is somewhat conducive to writing because of two factors: 1) time and the fact

---

10. The axle is not directly connected to the transmission. HMW

that you have an abundance of it, and 2) depression, specifically induced by either missing the only bus that runs that hour or by catching it.

Bus Thoughts

It's interesting how no one sits next to the man with the knife. (Some religious sect in white. I believe it's the Sikhs.)

One feels moved while observing the Ceremonial Exchanging of the Bus Drivers.

It is a very sadistic person who delights in farting on a public conveyance.

I was just thinking about relativity when I was deciding whether it would take less time to leave the bus by the front or the back door.

Relativity, the watchcry of the twentieth century, consumed Moose's thoughts while on the bus because when you have infinite time, you eventually get around to thinking about everything, even physics.

When I was around ten I would often read the Time-Life book on mathematics. In it was a cartoon illustrating relativity in the usual way: "Suppose there was a train that could go the speed of light and on this train there was a clock which was synchronized with the clock in town. After the train, traveling at the speed of light, went around the town once, would the clocks read the same time?" I willed myself to understand, but never really did. I accepted that it was true because it was a Time-Life book after all, and they had those nice color-coordinated covers. I still don't understand relativity, but that doesn't mean I can't cite it in conversation.[11]

Moose's Special Theory of Relative Good Looks

I was just sitting around thinking about the Principles of Relativity the other day. Special Relativity, that is, not General. Like what happens when you're going the speed of light and you turn on the TV? You know Einstein thought about things just like this. But I realized that there's an additional principle that Einstein overlooked. I mean, it wasn't his fault. He had a lot to think about. Actually I was roller skating when it came to me. See, when I lived in Venice, California, I spent most of my time roller skating. That's probably not too sur-

---

11. The train's clock would be behind the town's clock. HMW

prising to you. And I remembered – as you no doubt do too – that Einstein said as you approach the speed of light, buildings get taller and thinner. And also time slows down. Now I noticed as I approached the speed of light while roller skating that not only did people get taller and thinner, *they got better looking!* I swear. I've checked this time and time again and am convinced that this phenomenon is not merely a *trompe l'oeuf.*[12] People are definitely cuter the faster one goes by them. Indeed, common layman's knowledge has suggested this for years with the expression "She's passing pretty," which I interpret as, "She's pretty as one passes." Another case where folklore and common sense have beaten science to the truth. I have derived a mathematical equation for this phenomenon, which looks like this:

(picture of me roller-skating) $\rightarrow$ speed of light

$=$ (picture of stick figure) $\rightarrow$ (picture of Robert Redford)

(To be read: As I approach the speed of light, people begin to look more like Robert Redford.)

Indeed, as I speed past these better-looking individuals I feel certain that they are nodding absentmindedly to themselves, "Umm . . . passing pretty fast," as I momentarily catch their eye. Occasionally I ask these nodding people for the time and, to my astonishment, not only has time slowed down, but by the time they answer their watches have disappeared. I still haven't determined yet if this is merely due to the mercurial nature of Venice, California, or if it is in fact a true aspect of relativity.[13]

I've noticed a similar effect in New York, only there a more accurate description would be that the faster you pass someone the less your sensibilities are offended. That's why on the subway time slows down. I'm sure you've all noticed this. Especially if someone right next to you has forgotten to bathe. There's another principle Einstein forgot (!): as you approach the speed of light people have less body odor. I suspect that, had Einstein ridden the subway, this concept would not have eluded him. He did all his thinking in the car. It's lucky for us that Einstein did, in fact, think in the car because otherwise speed might not have been on his mind and we would be stuck with special theories like: as one walks toward Thrifty's, buildings get cheaper and shabbier.

---

12. Literally, "trick the egg." *Trompe l'oeil* means "trick the eye," probably what Moose meant. JMVB
13. Venice is known for its high crime rate. JMVB

So fond of his car was he, Einstein nicknamed it Doppler after one of Santa's reindeer.[14] And a consummate traveler, Einstein drove in many countries while he theorized. It's not known if he ever drove in England, but you can be sure that if he took a bath there, time slowed way down.

---

14. *None* of Santa's reindeer was named Doppler. NC

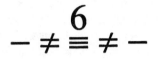

6

"Drugs filter reality, like seeing life without glasses" [1]

From the previous chapter it can be surmised that Moose went through the requisite drug phase, though it was generally mild. Her drug use was confined to marijuana (quite a lot of marijuana), some coke, LSD (twice), and whip-its.[2]

Los Angeles is an environment highly conducive to drug experimentation, due both to the prevalence of drugs and to the psychotic nature of the city. Much of her work from this period has to be read solely for its historic value. We reprint some of her drug-induced writing primarily for a flavor of what her mind was like at this time, but the reader will certainly agree that it lacks the concise perception and the grasp of life's enormity found in her other work.

5/10/80

Stoned in Venice. Boy, am I. I had a thought . . . hum . . . you know, all of a sudden you realize how stoned you are when you try to form consistent (concentric?) thought. No, no, stoned is concentric thought.

Randy says: You know, you can't have everything. (This is so brilliant, I ask her to repeat it.)

I am on a gay Venice beach just right of lifeguard station #3. Damn it, I had an insightful thought about romance. Now I'll never think it again and God knows, no one else will. Oh, well, maybe it'll go to Thought Heaven.

(I'm wondering if I'm funny and feeling somewhat certain that I'm just stupid.)

---

1. "Life without glasses" was the way Moose usually lived. She was too vain to wear her prescription glasses ("I only wear glasses when I need to see something . . . like other cars") and too poor to buy contact lenses. In moments of levity she maintained that she liked things fuzzy, that it made life impressionistic, "Renoir-esque." She was always trying to make life imitate art. JMVB
2. "Whip-its"—slang name for the nitrous oxide canisters used to dispense whipped cream. Nitrous oxide—more commonly known as "laughing gas"—induces twilight sleep at the dentist's office. HMW

Yet there were moments of lucidness, a realization of the drug's hold upon her, a questioning of her dependency, a knowing, a hoping that it wouldn't always be this way. Through it all—the drugs, the sex, the meaningless friendships—she was able to write. She needed to write; it was her "handhold," her safety valve, a way for her to know that she was still sane.

When I walk along Ocean Front Walk[3] I find myself wondering how many couples out here were married by Rev. Sun Myung Moon.

There are days when Venice is the most beautiful place in the world. The clouds form filigree about the sky. And the long claws of the palm trees fringe the picture. You who read this when I am but words on a page: know that I had some great days.

Late in the evening, as the sun burns a cigarette hole in your eye, the sky flattens to the depth of a Mexican pancake, the thick, soggy kind, and the air is sticky like watered-down syrup, making clothes cling to the skin between one's shoulder blades, a result of sitting too long against plastic car seats.

The setting sun throws capes of indigo shadows around the palm trees. Suddenly I realize that my eyes have lost their technicolor ability. Everything has shades of blue and sand. Sand mingles with my skin and loses its place. Molecules exchange. I am now part prehistoric dinosaur and the beach is now part Moose Minnion.

For the first year—no, two years—that I would get stoned, upon the first puff of pot I would always think of the same images in succession: a left foot, the "I Love Lucy" show, cottage cheese, and these toys that I used to play with as a child that looked like plastic puzzle pieces. There were more, but I don't remember them as well because the end images used to vary, almost in a kind of a pattern. I thought that it was some coded message from outer space and if I could just recognize the pattern, I would know what they were trying to communicate. *Very* shortly after I thought this thought, I convinced myself that this was probably not the case, but that it was instead conceivable that every time I got stoned, certain regions of my brain synaptically fired and the more I followed that line of thought, the deeper the ravine, the more my mind wanted to run off in that direction. It was a sensation of falling downhill, of being

---

3. A stretch of walkway paralleling the ocean that is found in Venice. On weekends, it often resembles a big party. HMW

pulled by suction, of how a fly must feel on the edge of a freeway as the still air has just whirlpooled into a giant wind tunnel.

Stoned, alone, and in L.A. — could be the theme song of my life

It was a time in my life when I drank a lot of wine, smoked a lot of pot, lounged in my bathrobe, stared out at the eaves and darkening sky, scratched my sunburn, and worried. I worried that the life I was leading was incorrect, but experienced a catharsis through worrying not unlike the kind that one experiences at Catholic confession. Worry to me is a method to allay guilt. I live my life, worry, and feel I've paid penance. No need to change: worrying is my salvation. It cleanses me. I can feel humble. I worried and drank. Worried and smoked pot. Worried and laid out at Venice Beach with neurotic Randy, my drug addict neighbor, and all her gay friends (chosen expressly because they were gay—they were so decadent and "in"). I tried to relax, and sometimes did, but my neuroses or drive or intellect or something kept prodding me on, trying to make sense, trying to find a pattern or construct one of my own. I thought myself brilliant but thwarted. Nicer than most but hesitant to admit it. At times I was far-seeing and even startled myself. But I was prone to being startled. I was restless, edgy, ready for action. I thought constantly, much to my distress, for I had too many thoughts and nowhere to put them.

I slept a lot and often in strange places. I even fell asleep while standing at Greg's Blue Dot. This caused neurotic Randy and all her gay friends to crack little witticisms and marvel, showing me off to passersby. Little did they know that I was dimly awake, that I rarely fall completely asleep in such situations, an animal reflex, really, a holdover from my previous life as a boa constrictor. I only feign sleep in order to escape, to alleviate boredom, to turn into myself and be saved from monotonous situations and inept conversations. I tired of telling Randy how beautiful she was when she wasn't, of telling her how many men couldn't keep their eyes off of her when they could . . . especially at Greg's Blue Dot.

Let me take a moment to say a few words about Greg's Blue Dot: a typical gay bar, a teeming anthill of a bar, body-to-body with bodies which explains why I could sleep standing up—there was nowhere to fall. At any other bar such close personal contact would lend itself to unsolicited fondling of women. Here, however, it was so safe for women as to be insulting. Suddenly I found myself nonexistent. How interesting to observe and know that I was unobserved. They only had eyes for each other. Or themselves. It amounted to the same thing. They served as each other's mirror.

I kept thinking of the Aesop fable about the dog with the bone seeing his reflection in the river. He jumps in to get the "other dog's" bone and of course loses his own. I don't know why I recalled this story—possibly because I had it confused with the story about Narcissus, who fell in love with his reflection in a river (ah! river motif, that must be it)—but both parables struck me as appropriate for the evening. The men here sought themselves in each other and were sexually excited. It was like out-of-body masturbation, similar to self-stimulation but with all the modern conveniences. They wanted what each other had, which was no more than a cheaper imitation of themselves.

I was in a room full of male clones all dressed in leather chaps, vests with no shirts, handkerchiefs tied carelessly around their throats . . . and Randy, queen of the "fag hags." I never knew what that term meant until I met her. Putting them together was simple math. The men at Greg's Blue Dot were crazy, safe, wild, zany, camp, wealthy, and tipped very well. They doted on the bizarre, the perturbed; they dealt in counterfeit emotions and good imitations. Randy was a poor man's Bette Midler, a deaf man's Barbra Streisand. She was camp. She was laughable. She said she loved life and then the paramedics had to break down the door to wake her out of her slumber. She always sang, "It's Judy's turn to cry, Judy's turn to cry," or, "It's my party and I'll cry if I want to," in her raucous, hackle-raising voice while she lay out in the sun, the ever-present joint nearby. Her face was that of a young apple doll, wrinkle lines in place but not quite dried enough to be irrevocable. The kind of face that was never popular despite her misconception to the contrary. She thought beauty lay solely in the kind of carcinogenic tans that people get in Southern California and thus her major aim in life was to obtain one. She lay out day after day, collecting unemployment but gainfully employed in the pursuit of the perfect bronze. This pursuit accounted for her parched and aging skin; having lost its elasticity, her skin stretched tightly over her face even after one of her starvation diets. (Her longest diet was a result of $6000 she owed to a friend for cocaine. She had offered, graciously, to sell some coke for him, but you know how things go. Somehow she thought she could make up the amount with her grocery money.)

I found in my dealings with Randy that the most dangerous times were when she was doing you a favor. She swore that helping others made her happy. She failed to notice, however, that her help rarely made others happy. When I turned twenty-two, Randy threw me a surprise party. She got me downstairs by calling to say that she'd just cut her wrists.

"Fifteen minutes," I said pointedly to my roommates. "In fifteen minutes you will call me up and tell me that my father has just died and I must leave town immediately." Of course, when I found out she'd only been thinking of me all along, I felt terrible. Somehow I always felt terrible around Randy. Needless to say, the party was a depressing collection of losers. And we all sat around and watched Randy, teetering precariously on her "fuck me" shoes, serve us cake and ice cream. (Her shoes, which were those slip-on kind, rose four-and-a-half inches above the floor because in her stocking feet Randy was barely tall enough to open her freezer. The freezer was where she kept her marijuana so you can understand her need for elevation.) Randy seemed to be always teetering, barely balanced on earth. This accounted for her constant clutching and grasping of one's arm, ostensibly in affection, more likely in a reaction to the earth's gravitational pull. Randy, however, had her own gravitational pull. She was a black hole, sucking you in with no hope of escape. She wanted everyone's attention so she could tell them how much life had made her suffer. Compared to how she had made others suffer, life had nothing on her.

One of the sufferers was Moxie, the pitiful, unkempt Irish setter that tried to roam around Randy's tiny apartment and would shit on the living room rug if Randy forgot to come home and take him out, something that happened at least once a week. I was forever walking Moxie because I felt sorry for him. I was also forever cleaning up the living room. As I think back now, I don't really know why I felt responsible, but for some reason I did. Both Randy and my mother could do that to me. And I chose to be responsible to them. Randy kept Moxie for the same reasons she tried to keep me. We both afforded instant attention and unquestioning sympathy, one of us with a furry shoulder and hot doggy breath, and the other of us (me) with analytical reasoning and a desire to help out the underdog. And I suppose I used her as much as she used me. Randy gave me someone to follow; she dominated everything and I needed domination. She gave me drugs and also a world where drug-related rituals made life meaningful, a dreamlike existence where I didn't have to think about the future or even the present. And occasionally Randy could be fun. She was larger-than-life, a Sally Bowles from *Cabaret*, a character out of a book to me, full of bodacious adventures and outlandish, attention-getting schemes.

One such scheme began when she borrowed Norman's cockatoo. (That's "Mr. Norman" to you.) Norman had a combination plant boutique/beauty salon. The hair dryers rested there under the potted date palms, the manicure table sidled up to the dieffenbachia. Maidenhair ferns (Norman's sense of humor) drooped over the large utility sinks. Ferns and ficuses obscured the checkerboard pattern of the floor (which was a good thing because the floor was filthy with bird droppings). There were baskets and rattan fans and witchy-looking brooms that no one ever bought to sweep anything up with and those Brobding-nagian teak forks and spoons that you always see for sale at Cost Plus, all quite festively arranged around the barber chairs. And there by the cash register was a four-foot-tall bird pedestal with this beautiful white cockatoo benignly cling-ing to its perch, quite happy to cry "Suck this, baby" to all the women who came in to get their hair done. I believe the women came just for the novelty of it all.

Randy loved this cockatoo. She had great affection for anything that she was bigger than and could smother. One afternoon she decided she wanted to take the cockatoo grocery shopping. She told Norman she'd be very careful with it. Norman had known Randy for years and somehow thought that meant some-thing. I'd known Randy a few months and would not have lent her my library card.

Now I suppose one would not think a cockatoo necessary gear when shop-ping for groceries. It would seem, in fact, to be just what one wouldn't want in a busy supermarket. But with Randy everything was provoked by her exces-sive need to be noticed. As a resident of Los Angeles she epitomized the inhabi-tants' thirst for fame. Randy told me that she used to be known far and wide as "Raccoon" because of the way she did her makeup (she said this proudly), and was always recognized on the Strip[4] and once even got her picture on the cover of a magazine, I don't remember which one. This was her crowning glory, her meaning in life, this proved that she was somebody. To be remem-bered, no matter the cost or the conditions, was her *raison d'être.* I confess, I occasionally fall into this mindset, but I control it. I don't sacrifice ethics or good taste or succumb to a poor use of makeup. I place limits, priorities on fame. It must be under my conditions or I'm not interested. (Or rather, I'm al-ways interested, but I shame myself into loftier ambitions.) Randy had no loft-ier ambitions. Her wants were all of a plebeian nature. Originally I thought that everything Randy did was provoked by her mating urge, but then I realized that this wasn't the true root. Mating came after getting attention in her Hierarchy of Values. (This is someone's theory, I forget whose—ask my mother.)[5]

Mankind's Hierarchy of Values
1. Survival
2. Food
3. Procreation

---

4. The Sunset Strip. HMW
5. This was Abraham Maslow's theory. Maslow was a forerunner in the development of humanistic psychology. His "Hierarchy of Needs" starts at the bottom with fundamental biological needs and

4. Success   (I'm guessing)
5. Philosophy (my addition)

Randy's Hierarchy of Values

1. Survival   (even though she kept
threatening to kill herself,
it was a ruse, merely a
technique for getting)
2. Attention
3. Drugs
4. Food   (#4 and #5 are actually
5. Mating   interchangeable, depending
on how starved she was and
for what)

Randy never got to philosophy. She rarely made it past drugs. Drugs were food and drink to Randy. They consumed her rather than vice versa. She wallowed in drugs, in the ritual and the paraphernalia, the accouterments to drugs. All her energy was spent getting drugs, using them, or showcasing them. She would roll EZ Wider cigarette papers around chopsticks and then pack them full of pot. It would take her hours but she had essentially nothing better to do with her time than get high—and rolling joints is a good pastime when one is high. She had a Chinese enamel box full of these perfectly rolled joints which

---

rises to the more complex psychological desires that can only be attained after the fundamental needs have been met:

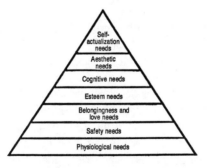

(*Introduction to Psychology,* by Rita L. Atkinson, Richard C. Atkinson, Ernest R. Hilgard, © 1983 by Harcourt Brace Jovanovich, Inc.) KLL

she would display, but no one was ever allowed to smoke them. They were hors d'oeuvres that she never offered her guests. Rather, she placed the joints in view as a tantalizing reminder that they weren't really her best friends. But then, no one was.

Because Randy's primary sustenance was drugs, the only time she became interested in food was when she could get it for free. This, not inexplicably, corresponded to when she was most interested in sex. (An example of the L.A. barter system.) During one of these bursts of mating frenzy Randy and I went to Trashy Lingerie, a place that sells "garments for the boudoir" and does so accompanied by a fake fireplace and ladies *en deshabille*. It was a marvel to me. As you enter the front door you are faced with a locked gate and a receptionist who informs you that in order to gain admittance all clientele must first buy membership cards. After the receptionist buzzes you through you are greeted by the "Madam" of the establishment, a buxom, down-to-earth woman with a husky voice and a face like Margot Kidder, who asks if you desire any help. Randy always desired assistance because it allowed her to relieve her vexations upon the unwary attendant. To anyone who waited on her she would only reply with senseless sarcasm.

"Would you like to see something in your size?"

"No, I'd like to see something in my dog's size." And then she would turn to me and giggle like a horse at what a wit she'd been.

I managed to escape from the fitting room while Randy had all her attention focused on the Madam's demonstration of the proper way to lace a corset. I walked around the shop, admiring the finery, fingering the silks and velvets, staring at the thinness of the shopgirls, whom I had earlier mistaken for mannequins. I perused the racks of corsets, sexy nighties, replicas of Victorian lingerie (all equipped with easy-access bindings). Randy tried on several of these and managed, in her haste and petulance, to snag a negligée on her dangling earrings; this she hid from the proprietress by stuffing the negligée into the cup of one of the corsets and then hanging it back up. Then, spying a fuchsia-colored brassiere pinned to the wall on display, she insisted that she be allowed to try it on. This meant that it had to be removed via stepstool and later replaced. She ended up buying only one pair of panties (chartreuse) and acted as if this was done out of an extreme benevolence on her part in return for all their time and effort, not as if she really intended to wear them. However, she later returned and bought a half-corset thing that leaves one's breasts supported but exposed. She bought it to entice one-eyed Simon, head chef of the Beverly Hilton.

Simon became Randy's "main man" because he could get her free lunches at the Beverly Hilton and she could even take her mother (whom she hated, but there's nothing like impressing people you hate). Simon looked a lot like Jerry, the orthodontist on the old "Bob Newhart Show," only not as good. He and Randy went round after round. They dated, fought, broke up, and then, realizing the kind of losers that losers attract, started dating again. This, for all I know, may still be going on.

Randy became most interested in Simon after Norman stopped speaking to her because of the cockatoo mishap. Up until then Norman had been her best friend. But Norman should have known better. I know I had misgivings as soon as Randy put her metallic blue Corvette into reverse and kamikazed out of the driveway, the cockatoo squawking in alarm and flapping its wings in Randy's face. She'd put the cockatoo on the steering wheel and it perched there precariously, raising its voice in distress and irritation at being taken from its tranquil spot among the coleus. Randy tried making little cooing sounds to it, but not being quite the motherly type (I would venture to say that she'd be the kind of mother children have nightmares about), she caused the cockatoo to further display its dissatisfaction by trying to peck at her pursed lips. And the fact that Randy's driving was extremely erratic didn't make the situation any better. She only occasionally stayed in her lane and, when the opportunity presented itself, Randy was quick with lewd gestures, foul words, and an assortment of racial slurs. She was the kind that drives by braille, as they say, meaning that she used the bumps in the road to keep herself within the confines of the lane. Moreover, Randy never decided until the last minute if she was going to turn a corner or go straight, so the cockatoo kept ending up at a ninety-degree angle to the earth, clutching with its little cockatoo feet and valiantly trying to right itself by walking sideways up the steering wheel. As soon as it made it to the top, Randy straightened the wheel and the poor frustrated thing repeated the process on the other side. By the time we got to the store the cockatoo was acting like it was drunk, reeling and lurching as it tenuously gripped the wheel. (Also, we were smoking the ubiquitous joint in the car, which may have made the cockatoo less agile but more able to handle it.)

We went inside and Randy set the bird on the handle of the shopping cart. It promptly pitched forward. It managed, however, with a diminished though still intact will to survive (see Mankind's Hierarchy of Values, #1[6]), to hang on to the chrome bar of the shopping cart. I looked in amazement at it hanging,

---

6. Like all animals, cockatoos have an instinctual desire to survive. Whether this can be likened to human need is another question. KLL

beak downward, by its claws. It looked like an albino bat. In fact, it looked dead.

"Randy," I said with concern, "Norman's cockatoo looks sick."

"Feh!" Randy monosyllabically replied. Her standard Yiddish retort, adequate for any social situation. "He's just playing dead. It's his favorite game."

Bending over and peering upside down at its slightly tilted head, I saw it open one leathery eyelid and then close it again.

"It looked a lot better when we were at Norman's . . . "

Sighing as if taxed beyond belief, Randy said, "Okay, we'll go get it some pepper beef. That'll revive it."

"Aren't birds vegetarians?" I asked. I thought over all I'd ever read about birds.

"Of course not," she said bitingly. "Norman feeds him falafels all the time."

Falafels are those Middle Eastern, meatball-looking things made from chick peas and I told her so in a how-can-you-be-so-dumb kind of voice.

"Not the kind Norman makes. He makes his with meat."

I gave up. Let her feed the bird pepper beef. What did I care? Then I remembered that of course birds eat worms and bugs and things. How much worse could pepper beef be?[7]

Off Randy went through the packed supermarket, pushing past people's carts in her impatience. The bird swung like a pendulum underneath the handle. I ran after her.

"Randy," I pleaded, "slow down. It's barely hanging on."

"Since when are you such a bird expert?" she asked, not slowing her pace.

"Excuse me!" a lady said quite loudly as Randy pushed the woman's cart out of her way and inadvertently rammed it into the woman's rear end.

"Ah, blow it out your ass. This is a store, not a library."

I was not sure what Randy meant by this and neither, I think, was the woman.

"You need to learn some manners," the woman finally retorted. By then we were already two aisles away.

Randy yelled back, "Yeah, and you need to do something about that mustache."

"Randy . . . " I said with exasperation as we approached the meat counter.

"Feh!" She gesticulated in a non-specific but still insulting manner and then,

---

7. Cockatoos are omnivorous birds, meaning that they will eat whatever presents itself in the wild, including animals and plants. HMW

without missing a beat, she ordered from the butcher, "A half a pound of pepper beef."

By now the bird had actually managed to right itself (with a little help from me) and was blinking in a confused fashion and trying out its neck to make sure it still worked.

Out of the corner of my eye I saw the woman moving toward us.

"Uh-oh," I said to myself.

She came right up to Randy. "You are a very rude woman. I was going to say young lady, but as I see now that you are neither, I won't. Not only are you rude, but you also are harboring a germ-carrying, disease-ridden animal which should not be in a grocery store.

"Sir!" The woman called for the butcher's attention as he handed the pepper beef to Randy. "This woman has a sick bird out here. Aren't there laws protecting people from diseased animals in food service areas?"

"Here, baby," Randy cooed to the cockatoo, feeding it some beef.

"Hey, you!" the butcher said to Randy, "You're not supposed to bring any animals in here. Get that thing out of here."

"It's not an animal. It's a bird." Randy's knowledge of the wild kingdom was spare.

"Didn't you hear him!" the woman shouted. "He said—"

She stopped suddenly and blanched. I looked where she was looking and winced as I saw the cockatoo suddenly spit out several small pieces of pepper beef.

"It's vomiting! That bird is vomiting in this grocery store!!" she shrieked. Then the cockatoo closed its little cockatoo eyes and fell forward onto the floor like a sack of something which doesn't sound good when it falls to the floor. Fortunately, the woman was standing close to it and the bird caught on the bottom of her blouse as it fell and then it landed on her shoe, somewhat breaking its fall.

"Oh, my poor baby," cried Randy, stooping to pick it up. She cradled the cockatoo in her arms. The woman was speechless. Her mouth kept opening and closing like a blowfish's. Little flecks of pepper beef spotted her blouse.

"I think we'd better try to revive it," Randy nodded, the concerned mother. A crowd had gathered around us by now wanting to know what all the shouting was about.

I said, "I think we'd better leave."

The woman gathered steam. "I am going to report you to the ASPCA. What is your name?" She searched for a pen.

"My name is Skeeter Blaizewell and you can report me if you want, but it isn't my bird."

Rolling my eyes, I whispered, "Wait here."

"Where are you going?" she demanded, but I was gone. I ran to the next aisle to get some ammonia to waft under the cockatoo's nose. (Where exactly is a cockatoo's nose? I asked myself.) Having read a lot of those old Gothic romances, I knew that ammonia is the main ingredient in smelling salts. When I came back they were still yelling. I opened the bottle and held it to those little portholes in the cockatoo's beak, assuming this was the right place.

"What are you doing?" asked Randy.

"Miss Blaizewell, I'd like to know when you're going to remove this health hazard from the store! Doesn't anyone else care that their life is being endangered by a rabid bird?" The woman was attempting to pull in some support.

"He's not rabid!" Randy shouted at her.

"He was vomiting!"

"When you barf are you rabid?"

This prompted an all-out yelling match contributed to by other individuals standing around who obviously didn't have enough to do during their days. It ended when Randy yelled, "Oh, blow it out your—"

"Blow it out your ass. Blow it out your ass." The cockatoo, having responded to treatment, came to and, as if cued, said the words it loved to hear. Randy cuddled the bird.

"I know that bird," another woman cried. I cringed. "That bird belongs to Mr. Norman."

"Who's Mr. Norman?" the woman with the beef-flecked blouse frowned.

"Mr. Norman, my hairdresser. His shop is on Overland a few blocks above Venice Boulevard. You can't miss it. It looks like a plant store. This cockatoo is always there saying funny things. He's a scream."

"That's wonderful . . . " the woman said snidely. She pointed her finger at Randy. "You'll be hearing from me. That'll teach you to bring a diseased animal into the grocery store."

"I'll bet it has less diseases than you do and none of them sexual." Randy smirked at this last bit, proud of herself.

The woman looked daggers at Randy and walked away. The bird croaked, *"Voulez vous coucher avec moi ce soir?"*

A few days later I saw Randy and she was all pissed off. "What's wrong?" I asked.

"Norman won't talk to me anymore."

"Why?"

"That woman called the ASPCA and reported him as mistreating his cockatoo and he has to pay a fine."

"You could've paid it for him."

She looked at me as if I was stupid. "It's not *my* bird."

I think she managed to appease Norman later with drugs. It was the one commodity that Randy could always pacify her friends with—that's why they were her friends. Enough drugs can make you accept anything . . . for a while.

The day I first met Randy she was returning from the hospital after almost setting her face on fire. (Many years later I would see Randy at Cedars-Sinai—I was just getting out of the emergency room, having had an allergic reaction to something my allergist gave me—and I would remember that Randy and hospitals always struck me as synonymous.) Originally she told me that the bandage over her eye was due to her oven exploding when she went to pull out a casserole. Had I known Randy for even a week I would have realized that she didn't know what a casserole was. Shortly after that (roughly an hour later, when we were free-basing cocaine), she told me that she had been free-basing and it had exploded in her face. The patch over her left eye served as proof. She invited me down that same first day to join her because she had to free-base in order to "ease the pain." I had smoked pot at this point, but not a lot. I had never done coke. I was quite naive about most things.

The whole free-basing process is a tremendous ritual. Randy took the coke, which was in a vial the size of a Barbie doll thermos, and proceeded to submerge the vial into boiling water, then into cold, then back into the boiling, back into the cold, repeatedly. I think she may have also put some baking soda in with the coke; I forget. She wouldn't tell me how she did it because she said it was a terrible habit and better that I not know. Randy the Altruist. I have since learned from more informed people than I that her method was very tedious and dangerous. She then took this vial, poured the contents onto a paper towel, let it dry a bit (though not long, as she couldn't wait), put a small amount on the screen of her special water pipe, picked up a cotton ball with those long, bent suture scissors that doctors use, soaked the cotton ball in 151-proof rum, lit it with her ornate cigarette lighter, applied it to the free-based coke, and then inhaled while I watched the spiritual smoke swirl around inside the glass pipe, thick, sultry smoke, weaving its way, snakelike, through the pipe and into her lungs, then into her brain where it induced this tremendous awakening, peace of mind, all-is-right-with-the-world, dam-the-torpedos feeling. If she had a lot of coke, she would let me have my own hit, if not, she would let me have seconds on hers. I found this odd but exciting, applying my lips to hers and inhaling of the drug. It was like a witches' ritual only instead of a black cat we had a ruddy Irish setter that would bound around knocking coke on the floor and causing me the most violent allergic reaction. Because of this lip-to-lip contact, breathing another's breath, I began to wonder if I was lesbian, but the coke made me know that this was all right. Everything was all right.

And I sat, anesthetized, in her room, a monument to Haight-Ashbury with its waterbed and simulated brown fur bedspread, her abundance of wood-framed mirrors, plant holders, wall hangings, her stereo playing a Barbra Streisand-Barry Gibb record with which Randy would sing along. On her bureau lay her drug equipment: the grinder, the sieve, the water pipes, the vials, the mother-of-pearl inlaid spoons—everything was top quality and expensive. She spent all her money, when she had it, on what my father would have called gimcracks: gold coke-spoon earrings, mushroom candles, decoupaged prints of two people against a sunset with corny inscriptions like "Do not follow me for I will not lead. Do not lead me for I will not follow. But stand beside me and we will walk together forever." Randy was able to buy these frill possessions from the money she made renting out her spare bedroom. Her monthly rent was $250, but she charged her roommate $300, letting him think that her rent was $600 a month. And this amount wasn't inconceivable because my apartment went for $500 a month. (Randy had been there for years.) However, she went through roommates quickly because, viper that she was, she wrapped around them so tightly that they had to leave in order to breathe.[8] And her apartment left you feeling just as claustrophobic. The air was thick with dog fur and marijuana fumes. The place hadn't been cleaned since before she lived there. One time some wild pilot friends of mine came over and we went down to Randy's. When she was in the other room they threw a beer can behind her TV. (The condition of her apartment motivated them to do this.) A year later when I moved out, curiosity overcame me and I bent down to look under her TV. Sure enough, there it was, coated with a layer of dust. And I know it hasn't moved since.

You would have thought she'd have had time to clean, so seldom did she work. Her profession was as an automotive service support representative, which meant that when someone brought in their car to the dealership and they would tell her what was wrong with it, she would tell them what was really wrong with it and what an incredible amount it was going to cost, and then she would go into the bathroom, snort a little coke, and come out ready to handle the next customer. While I knew her she was on unemployment or disability

---

8. Vipers do not kill by suffocation. HMW

fifty percent of the time. Because I was going to school, we found that we often kept the same hours. We driveled them away in worthless pursuits, mostly drug-oriented. It would take hours just to prepare the free-based cocaine. But we had hours. We had days. We weren't going anywhere. And so we would languidly inhale this exotic drug, our friendship existing solely out of need: need of drugs, need of a mother, need of a friend, need of not being alone, need of power—all negative conditions. Other than that we had nothing in common. She—with her blood red, Mata Hari fingernails finding tiny grains of coke in her matted bedroom rug (she once knocked over $300 worth of coke in her sleep and the next day was kind enough to let me inhale it from the floor . . . which I did), her rouged, Indian Earth cheeks and tautly tanned skin, her lexicon of Yiddish put-downs, and, most of all, her fierce desire to claim a friend, forcing them to come to her aid at every little crisis in her life—and I—with my philosophies, my desire to experience life, my acceptance of all realities, and, especially, with a mother who raised me with an Achilles Heel of feeling compelled to come to the aid of anyone who throws a temper tantrum—were a symbiotic unit. It was an almost sadomasochistic relationship, for Randy was very like my mother. Both have threatened suicide to me, both desperately needed me to tell them things that they didn't believe themselves, both lived through me, and both disliked the little bit they knew about the other. They would both be appalled at my finding them similar, but only their methods differed—their effect was the same. In all fairness, I must say that my mother was eminently preferable to be raised by, but she was also by far the more frightening of the two.

Randy was never frightening, just pathetic. Like the time we went to the Date Room, heart of Culver City, and she wore her skin-tight, hot fuchsia stretch jumpsuit and looked like a more modern version of death warmed over. She kept standing up to go to the bathroom and on the way would whisper in my ear, "Now watch how many men turn and look as I walk away." And I watched and none did. When she returned she asked, "Was I right?" And I, never one to question anyone's reality (if she wanted to believe she was a sex object, she was), said, "I'm sure several men did." She never listened to my words, never noticed that I didn't completely validate her theories, and if I had said, "No, no one looked," she would have accused me of not paying attention and argued with me until I concurred. She knew what she believed and no amount of external information was going to upset her internal knowledge. Randy's concept of reality definitely oriented itself around the facts which suited her best, specifically the facts which would get her drugs or money. I once lent Randy $200 for her rent which she was supposed to pay back within the week. (Okay, I was stupid. Get used to it; it will happen again.) Two days after I lent her the money her stereo was stolen from her car. Randy maintained that I had left the passenger door unlocked the day before. This made no sense to me because if the door was unlocked, why would they have had to break the window? She also maintained that her stereo cost exactly $200. Do you see where I'm going with this? So I bided my time and managed, as I moved out, to steal a rust-colored coat which she had lent me. It was probably worth twenty dollars.

It took her two months to discover that it was gone. One day while in summer stock I got a message that Randy had called. I'd completely forgotten by this time that I'd stolen her coat and I was sure that she was calling because she was going to commit suicide and I must talk her out of it. I geared up for the ordeal, saying to myself, "What are friends for but this?" I called her and she started yelling at me about her coat. Shaking my head at my naiveté, I hung up. Months later an old boyfriend of mine called me at my parents' home. I had been dating him at the same time that I lived above Randy and they had *hated* one another. Each had viewed the other as competition and made my life miserable trying to bend my ear in opposite directions. My old boyfriend confessed to me that he had been there the night I called Randy, the night she'd discovered her coat stolen. He laughed, "We were in bed together. Don't you think that's funny?" He wasn't trying to taunt me, he genuinely found it humorous.

"I think that's very sad," I said, depressed at their pitiful need to possess me, and instead possessing the only person who reminded them of me, the person they hated, yet the last link that connected them to me. They personified a desperate, quailing, foul-tasting L.A., an L.A. which makes people wizened, tortured creatures succumbing to the basest of needs, grasping for petty advantages over other such creatures and coming away empty-handed.

Randy never came away completely empty-handed, however. She always managed to grab someone, pulling herself up hand over fist until she no longer needed them for support. She was a survivor, the thing that floats, somehow always managing to rise to the top though never getting there under her own power. She could climb over you and then make you apologize for getting in her way. Her reality was a test for me. How much of an existentialist was I? Could I accept her reality and mine both? What sacrifices must I make and was it worthwhile? I created running dialogue in my head to counteract her arrogance, her treatment of waitresses, department store clerks, friends of mine she didn't like, and sometimes (ofttimes) me. It did no good to make honest comments, to put forth an idea differing from hers for she would browbeat you into submission. So I thought my own thoughts and planned my revenge.

Ah, but revenge is too harsh a word to describe my freedom, for all I plotted was how I would never again see, communicate with, or have anything to do with her. Some people drain you. They are vampires. They allow you no choice but to lose them in the melee of life. There's no half-and-half, give-and-take, nor amicable disinvolvement. I was too, too much smarter than she and too far beyond, using a vocabulary she couldn't comprehend. What a bitch I sound, and yet in reality (mine), she was the bitch. The difficult, defunct princess still trying to lay Prince Charming but, due to haste, only finding frogs in her bed. Her relationships were all of the two-week variety and ended with her changing the locks on her doors and moving all her valued possessions (her drugs and ermine coat – the one I should have stolen) up to my apartment. With all the coke and Black Beauties, Quaaludes and pot, utensils and paraphernalia, I could have opened a head shop.

Randy was a storybook character, which is perhaps why I stood her. But she was only interesting on the periphery of the plot. There was no empathy for her condition. Sympathy was the closest I could come and it was more for those around her than for Randy herself. And yet, almost anything was preferable to being alone. I wanted friends, but motivated ones, not those who had succumbed to the blasé of L.A. Not resigned to waiting tables, waiting in traffic, waiting for roles, wading through life.

And it was at these intersections of life and philosophy that drugs became so very important to Moose.

Oh, there is such relief when the drug inches in and consumes my brain. It pervades upon the pervading gloom. And no longer am I sullied but subtle. No longer wretched but resigned. It makes me even think I have a way with words. Am I addicted? Probably. But it is such a good addiction. I have need of an opiate. I learned in Biological Psych that our minds have opiate receptors. I figure why not fill them? My body is not adept at making enough of its own.[9]

I will remember these days. These days of snorting spilled coke off of Randy's floor. Days of hedonistic pleasure. Drugs and more. Aimless searching. Wondering where I'm going and if. See, I don't know the sort of person I am yet. Will I continually be writing my memoirs thinking I'll eventually have something? Will I be forever thinking of fame and never reach it?

I think, thick with drugs. I've accepted this softness of mind, this euphoria. I am a captive of a time and of a city. Tied down with drugs and an Audi, tortured by mediocrity, but fed well and entertained royally. My relationship with

---

9. Neither THC nor cocaine interacts with opiate receptors. HMW

L.A. and Randy is synonymous: I am as seduced by the city as I am by its inhabitants. So I will move to Greece. I *must* move to Greece to get away from traffic, drugs, and Randy. She is a harpy, a clinger to my life. Parasitic. She is mistletoe. She means well yet smothers you while she's doing you a good turn. I cannot fight her. I must sever my ties. I need a new life and one that isn't festering in L.A. I feel like one sore on a syphilitic L.A. I want peace of mind. I want to choose my friends, not by what they can do for me, but by how our minds interlock. The synapses we create across our collective brains.

People here seem to live life without passion. L.A. breeds this passive existence. Nothing is crucial. It's not a life, it's an offramp. I need expansive emotions. Life or death causes. I need thickness to my existence. I must leave L.A. This chapter has lasted too long, for I don't recognize myself in the mirror anymore. The eyes I see reveal someone else. And they shed their tears, not mine. They possess not only my soul, but my sense of humor, and keep it captive somewhere in the sulci and gyri of my mind.

There's got to be more to life than L.A.

—Ibsen

7
$$- \neq \equiv \neq -$$

It's not clear that Ibsen ever visited L.A., so a discretionary "writer's prerogative" might be appropriate here. Forever irreverent, Moose had no qualms about embellishment, in art *and* in life. If a quote didn't readily come to mind, she would simply make one up, attributing it to whomever served her purpose. The flow of the words and the tilt of the line she considered of greater importance than the "apparent" truth of the prose.

Literature was often a source of controversy for Moose. She respected well-known writers, yet lost no time in satirizing those who quoted them. She read great works, but despised those who taught them. Indeed, in presenting her work in this manner, we acknowledge that we might well be causing her to roll over in her grave, were she in one.

Always somewhat defiant when it came to her disregard for formal schooling,

Education, after all, is merely a vicarious experience,

Moose regarded college as a way station, a halfway house, allowing an individual extra time to grow to an adult without forcing the real world upon him. This, she believed, was the true purpose of college. Real learning was something done furtively, sporadically, more often at night and in desperation.

Moose's distaste for higher education lay with authority, not learning. Rather than question authority, she simply chose to ignore it. This was most easily done by avoiding class. Instead, she sat at the UCLA coffeehouse and wrote. This helped dissipate the frenzy which welled up inside her.

Moose's comments about school were terse:

When one considers infinity, theater history seems somewhat silly.

Notes taken in class were cryptic:

Amer. Lit. 1/15/79
Poe: offended times by not being didactic, moral. Attempts to penetrate sounds where human mind cannot go. Ex: Melancholy effect (100 lines). Refrain arbitrary (adds piquancy). I don't want to be here. I don't want to

be anywhere. I want to stop having hopeless love. I want to stop. Why wasn't I born a Muppet? 1836 – Poe can write to benefactor, Kennedy; then married 14-year-old Virginia, she died at 22 breaking a blood vessel in throat singing.[1] I need a benefactor. How can people who marry their 14-year-old cousins get benefactors and I can't? Why can't I take notes like most normal students?

Sitting by this open window, with the leaves making dry music outside, I feel like Tom Sawyer or Huckleberry Finn or any such child knowing the frustration of sitting in a tight brown desk listening to a tight brown lecture by a plump pompous teacher who knows no higher truths than Melville used Shakespearean imagery.

She worried.

I began to get nervous when I realized that everyone else had three blue books and I had but one.

She drank.

If I have to study, I might as well be plastered.
– Good Earth Restaurant, circa 1980

She complained.

They never tell you in directing class what to do if no one shows up at auditions.

She parodied.

Hope is the thing with feathers,
I am the thing with dandruff.

During class much of her time was spent writing, though it had little to do with the subject at hand.

Quiz:
There was a deer, a doe, a man, a faun, a tree, a brook, twelve branches, one hundred and forty-three verbs (including thirty-seven modals), one conflict concerning race relations and one concerning time travel (both for-

---

1. According to *The Norton Anthology of American Literature* Volume I (pp. 1203–1204), Poe actually secretly married a thirteen-year-old Virginia Clemm in 1835 and then publicly remarried her in 1836. "In January, 1842, Virginia Poe, not yet twenty, burst a blood vessel in her throat (she lived only five more years)." HMW

ward and back), eighty-three marks of punctuation (though no colons), and a moral, unclearly defined so as to be ambiguous, providing much literary dispute. Reconstruct this story and analyze whether or not the school of thought which supports the argument of neglect in parochial schools is valid and, if so, what are the ramifications which challenge a belief in God?

Okay, go:

Her basic belief was that

Literature is not good solely because of its structure. In fact, if its best quality is structure, then it's not good literature.

Structure, that all important literary scaffolding, would continue to plague her. She argued not against its necessity, but against its limited styles and colors, and debated specifically whether or not to "plot."

June 1984 — Some thoughts about plots

I guess it's kind of important to have a goal when writing a book. I think it might be more commonly called a plot. But when my life has neither goal nor plot I find it hard to manufacture one just for a book. In order of importance it would seem as if my life should have first preference. Maybe, maybe not . . . it's all water under a gift horse (you get an extra bonus point if you can pack two clichés into one), because I'm out of plots, goals, and Bailey's Irish Cream and have been for a while. (In actual fact, the Bailey's Irish Cream was my parents' and they probably have my plots and goals as well.)

To me a plot is too simple an answer. It's given that everything will turn out, maybe not well, but something will change and in a cute way. Plots are all cute. They all tie up attractively. A plot with loose ends is a sloppy plot and probably won't be found in the Book-of-the-Month Club. No wonder everyone is neurotic and unhappy: we are raised on plots, raised on everything turning out properly. The good are rewarded and the bad must pay the price, from "The Three Bears" to *Moby Dick*. Of course, now we have plots with anticlimactic endings. Like they are fooling someone. It's really worse. They set you up like it's a traditional plot and then whamo, you find out that the neighbors are getting a divorce and you don't even know their names.

About this book people will say, "She didn't have a plot because she's not bright enough to write one." They won't say, "She has no plots because of a socio-philosophical desire to question, existentially, whether people can afford the luxury of believing in something which, like justice or equality, doesn't exist." Even Santa Claus has more reality than plots do because it's accepted that he is fantasy. But I digress.

Life has no plot. Loose ends rarely become less loose. People die and then their fascination for plots becomes fairly academic. Plot is only the interweaving of characters and events with the boring days left out. The days when the characters did their laundry or took the wife and kids to the beach. (Which brings me to the question I just asked my roommates: "Do you think cavemen ever went on vacations? They had beaches.")

Why should I have a plot just because everyone else does? Why should their insecurities dictate my work? Are plots really that necessary to good writing? And if not plots, what? Varied punctuation? An easy-to-read typeface? Funny cartoons?

Okay, so maybe I don't really know what makes a plot. I mean it's obviously re-introducing the characters over and over again and making them a little bit better people each time (unless they're villains). But I'm sure there must be more to it. Who taught Steinbeck or Hemingway about plots? How did they know? Is it recorded on their DNA? Did some dead uncle will them his set of thirty as-of-yet unused plots? Can one win a plot on a game show?

Ultimately the crux of the issue is: why plots? Why not everything has to end in "o"? Or you have to be able to sing the moral to the tune of "Swanee River"? That makes as much sense to me. Which is probably why not many people understand my logic. Plots are just too foreign to me. Too contrived. Too satisfying. Too Spielberg. I'd rather have single words, a past participle, three geese a-laying, a stone's throw from eternity, than try and manufacture a plan, a pattern, logic, rules, rationality. We only think there is logic because we created it. Once when I was little I took a pencil to a piece of paper and, without looking, quickly made a lot of scribbly marks in the hope (somewhat faint) that a masterpiece would be created unwittingly. Instead my parents got mad at me for wasting paper. Now I write scribbly fragments of thought in the hope (somewhat faint) that a plot will come of itself. And I look around for an angered party.

I suppose that'll be the critics. I can already sense that they'll be ruthless. They always are. Why else call them critics? They've built their careers by abusing others' work by unraveling their plots. They don't care that a plot is the demise of arbitrarity [sic], that it's an unfair advantage characters have over real people. And the saddest thing is that characters seem more real than most people I know. Maybe more of us should have plots. Let's take them out of books and put them back in life where they belong.

Face it, I'm jealous. Why should a fictional character have more motivation than I do? I look over my past and think, where is the mysterious message, where are the clues leading me to the answer? Whenever I meet new people

I reveal to them things one would normally only reveal to a close friend, all in hopes that they will make the connection or see a pattern I have missed. "Compulsively Intimate," I call it – the need to tell strangers all the dark secrets in one's life in the hopes that they will furnish the missing piece of the puzzle, the piece that I can't ever figure out. But the piece that I can't figure out is why do I so badly need to reveal to others all the private and tortured parts of my life? For mere attention? Or because their own revelations are so damned boring? I feel guilty that my life is so much more interesting than other people's. I feel guilty that they like listening to my exploits and I dread listening to theirs. But why have a conversation that doesn't touch any emotion or reveal anything sordid? Life is too short to continually discuss the weather.

That's why I like to travel abroad, because even though everyone says the same mundane things over there, they have those great accents! And you can ignore, for instance, that they are only asking you to pass the salt because of the sheer joy you feel at understanding them and *actually passing them the salt*.

I prefer Europe to the U.S – it's better not to know what people are saying and to retain an air of mystery. That way conversation becomes a game. (Unless of course, you have no place to stay at night and it's already dark and the operators just hang up on you.) But I figure as long as you know how to say "Where are your bathrooms?" what else do you really need to know?

*Short List – Free to the Reader – Of the Number One
Question to Ask in Every Country*

Spanish:
¿Donde esta los banyos? [sic]

Korean:
Wha jong shi e o di e yo?

Thai:
Hong nám u tinai? (Room for water, where is it?)

Chinese:
Ki my young how?

Hebrew (Formal):
E-fo hno-chi-yout? (Where is your place of ease?)

Hebrew (Slang):
E-fo habet she moosh? (Where is the house of use?)

Polish:
Gdzie jest ubikacia?

Greek:
Poo in e tuelta?

French:
Où est la salle de bain?

German:
Wo ist die toiletta?

Marathi (a dialect of India):
Tunche shangeiha kothe aahe?

Russian:
Pajawistia goody ay oo-born eye ah

(And I'm a bit suspicious of this one)
Hawaiian:
Imua to the lua?

Once you can ask a native where their bathroom is you begin to be on equal footing. You've done them the honor of speaking their tongue rather than making them speak yours. Plus you increase the likelihood of actually being told where the bathroom is.

I didn't go to Europe just to use the bathroom, though; I originally went there to lose weight. Europe, it turns out, is not the best place for this so I don't advise it. On the other hand, Europe can put feeling overweight into perspective. Thin there is considerably fatter than thin here. I believe this to be a result of the metric system.[2]

Don't let me dissuade you from going, though; there are other reasons for visiting Europe, if just to remind ourselves that there are cultures that still haven't mastered the art of making toilet paper.

I also went to Europe to find myself a plot. To lose myself in adventure. I thought I loved someone over there. That's about as much plot as I had. I try to follow threads through my life, like playing a very loose game of Treasure Hunt where not only are you searching for clues, but also for clues as to *which* *are* the clues. But I figured that I could do worse than go to Europe, so I went.

Moose thought she loved a BBC producer whom she had met in Los Angeles after he had filmed her for a British documentary on game shows. (She had appeared on seven game shows in Los Angeles and, conse-

---

2. Having lived most of her life in California, Moose had a skewed vision as to the general svelteness of Americans. JMVB

quently, was of interest to the British public.) After having an affair with this producer in America, and thinking perhaps that love with an Englishman was a suitable plot for her life, Moose took a six-week vacation to Europe later that same year. (She had just won $9400 on "Body Language," a somewhat obscure game show.) When Moose arrived in England, it was apparent that the relationship was of a different variety than it had been in the U.S. (It's easier for some to have affairs on foreign soil.) Though he politely let her use his house as home base, the producer was obviously no longer interested in romance. Moose slept on the couch.

Saddened, she traveled.

When you travel on your own, you learn a lot about self-reliance, especially on that first day in Paris when, within the space of twenty-four hours, you:

1) Lose your umbrella in the middle of a rain storm,
2) Have a man expose himself to you with definite hopes that you will do something about it,
3) Get horribly drunk and cry in a restaurant,
4) Have the worst, the absolute worst cramps of your life, and,
5) Finally, throw up.

But this gives you a measure. You know you've hit bottom when you throw up in a foreign country where you can't even get the operators to give you the time of day.

Life got better (I finally got out of the bathroom), and I awoke the next day at most likely two in the afternoon (the operators absolutely refused to confirm or deny my *"Est-ce que deux heure?"*)[3] with the overwhelming desire to see the *Mona Lisa*. I went to the Louvre and stood behind a crowd of thirty or forty people all carrying "listening wands," which are large, short-frequency phones. You hold a wand to your ear and, as you come close to the work of art, a sonorous-voiced Ricardo Montalban type describes the painting to you and tells you a little bit about the proclivities of the artist.

Now when a group of ten people or more (and in the Louvre everyone comes in groups of ten or more) are carrying these things, the art is so obscured you might as well have brought a book. So go home. Go eat. That's why you came to France anyway. Let me tell you, the *Mona Lisa* looks just like all the pictures. That's exactly why people like it—it's familiar. "Yep, that's art," they

---

3. Correct phrase: *"Est-ce que c'est deux heures?"* No doubt a clue to the operators' reticence. HMW

say to themselves and feel happy that they were able to recognize art when it came along.

Maybe I wouldn't sound so nasty if I'd actually been able to *see* the *Mona Lisa.* I like art because it moves me, but among masses of people I can't be moved because there is nowhere for me to go. Any closer and I'll have to enter into their conversation which has already been foisted upon me by their immoderate decibel level.

So I left the Louvre and the teeming hordes and sadly walked along the Seine and decided that Paris was very different from the way it was depicted in *Gay Purr-ee.* (I thought there'd be more cats.)[4] I laughed to myself briefly, remembering someone, who knows who it was, telling me about a French girl who hated Americans because once she saw "Saturday Night Live" when the Coneheads were on. The Coneheads' neighbor asked the Coneheads where they were from and the Coneheads intoned, "France."

See, she thought that Americans *really* thought French people acted like the Coneheads . . . [5]

I traveled alone in Europe and so I must constantly water my own memories as I have no one else to rekindle them with. (Basic elements metaphor.) What I remember most vividly about Europe is a passionate conversation on a Venice-bound train (with a girl who drove a taxi in San Diego) about the incredible diversity of European toilet paper.

We were both stoned.

The taxi driver's name was Margaret or something rather tame like that. Maybe Cassandra. No, too exotic. Tillie? I would have remembered. It doesn't matter because she was ineffectually named. I suppose her parents had no idea how she would turn out. She was wiry, mouthy, full of kinetic energy. A real cab driver. A writer, pulling her out of thin air, would have called her Babs or Dido or Chuck. I'll call her Bitsy just to be difficult.

Anyway, Bitsy was traveling with her whale of an aunt who addressed me in a Brooklynese accent from a prone position in her couchette (pronounced "coo-shet"). There are six couchettes to a compartment and she seemed to fill two of them, though rationally I know this to be impossible. Bitsy's aunt was

---

4. *Gay Purr-ee* is an animated musical about cats in Paris. HMW
5. "The Coneheads" was a running skit on the comedy show "Saturday Night Live" about aliens with abnormally distended craniums who lived in suburbia. When asked to specify where they were from, Beldar Conehead, the father, would say immediately, "Remulac, a small town in France." JC

a good woman—I don't mean to be snide—the salt-of-the-earth type. The two of them reminded me of Jack Sprat and his wife who could eat no lean.

Bitsy's parents had either died, or no—I remember now—they had given her, at the age of three, to her aunt to raise. Bitsy said that it didn't make any difference to her, but her whole being denied this. She was like a mutt, a stray dog used to being kicked around but still barking in a good-humored way. She was scruffy, tough, the salt *of the* salt of the earth. I liked her but I could tell she was the clinging type. She kept saying how we just had to "do Venice together." This is the kind of expression that makes me travel alone. I rarely find congruence with others for a long enough duration to promote traveling in tandem. (One always leads and the other must always follow.) But I do love a good story. Within ten minutes of meeting me Bitsy had told me 1) that she'd punched a guy in the mouth in Nice, France, and 2) that she had a joint—always good news to me. As a show of camaraderie and good cheer, I encouraged her to tell me the story. (I really wanted to get stoned.)

"Yeah, this asshole . . . What an asshole! He got all pissed off at the way I was driving. He was on a fuckin' moped and he was trying to pass our rental car! I mean I get a lot of jerk-offs in my line of work, you know, but these foreign bastards, they really take the cake. So anyway, he signals me to pull over and I flip him off. The universal language."

She grinned and showed the finger. "So he tries," her already high, Minnie Mouse voice modulated up a key, "to kick my car with his boot! His fuckin' boot! What a fuckin' asshole. So I pull our car over—"

Her aunt interjected, "Yeah, I was afraid she might be gonna hurt him."

Bitsy grinned, "Yeah, she was all worried," nodding to her aunt affectionately. "I gotta mean punch," she explained matter-of-factly.

"So anyway, this guy grabs my lapels," another modulation, "through the open window and starts swearing at me in French. He's saying *merde* this and *merde* that. Well, nobody swears at me in a language I don't understand. So I fling open my door, which takes him by surprise and knocks him back. He goes for me and has me down on the ground. So I fuckin' punch him in the eye so hard he starts bleedin'."

"Noooo . . . " I said in disbelief.

"Yeaaahh . . . " she and her aunt chorused, nodding together.

"I told ya, I gotta mean punch. You gotta to be a cabby. Even in San Diego."

"But he didn't hit you back? That's—"

Her aunt interrupted, "These men jumped him—"

"I'm gettin' there," Bitsy said indignantly, rolling her shoulders and waving her arms in order to give herself some room.

"See, there was this construction site and all these guys were watchin' and as soon as that asshole has me down on the ground, they start runnin' over. But not before I give him somethin' to remember me by."

She grinned again. Her grin was the expression of the common man. There was no hierarchy of emotion, nothing noble or self-conscious or calculated about it. It yielded a clear view to her cut-and-dried philosophy, a portal to her tit-for-tat world.

"When they pulled him off a me, he was yellin', 'I kill you, I kill you,' " Bitsy said, imitating his broken English.

"He kept swinging his arms like some fucked-up kangaroo. I just kept yellin', 'Come on at me buddy! I'm ready.' Boy, he was mad . . . !"

"I hadda hold her back," the aunt interjected again, nodding.

"Yeah," agreed Bitsy, laughing. "She was afraid I was gonna hit him again. I woulda too. You shoulda let me," she added ruefully.

"The guy was already bleedin'. He shoulda bled more?" Her aunt raised one eyebrow in an attempt to impart a little lesson in morality.

Bitsy, from the "eye for an eye and a tooth for a tooth" school, merely said, "I just wanted to teach him not to mess with American women anymore. Fuckin' Frog.

"Oh, but, it was great . . . the men at the construction site couldn't believe I hit him and made him bleed. They were all shakin' their heads and exclaimin' things in French." She smiled and shook her head slightly.

"I guess in France women tend not to punch men in the eye," I said dryly.

Bitsy was so American. You can spot Americans in a second in Europe. For one thing, they usually talk louder than everyone else. I guess this is because the United States is so big, consequently people live farther apart, ergo: you have to talk louder to be heard.

Is my theory.

Americans also rarely try to speak the language. When I lived in L.A. I always heard the same complaint about the emphasis on everything (signs, bathrooms, voting materials) being in both English and Spanish: "They live in America, make 'em learn English!" (Which is, in itself, quite ironic.) And yet, when Americans go abroad they expect, demand even, that everyone speak English. Americans see no reason to assimilate or even try. And if they do ask haltingly in French where is a nice restaurant, it's in that gauche, verbally kitsch way: "Oo . . . ay . . . la . . . belle . . . restaurant-ay, peu expensive, but tres clean, with-a-kid's-menu?" The last part they say fast, hoping that if they rush it all in it will be understood. After all, we know foreigners are just pretending not to speak English.

The United States of America, a youthful nation in comparison to a more mature Europe, gives rise to an unruly populace. Advanced technology, a strong dollar,[6] a young upstart of a country, all produce rambunctious offspring. It's chilling to realize, however, that the major countries in Europe once held a similar position: they were the seat of world power. Other countries looked up to them. Everyone talked about how strong the drachma was or bought the latest in Florentine fashion. I say it is chilling because one could assume that North America's power will be similarly short-lived. In five hundred or a thousand years (or perhaps tomorrow), who will be touring our country, demanding we speak their language, taking their equivalent of snapshots and exclaiming, "How picturesque!"? Perhaps Africans, Antarcticans, even residents of the moon. Will we, too, develop into a parasitical society, our host being the ruins of our past? Will our chief commerce be tourism? And will we settle for selling trinkets beside the Lincoln Memorial and ashtrays painted with lewd renditions of Mount Rushmore?

It has been said that this is called "The Age of Information," but I call this "The Age of Tourism." They are not incompatible. Perhaps they are less and more honest names for the same thing. I prefer "The Age of Tourism" because it suggests our true character a bit more than a rather generic, Time-Life-ish title like "The Age of Information." More than being informed, we have learned to tour information and store it, keeping it on a back burner in our minds, saving it to bring out at dinner parties: informative half-baked chit-chat, stale tidbits of fact. To this end we travel, tour, and primarily sightsee. Even if we can't leave our homes, our TVs bring foreign lands to us. Not so we can experience them, but so we can *know* them, be informed. We are told in a "Real People,"[7] snappy, quippy sort of way what it is that we are seeing and why we should see it. We have refined travel into a pastime that has little to do with actually seeing a country or its inhabitants; we have boiled it down to its derivatives: how many antique shops can one visit in an hour, how many pastries can one devour in a day, and, for some, how many nationalities can one sleep with in a week? In our pedestrian way we wander through cemeteries as if they were

---

6. When MM wrote this the dollar was strong. HMW
7. "Real People"—a TV show popular in early 1980. It depicted famous people, curiosities (e.g., a man who had been hit several times by lightning), and pagan practices in foreign countries; basically a show which ran the gamut of sensationalism. HMW

I liked it. NC

shopping malls and shopping malls as if they were temples. Ninety-nine percent of tourism is actually consumerism, for the only way you can prove you were somewhere is if you have a T-shirt, preferably with fringe, stating the name of wherever you were. And many people would just as soon the T-shirts be mailed to them, thus saving them the expense of the trip.

The verb "to experience" is becoming archaic. Soon it will fall by the wayside, to be replaced by "to observe" or "to watch color TV." Experience will become meaningless. We'll remember that it had something to do with information, but in a very messy, hit-and-miss, unmethodical sort of way. Experience is the antithesis of tourism, the bastard cousin of observation—a dirty, heathen, incredibly vulnerable way to go through life. And more often than not, one's range of experience is inversely proportional to how many tooled leather wallets one buys for the folks at home "because leather is so cheap here!" Life—and Europe especially—is harder to experience if your major fear is that someone'll steal the very things you bought to prove you've been somewhere. I didn't bring enough money to buy things when I went to Europe, so I knew I had to have some good stories.

It was for all these reasons (though doubtless I couldn't have told you at the time) that I threw caution out of a dirty train window and decided to smoke a joint in a smelly w.c. at one in the morning with a ballsy, scrappy wisp of a cab driver. I'd read *Midnight Express*; I knew Italy could be ruthless.[8] But I just couldn't visit Europe for the sake of taking pictures.

My life has set me up for risks. I excel in crisis situations because I can remove myself emotionally and therefore act calmly. I've had years of practice with my family. And consequently, I find that the rest of my life is boring. It's too easy. I thrive during catastrophes. At age thirteen I realized I had this ability to step out of life, to suddenly become disinterested, a mere spectator. It happened one day in the bathroom as I stared at my mother recklessly handling a rifle and realized once and for all that life isn't how they depict it in books.

My mother was the type of woman who always folded her towels in perfect thirds, a practice she insisted upon. She was the type who would banish you from Thanksgiving dinner for taking the Jell-O out of the Jell-O mold incorrectly (I melted too much of the lobster design). Every week we had to restain the two-inch high baseboards below the kitchen counter where the bottom of the bar stools nicked the wood. I always wondered who we were doing this for. No human being could see it unless he got down on his stomach. I figured we

---

8. *Midnight Express* took place in Turkey. JC

were trying to impress the ants. Imagine living in a house where even the insects were guaranteed aesthetics.

Perfectionism wasn't my mother's quirkiest behavior. It's hard to say what was. She was an unstable chemical compound. There was no procedure for evaluating, nor any point in trying to determine what would set her off. My mother's emotions were their own random number generator.

I see myself fixed at some point, responding to my mother. Her face personifying evil. I had a dream about the devil and he sang like my mother. Actually the dream was a musical version of *The Exorcist* where Julie Andrews played the part of the girl and Woody Allen, the devil. And when I listened to the record in my dream, I heard "On a Clear Day" in that husky, guttural, your-mother-sucks-cocks-in-hell voice. It was my mother. No question. If she were the devil, she would sing songs from Broadway.

At that moment in the bathroom when my mother said she was going to kill me, life became most clearly defined. I watched myself go through the motions of defending myself, which were pitifully few. You tried not to antagonize her any more than she already was. You agreed, but not too quickly or she'd think you were patronizing her—and she'd be right. Dealing with someone who is temporarily unhinged is like handling nitroglycerine: every moment you are waiting to be blown up. There are no two ways about it—when someone has the power to destroy you they ultimately have all the power. The only power that you can hold over them is not to care. But death is a large price to pay for pride. Suddenly even one's patina of indifference starts flaking off. It was never more than skin deep. The enormity of death makes one feel a hypocrite. Thoughts like this flash through your mind faster than you can think them. Time slows down.

At thirteen, perhaps at any age, but especially at thirteen, something like this gives you a reference point. No matter what happens it'll never be as bad as having your mother point a gun at you and say she is going to kill you. And this is where my duality started, the awareness of my theoretical and practical self, the continual dispute between my logical brain and illogical heredity. I recognized that I differed from my family. I fancied that I was a changeling, a baby the fairies stole and put in someone else's crib. Or somehow a survivor from another world, another dimension. I've always thought that I was a person for subsequent generations. This is only because my real concern in life is to get along, to get from point A to point B without any serious battles. Battles don't interest me.

Having mulled over what I've said so far, you're probably saying to yourself, "Come on, no one just points a gun at her daughter for no good reason," thinking, perhaps, that I had provoked her. However, my mother lost control because my brother and sister were playing slip-and-slide on the hall rug. They ran into a full-length mirror and broke it. The mirror cost ten dollars. My mother was furious. She had been in one of her other personalities all that week. (Maybe it was PMS – Pre-Menstrual Schizophrenia.)[9] When my mother got mad suddenly everyone was at fault. There was no sideline position. My crime was that I was her daughter.

And what of my father? you wonder. First, understand that my father is completely passive. I could psychoanalyze him and say he needed a mother because his mother died when he was three, but that kind of thing bores me and is too pat an answer.[10] I'm not sure where he was when my mother burst into the bathroom, her eyes transformed into what I call "little pig eyes," wild, violent, and pitch black. Her voice as if from a different throat. She sounded like gravel.

She growled hoarsely, even smiling a bit with her new-found power, "It's too late. You should have thought of me before. You should have helped me when I begged you all. When I asked you to unload the dishwasher. When I asked you to help me fold the clothes. But no, you were too busy prancing around playing theater. Well, I'll show you . . . Now you're going to learn what life's about. So. What do you have to say for yourself?" My mind reeled. I knew her question was only a ploy. A way to suck me further into her web. She wanted to take a magnifying glass and fry me the way my brother used to fry caterpillars.

"I'm sorry," I said.

She laughed vulgarly. "I'll bet you're sorry. You worthless piece of shit. Your father's a bastard. Your brother's a son-of-a-bitch. I'm not living in the same house with them anymore. I'm going to kill you all. You treat me like your slave. I'm sick of each and every one of you. It's too late to say you're sorry. You should have thought of that before."

I made an involuntary sound that one makes when one has been crying a great deal, a kind of hiccup.

"What!?" she yelled. "What did you say?!"

Crying, I pleaded, "I didn't say anything."

---

9. The use of the word "schizophrenia" is incorrect here, as schizophrenia does not denote split personalities but rather a variety of thought disorders, bizarre behavior, and social withdrawal, including, but not limited to, hearing voices, clanging (rhyming words), delusions of grandeur or persecution, hallucination, etc. KLL
10. Though correct, according to Freud. KLL

She started hitting me with the end of the gun. The gun was too heavy for her to swing at me, though, so she ended up slapping my face with one hand and carelessly holding the gun with the other. "That'll teach you to mock me. You worthless slut. All you ever think about is yourself."

After hitting me a few more times she left. Some time later my father got the gun away from her. I don't know exactly what happened after she left me because none of us ever talked about these incidents after they happened. I think we felt too embarrassed.

Many years later, when my parents were in the process of disowning me for the second time, my father, on the phone with me, claimed not to remember that day.

"Dad," I said, trying to reach into the little bit of rationality that I knew he'd sequestered away, "Mom pointed a gun at me when I was thirteen. It's hard to have much trust after that."

Pause. Then, as if wrenched from him, "I . . . don't . . . remember that."

"I didn't think you would," I sighed, knowing that he had lived with my mother too long to know what he remembered.

Next to my mother's violence, nothing else measures up. The possibility of getting caught while smoking pot on a train seems a trivial concern. The only way I know I'm alive is if I take a fair amount of risk because my life has prepared me for adventure. Risk is a habit, like brushing your teeth, only more pervasive. It is a drug, its effects addictive. Friendships are firmer, moments greater. Life becomes heightened when its span appears limited. If there is a choice between a simple and an extreme condition, for me there is no choice. I always succumb.

Knowing that I would give in and get stoned, it was of no great concern to me that added to the inherent danger of the situation was the irritating but ultimately fortunate happenstance that the train conductor could not seem to leave me alone. I say this without vanity. Some professions have a lower threshold of entrancement. It's logical. A train conductor, if he wishes to fall in love along the trip, has only the occupants of the train from which to choose. As an American I suggested novelty, as a lone woman I presented obvious advantages, and my inability to tell him to "haul ass" sealed my doom. He, in his little, mincing French way, kept cooing over me, touching my arm, my hair, saying how nice I was and that he would be all mine when he finished work in five minutes. I rolled my eyes at Bitsy. We received this news with minimum excitement having just decided to smoke the joint in the bathroom.

"We got five minutes," I said to Bitsy after he left. So we situated ourselves in the cramped quarters of the w.c.; I sat on the toilet seat, she stood in the only other space one could stand in and, amid the jolting of the train, we got deliciously, euphorically high. We talked in that easy, lilting way Californians talk and drank the demi-bottle of Bordeaux that I had bought in Nice for tomorrow's breakfast. I knew this would be the story that I told my friends, that the exhilaration of our daring would cause little scurrying neurotransmitters to synaptically, vividly imprint on my mind the dingy yellow of the walls, the streaked mirror, the smell of quietly growing grapes wafting through the tiny window we opened for air. We giggled. Discussed men. Discussed crazy European customs. It was like putting on a ratty old bathrobe after wearing a high-necked dress and spike heels. The relief at being able to be one's natural self, the proverbial "letting down of one's hair," was overwhelming. I felt I was home.

Suddenly—a knock.

We froze. Looked at each other. Didn't look.

Another knock.

"I'm going to be a few minutes," I said loudly.

Pause.

Two knocks.

Complete fear makes me brilliant. "Look, I accidentally drank some water and I'm not feeling too good. I'm gonna to be in here awhile. You might want to find another bathroom."

The funny, fortunate thing was that I *had* accidentally drunk the water. The sign above the tap read "*Eau non potable.*"[11] I thought it meant you couldn't carry the water away. Earlier in the trip I had mentioned to my good friend the train conductor that I had drunk some of the water and he had been most concerned that I would be ill. I just knew that was him outside the door; everyone else was in bed.

The train stopped with a shudder. It stopped often during the trip from France to Italy, but our paranoid, pot-infiltrated minds knew the *polizia* were now on board, going from compartment to compartment with those dogs that sniff out narcotics and piss on your luggage. By this time I was troubled by a severe stomachache. (I think that I hate to lie so much that my body subconsciously makes me honest by creating the truth.) With a nervous laugh I told Bitsy that perhaps I could fart and then no one would smell the pot. (Surely it would fool even the dogs.) But of course, there are some things that women just cannot do on cue. Bitsy was doing her part by smoking several cigarettes

---

11. "Water undrinkable." HMW

furiously and leaving them conspicuously in sight. She had already tossed the roach out the window.

Suddenly the door was fumbled with, unlocked, and opened a crack. I hurriedly jumped up. That "fight or flight" adrenaline continued to race through my body, anachronistic to a modern day when one can do neither. However, these surges of adrenaline make me exceedingly clever. Perhaps the condition should now be known as "fight or flight – or lie." Fighting seemed inappropriate, there was nowhere to flee, so I launched into an in-depth report on behalf of my stomach. Anything to seem completely natural – like I always go to the bathroom with another woman.

The conductor was quite solicitous, apologizing profusely for opening the door, explaining that he was afraid someone was hiding in the bathroom so as not to pay for a ticket. I didn't buy it. He knew we were in there, but so long as nothing happened, I didn't care about the reason for his intrusion. I suspect he missed having company. He probably heard us giggling.

Bitsy offered him some wine. He didn't seem to find it odd that we were drinking wine in the bathroom. His response to her offer was, "Oh, no, no, no . . . " in an Inspector Clouseau-esque sort of way.

"He can't drink when he's on the job," I chided.

He corrected me, "Oh, no, no, no . . . I'm off now." And smiled.

"Oh, well then, you must have some wine!" I insisted, wondering what business he had checking for stowaways when he was off-duty.

I tend to have an infectious, "Life is a cabaret, old chum" conviviality to my voice that often succeeds in getting people to break loose and let themselves have fun. At 1:15 a.m. on a French train I thanked my personal corporate god for this wheedling ability because the conductor, with minor prompting, capitulated. I knew that if we could get him to take one drink we were home free. And we were. We ended up in his private compartment (which sounds as if it were elegant but it wasn't, merely four of the six couchettes were folded up so one could actually sit on the other two without hitting one's head) drinking Bordeaux and discussing the differences between Europe and "The States." (Our country is never called anything but "The States" in Europe. Not "The United States," not "The U.S.," and especially not "America" because, as someone pointed out, there are several Americas and we are a little presumptuous to try and claim them all for ourselves.) It was during this comparison of Europe and The States that the question of toilet paper arose. I say "the question of toilet paper" because in Europe it is questionable that toilet paper even exists. They do often – not always, but at least fifty percent of the time – have paper beside the toilet. This paper, however, would be more recognizable to us as waxed paper, or crepe paper, or even newsprint. Now to be perfectly honest, these types of paper are not unfamiliar to us, we just don't use them in matters of hygiene. I suppose we too have our anomalies. I've been saying for years that the paper one puts down on the toilet seat[12] looks suspiciously like the paper that Winchell's[13] uses to wrap their doughnuts.

But it isn't just the paper that lets you know you're in a foreign country; the manner in which one flushes is a dead giveaway. To "flush," according to my reference, *The Random House College Dictionary*, is to "wash out (a sewer, toilet, etc.) by a sudden rush of water." The two major discrepancies between Europe and the U.S. lie in the words "wash out" and "a sudden rush of water." According to this definition, one does not "flush" a European toilet. Rather one pushes, pulls, kicks, prods, or dislodges a choice of buttons, strings, pedals, oval-shaped objects, and potential projectiles which *can* lie across the room from the toilet, seemingly uninvolved and disinterested. This action then can, though in all probability will not, cause a trickle of water to lethargically wind its way down the basin, and maybe stew around a bit, the ghost of a whirlpool will appear and then, after what seems to be a monstrous effort on the part of the toilet, it will relax (with a palpable air of exhaustion) and refuse to disrupt its serenity no matter how many additional times one pushes, kicks, or dislodges whatever one pushed, kicked, or dislodged in the first place.

Bathrooms—all right, all right, I know the term "bathroom" is a euphemism; I saw *Who's Afraid of Virginia Woolf*, but I admit I prefer a soft, polite euphemism, to a hard, calling-it-like-it-is term like "toilet" or "john" or "head" or "shitter." Or even "loo," which, though it does have a bit of charm said with an English accent, is an agnostic word: it isn't polite enough for polite company and it isn't filthy enough to derive any real satisfaction. Not only that, "loo" isn't even English, it comes from the French "*lieux d'aisances,*" literally "places of ease"—a euphemism if I ever heard one. Obviously the British are too embarrassed to use their own euphemisms so they must borrow someone else's.[14] Admittedly, most language is borrowed. However, this, I believe, is an evolutionary process and didn't happen with the advent of lavatories. (When I was a child my mother worked in a laboratory and I always wondered what she did all day in a little room with toilets.)

---

12. Moose's husband jokingly referred to these as "butt gaskets." JMVB
13. A western U.S. doughnut franchise. HMW
14. I was recently told by a Welshman that he believed the term "loo" was derived from "leeward" (corrupted to "looward") because on a boat you would want to piss on the leeward side so that you wouldn't end up getting it back into your face. It's a good theory, but I prefer the other one because it fits my conception of the English. (MM)

I personally feel that "water closet" is the most logical choice for that indescribable room. It is small like a closet and houses water. The problem is, in The States, bathrooms are large like hallways and house any number of things, including water and closets. "Water hallway" makes me think of the showers in my junior high school (where I once slipped and fell, sliding completely nude through the stagnant water, humiliated and convulsive at the thought of my entire body getting athlete's foot) and doesn't adequately describe what I think of as the rest room, the comfort station, the indoor privy, the powder room, the little girl's room, the can, the convenience, the necessary, the latrine, the pee parlor even. Eskimos allegedly have fifty words for snow and we don't even have one adequate word for that room in which we are our most honest selves. I mean face it, everyone farts. (There used to be a time when I wouldn't even let myself *think* that word.)

But I was talking about bathrooms . . . They are a context to understanding other cultures in much the same way that you can tell a lot about people by the way they dance. We think of The States as being free, and though other countries tend to dispute this, when it comes to taking a whiz there is no country that considers this need an inalienable right other than the U.S. of A. I'm not irritated by much, but in Europe my patience was sorely tried by having to pay to perform bodily functions. Now my liberal sense says, "Moose" (it always addresses me in the familiar), "perhaps this is the only revenue these bathroom attendants get . . . What is a couple of francs (pence, lire, drachmas)?"

But I answer back, "It's the principle, it's the inconvenience (no wonder we call ours 'the convenience') of searching for fifty lire and it pisses me off to pay and then find that there is no goddamn toilet paper."[15] And by "principle," I really do mean the principle of having someone in charge of whether one has the right to go to the bathroom or not, because this sort of power and authority leads to little (water) closet Hitlers even if their domain is only the bathroom. Nowhere is authority flaunted so much as in lowly jobs.

I challenged such a bathroom Nazi in Nice in the train station's w.c. Ironically, I didn't even have to pee, I merely needed to change my clothes. I went into the w.c. and, as a matter of form, paid one franc thirty centimes for the right to go into a stall, ostensibly to urinate. I had with me my backpack, my

---

15. It's interesting to note that the term "pissed" means inebriated in Britain, probably because of the relationship between heavy drinking and urination, whereas in the U.S. pissed means angry, possibly because that's how North Americans find themselves feeling when they try to use the bathrooms overseas. (MM)

Doubtful. JMVB

coat, my camera, and a book. As I started for a stall, the matron of the w.c. called me back.

"You non chonge zoo clue-zez," she said, waving her finger.

"Sure," I said, knowing full well that I was going to do whatever the hell I felt like.

Intuitive busybody that she was, she sensed this and told me in her infuriatingly French accent that I must "leave zoo bags on zoo chair."

"I'm not about to get my stuff stolen!" I said with exasperation.

She was adamant about me not taking my backpack inside the stall. Her cleaning minions (there were three) started chiming in in French and I, the voice of reason, said as if to a much younger person, "Look, I'm not going to use your water, I'm not even going to flush your toilet, I'm just going to change my clothes." Aha! but to change my clothes cost three francs twenty centimes. It was more money to change my clothes than to pee!

I was exceedingly tired from having slept on the train and in no mood for medieval thinking, so I shouted at her, "That is ridiculous!" I gesticulated wildly as she began to pull at my backpack. I then performed a typical, perhaps genetic behavior which is common to my family and threw a scene. I yelled, "Okay, then I'll just change my clothes here!" and began to undo my pants.

We were in the anteroom of the w.c. It looked to me like this building might have been an old bath house at one time. There was a staircase leading from the street down to the anteroom where, sitting near the back, directly obstructing immediate access to the men's room on the left and the women's on the right, was the matron's desk. I was standing between her desk and the entrance to the women's room as I started to take off my clothes, still visible to anyone coming in off the street. A couple of men were now hanging back hoping, I imagine, for an interesting exhibition by a crazed English-speaking tourist. The matron, the soul of propriety, shrieked at me, "Zees is no Angleterre, zees is Frannge and we do sings different 'ere! When you come to Frannge you follow zoo rules of Frannge." (She didn't know the Romans had a better way of putting this.)

"You must pay to chonge zoo clue-zez, you non chonge zoo clue-zez 'ere!" she yelled as she attempted to wrestle my backpack and camera away, her helpers providing a sort of Greek chorus effect by yelling, "Zees is no Angleterre, zees is Frannge," over and over again. Later I found it funny that they thought I was English, for I can't quite imagine an English girl threatening to disrobe in front of the opposite sex for the sake of a principle. I believe it is a phenomenon peculiar to an American, indeed, peculiar to a Californian. Indeed, my friends would say, peculiar to me. However, principles can weigh you down sometimes in trivial situations. I just wanted to change my clothes, not their culture. So I acknowledged defeat, knowing that I couldn't apprehend my possessions and adhere to my beliefs without possibly being arrested. Besides, I was late for a Robert Redford movie and I was deeply in need of some basic American righteousness, goodwill, and common sense, not to mention boyish good looks.

8

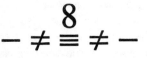

I'm tied to a train track and Robert Redford rides up on a horse all dressed in white (Redford, not the horse) with a white ten-gallon hat. The train is in sight. Redford looks at me, then at the train and says, "I guess there's not enough time. Do you still want 'She was funny' put on your tombstone?"

Denying fate is the condition of two women stuck on an island for the rest of their lives and refusing to become lesbians.[1]

Actual conversation circa 1967:
"Mom, how are babies made again?"
"I already told you. The man sticks his penis in the woman's vagina; now go away, I'm making dinner."

When I was about seven I came up with the word "contation" which meant something that I knew needed a word but try as I might, I can't remember now what it was. Solely on the basis of this one word, however, I decided to write a dictionary. The next words I invented were useful in describing every possible combination of siblings. Say you had three brothers and two sisters, you would say, "I have zswedlov," which meant that you had three brothers and two sisters. The obvious drawbacks of sheer memorization and the unlikelihood of various sibling combinations (eight sisters and twenty-nine brothers, for example) did not occur to my seven-year-old mind. Then, needing more words for my dictionary, I came up with a word for a Martian fish. Suddenly I realized that not only was I inventing words, I was also inventing the things themselves out of a sheer desire to invent words. This bothered me. I rather doubted that there were any fish on Mars and I wanted this to be a credible dictionary. So I stopped working on the dictionary because I couldn't think of any more words that needed inventing—unlike now. Now words that need inventing barrage my mind. And I suppose I am inundated with new words because they either describe me or things I perceive.

"Amouricious" is a word that fits me probably better than any existing word. It means "1) to strive for love, to actively seek it; 2) to be in love with love,

---

1. I think that's sick. NC

desiring love for love's sake; 3) to be easy (though not necessarily in a cheap, tawdry way)." Being compulsively intimate is the result of my amouriciousness. When I tell people supposedly intimate details they suddenly think they know me . . . and I think they do too. I'm not sure what it is that I am, so the person that they think they know could very well be me. I give them the benefit of the doubt.

Being amouricious also infers that in striving for love one generally finds, if not love, some pretty interesting counterfeits.

On Becoming a Femme Fatale

I'm not sure what drugs they give you in surgery, but I sure wish I could find them for everyday life. As I rode along on a gurney (on the verge of getting my nose undeviated),[2] I pursued an untrammeled path of thought. For instance: What did Robert Frost really do for a living?

It troubled me that I didn't know, but trouble is a delight to one in such a euphoric state. I kept waiting for an intern to ask me what I was thinking so I could startle her with what I considered a burning question. Somehow I thought that if I wasn't just the average patient they would take more care with my surgery, that if they knew I was profound they wouldn't just slap the scalpel around.

I started to fixate on the medical profession's indiscriminate use of the scalpel. Quickly I switched to my indiscriminate use of men. I began counting up all the men I'd ever slept with. (Women just love to do this and it is something that will keep me occupied for hours.) I managed to get to eight several times but kept forgetting which fingers I had used. Once I had considered the subject, however, I found that it was permanently affixed in my mind. Days later another paramour would occur to me. The Con Ed man came to read my meter and in his face I found the features of yet one more past conquest. I smirk now about my deborous past. (Though I cannot find "deborous" in any dictionary I know it is a word because Oscar Hammerstein II used it in *Camelot*.)[3] I smirk because it can no longer touch me.

Or can it?

Why do I write but to excise these devils? To surgically remove them to these pages where I remember them only if I choose to open this book?

Though I may reduce my past loves to print, they can still write me. It's my

2. Summer of 1987. HMW
3. Possibly "debris" (deb-ris) pronounced with an Old English accent. JMVB

fault, really. I wrote a former lover of my impending marriage, perhaps to brag, perhaps to let him know I was doing well, perhaps to get a nice present (he's very wealthy). He wrote back:

Married?!
Hard to believe.

Elected to Congress, scaled the Matterhorn, sent to the electric chair, could believe all the above before married!

The moral is, former lovers do not send presents.

I met Marty Rawlins in a class he taught on musical comedy at UCLA in the spring of 1980. I knew he liked me when he asked me to do some typing for him. I said I didn't type. He said that didn't matter.

We went to lunch. He propositioned me over a crab tostado at the Famous Enterprise Fish Company. Actually, he was smoother than that. He told me how, when he was a young man, he was kept by an older woman, a famous actress. He regaled me with interesting stories and enumerated the perquisites of that kind of life (boxes at Broadway shows, expensive dinners, silk ties, the usual rot) and how one day he came back to their apartment and found all the locks changed.

He laughed, "I was twenty-one, I was out on the street, mmm . . . " (He drew out a suggestive, guttural sigh.) "But it was a fascinating life. I loved it," he said, clenching his false teeth.

Marty wasn't an attractive man. His hair thinned badly. His build was more of an old woman's. They say that as you get older the differences between the sexes become less distinct. Like babies. External plumage is only necessary for mating purposes. Humans have managed to overcome this lack by using large amounts of money and fancy lunches to attract the opposite sex.

"You remind me of a younger me," Marty chewed his words lazily. He spoke the way Mick Jagger might, were Mick Jagger sixty-five and American. "The wild, outspoken way you are in class. I was outrageous too, always up to something. That kind of life takes a person who isn't afraid to live."

"Are you propositioning me?" I asked between mouthfuls of tostado. It wasn't that being propositioned bothered me, I just wanted him to admit it, not beat around the bush, not think that I would so simply fall for a thinly veiled attempt to get me into bed. I knew I wasn't worth it. I had recently lost my virginity and still didn't care much for sex. But not caring much for sex doesn't mean you can't realize its power. I wanted to know exactly what having an affair with someone meant. Where it would lead, who I would become. I yearned for excitement, for adventure, for anything to offset my staid college existence. There's something naughty about having an affair with the teacher and I liked being naughty.

Our affair lasted three years, but that time was porous, riddled with my various boyfriends, excursions to far-off places, and occasional disinterest. If run without interruption, it would have lasted no more than a month.

In the beginning Marty would come over in the afternoon, usually once a week. We would work on the musical I was writing. Then he would touch my breasts. Have me touch his. Ask me if I thought this odd. I thought *he* was odd, but never said so. I admit, I liked him. We were both societal renegades. Savvy and cynical. We both liked the fact that this was an affair and we played it to the hilt. Only eating in dark restaurants. Meeting at corner flowershops where he would whisk me away to his house when his wife was at work. It made me very nervous just to be in his house, let alone naked on his bed. However, his wife was a radio announcer whose show was produced live. Marty could always turn on her station to check her whereabouts. Anyway, as he conversationally pointed out to me, his wife was a very practical person and her life was quite good. She would be foolish to get upset. A previous amour, whom Marty had set up in an apartment, had threatened blackmail. When he didn't front her the money, she called his wife. Marty dumped the girl and that was that. Nothing more was said.

He told me this as an interesting story, but I knew it was a warning. I had no interest in calling his wife, however. I didn't do this for love or money. I did this because I was amazed that I could, because he had written music for Broadway and yet still found my conversation interesting, because my life had no plot and I thought, maybe, that sexual entanglements were my throughline, my hidden path to meaning. An odd way to look at it, perhaps, but when you have no meaning you think it could be anywhere—under a rock, inside a toilet, in someone's bed. And he did give me something: belief in myself, belief in my sexuality. No one my age could handle me. I scared boys off. Marty liked my mind as well as my body. He could have had much better looking women (maybe not as inexpensively), but my having a brain held an enticement for him.

Sometimes he would play me musical ideas he had. One time we watched *Carnal Knowledge* together because he was considering it for musical possibilities.[4] I was flattered that he sought my opinion. No one else at UCLA even knew who I was.

---

4. Sure he was. NC

Early on in our relationship we fooled around on my roommate's bed. (Hers was a queen, mine, a twin.) Marty lost his wallet. I know he thought I took it, though it would be tacky to accuse me. As he was walking down the street I found it and ran out to him. I didn't want his money.

Okay, maybe I did, but not that way.

Occasionally he would give me cash, little gifts marking milestones in our relationship. He moved slowly with me, knowing that I was inexperienced. One day, when I'd actually touched his penis, he gave me fifty dollars to buy food. I said, "Oh, I get it—sex for groceries." (I like to keep accounts straight.)

"Well, if you must put it so baldly," Marty drawled, smiling. He had a low, drawn out, purposefully sexual voice, even during class, a voice that made you look for the innuendos. It was his voice that made me sometimes want to end our affair. I don't like innuendos. Sex is great, but I wouldn't want it to encompass my personality. He wasn't so particular.

I didn't see Marty for quite a long time after those first few liaisons. I graduated from UCLA and moved, first to Montana alone, and then later to Chicago with T. Rex. It wasn't until a year and a half later, when I decided to move back to L.A. and form a comedy team with my friend Tuesday, that I saw him again. When Tuesday and I arrived, both of us poor and not greatly skilled, we were forced to live at a middle-class poverty level (which means no furniture, but great hairdos). I managed to get us food stamps by waiting in a welfare line for three hours in West L.A. I'd done it before (when my parents disowned me for the first time and I still had two quarters of school to finish) and had the routine down. It's not a pleasant method of survival, but I deemed any successful method acceptable and tried to distance myself from my circumstances by being hyperaware of my surroundings, viewing the welfare office as "60 Minutes" might. I fully believe that everyone should try it once (although the government might have some thoughts about that) just so every person knows what it is like to be dependent upon the whims of the government (and specifically its agents) for sustenance.

In general our poverty was stimulating rather than depressing. We were young actresses ready to take on L.A. We didn't mind that our apartment was bare except for the lawn furniture my aunt had graciously given me. I found sleeping on the floor amusing; piles of books, papers, and artwork lay in an orderly fashion around my bedding. Our refrigerator was a Styrofoam ice chest. It barely kept the cheese from molding. I mentioned our prehistoric method of refrigeration to Marty (in a discreet letter letting him know I was back in town) and he gave me money to buy a real one (used). We always referred to it as "Marty Rawlins' refrigerator." In fact, we painted his name on it. That's probably why we could never sell it.

Perhaps you're puzzled at my upfront presentation of our affair. Wondering why I didn't exchange the touching of my breasts for a higher price. But that would have been prostitution for money and my conscience wouldn't let me do that; instead, this was prostitution for obscure stories at parties later in life, for history, for some insatiable desire to live a life that didn't put me to sleep. And I thought maybe his fame would rub off on me. If you laugh because you've never heard of him, well, he was all I was offered. *Someone* had to write "How Much is That Doggie in the Window." I thought maybe he would introduce me to people. Because he was married, this never happened. He even asked me to marry him once, but, because he was already married, he probably wasn't serious.

I guess I did want *something* from him, so I deserved what I got, as does anyone who exchanges commodities on the sexual market. I say I deserved what I got, but it wasn't anything so terrible: perhaps a bit of a jaded attitude, occasional remorse at my past. You only regret your past if you're unhappy in the present. As long as the sum of your life leans toward the positive, the irrational numbers or irrational acts which litter your youth don't matter. I don't regret the affairs I've had with older men because they've given substance to an already existent depression; they justify my belief in my ability to write an interesting book, if only because I've lived such a flagrant life. I don't regret these affairs, but I'd rather my daughter didn't have them. I'd rather females inexperienced in the ways of L.A. didn't have them because when you get right down to it, being sexually intimate with someone fifty or more years older than you are is downright seedy. It's not quite like *Harold and Maude*. You feel the need to scour yourself with Brillo pads or steam yourself in a sweathouse and then plunge into a river of recently melted snow. Your soul feels unclean. You feel the need to write. To purge your mind on paper. To try to figure out what masochistic tendency is pulling you toward whoredom. Writing about it is the only way that I can avoid regretting someone like Roman Babbiack, dime-a-dozen concert pianist.

I met Roman because I won a voice scholarship through his studio (sponsored by the guy who owns Barbie dolls, Roman confided later—I don't know if he meant that the guy owned Mattel as well, or if he simply had a thing for Barbie dolls). Only three girls auditioned. I had the bad taste to win.

I go to have my first lesson. I wait in the foyer along with a few copies of *Time* magazine. Twenty minutes pass. Finally a short, asthmatic man with silver hair ushers me into his studio. We begin the lesson. Within fifteen minutes he has me crying. It occurs to me that this singing scholarship has become something he regrets.

Trying now to recall what set our affair in motion, I haven't a clue. Perhaps I wore more makeup the next time or took him up on an offer for a drink or any one of a number of things that suddenly catapults a nondenominational relationship into one named.

It was a drink, I believe, one drink accepted in a moment of unguardedness, that encouraged him to ask me to dinner. And so unloved was I, by myself and others, that I went.

Roman was seventy years old, a virtuoso piano player. Not really someone you'd take home to your family, but then I had no family.[5] He said that he was better than Liberace and perhaps he was, but Liberace had style and flamboyance. Roman was flamboyant in a small-town sort of way.

I sang once at a club that Roman played at in Beverly Hills—Romeo and Juliet's. This was the only time I sang there as I only had an affair with him for one week. That was as long as I could lie to myself.

Every day (for a week) he had me meet him at the Polo Lounge. The Polo Lounge, if you haven't been there, was, perhaps still is, one of the *"tres chic"* places to go in Los Angeles. It is found in the Beverly Hills Hotel, just off Sunset (as you go toward the beach, take a right). It is done in dark green with plush velvet seats that wrap you intimately around little tables. Supposedly much of Hollywood hangs out there, though I could never tell because I never wore my glasses. You can't wear glasses to an affair.

After the Polo Lounge, Roman would take me to dinner somewhere on the Sunset Strip: the Cock 'n' Bull, Butterfield's, Mirabelle's, or his favorite, Tony Roma's, where cheap wealthy people can get a lot to eat for not much money. Then we'd listen to some music at a club and, finally, we'd drive around in his car until we found a place to park. I convinced myself at the time that I honestly liked him. He wasn't a bad man, just stupid, just out for himself so much that he always ended up being taken by others who were out for themselves and smarter. He was always picking up whores and thinking that they liked him for himself. He'd give them $500 for orthodontia (or electrolysis or some other life-or-death need) and then they'd ditch him. Even lost little girls like me would try it for a while, would wear his "slave" ankle bracelet, would play the role, listen to his wise philosophies, would let him make them a "star." I got a few good voice lessons out of it, an expensive dress from Frederick's of

---

5. This was one of the periods during which Moose had been disowned by her parents. JMVB

{ *126* }

Hollywood, and to meet Tony Perkins for a brief conversation where I said nothing and Roman told him how nice I was.

In retrospect it seems fascinating, but in reality it was primarily boring. I would eat so much food for dinner because I had absolutely nothing to say. When I talk it's usually to make humorous observations, but Roman only knew I was being funny if he looked up and saw that I was smiling. Then he would try to catch up on the laugh, but only halfheartedly, perhaps one low, hesitant chuckle and then he would go back to eating.

Occasionally Roman would tell me stories, mostly about old friends of his. He had a friend who was a millionaire several times over and had once dated Marilyn Monroe. (Like only two or three people ever dated Marilyn Monroe . . .) This man now lived in a matchbox apartment and wouldn't even own an air conditioner because of the expense. I met this guy at his apartment after hearing his character detailed in depth by Roman. He was a fat, hairy slob. The kind of guy who directed movies like *Attack of the Killer Tomatoes* only the movies he directed weren't as good. Every time he left the room Roman would whisper, "He's a millionaire," knowing that I would look around this depressing little dump and be amazed at the squalor. It didn't matter how much money he had, he was sleazy. He kept trying to paw my dress and then act like it was an accident. After I broke up with Roman he called me a couple of times, reminding me that he was the guy who once dated Marilyn Monroe and saying that he could help my career. I told him that I had no career.

Although I didn't consider going to bed with older men a career, it occurred to me that I could live like that for a while. Even ancient sex was preferable to a nine-to-five job. Working nine to five makes me go insane, makes me hyperventilate over the Xerox copier so that I can attend boat christenings during working hours,[6] makes me do sit-ups on the floor of my office to get in shape on someone else's time. And fooling around with Roman was okay except for when I could see the netting of his silver toupee — which was always. Seeing evidence of your lover's hairpiece is just too intimate for me. It's like knowing how regular they are, or their semen count, or if they've been incar-

---

6. Moose is referring to the time she wanted to go to a friend's three p.m. boat christening and knew that the head secretary at the Brentwood Country Club where she worked wouldn't let her off, so she hyperventilated in order to make herself appear sick enough to go home. (Her plan was to fall down a set of stairs with a pile of documents, flinging them in the air as she fainted. She settled for passing out over the Xerox copier.) The thing she didn't consider was that country clubs generally have an abundance of doctors and, sure enough, the head secretary went in search of one. In her self-induced daze, Moose worried that a doctor would see through her ruse, but fortunately, all the doctors were too busy playing golf to see her. JMVB

cerated for child molestation. I suppose toupees are better than hair implants. You see a lot of implants in the subway stations of New York. It's like some farmer is cultivating a crop on someone's head: the rows, the sprouts, the furrows in between all resemble a field of hair. Even a bad rug is better than that.

Roman could have afforded a decent toupee, though. His miserliness in personal appearance irritated me. I pretended that I didn't see his wig; I stifled my gag reflex by keeping my mind as occupied as possible. I would do this by counting "One, two, three, four . . . " and then while I was counting I would add in the alphabet. Once I got the both of them going I would start singing "Row, Row, Row Your Boat" (in rounds) until every part of my brain was involved and I had only my spinal cord directing motor activity. It worked for a week. When I told my therapist later that I did this she told me never to do it again. That frenetic neural stimulation was not something I needed more of. Roman was one of the reasons I went to a therapist. I didn't think it was normal to have sex with someone almost three times my age. Though Roman and I never had sex, per se. When men approach their seventies, they want to climax as simply as possible. Penetration takes too much effort or, more to the point, is simply out of the question. (At least it appears so from my limited experience.) However, we fooled around extensively in his big fancy car, usually along Mulholland Drive, and said dirty things to each other.

And Roman liked the fact that I wore no underwear. My friend Tuesday was appalled. She would always stop me when I left the house. "Marissa! Are you wearing a slip? I can see right through that."

I'd yell back at her, "I don't own a slip." She'd offer to lend me hers, but I'd be gone.

Tuesday was the type of girl who would laze around in a T-shirt all day, leaving cereal bowls strewn wherever she last watched "All My Children," and her diaphragm on the kitchen table whenever she happened to clean out her purse (this would piss off Clay, our gay roommate, possibly because he never had any use for one). In other words, it was hard to take Tuesday's counsel seriously. I borrowed her slip in the beginning, until I got tired of being mothered. After cleaning so many tins of sardines and mustard-smeared knives off the floor, I began to stop caring about what Tuesday thought.

I began to stop caring about what Roman thought when he wanted me to spit in his face. I did it a few times . . . with complete loathing. I have no interest in humiliating people. Besides, I could never work up enough saliva. (Ultimately, the impracticality of someone's fetish is more of a deterrent than the moral aspect . . . okay, perhaps aesthetics enter in there too.) It makes you wonder: where in a person's past would they get conditioned to think that having someone spit in their face is sexy? I can understand bondage, especially if you're raised by someone who ties you up when you're bad, but unless someone actually spits on you when you're a kid . . . probably some little girl used to spit on Roman when he was in kindergarten. I wonder where she is now and if she realizes she's ruined him for life.[7]

Perhaps because I spit so well, Roman was going to fly me to Las Vegas and meet me there after he played a concert in Delaware for the governor. But our week together came to an end when he insisted I buy him a whip. He didn't want to whip me. He wanted me to whip him.

What an odd sexual device a whip is. How like a snake. How like the Bible. I looked up whip in my dictionary. It made no mention of sadomasochistic acts. Surely they're not so uninformed. You know, you hear about people using whips, usually gay men who wear a lot of leather, but you never think that it will come up in the context of your own sexual life. That you will be the one to use it. And so I found myself, a simple girl, standing in the Pleasure Chest about to buy a whip. I had to laugh. It was so Hollywood.

I went in while Roman waited in the car (because, of course, he couldn't be seen in a place that sold whips). I didn't have much time to browse so I asked the man behind the counter, "How can you tell a good whip from a bad whip?" (I wanted to say it just like Glinda the Good in *The Wizard of Oz,* but I didn't have the nerve.) The man had no reaction (probably a lot of people ask him that question) and he quietly showed me where the whips were. Not only did they carry whips, they also carried any utensil—no, no, that's not quite the right word—any device one could possibly want for any type of sex one could possibly think of: all varieties of handcuffs, ropes, straps for one's penis, dildos, vibrators with various attachments, black leather masks with zippers for the mouth (scary stuff), gloves, breeches . . it made me feel so pedestrian buying a skinny little thirty-dollar whip. They had whips that ran up into the $100-plus range. Mostly these were longer (thirty dollars bought you about a three-foot whip), but some whips had further embellishments, like being split off at the end into three fingers with little pieces of leather knotted on.

I brought our two-bit little whip back to the car. Roman was so excited; I shuddered with revulsion. I wanted to go back into the Pleasure Chest and talk

---

7. In a case such as this it's quite obvious that the act of expectorating (spitting) is symbolic of ejaculation. Roman, in this instance, desires to play the submissive role. His passivity allows him not to be responsible for having sex, thus alleviating the guilt that being raised in an era of sexual taboos promotes. KLL

to the humorless salesman about the best way to flail, or who makes the sturdiest Ben Wa balls, or anything but watch Roman salivate in expectation.

Fortunately, even though we had the whip, we couldn't do anything with it because it was daytime and not only was his house his studio and other teachers worked there, but there also lived in the back of the house a woman who had agoraphobia and had been there for thirteen years, only leaving once to go to New York. (Apparently New York doesn't have enough open spaces to warrant an agoraphobiac's fear.) Roman assured me that he didn't have sex with her, but I think he must have loved her at one time. I sensed some deep, dark secret there.

I said to him, "Well, how did she end up in your house for thirteen years? I mean after the first year or two I could see how all of a sudden thirteen years could pass without remark, but it's that first week that would make me wonder when someone hasn't left their room, not even to pee."

"She has a bucket."

"You let a woman live in one of your bedrooms and pee in a bucket!?" (My therapist had a lot to say about this one.)

"She had a back problem and the doctor confined her to bed. I never had sex with her." He kept bringing up that little fact out of context, certain that this was what bothered me about the whole situation. He explained that her back was okay now, but she preferred to stay and, as she slept in a chair and didn't eat anything more than a bird would, he had no problem keeping her.

I saw her once when she peered out of the rear of the house to say that the phone was for Roman. She did kind of look like a bird, a bird with a housewife's turban on, all bony and knobby in her face and hands. She chirped her message and then disappeared. I wanted to tell her that I knew all about her. I wanted to ask her what she did in New York. Why did she go there once and then come back to live like Emily Dickinson except without the poems? How could she sleep sitting in a chair? What did she do all day? Did she sew? She looked as if she must have had arthritis. Did she ever play the piano? Is that how she met Roman? Were they going to get married once? Did she love Roman? How could she love a man who wanted to be beaten with a whip? Oh, didn't she know about that? Had they ever had sex? How many years ago? Why did she wear a turban? Did she have any hair? Did that have anything to do with why she went to New York?

But she went back into her free zone before I could tag her out and ask her my questions.

I asked Roman once, "Have you ever read *Jane Eyre*?" It all seemed too funny, too coincidental—a twenty-four-year-old, unemployed actress having an affair with a wealthy seventy-year-old pianist who had a crazy woman living in the back of his house in Beverly Hills. I kept waiting for the fire.[8]

Sometimes I still wait for the fire. For the catastrophe that will finally catch up with me for all the debauched things I've done. It's not guilt I feel while waiting, just coolness, waiting for that spark to warm me to life, for that crisis to make me interested in my own outcome. It was coolly that I had decided if I couldn't find love, I'd find the next best thing: money. But I wasn't ruthless enough to see it through. Money just doesn't compensate for boredom, for having absolutely nothing in common with the person you're seeing; money doesn't compensate for intimacy with relics.

And then, just as I was working this out, as I was realizing that I didn't have the fortitude to be a concubine, love showed up. At four in the morning.

I said, "You can stay two nights and no sex." A week later Justin, love, and I moved to Venice, California.

I had met Justin in summer stock a year before.[9] He had driven from Sacramento to Bigfork, Montana, on his motorcycle. It almost killed him. His motorcycle was only a 350 cc and had no windshield. He loved doing these robust, manly things, but was just the wrong type of person for them. He liked cats too much. Justin had one of the driest senses of humor I've ever seen, a well-developed instinct for irony. He threw subtle barbs at you that others would miss. He also threw a camp skillet at his tent in Glacier National Park because he couldn't make dollar-size pancakes. He had a hard time with incompetence, his own especially.

I started having an affair with Justin that same summer, even though I was still living with T. Rex. Naively, I figured Rex wouldn't care since he hadn't shown any interest in consummating our relationship in some time. If I could have worked my passions out onstage it might have helped, but my biggest role had only fourteen lines and I felt the boring, sexless summer stretch ahead of me. I decided if I couldn't have a lead onstage, I would be a lead in my own life. I would climb behind Justin on his motorcycle and go roaring off, despite costume-shop gossip and petty criticism. I moved out of Rex's and my bedroom one night and moved in with three other girls, putting so many clothes in their closet that I broke the dowel. In the midst of all the summer dresses I sat down and cried. I was so lost.

---

8. In *Jane Eyre*, Mr. Rochester's house catches on fire and Bertha, his crazy wife who lives in the attic, burns up. HMW
9. Moose acted in Montana summer stock for four summers; this was summer #4, 1982. JMVB

Women are funny. You can go from having no boyfriends for a long time, feeling independent and strong, and then suddenly you have a string of entanglements. You live with men and abruptly forget how to do simple things, like cope. Hammering nails, calling taxis, figuring out a tip, these are trivial matters compared to the thing that men really supply, which is a place to go when you need to cry. Men never understand that that's all women want when they get upset. We don't want anger in return for our tears, nor a lot of logical explanations about menstrual cycles. We just want comfort. Some of us have an excess of salt water and nature has decided that crying is the most efficient method of excretion. I'm not sure if all women cry. Some claim not to, but I think they're carriers—they make others cry. They're all office managers, or they teach third grade in a town where corporal punishment is still accepted—or they're men.

At the end of the summer Justin and I decided to rent a U-Haul trailer for his motorcycle and leave Bigfork together. We weren't planning on living with each other, but we didn't want to part yet. Tuesday and I were moving to L.A., and Justin didn't like L.A., so there it stood. The U-Haul ended up pulling the bumper off my car, which had to be fixed somewhere along the Oregon coast, but the scenery was beautiful, sex was good, and we tried not to notice that we really didn't get along. Theoretically we liked each other a lot, but in reality we kept ending up in fights, little tiffs that make you want to disagree with the other person because they're being so pettish. It's a sad time in your life when you realize that romance is wonderful, but it doesn't ensure happiness. Romance is a fleeting thing. It's appliqué, but so well done. It's all sequins, bows, piping, and lace, but useless when there's no fabric to adorn. It's the accouterments. "All the attachments but not the vacuum cleaner," as my grandmother used to say.

So I left Justin in Sacramento, a fusty little town that's grown too big to be charming anymore. We wrote each other for a while, but we both felt long-distance relationships to be silly. We stopped writing.

Now, suddenly, out of the blue, a year later and certain to disrupt my life again, Justin appeared on my doorstep ready for me to take him in. And I did. He could hardly be worse than seventy-year-old men.

Justin and I moved to Venice in November. We lived there together for five months—happily until Christmas. I think it was Christmas that tainted our vision of romance. We went to Joshua Tree Campground[10] for Christmas. We did acid, always a festive activity. Neither of us had done acid before. Just the

---

10. East of Palm Springs. HMW

thing to renew a tenuous acquaintance. As soon as we got there we set up the tent and then went to sleep for a few hours. We woke up at two in the afternoon, took half of a tab each,[11] and went hiking. Excluding the sensation of needing to throw up (which eventually went away), it was the closest I've ever come to feeling enchanted. There were red, blue, green, and violet sparkles all over the ground. Gems, rubies, sapphires, diamonds, there for anyone to pick up. They grew on the cacti, on the hummocks, on the fauna and flora. When I peered closely they dissolved into the miasma like Brigadoon, only to reappear on the next outcropping.

Joshua Tree has naturally beautiful rock formations that anyone would find stupendous even without the aid of drugs, but the drugs made the landscape breathe. It was an entity. I was reminded of a book I'd read as a child (and have never found again) about an invalid girl who had a magic pencil that caused whatever she drew in the daytime to reappear in her dreams. In a fit of anger over her inability to leave her bed, she drew large boulders outside her house and gave them eyes. During the night they moved progressively closer and she began to regret what her petulance had caused.

The boulders I saw didn't portend evil, but they almost certainly had eyes. They were monoliths, spires, hobbit homes, eloquently talking rocks kindly beckoning us to climb them. And we did, we had so much energy. We ran, bounding into the air like gazelles. We jumped at least six feet from the ground with each leap. The air was on our side, conspiring against gravity. The ground was a sponge, a trampoline, it gave way with every step, shooting us on, higher and farther.

Suddenly we stopped. We looked ahead. We turned to each other and said in the same instant, the same voice, "That can't be a Chinese pagoda." (I *swear* we said this simultaneously.) We ran to it in disbelief. We were right—it couldn't be a Chinese pagoda. It was a deserted mineshaft, burnt and desolate, clinging to the rocks behind it, yet no less mystical for not being oriental. In actuality, it was probably built by the Chinese and that's what we were intuiting. We knew things from other lives, other voices than our own told us things in foreign tongues. Our lunch spoke to us in an educated and refined manner about the ways of wheat and crazy paving.[12] The air sang us songs from old cowboy movies. It "Git Along Little Dogie"-ed us. It was so light that when we spoke our voices buzzed like Donald Duck's. We felt we were in a 3-D movie or that it was prehistoric earth and all the dinosaurs had gone home. We

---

11. A tab equals one quarter-inch square of paper soaked in lysergic acid diethylamide. HMW
12. A type of paving common in the United Kingdom. HMW

danced and sang and leaped and bounded as, unbeknownst to us, the sun sank. Unfortunately, our lunch never spoke to us about the time. Suddenly the light was dimmer. I said, "Justin, it's getting dark, we'd better get back to the campground." He agreed, but kept finding more sparkles, more precious stones with which to be engrossed. I urged him on. We began running. Seriously. We didn't even know if we were following a trail, but we ran anyway. I began to worry about wolves.

"Justin, what kind of animals do they have in the desert?" I panted as I ran.

"Oh, jackals, wolves, maybe coyotes." He thought it over and seemed satisfied with his list. I was not.

It began to get very dark and I hadn't worn my glasses to this affair either. Our buoyant galumphing had long since stopped and I was doing all I could to run as fast as possible without hitting anything, especially anything that breathed. I kept thinking of *Lord of the Flies* and confusing myself with Piggy. I wondered why I didn't have asthma.[13]

We stumbled upon an oasis. Palm trees suddenly sprang up from behind the rocks. A beautiful little spring trickled into a pool of clear water. We rubbed our eyes, certain that the acid was making us see things. I thought that we should stay there, mirage or not. I was convinced that we'd never make it home. Justin urged me on. He thought it was only a little bit farther. We went over a rise and found a paved road! Justin was so excited. That scared me because until now he'd been acting like we were in no danger. If there was such little danger of us being lost why did a paved road make him so happy? And why did a paved road mean we were any less lost? We could walk on this road for days! Suddenly I knew we were going to die in the desert. We were going to be those people you read about in the newspapers who get lost in the desert on acid! It hit me so hard, I stumbled: I DIDN'T WANT TO DIE.

"Justin, I'm scared."

"Come on, we don't have time for you to be scared right now. Be brave."

"I'm trying to be brave. I'm trying to be Katharine Hepburn."

"That's it, be just like Katharine Hepburn."

And so for about five steps I straightened my posture and tried to think about what Kate would do in this predicament and then I realized that she probably wouldn't have been on acid and therefore she wouldn't have been lost in the des-

---

13. *Lord of the Flies* is a novel by William Golding about a plane full of English boys that crashes on a deserted island. The boys create a social order based on who can bully whom. Piggy, one of the smartest but weakest boys, suffers from the inequity (and from asthma). HMW

ert and so what good was there for me to pretend that I was Katharine Hepburn when she would never have been this stupid?

"Justin, I just can't help it, I'm really scared. We're going to die, aren't we? Tell me, are we going to die?"

"I don't know."

My mind screamed. He didn't know? What kind of answer was that? What kind of man was he? Didn't he know that you never say that kind of thing to a woman? Especially one on LSD? My life passed before me, but I'm not sure if it was my life or Katharine Hepburn's. I think it might have been Katharine Hepburn's because I don't remember ever kissing Cary Grant.

Suddenly salvation appeared. It came in the form of a recreational vehicle ahead of us on the road. How did it get there? Divine intervention, I guess. Its red brake lights gleamed at me like a beacon. I ran after it yelling, "Stop, stop, please stop. We're lost." It slowed down and pulled to the side. I couldn't believe our luck. We were saved.

And then, inexplicably, as I ran closer, *it drove away.*

"NO, NO, NO, PLEASE GOD STOP! LORD OF GOD HAVE MERCY UPON US! HAVE MERCY UPON US! OH, GOD . . . " I collapsed onto the pavement crying. Why would God play tricks and then leave us to die? I didn't understand. Just because I'd never believed in God before, was that a sin? (I wasn't too clear on religious doctrine.)

Justin picked me up off the ground and he said, "Look!" There were colored lights of some kind, but I couldn't make out what they were. Acid impairs your eyes' ability to focus on things. You feel as if you can trust none of your senses. So, senseless, we stumbled together toward the lights. We came over another small hill and lo and behold, there was our campground not fifty feet from us. The lights glistened at us as we approached. What could they be? Finally, when they were about fifteen feet from us, Justin laughed.

"What?" I demanded suspiciously.

"It's a Christmas tree." And it was, a four-foot Christmas tree fashioned out of colored lights and aluminum foil. It was attached to the ranger's trailer and would have been hard to miss under most normal conditions. Sheepishly we ran for our tent, crawled inside, and lay down. We didn't even take off our shoes. We were home (sort of). We were safe. We weren't going to die.

"Marissa, I really love you," Justin said as we lay there. He had never told me so before. If I had to get lost in the desert on acid to get him to admit that, then I guess it was worth it. So I thought.

We may have loved one another, but we couldn't look at each other because there, in the hesitant moonlight that wriggled through the weave of the tent, we saw monsters in each other's faces. Ghastly creatures with sunken eye sockets and no noses, striated muscle, webbing for ears, undulating and frothing at our slightest movement. This is the horrific part of LSD, the part you occasionally hear about, where you think you know the story of the world and it isn't good. You are one little microorganism in a vast galaxy and no one is looking out for you. Though this is probably true, it seems unsupportable on acid. You feel ready to go in hands up. Why even fight a losing battle? Everywhere you look is shrouded in spiderweb; everything living, dead, or undeclared struggles to shake it off, but it just knots tighter. LSD takes you to the fever dreams of your youth, both the fantasy and the grisly nightmares. But the fantasy begins to pale. Suddenly you notice that the colors you see, the sparkles on the ground, the rainbows that materialize and then dissolve at every turn, are the colors of cartoons, of Kool-aid, of cheap comic books that rub off on your hands. And things smell as if they're faintly burning. Or is it you that's burning? No, not burning but . . . wrong . . . they smell wrong, which smells very close to burning.

For hours we lay awake; the demons wouldn't let us sleep. Finally it was morning. I felt a curious elation. I think it was joy that I wasn't dead.

The camp ranger came by with fudge. She said to us, "Merry Christmas."

As we ate the fudge she nonchalantly added, "By the way, if you ever happen to get lost while you're hiking, just look for Cathedral Peak." She pointed to it. "That's west and you'll get your bearings." She walked away to greet other campers.

We looked at each other, embarrassed.

"I guess sound travels pretty far in the desert," I said.

Justin smiled his dour smile, "Especially if you're only fifty feet from the campsite."

Despite the fact that Justin now loved me, or perhaps because of it, our relationship was downhill from there. I think the LSD helped it along. We couldn't shake those nightmarish visions we'd seen of each other. We had expected to be with stronger people. We felt deceived.

A week later, still having the other half of the tabs left, we decided to do them and go to the beach. (We walked, as the beach was only a block from our apartment.) This time the acid made me impatient. In the desert it had been magical though ultimately scary; here it was just disorienting. I kept returning home to change my clothes and come out as another person. I tried on all my hats and shoes, long gowns and makeup, attempting to recapture Justin's love. I knew it was already lost. I wanted to be dying in the desert again, the two of us alone, clinging to each other.

Justin just sat on the rocks along the beach, watched the waves, and thought. I decided, that's always been his problem: all he does is think, he never acts. I felt disgusted with him and disgusted with myself for liking him. I flounced into the apartment and tried to write. Tried to capture my anger and stick it into the refrigerator so I could have it later for dinner. I wrote:

I lived several childhood summers today.

It was such a nice beginning that I couldn't get past that thought. It was just so beautiful. I thought of all the family trips that we went on in the trailer during summer vacation—going across the United States, up into Canada, through Mexico . . . I thought of the time when we were going to L.A. and stopped the night in Santa Barbara and I forgot and got my hair wet and my mother got all mad because she'd just given me a permanent and then curled my hair on large rollers and now she said it was going to be all frizzy and I said I didn't mind but she slapped me and said she did. So the next day she slapped me some more and we turned around without ever getting to L.A. We went back home to Placerville and my mother cut all my hair off. (Well, not all of it. It was one of those bowl cuts. You know, where they put a bowl on your head and all the hair that can be seen gets cut off.)

I sighed, realizing that my childhood was better in retrospect than in live action, and I changed my clothes again and went out to entice Justin.

"Why don't you just sit down and watch the waves?" he asked.

So I did. But it was boring. And he hadn't noticed my hat. I got up after a minute. "Don't you want to do anything?" I whined.

"I am."

I sighed again and went back to write more.

Today, Venice, 12/30/83, On Acid

Venice is a waiting room for artists. I, as much as others, wait. Oh, we dabble while we wait. I paint eggs. Portraits, hangings; I perceive the world through eggs . . . for a time . . . and then I flit. I haven't the stomach for more. I'm quaint until I want to throw up and then I go dress differently and come out quaint again.

I yearn for travel, for input, for spice. (That's what sent them traveling in the first place: spice. Perhaps that's where the expression "Put some spice in your life" comes from—they're suggesting you travel, not eat more.)

And there I am, quaint again.

I'm haunted by it.

And haunted am I still, as I lie here recuperating, my nose aching, with nothing better to do than count up past lovers. The ghosts of departed conquests still echo in my brain. I think the number of men I've slept with is enough for any two people's lifetimes. It's a good thing I'm married now and don't have to go through those rigors anymore. It's not sex that's so exhausting, it's the dating, the wasted energy and bated breath. The effort. What was the purpose, I wonder? Where did all that energy go? It has volatilized along with my desire. Or is my desire merely on hold, waiting to spring upon me at inappropriate times? When you're younger it's difficult to contain your passions. I suppose as you get older passing gas is really the more troublesome. Passion has long since winnowed away.

Do I miss it? I don't miss the men near as much as the itch, the burning, the pining and yearning. I've always said the worst thing about goals is achieving them because then you have to get new goals. And the worst thing about love is finding it because then you need never look again.

But does that necessarily mean you won't?

9

$$- \neq \equiv \neq -$$

Eavesdropping

"I don't go into sharky bars, I'll tell you that."
> —Tall man, curly hair

"A lot of cute guys get ordinary girls . . . you know what I mean?"
> —Girl in stall #3, North Campus bathroom

"I've only got one light with me, Bob."
> —Somewhere dark

"Those people who are fortunate enough to know German like the Germans . . . are German."
> —UCLA Sculpture Gardens, 5/29/80

"The Jewish have to buy tickets for high holidays. Doesn't that crack you up?"
> —South Campus, probably some Catholic

"And I know damn well I wasn't mad."
> —Fat lady talking to another fat lady

"Well, what's going to happen when you guys get married? Are you going to buy a bed?" "We have a sofa . . . "
> —Two girls, one of marriageable age

"I want a Looney Tunes lunch box."
> —South end of campus near Engineering building

"Most people resent being used . . . "
> —Inside Theater Arts building

"Boy meets girl, boy fucks girl, boy cuts girl's head off and feeds it to the sharks."
> —Bergin's Bar, two scriptwriters? psychopaths? marine biologists?

"It's always nice to be greeted by balloons!"
> —Old lady in wedding dress at BBC Soap Opera Party, Casa Cugat's, 1985

"Well, so far we're still two steps ahead of the sheriff."
—Bank employee, October 2, 1984

"My ex's brother manages it."
—Heard in an L.A. bar, 4/30/80

Comments at an art reception:
"It's like a very young Swiss."

"Where did the last person I was put my keys?" (I said this.)

"Did you see the fish? Marvelous!!"

Expressions

Just when you're finally feeling truly satisfied, remember: cows are content, but they're not real creative.

Ambivalent about accomplishment, Moose's adage, "The worst thing about goals is achieving them because then you have to get new goals," demonstrates a fear, not of success, but of boredom. She never wanted to be completely satisfied with her life because to her, satisfaction culminated in the desire to watch television.

Accomplishing goals was something Moose did, but with great obstinacy. Moose was an achiever, but a reluctant one. It was this reluctance, this hesitation toward the future, that sparked her philosophizing.

"Philosophy is merely a way of labeling a lifestyle. If I was really living it, I wouldn't have to label it." Yet another example of her ambivalence. Moose was a philosopher who despised philosophy. She was actor and critic in one. Parent and child, voyeur and viewed. Moose observed herself, penned what she found, and then scoffed at the findings. She summed up her personality, but recognized the danger: one is left with too pat an answer, something that sounds too much like a rhyme. But rhymes, like expressions, are pulse readings; they earmark a generation. Expressions are moments of secular poetry, nonpartisan but moral. Expressions fascinated Moose, but their frequent use often made her roll her eyes. Familiar expressions that she particularly despised include:

Children should be seen and not heard.
A stitch in time saves nine.
You can't judge a book by its cover.

{ *140* }

C'est la vie.
An apple a day keeps the doctor away.

An expression's existence rests on the fact that, rather than think for themselves, people prefer to cite someone else's platitudes. (In observing stand-up comedy Moose noticed that "Most people have mostly other people's humor.") Expressions provide people with quick answers, bits of pop philosophy, proof that they "know a thing or two." Expressions are also easy to remember because they are concise, clever, and often rhyme. "Even the ancients realized the power in rhymes. Rhymes are satisfying. They sum things up. They are the last word in a conversation and everyone likes to have the last word."[1]

The trivial examples above aren't the kind of expressions Moose liked, however. It wasn't the everyday, common household expression that gavotted in her mind, rather it was the odd aphorism and antiquated maxim that she found most interesting—expressions like "Dig deep and get dog" (which her grandmother insisted was handed down from her Indian ancestors). "Grandma explained that the dog was always at the bottom of the stew. I told her that I didn't think the Indians ever said this, but she said they were her ancestors and she should know."

Another expression Moose's grandmother frequently used was "Eat your dessert first before the Indians get it."

Grandma explained that when her white ancestors (she claimed both kinds) came across in covered wagons, the children always wanted to eat dessert before the meal in case the Indians came before they had time to finish. It was a practical decision; however, it was based on the assumption that the Indians wanted their dessert.

I feel there was a deep, residual conflict between the genetic strands of my grandmother's differing ancestry and this manifested itself in a sheer lunacy of an amiable nature (except less so to my mother).

Moose's grandmother often expressed opposing views even within the same sentence. She harbored a variety of opinions that had no basis in fact.

[Grandma] thought that Watergate was a case where the Democrats bugged themselves just to blame the Republicans. She thought that killer bees were migrating from Brazil in a couple of weeks and used to send us newspaper clippings about them because my father wanted to keep bees on

---

1. Moose Minnion Diaries, Volume XII. JMVB

her property. She also thought that black people had such lovely white teeth which was why they were in all those toothpaste commercials.

My grandmother had the proverbial bats in the belfry, bees in the bonnet, maggots in the brain, *il a des rats dans la tête.*[2]

As Moose illustrates above, expressions are often analogies, not actual facts. (For of course, Moose's grandmother had no repugnant wildlife roaming her gray matter. Though Moose notes that her grandmother did have this picture of herself at age twelve posed with a baby carriage. "Every time we happened across it Grandma would boast, 'That was when I had worms.' ")

Analogies form the basis for most common expressions because they illustrate a sentiment graphically. "When you go fishing for compliments, be careful you don't hook yourself," Moose's grandmother warned. This expression is actually a more complex form of the well-known "fishing for compliments" metaphor. It suggests that if you throw out leading questions for others' praise, you may be caught in the process. It uses fishing as an analogy to illustrate both the activity and the consequence. Moose was amused by her grandmother's expressions and realized that they represented the theory that came after the practice, literary counterparts to real life events. Moose thought quite a bit about the derivation of expressions.

Expressions find themselves quite far afield from the situation that originally provoked their existence. A good example is the expression: "To eat humble pie."[3] This means

to come down from a position you have assumed and to be obliged to defer to others, to submit to humiliation. Here "humble" is a pun on *umble,* the umbles being the heart, liver, and entrails of the deer, the huntsmen's perquisites. When the lord and his household dined off the venison on the dais, the huntsman and his fellows took lower seats and partook of the umbles made into a pie.[4]

These days when someone says "I ate humble pie," one doesn't think of Swanson's Chicken Pot Pies (what I figure to be our contemporary equivalent

---

2. Moose found the expressions listed here in one of her favorite books, *Brewer's Dictionary of Phrase and Fable,* edited by Ivor H. Evans, © 1959, 1981, Harper & Row. JMVB
3. This expression may be familiar to some due to the rock group, Humble Pie. JC

I like their music. NC
4. *Brewer's Dictionary of Phrase and Fable.* (MM)

of deer entrails made into a pie), one knows rather that the speaker feels like an asshole (our modern day analogy). So an expression is a holdover from the past. It is the same words, but the meaning has changed from under them. Yet we still use the expression *as if it made sense.* And it does. It makes sense because everyone knows what it means even if the words no longer mean it.

Because an expression does make sense, even though the words themselves do not (we know "distaff" refers to women, but we don't know why[5]), an expression can be considered to be the emotional leavings after the meaning has been siphoned off, the distillate, the extract of sensation. An expression is a representation of an experience in much the same way that math is a representation of a physical operation. They are both languages. They represent reality abstractly. In the first, a string of words stands in for feelings as the original meaning is now archaic. In the second, symbols stand in for quantities or functions, the original pictorial representation having been left behind with the cavemen (or in first grade). When we think of "three," we no longer need to have three stones before us. Neither, when we call someone "an asshole," do we need to have this graphically depicted.[6]

Expressions illustrate implicitly, not explicitly. The reason for this is that retention is a more valuable commodity than accuracy. When something is said cleverly it may have to sacrifice clarity to do so. (Much of my conversation is this way.) This allows for a great deal of change in the meaning of an expression over the years. I use the expression "Never look a gift horse in the mouth" as an example. I'm sure everyone would swear they know what this expression means. "Don't stare at good fortune because it is rude." Or, "If someone's giving you a free horse, don't be so ill-mannered as to check how old it is [the horse's teeth being the only way to determine this] because at least you've gotten a free horse."

I question these interpretations. Or rather, I question that this is where the interpretation leaves off. Why would one even suspect that there was anything aged about the horse unless one was a bit cynical about human nature and the giving of gifts? In ninth grade a girlfriend of mine got a gift horse and within two weeks had to have it put it to sleep because it was so old. It cost her $200. To say, "Never look a gift horse in the mouth," implies you won't like how many teeth you find there, otherwise the expression might be "A gift horse is a thing of beauty forever" or some such bullshit. The first person to ever say,

---

5. "Distaff is the staff from which the flax was drawn in spinning; hence, figuratively, woman's work . . . " ibid. (MM)
6. Moose here broaches her theory that math is a means to define human exchanges. JMVB

"Hey Jonah, don't look a gift horse in the mouth," did so with a little cynical knowledge. Just as "necessity is the mother of invention," so, too, experience is the author of expressions.

Expressions are indicative of an age. They reflect the beliefs of the culture in which they were coined. My grandmother, quoting her mother, would scold, "Whistling girls, like crowing hens, always come to some bad end." The obvious message here (obvious if you know the habits of poultry and the fact that only roosters, the male of the species, crow) is that if girls act like boys, something terrible will befall them (as befalls the rooster when he is eaten for Sunday dinner, the hens being too valuable to eat as they provide eggs). My mother said that with a family of ten children (predominantly female) my great-grandmother would say anything to get the kids to shut up. I often jokingly tell the expression to friends (usually whistling girls) and until I explain it to them they haven't a sense of the meaning. We no longer grow up on farms. Girls are not so obviously put in their place. Whistling is no longer considered "the devil's music." Consequently, to use that expression now elicits only derision. It has lost its meaning.

And then there are the expressions that have lost their meaning but still seem to get said. Expressions like "Long time, no see." I believe that this expression has lost its meaning based on the fact that I only hear phony people (specifically those away on business weekends) forced to make this observation, and phony people, by definition, don't mean what they say.

In considering the derivation of this expression, I have come up with several theories about its origin. Obviously this expression came about before they had verbs (circa 40,000 B.C.). Now I've read a theory that verbs actually came into being before nouns, but purely on the basis of this expression that would seem to be incorrect. This was also certainly before they had conjunctions, personal pronouns, contractions . . . basically when life and speech were simpler.

(I'm taking as my translation *Bartlett's,* "It's been a long time since we've seen you," rather than *Foote's,* "It has been a long time from the time we last saw you," which I find a bit stuffy and I completely shun *Hofmenngeger's,* "The time in which we saw you before is quite a space apart from the time in which we are seeing you now." [I don't know how Hofmenngeger manages to get through life if he speaks like that all the time. He must drive his wife bananas, especially during sex—but perhaps he's not a talker.])

Of course, this expression could have originated much later than 40,000 B.C. in a culture not as vernacularly advanced as Indo-European or Asian culture. Say, the American Indians. When communicating to other tribes Indians had to use smoke signals. No doubt brevity of expression was a prime consideration. Perhaps the expression was more correctly, "Many moons since last saw [smoke signals of your tribe]." White man logically took "many moons" to mean a "long time."

Indeed, the more I thought about it, the more the theories abounded. (Which is often the way with me and theories. I figure hey, let them breed; it's more than I'm doing.)

Biblical implications occurred to me. "Long time, Noah, no sea" could have been the neighbors making fun of the Ark. ("Noah" and "no" eventually forming a contraction.)

Or perhaps in some Aztec village a jilted lover spat the leading fertility curse, "Long time, no seed," thus rendering the cursed infertile and demonstrating the sheer susceptibility of primitive minds.

The words could have mutated slightly as the expression made its way through history so the original idiom might have been, "Wrong time, no tea," as the radical elements of a newly established colony waited for the ships from England to dock so they could dump tea into the harbor.

And, of course, there is the ever popular: "Wrong chime, bro Quasi" — humorous monk expression.

And lastly, the furthest from our present day utterance, but still a possibility judging from the way some people listen, a king, with as little patience for non-speaking theatrics as modern day audiences, might have said, "Flog mime, slowly," to his henchmen, hoping that the administration of pain might make the mime think twice about wearing white-face in public again.

I confess, the last theories are perhaps a bit farfetched, but it takes the farfetched theories to put the more legitimate ones in a good light. Until one gets completely stupid one often doesn't realize how very bright one is.

Speaking of stupid, most people who use expressions consistently are. I mean the kind of well-meaning people who say, "Don't count your chickens before they hatch," when you tell them that you are writing a book (always a sore spot with me). Or those people who apostrophize near the Xerox copier (because no one else will listen), "Ah, virtue is its own reward . . . " I say hardly. The real reward for virtue is the mawkish jubilation felt by those who think they are the only true Christians left in the world. (The kind who bring coffee to their boss, who stay late to finish filing, who say things like, "Oh, are we keeping bankers' hours now?" when I arrive at 10:05 a.m.)

Obviously, I'm not cut out for this work.

—Old seamstress expression

You see, expressions are accepted as truth. Consensus is so strong among the masses that if one reiterates that which has been said before, it becomes etched in the stone that encloses their minds. Reiteration carries clout. It is like quoting a source, even if the source is Mother Goose. The expression "See a penny/pick it up/all the day you'll have good luck./See a penny/let it lay/bad luck you will have all day" isn't true. It isn't even good poetry. But you hear it often because people have so little else in their minds that it shakes loose and falls out. I'm convinced that this paltry, needling little rhyme was merely justification for those who were cheap enough to pick up pennies but not man enough to admit it. People say these things with irritating regularity in little singsong voices that claim their right to free speech. They can have their free speech, but remember: one who speaks in aphorisms is seldom invited to parties.

And yet people who coin expressions are often considered witty, sometimes even "the life of the party"; it's the people who constantly repeat expressions that are bosky—you know, thickly-wooded, dense—those are the people who can't think for themselves, the ones who have to say "Long time, no see" because they think sparkling conversation is something only found on "ALF."[7] I am reminded of machines when I meet these people because, similar to automatons, they are only able to function with preprogrammed speech. It is for this reason that I believe man will eventually be able to reproduce himself as a machine, at least for the clerical and manual tasks. A civilization of electronic masses is my prediction for the future. And the language and expressions that evolve will be a hodgepodge of vowel-less, circuitry-inspired scratchings and whinings—sounds left over from when words actually meant something.

Act II Scene 1[8]

Cat: Come on, Nils.

Nils: Hmmm . . .

Cat: Just listen. I'm going to speak another language.

Nils: (Out of his reverie) What?

Cat: No, really, I'm gonna say something in a different language and you're gonna just hear the air and make sense out of it.

---

7. TV sit-com about a long-nosed puppet from outer space. HMW
8. From Marissa "Moose" Minnion's unfinished musical, *Higher Math—The One-Woman Show*. (Both characters are to be played by the same actress.) JC

Nils:	What are you talking about?
Cat:	Haven't you ever heard of speaking in tongues? Where a bunch of guys in the Bible got together and spoke the same—no, different—I'm sorry, I meant different languages, *but they understood each other.*
Nils:	Are you stoned?
Cat:	Yes, now listen. I'm gonna say, "Lulu gug wum. Bosh il tuba fu meeter sky likle sprot. Fliester twy-n'-twy."

(Pause)

Nils:	You don't know another language.
Cat:	Right, but it's not an *existing* language. I don't know any *existing* languages.

The Poems

Moose didn't know any existing languages either, other than English, but she used English as an artist uses a palette: a dab of sound here, alliteration there, a subtle hue of assonance, all running together in one complex, slightly chaotic picture. She even tried her hand at poetry, declaiming, "I could never take poetry completely seriously." She thought poetry pretentious, much more suited for music because "then the words don't obligate you. I mean, who in their right mind really *wants* to read poetry?"

Most of these poems were written during Moose's college days because she found she had to be really depressed to want to write poetry, and college did that for her. Though not set to music, her poems seem to imply melodies. However, we should not circumscribe your enjoyment of her work—critics though we may be—but rather, leave you here with Moose alone. We'll be back later.

Salt

Why is only one eye crying?
I feel lopsided.
Guess my heart's divided.

But I confess, it's not my fault,
For tears are nothing but wet salt.
And I haven't eaten enough salt lately to cry.

So why am I
Crying only with one eye?

Heart——[9]

I've got seams on my heart
Where it's coming apart over you.
Seams on my heart
My life's pulling apart over you.

No rips, no tears,
The material has just frayed,
The pattern's begun to fade,
I've just been laid.

But those seams on my heart
Keep on coming apart
They're much the worse for wear.
Those seams on my heart
Are not *objets d'art,*
Nor in vogue,
Just in disrepair.

Thanks to you,
A new heart is required,
But I don't feel inspired
To go shopping for a while . . .

So I'll take the seams,
Frayed hopes and faded dreams
Of you, due to you,
If you knew how I need you,
You'd use that too.

And those seams on my heart
Would be all, not just part;
I'd be more seams
To much less heart,
A ratio I am partial to,
For heartless now, I'll use you.

---

9. Referred to by Moose as "Heart Blank," because every other combination of words that included the word "heart" in them seemed trite. JMVB

Metaphors

Poignancy is pensive lips, peering through raindrops.
Respectability is clean glasses.
Charity isn't.
Graciousness is cloth napkins and chilled salad forks.
Lusty is in the tilt of the lips.
Rickets is in the legs.
Crimson evokes a rustly blush of excitement.
Gray is maligned.
And vulnerability is in the swelling of French horns.

Silence

A non-existent day,
Few higher truths, maybe none at all.
Potential hurt from several sources.
Many sighs,
Not enough tears to fill one eye.
Grasping,
No clear thoughts.
"*Ennui*" is too exact a word to describe too vague a day.
With pursed lips,
I've nothing to say.

Bookend Poetry

Left Side
Can I help it if I think better in pictures
than scripture or lecture?
(This is merely conjecture.)
Or melodies.
(Please . . .)
Bad jokes, especially puns.
(My mind has the runs.)
But better me than Sammy Davis Jr. or
                    Chris Evert or
                    Genghis Khan.
They'd cry before long.

I cry before breakfast.

Right Side
My mind has no divisions between thoughts:
past and present memory,
equations + rhymes = times, schemes, motion picture
   dreams,
snippets of song, wrong #'s
π, the $\sqrt{i}$ all flow along.
I flow, glow, glisten,
seldom listen;
but I observe and watch, which tells me more than
verbal lies.
My eyes are wise(r)

Miser, tinker, soldier, sailor, travel trailer:
all sift together
and I'm left with as much thought as I started.
My mind farted.

I didn't with this

(She did.)

Untitled but full of meaning
Toffee and butter creams,
representing dreams;
Both forbidden food,
dreamless, I brood.

10
$- \neq \equiv \neq -$

Broods[1]

When I awoke this morning my first thought was, "Okay, regroup." I think I must have meant my bones.

I had a dream once where my perfect pitch was actually delayed precognition.[2]

I'm in a museum. Monkeys are sitting in glass display cases after having been part of a psychological test on the effects of cannabis. They look so pitiful, right on the verge of dying, that Theresa and I decide to put them out of their misery. Unfortunately, we don't have any chloroform, so we settle for Stridex medicated pads. They do the trick.

10/20/85
Last night I dreamed I had to move from New York to New York via Mexico. I kept saying, "Wait, why do I have to leave if I already live here?" In Mexico—I was traveling in a station wagon with three other girls—we went to this museum that was an actual artist's home. It was adobe. The Mexican artist was out in the back field doing a huge pastel of Larry Storch.[3] At the bottom of the pastel in big letters it said, "What a Great Guy!" I thought this an odd thing to have at the bottom of a painting, but the artist explained to me that it was an old Mexican saying.

A Chronicle of Our Arrival in New York

We weren't really ready for New York, but then—is anyone? We arrived on People's Express[4] with little sleep but all our luggage. Sam slept not at all . . . me, I can sleep anywhere. I once fell asleep in front of his amplifier when the whole band was playing.[5] But still, sleeping on a plane isn't real sleep.

---

1. Marissa referred to her dreams as "broods" because she felt only other people dreamed. She mused. KLL
2. Marissa "Moose" Minnion didn't have perfect pitch, she only thought she did. JC
3. Larry Storch was a star of the TV show "F Troop." JC
4. Defunct airline. HMW
5. Marissa "Moose" Minnion played the French horn in a rock band in L.A. Sam, her future husband, played the guitar. JC

It's powdered milk sleep, sleep of an artificial nature. You pretend to sleep so well that every two minutes you actually do.

We rented a car when we got to Newark and drove to Sam's father's old college roommate's apartment because he was the only person we even distantly knew in all of New York and we hadn't the finances to stay in a hotel. I had to drive because Sam kept asking me when we were going to land.

It's very specific when you arrive in a new place. You remember things you would never remember if you grew up there. You remember the way the air rubs your skin. The smell of a place as it interrupts your nose. You feel excited and, to varying degrees, overwhelmed. And then, because you're an adult, you get to drive. Driving in a new place is exhilarating. Because you're feeling like a kid—disoriented, out-of-sorts, like someone's just asked you to spell a word you don't know—and then suddenly you find yourself driving: the major perk of being an adult. No matter how unusual the scenery, there is still a road beneath your wheels. You feel a common denominator. New York isn't so pagan that it doesn't have a dotted white line dividing the road into workable pieces (not that anyone really pays attention to it, but I didn't know that then).

Sam and I moved to New York together because I got really drunk one night (I think it was a Thursday, about eleven p.m.) and called him up at the lab and said, "You know, I've known you for eight years and I've always liked you and I've always sorta figured that every now and then we would run into each other, but *now,* all of a sudden I find you're moving to New York and—" the next I say like it's a given, in a somewhat singsong manner, "I figure you'll probably end up marrying Trudy,[6] and I feel kind of sad that we won't be able to fool around like we used to and I just wanted to know—" I was laughing by this time, "if you wanted to have sex just one last time."

Lemme explain: I knew Sam like you know the guy next door. I knew Sam so well that the first time I met him wasn't cataclysmic. (I don't even remember it and neither does he.) It must have been at some college party. He was friends with the guys that lived next door to me. I think we must have been so similar as to have been unimpressed with each other. Maybe "unimpressed" is the wrong word because of its negative connotations; I mean unimpressed in the way that one avoids becoming bedazzled by the opposite sex, unable to do much more than worship them. In being unimpressed we were more real. We were never boyfriend and girlfriend, but we had nice sex every now and then, between and during boyfriends and girlfriends. I admit, I'd kind of always taken him for granted. That's what you do with the guy next door.

---

6. Trudy, an organometallic chemist, was Sam's girlfriend of two years. JMVB

So after I asked him if he wanted to have sex, Sam, laughing, said, "Weeeeeell . . . I'll have to think about this," and I knew that he wanted to because I knew him. I also knew that sex between him and his girlfriend had somewhat dwindled, but I also knew that Sam was a really loyal guy because one time, years ago, when we were completely naked and in bed, he wouldn't have sex with me because of his girlfriend Elizabeth. And I'm yelling at him, "Oh, so *Elizabeth* doesn't mind if you lie *naked with women,* just if you have *sex* with them, huh?!" I was pissed at him for about a year. But ultimately I suppose you have to admire that kind of stupidity in a guy; it's nonsensical, but it's touching.

We joked a bit more on the phone and then he said, "I'd really like to, but there's Trudy and she's really smart. She'd know. I don't want to hurt her. Did I ever tell you that she found a picture taken at a party that we went to three years ago and there's a lot of people in the picture and she immediately singles you out and asks, 'Who is that?' " He imitated her voice in his generic woman's falsetto.

"Oh, Sam . . . " I said, pretending to be disgusted. "How come every woman you imitate sounds exactly the same?"

"Only one reason I can think of."

"That you're bad at impressions?"

"*You* laugh at them," he said.

"I have a lousy sense of humor," I said.

"I know, I've seen you do comedy." He laughed uproariously at his insult.

"You're stupid," I said, smiling into the phone.

"Hey." I said this with a silence, just to let him know that I was really talking to him. Sincere. Not rehearsed. (It's a technique I have.) "I probably shouldn't have called you, but it's good to talk to you and I'm really very drunk right now and I just felt like I needed a friend—"

"I'm your friend, Marissa."

"I know, it's just that I haven't seen you for over a year. It wasn't until after I joined the band that I suddenly remembered how you never put any pressure on me to call you or be your girlfriend. We would go out and then I would decide that I didn't like your politics because of some stupid, conservative thing you said," I was laughing again, "and then I wouldn't call you for another year. But you know, I've come to realize that there are a lot better reasons not to like someone."

"Yeah, like if they've got a little dick."

"Why are you such an idiot?" I asked, shaking my head and trying not to laugh.

"Because you like it."

"Remember that time when we got in a big argument and I said, 'If there's poverty there's gonna be crime,' and you disagreed?"

"And then some son-of-a-bitch broke my fucking car window and stole my best 501s. I know where you're going with this." I could sense Sam shaking his head at me.

"I just like it when life proves me right."

"Is that why you came into the bathroom that night while I was taking a shower? For an 'I told you so'?" Sam asked me.

"You know," I said pensively, "I don't know why I did that. It felt comfortable being there until you said that I only did it to see your dick and then I felt embarrassed. I didn't want you thinking I wanted to have sex with you 'cause I didn't."

"So what's changed?"

"I think it was that rehearsal when you said you'd been up for forty-eight hours because you burped your flask wrong and got five years' of work all over the lab and then you used three hundred KimWipes and still only got back half of your stuff and you were bummed because you thought you should have gotten back more."

"Why would that make you want to have sex with me?" he asked, incredulously.

"'on't know . . ." (That's how I say "I don't know" when I'm feeling cute.) "I think because your hair was all messy and you looked desperate."

"Great."

"Sam, I would never want to put any pressure on you . . ."

"I know." He paused. "I have to think about it."

"Just ignore me. You know I'm a bad influence. I wish you weren't going away. I don't even know why I want to have sex with you. I'm just drunk, I guess."

"That's okay, I'd like to have sex with you too. I don't know that I can, though. I might like it too much, and then where would we be?"

"Yeah."

There was silence for awhile.

I started laughing, my way of easing situations.

"I am *really* drunk; I was at a 'drinks party' for this BBC soap opera documentary. It was weird. There was this aging soap star—she looked like a corpse—and she was wearing a wedding dress and acting really coy. It was kinda sad."

"Is that the thing you're working on for Colin?"

"Yeah, Colin's weird too. He has another American girlfriend—she's blonde—but when I was at his apartment the other day, he kept trying to pull off my shorts in the living room. I don't know why he plays these silly games. It makes you understand why romantic farce is so popular in England. He doesn't want to have a relationship, he just wants to play at sex."

"He grew up in a boarding school . . . "

"Yeah, I know. I'm just still somewhat susceptible so when he does shit like that it kind of pisses me off."

"Is that why you called?"

"No . . . well, maybe just a little bit. I know that you like me and I needed to talk to someone who liked me. Maybe you should just forget I called. I'll see you on Saturday."

"Marissa, you can call me again . . . "

It took three rehearsals for Sam to fall. We were standing in the parking lot of Fat Burger. (That's where the band would go to eat after practice). It was about 11:30 p.m. He and I were standing talking; the others had left. We were feverish, nervous, not touching; laughing, joking, and trying to accidentally fall on each other. We were both twenty-seven. It shows you that age is immaterial when it comes to attraction and nerves.

Suddenly Sam simply said, "OK."

I looked at him. I had the shakes. When had I ever felt this way about him before? I was nuts. *It was just Sam.* I couldn't remember ever wanting to have sex with someone so badly.

We went to my apartment in Venice. We just made it through the door before we were on each other. We had sex like I never remember us having sex before. I thought to myself in amazement, "I could love Sam."

It's funny, but when I think back over our friendship, I hardly remember us having sex, I only remember us *not* having sex. As I lay there exhausted, cradling Sam in the crook of my arm, I remembered the first time I ever got into bed with him. It was my first quarter at UCLA. I was wearing a cross-your-heart bra (back in the days when I used to wear a bra) and panties. There were two other people in the room, so we just cuddled on the lower bunk and fell asleep. I hadn't lost my virginity yet, so this was fine with me. I have a lot of memories where Sam and I just slept together. We liked each other. We liked making conversation but we didn't always want to complicate it with sex, especially since we had other people we were already complicating our lives with.

One time we went skinny-dipping in Sam's research advisor's swimming pool when Sam was house-sitting for him. He had to watch his advisor's dog, the dog he called "Shitzy." I don't know what the dog's name actually was, but

Sam was scared to death that the dog would die before his advisor came home. (A research advisor is like God to someone in graduate school.) The dog was approximately 300 years old. It looked like it wanted to die any minute.

All through college it never dawned on me that Sam was smart. He wasn't a person that exudes smartness like people who wear double-breasted suits and carry briefcases. Sam wore jeans. I never knew that all that time he was getting a Ph.D. in chemistry. I just thought he was having a little trouble finishing school.

Our affair continued through the summer. No one knew. Not the band, not Trudy. We felt guilty but that didn't stop us. Sam would most always come over after Wednesday night rehearsals and stay until three or four in the morning and then he would run with his guitar back to his car (Venice is a dangerous place at four a.m.) and drive home to Pasadena. One night, several weeks after this started, we were over at Jasper and Stan's and there was a small party and we'd done some coke. (I just hate snorting it because it makes my jaw wiggle from side to side, but I felt out of control and needed to do something wild because here I was having sex with someone else's boyfriend and he was moving three thousand miles away in a month and I suddenly felt like I was going to care. I had spent my life not caring—why couldn't I get it to kick in now?)

While we were upstairs making love in Jasper's bed, I heard myself say to Sam, "I think I'm falling in love with you." But inside I cringed. Was I making that up? I'd lied about stuff like that for so long, I couldn't tell if I was for real or not. And I thought, I can't fool with people's lives like this. Sam's a nice guy. Was I going to lure him away from his girlfriend and then dump him? What *did* I want out of this? I was very confused.

Sam was days away from getting his doctorate. People become less rational as something they've worked on for years approaches. Sam wrote me a letter. Wait, I have it here.

7/1/85

Dear Marissa:

I figured I'd write you a letter, not just because you have written me so many without return, but because for some crazy reason I thought I might be able to express how I feel in a more consise [sic] manner. When I got into this thing, how the hell was I supposed to know I was going to go bonkers over this girl I knew for eight years. I'm asking you to go to New York. I would like not for you to go to New York with me, but for us to go to New York together. Did you get that? What I am asking you is not a logical or practical thing to do. Therefore, you can't base your decision on logical grounds. The decision must be from your heart. Never in my life have I ever asked a woman to make what some people might call a sacrifice for me, but I figured I can't let this chance slip away just because of some bogus principle. I will not leave until late August, so you have a while to decide. I will try not to put pressure on you. If you decide not to go I guarantee the offer will stand after I leave. If your therapist says you are crazy, have her give me a call and I'll straighten her out.

Remember, don't think about it too hard though because logic and reason might overwhelm you and make you stay.

Love,
Sam

I had to say yes. When would a scientist ever again ask me to not be logical?

I churned the past few months over in my head, as one is wont to do when very tired and far away from home. The New York skyline loomed ahead. I was wondering why I didn't feel scared. Sam and I had never lived together before, but we knew each other so well. It had to be right. And if it wasn't, well, at least I would have lived in New York.

As I drove over the George Washington bridge, I glanced at Sam and he looked so exhausted. His little pink rabbit eyes were bloodshot.

"What?" he asked.

"Nothin'," I smiled back.

I drove us to the Upper West Side near Columbia University where Sam would be working as a research chemist. Columbia is about as close as one can get to Harlem without actually being there. Columbia covers the blocks from 114th Street to 119th. Harlem unofficially starts at 120th Street and Broadway on the West Side and goes north (to the higher numbers). For thrills, many of the Columbia chemistry students would walk to Kentucky Fried Chicken on 125th Street. I went once in a taxi. I don't need that much excitement.

Percy, Sam's dad's college roommate, and Thelma, his wife, lived at Eightieth and Broadway, a very nice area. Percy and Thelma were both therapists. They found no shortage of work in New York. Percy held a Ph.D. in both psychology and divinity – a pretty lethal combination. Sam, investigative reporter that he is, managed in the two weeks we were there to uncover that Percy was attempting to start not one, but two pyramid scams, à la Herbal Life or Amway. We even found manuals for several pyramid companies on his bookshelves. What a sleazeball.

I had to disentangle my friend Tuesday from an amorous Amway distributor once. I came to his apartment where Tuesday and some others were listening to him intone, "How would you like to make *a million dollars?* But wait . . . Why stop there? How many of you would like to make *ten million dollars!?* You can, you know. I'm going to show you how." I yelled at her from outside the screen door, "Tuesday if you don't leave right now I will not take you to an expensive dinner for your birthday." She was still hesitant. (I think she was dating the guy as well.) I had to go in there, take her by the arm, and talk to her like I was bringing her down from a fix.

These kinds of companies are business/religion. They thrive on the Southern Baptist approach. They work by using a form of hypnosis, chanting promises of money till you are mesmerized. And the way that you make so much money is not by selling Amway door-to-door, it's by getting others to work for you who in turn get others to work for them, all the while pushing you higher up the pyramid because you get a cut from everyone. Kind of like the Mafia.

Percy was attempting with one marketing scheme to sell holistic vitamins, and with the other to sell tapes that convince you to change a bad habit. The way the tapes work is that on one track is the sound of the ocean or bird calls or ambient music and softly recorded on the other track is someone insisting, "You will lose weight, you will lose weight . . . " on and on. I suppose he got this idea from those subliminal advertisements that were outlawed in the fifties, advertisements that were injected into a motion picture show but only lasted one frame. Since the suggestion to "Eat popcorn" flashed past your eye faster than you could consciously perceive it, you never knew that you had received this suggestion, yet your mind subconsciously retained the information. The problem with subliminal audio messages is that it's never been proven that there is such a thing as a "frame" when it comes to hearing. Either you hear it or you don't. In other words, these tapes were a hoax.

What truly amazes me is that not one, but two colleges gave this guy a Ph.D.

Nevertheless, Percy's clients found him a soothing influence there in his leather-and-wood encased study, books lining the walls, all very masculine, knowledgeable, and comforting. Thelma's clients, however, were relegated to the tiny sewing room off the kitchen. In the adjoining bathroom, half of a dressmaker's dummy lay facedown in the tub. I suppose one look at that ensured repeat customers.

Thelma's office was barely big enough for one person and Thelma was one of those larger-than-life people who appear to take up more than their fair share of body space. The fact that Percy and Thelma spouted feminism made the inequity in the division of rooms all the more peculiar (unless you know that therapists generally sport such incongruities).

Basically, Sam and I couldn't stand them—and have you ever noticed that once you can't stand someone, you absolutely detest what they eat? Percy and Thelma ate food that was either whole wheat or some derivative of a soybean by-product. Everything in the kitchen was wrapped in sordid little plastic bags that had already been used for something else. They ate natural peanut butter, unsalted of course. They bought plain yogurt in the big, economy gallon-size containers (which always had little flecks of old, discolored yogurt falling into it from the sides) and they would mix this with a variety of seeds and bulgur wheat and other things that could make you throw up just by looking at them. The one good thing about this kind of food was that it didn't encourage roaches. (Although last night in *our* apartment Sam woke me up to tell me that there was a bunch of roaches huddled around a piece of lettuce. Just our luck to get the vegetarian roaches.) One night, when Percy and Thelma were gone, we made nachos with sour cream and tons of cheese and all the fattening, bad things we could think of. And Sam went around their kitchen pulling out items that offended his eyes and yelling obscenities into the cabinets for relaxation.

During the two weeks we were there, the best thing Percy and Thelma did was to go away to their house in the country on weekends. Then Sam and I had the place to ourselves. Well, sort of . . . There was still a summer boarder living there who was then replaced by the winter boarder. Then this engineer, who barely spoke English, came from France. His parents were friends of Percy and Thelma's. He was sent by his company to learn English by working at JFK Airport. Right . . . like he's going to learn English in the middle of Queens. Everyone in Queens talks like Sylvester Stallone.[7] Who wants to speak English that sounds like you've got food in your mouth? Anyway, we showed him around. (Like we'd been here long enough to show anybody around. We didn't understand the language either. It was a foreign country. In fact, I was thrilled every time I bought something because we used the same currency in California.)

Besides all the guests, there was also Thelma's sister, Gladys, who lived with them, their three cats, one of which was in heat and was trying to get some action with the other two who, at seventeen and eighteen years old, were lucky if they mustered the strength to fart, and lastly there was a hyperactive dog and some rather dingy fish, all of which (except for Gladys and the fish) I was allergic to. Let me tell you, it was hell. We didn't even have a real bed. Sam and

---

7. Sly Stallone has an accent from Philly. NC

I had to sleep on sofas that were at right angles to each other. We were sleeping in the dining room and even though I kept wheezing due to the animal hair, we couldn't have the door closed because it "depressed the cats."

No, really. It "depressed the cats."

If this wasn't bad enough, we also had to get up at four in the morning to go wait in line at Columbia's housing office for an apartment, though Sam had been promised a place to live the day we got here. (Believing this was our first mistake.) For four mornings we woke up at 3:30 a.m., stealthily tiptoed through the menagerie, descended on the elevator that smelled of morning urine (find an elevator in New York that doesn't smell of urine and you can't afford to live there), and waited on the corner of an empty street (with the occasional insomniac and potential mugger) for the bus. We rode up to 118th and walked the chilly and treacherous way to 119th and Morningside, only to wait four hours until eight a.m. for the housing office to open and tell us that there were no apartments today.

The fourth day we got dibs on an apartment. We were sure it was a fluke. We walked to the apartment with vigor. Excited, we claimed that no matter how bad it was, we'd take it. We got to the building. It looked promising. We couldn't say enough good things about it. It appeared to have indoor plumbing. We were thrilled. We went to talk to the super. He looked confused. There was someone living in that apartment. We told him he must be thinking of a different apartment. We went with him and knocked on the door. No, he had the right apartment. There was someone living there. Two someones. They'd paid a third someone off. We were too depressed to be mad. Were there any other available rooms in this building? The super showed one to us but we couldn't tell anyone that we'd seen it (otherwise I suspect the housing mafia would shoot him). The apartment was beautiful. Gray carpets on the floor, wonderful view. Who was getting these apartments? We were too naive at the time to figure it out.

That night Sam and I went out walking. It was eighty-seven degrees and the humidity was higher. Everyone was on the street. There were people in every cubbyhole of a bird's-eye view. One of those "How many people can you see in this picture" pictures. But there was still more privacy on the street than in Percy and Thelma's apartment. Psychologists ask too many questions and then think too much about your answers. Percy asked Sam questions about his dad. Sam, always open, gave him straight answers. Percy said, summing it up, "So, you think your father's more of a gambler than you?"

Sam said, "I have to go buy groceries now."

While we were out walking, I saw a bag woman crying. I'd never seen a bag woman cry before. I thought they were too oblivious. Tears were pouring down her face. Everyone walked by without a glance. I started crying. I wanted to help her. I tried to stop but Sam said, "What are you going to do? Bring her back to Percy and Thelma's? We don't have a place to live either."

Finally Sam's boss wrote a scathing letter to the housing office. The day after the letter was delivered five apartments came open. (We had been told that nothing would be available for two more weeks.) We got a beautiful apartment in faculty housing. We even had a doorman. Thelma let us borrow her car to move. The only problem was that she had a great parking space right in front of her apartment and we knew we'd be up all night trying to find another one. As we were carrying our luggage down I noticed a guy just sitting across the street on a chair doing nothing.

"Sam, you think we could talk that guy into sitting in this space while we're gone? He's just sitting over there. He might as well sit here where it'll do us some good."

"Marissa . . . " Sam shook his head impatiently and then shrugged. "Ask him if you want." He left for another load. I was guarding the car.

Sam came back.

"What d'ya think? Should I ask him?" I bugged Sam as he put our suitcases in the car. "We could offer to pay him."

"I doubt if he'll do it. We should get some bag people," he said jokingly. "They need the money."

Sam came down with the last load and before he could say anything I started off down the street yelling over my shoulder, "I'll be right back." I dashed to the island that ran down the middle of Broadway. I found this black couple who appeared to be bag people and asked them if they'd like to sit in our parking space. (I was hesitant to ask them because bag people don't usually come in pairs.) I explained that we only needed to drop off some stuff and we'd give them $2.50 now and $2.50 when we returned. They seemed excited to help out. (They weren't going anywhere anyway.) I introduced them to Sam. Sam thought the situation very funny, though he suspected that they might not be there when we returned. I told him he was too suspicious of human nature. Not only were they there when we came back, they also shared with us an amusing anecdote about their hemorrhoids.

This incident later showed up in Moose's comedy act. Many things that happened to Moose in New York provided her with material because, according to Moose, "Life in New York is like a bad Neil Simon comedy . . . or for that matter, *any* Neil Simon comedy."

The following was performed at the Comic Strip Thanksgiving Night, 1986, while a man yelled, "Play the horn!" all during the routine, even when Moose *was* playing the horn.[8]

I've just moved to New York. And I only have one question. What's all this contraception doing on the street? I've only been here a few months and already I've seen four rubbers, two contraceptive sponges, and a diaphragm lying on the ground. And I wanna know, where are they all coming from? I mean, it's not like you wear these things on your head.

Every time I see one lying on the ground I want to stop people and ask if it's theirs, but you know, it doesn't match anything they're wearing—which is perhaps a good thing—and I wouldn't want to insult them. I can just see the scene in Planned Parenthood when the guy says to his girlfriend: [male voice] "But I thought you used something." She says: [generic female falsetto] "Well I did, and it's lying on the corner of Seventy-ninth and Broadway . . . You wanna go get it?"

No wonder so many people live in New York.

I met a product of such carelessness yesterday at a party. She was a Rastafarian computer programmer who said that she uses "mental birth control." MENTAL BIRTH CONTROL! I met this girl at a chemistry party. *These* are the people chemists hang out with . . . people who believe in mental birth control. I mean, this girl thinks she can use her mind—like a rubber? Well, I guess she doesn't have to worry about losing it on the sidewalk. Now, let's be serious . . . mental birth control? Okay, I could see it if you're Carrie. I mean, Carrie could make knives fly around the kitchen, she could probably make jism spontaneously combust. But a computer programmer? I'm not convinced that someone who believes in mental birth control even knows how to have sex. Which is perhaps why it is so effective.

[mincing computer programmer voice] "Well, I've been using it for a year and a half."

Now the first thing that occurred to me, and I confess it wasn't nice, I said, "Maybe your boyfriend's shooting blanks. Did you ever think of that?"[9]

I mean, what makes her think she's so special? Yeah, like when I'm having sex I'm saying [very calm voice], "Boy. I sure hope I have an illegitimate child."

---

8. Marissa "Moose" Minnion opened her set by playing the French horn. JC
9. In actuality Marissa "Moose" Minnion suggested, "Maybe you're sterile." Apparently this proved too much for her audiences. JC

[screaming] Are you kidding? I'm saying "Please, God. Just this once don't let me get pregnant. I promise I'll *never* do it again."

Do you see what I mean? *Everybody* uses mental birth control. The problem is, those sperm don't have any brains.

This woman also told me that "periods should be a time of celebration." Some people will use any excuse to have party. Hell, I'd celebrate too if I was playing Russian roulette with my ovaries.

Now I don't know about you, but I think these people shouldn't be allowed to have sex. Somebody—I don't know, the government—should step in. "You can't have sex until you can stop being an idiot." Because this is where evolution has failed us. There are no mental requirements for sex. Anybody that's been through puberty knows that. And between the people practicing mental birth control and the people losing their contraception on the sidewalk, it's no wonder there are so many bag people around. If you were born because your mom's frisbee—that's the term most scientists prefer—fell out on the street, doesn't it seem more likely that you'd end up there yourself? I'll bet if you counted them up, the bums would equal the number of lost contraceptive devices. In fact, I just know some sociologist has already done this for her Ph.D.

But you know, sometimes bums are kind of handy to have around. Like if you want to keep a parking space for a while. Say you wanna go to the grocery store for ten minutes and you don't want to hunt for three days for another place to park. What I do is go out to Broadway where there's a whole sector of mankind perfectly willing to stand in one place for two bucks, maybe two-fifty. I see this as a form of public assistance. It's already higher than minimum wage. I'm gonna make them work for their handouts. I mean why should I give them money when there already is a bum tax? I can see some puzzlement in your eyes. Bum tax? What bum tax? Okay, who here actually packs up their bottles, takes them to the grocery store, and waits in line for thirty cents?[10]

[Answer if they yell "I do": "Yeah, and you probably send that thing back to Ed McMahon too."]

Now when bums ask me for money, I just give them bottles. Make *them* return 'em. But have you noticed? There's two kinds of bums now. Ones that take bottles and ones that don't. There's this guy on Eightieth Street that only takes Swiss francs. Really . . . He's on the west side of the street.

---

10. In New York there is a five cent deposit on each bottle, refundable if returned to the market. Bums search garbage to find them. MM used to separate garbage (hers) to facilitate this process. HMW

So you know what I say?

"Teach 'em how to hunt!" [pause]

Have you ever noticed how many pigeons there are in New York? [pause]

With a minimum investment by the government we could teach these people how to kill and cook pigeons. And this would solve several problems: not only would these people get some meat in them, it would give them something sporting to do in their spare time (and we all know they have a lot of that). Plus, it would reduce the number of pigeons that plague our major cities. And most importantly, it would get rid of all this fucking pigeon shit. Now if we could just teach the pigeons to eat those old rubbers and sponges, we'd have a perfect food chain.

11
$$- \neq \equiv \neq -$$

Food chain *n:* a succession of organisms in a community that constitute a feeding chain in which food energy is transferred from one organism to another as each consumes a lower member and in turn is preyed upon by a higher member.[1]

An urban food chain is the best depiction of life in New York, the only difference being that people thrive on the next lower member (i.e., the person standing next to you) as a source of entertainment rather than food. It's the kind of sensationalism that you won't find on TV. New Yorkers love to watch other New Yorkers. This is why you never want to get too close to the subway tracks because someone could push you, not out of anger, but out of a desire for spectacle, a few sparks, a lot of yelling; it's street theater. There are so many people in New York, what's the harm in sacrificing a few for excitement?

This philosophy extends into the New York comedy clubs. You often see comedians being sacrificed for the amusement of a heckler. The competition for stand-up is fierce and audiences won't put up with inexperience or ineptitude. They have been spoiled by so much inadvertent street theater. I used to think that being a comedian just meant spacing your jokes closer together than normal people; I now know that in New York, everyone has their timing down perfectly. They learn it from the cab drivers, from the street vendors, even from the bag people. Sarcasm is as indigenous to New York as the mob. Even the little old ladies will beat you to a punch line if you're not careful. They've learned that in New York, a smart mouth will get you much further than any amount of social graces.

Stand-up comedy was something Moose dabbled in, never really attaining professional status, but quickly rising above rank amateur. Her first stab at it was in 1979. (She was twenty years old and still in college.) We have an account of that performance from a roommate who chose to remain anonymous. The roommate was not extremely impressed with Moose's

---

1. *The American Heritage Dictionary,* Second College Edition, © 1982, 1985 Houghton Mifflin Company. (MM)

efforts, but we remain uncertain as to whether this is due to jealousy on the part of the roommate or Moose's actual incompetence on the stage.[2]

The following is a transcript of the routine, performed January 3, 1979, at the Comedy Store on Sunset Boulevard in Hollywood. She added the heading later:

Why I Never Made it as a Stand-Up Comic

Good evening, ladies and gentlemen. Are you ready to laugh? [pause] Good. For my first joke of the evening, I'd like to start with an old stand-by. This was made popular by Bennett Cerf in the late 1950s. Here it is. [She reads it first to herself and laughs.] Oh, God, it is great. Okay, what did the mayonnaise say to the refrigerator? [laugh] This one gets me every time. Close the door, *I'm dressing.* [laugh] Remember that one? Doesn't it bring back memories? [pause, realizing that no one is laughing] Do you get it? It's a play on the word "dressing." [pause] Don't worry, I got lots more. We're sure to find one you remember.

How about, why did the deviant cross the road? [laugh] This is a re-working of an old standard. The deviant crossed the road because he had a chicken stuck to his dick! [When no one laughs . . .] Sorry, a friend of mine told me that joke. He said people like jokes about genitalia.

Okay, how do you tell a chicken from a chicken? [chuckle] One lays eggs and one lays eggs. ["And you just did, buddy"–simulated drunken response.[3] She gets very excited.]

Oh, God, my first heckler! You probably couldn't tell, but this is the first time I've ever done stand-up comedy. Oh, wow. I have a camera just to record this moment. The rest of you hold on a moment. I just want to get a shot of me and the heckler so I can send it to my parents. [She runs into the audience with a camera and poses with the heckler. Then . . .]

What is smaller than a bread box? Bread! [Realizing not many are laughing

---

2. I would like to go on record as saying that I feel certain that the roommate was indeed jealous. At the interview she was quoted as saying that Marissa "Moose" Minnion's taste in clothes was "painful to the senses." This girl seemed accustomed to lengthy discourse on others' faults. Her obvious proletarian upbringing, living as she did in the City of Commerce, rendered her somewhat petty, though I did pick up some nice Tupperware from her which she let me have at half-price because she'd recently had a Tupperware party and had accidentally ordered too many party ice cube trays that froze ice cubes in the shapes of hearts, diamonds, clubs, and spades. Oddly enough, I'd been looking for these for years. JC
3. Marissa "Moose" Minnion was anticipating her heckler here because any heckler worth his salt would jump to such an obvious lead. JC

she says] You know, we'd all have a better time if you'd just lower your standards a little. Actually, you do me a favor when you don't laugh. I don't have to worry about success going to my head. And no one's tempted to steal my material.

Since this is my first time as a stand-up comedienne I'd like to ask you a big favor. Would you mind filling out a little survey to help me? [She passes out survey and unsharpened #2 pencils.]

And remember, the first rule of comedy says that anything's funny if you surround it by jokes that are worse.

Sample of Comic Survey

1. I _____ the joke about the mayonnaise and the refrigerator.
   A. Liked
   B. Loved
   C. Fondly recalled

2. What punch line would you end this joke with?
   There was a sanitation engineer, a United Nations interpreter, and a three-foot armadillo all trapped in an elevator between the second and third floor in L.A.'s Bonaventure Hotel. The armadillo peed on the interpreter's leg and the sanitation engineer said, chuckling, "_____."

3. If your punchline is accepted, would you sue if I borrowed it?

4. Which of my jokes would have been funnier if I hadn't said them?
   A. _____
   B. _____ (that's enough)

Marissa "Moose" Minnion even had additional material on the possibility (though she knew it was slight) that the audience liked her enough to continue listening to her.

Excess Lines (if they let me stay onstage)

It's a good thing that we don't have eyes in our feet because that would make it very difficult to wear glasses.

Q: What did one turtle say to the other turtle?
A: Nothing, turtles can't talk.

{ 167 }

Alternate joke for intellectuals:

Q: What did one copy of Plato's *Republic* say to another copy of Plato's *Republic?*

A: (See above joke and replace "turtles" with "copies of Plato's *Republic.*")

Thoughts to Ponder (if they let me ponder)

You know how dogs bark in Japan? *"Wong, wong, wong."*
(I file this under foreign facts.)[4]

A listing of higher truths:
1. Glass is a liquid. Ask a chemist.
2. A palm tree grows from the top downward.
3. It is legal to drink the day before your twenty-first birthday.
4. Sarah Bernhardt had her lovers make love to her in a coffin.
5. Mike Nesmith's (of the Monkees) mother invented liquid paper.

Whatever happened to Josie and the Pussycats? Or fertilizing the crops with menstrual blood?

Obviously, Moose had much to learn in the way of comedy. You can see why her roommate said to her after this performance, "I wish I had the guts to get up there and make a fool of myself like that." Moose acknowledged,

The problem is, my idea of funny is an unfunny stand-up comedian.

Unfortunately, most people's idea of funny is a *funny* stand-up comedian. While Moose was in college, she tried comedy a couple more times after this first performance, but eventually quit because she kept feeling that she'd heard all her jokes somewhere else.

Sometimes I don't think my humor is very original, but I can't think of anyone who's done it before.

It was many years later in New York when she finally achieved slight success as a stand-up comic. She was a regular at the Comic Strip and performed at other local clubs as well. She maintained that her best performance (for herself, not necessarily the audience) was the night she brought her bathroom scale and weighed the audience and then passed out fortune cookies. A cook even came out of the kitchen for this event. He had no interest in comedy, he merely wanted to know how much he weighed.

---

4. This was a fact acquired from Sam who had, during a certain period of his life, several Asian girlfriends. HMW

She eventually quit comedy to work on *Higher Math*. She tired of making "one-liner small talk," of the competitiveness of comedians; she began to fear that she would end up like them, firing witty repartee at whatever audience happened to be around, measuring the quality of conversation by the laughs it provoked.

We reproduce some of her comedic monologues here, but bear in mind that, as comedy is meant to be performed, it would be best if you read them aloud, preferably to your neighbor, in order to get a flavor of what it is like to be a stand-up comedian. (If your neighbor would yell out obscenities it would help greatly with this exercise.)

First, imagine standing on the stage before you a nervous girl in a black, forties-style dress of her grandmother's. It has tiny studs decoratively placed, spewing light as she talks. She has a French horn in her hands and has already explained that she only plays it because she thought it went so well with the dress and she needed another accessory. You've missed the beginning of her act where she plays "The Munsters Theme"[5] on her French horn. She then says:

You know, surprising as this may sound, not a lot of guys ask out the girl that plays the French horn . . . Especially the ones with the motorcycles . . . But it doesn't matter because this chemist asked me to move to New York with him. I wasn't doing anything, so I figured, "Why not?" See, I tend to fall in love and move to major cities. I know, it's kind of crazy, but at least I see a lot of the country that way.

I met this chemist in a rock band; he plays guitar and I play lead French horn. Really. And the best thing about him is that I'm really loud and he doesn't mind. The thing about being loud and funny is that everyone thinks you're Jewish. I'm not, but when I was a kid I really wanted to be Jewish. See, I thought it was a profession. It's kind of like a regular job only with more days off. In fact, when people asked me if I was Jewish I'd tell them, "In my family we had all the guilt and none of the holidays." I either wanted to be Jewish or join a nudist camp. Tough decision. I was going to do both, but it's hard to color-coordinate when you're naked.

I really was kind of an odd kid. I used to think that Walter Cronkite and Captain Kangaroo were the same person. In fact, I'm still not sure. You know, you

---

5. "The Munsters"—a TV sit-com in the 1960s. Herman Munster, the father, slightly resembled Frankenstein's monster. This is where similarity to great literature ends. Later it became a cult show during reruns. JC

never see them together. I was also deathly afraid of Josephine the Plumber. Every time she came on TV I would run screaming from the room. I think this was because in my house, a plunger was a disciplinary tool.

I was also very lonely as a child. I had two imaginary friends. Actually, that's not true . . . I only had one imaginary friend . . . and she had a friend . . . that neither of us liked. We kept trying to lose her but she had really good drugs. And we all know how hard it is to stay away from *real* friends with good drugs.

See, I think one of the reasons I was lonely was because I never had any pets as a kid. I kept bugging my parents for one until they finally had my sister. She was great. Actually *she* was the one who was afraid of Josephine the Plumber. I was afraid of Manfred the Wonder Dog. See, I'm allergic to everything with hair. Horses, dogs . . . even coconuts. I almost went into a coma when we went to Hawaii. And they used to have to shave my sister. I can walk into a room and tell if a cat has been there within the last century. It's kind of like ESP only it's all in my nose. In fact, when I was a kid, every time I sneezed the channel on the TV changed. Whenever I'd get a cold my parents would send me over to the neighbors. (They hated the neighbors because they were Amway distributors.) I thought maybe this sneezing thing was hereditary so I went to this psychic to contact my dead grandmother . . . but all we could get was her dog.

Why is it I'm the only person who thinks that's funny?

So anyway, I finally figured out a solution. I mean about being allergic to pets. I bought an ant farm. About a month ago. Think about it: ants are the perfect urban pet. They don't shed, they don't shit – and if they did, who'd notice? They build little subways and walk all over each other. They make New Yorkers feel comfortable. Ants are man's best friend. They don't take up too much room, they're great company, they make you feel very powerful – and if they bite you, you kill them.

But you know what pisses me off about ants? They all look alike. Some of you have probably already noticed this. So if one of 'em bites you, you don't know which one of the little pissants did it. And then you have to kill a whole bunch of 'em. I just hate that. It used to really bother me when I was a vegetarian because I didn't believe in killing animals, but if they bite you, it kind of changes things, you know? Anyway, I only became a vegetarian because I thought I needed more convictions. Now I just think I need more ants.

Aside from the fact that all my ants died, it was pretty neat to see them running around. Except they stopped doing that after about three days. I don't know what the problem was . . . I watered them. You're supposed to do that!

I got really attached to them. I'd let them out to exercise. And I had them almost trained to come back right about the time they died. See, I got kind of fond of them while reading this book on scanning electron micrographs; you know, where they take a pointed Tungsten filament and apply a high negative polarity accelerating voltage (normally 1000 to 30,000 volts) causing the electrons to be emitted into the vacuum—oh, you probably already read this book. Anyway, they've got these enormous portraits of ants.[6] And you know what?! Ants don't all look alike. Of course, that's before you step on them. Then they look pretty similar, even if they are magnified a thousand times.

I got my ants from this company called Auntie Em Industries. It's based in L.A.—and I'll bet that doesn't surprise you. I think Auntie Em made her fortune by sending diseased ants because the second batch died even faster than the first. They lived longer in the mail than they did in their ant farm. I did everything they said to do. I didn't feed them too much. Auntie Em says that overfeeding is the most common reason for ant fatalities. Of course, that excludes the inability to support a 130-pound person on your back.

I'm thinking it was a cult thing. One of the ants made the other ants drink aphid Kool-aid.[7] I'll just bet Auntie Em encourages them. It keeps her in business. She should at least send an ant cemetery to bury them in 'cause now they're all just lying on their backs . . . well, some of them are kind of curled up on their sides. And they didn't even make any tunnels or anything [pouting]. It cost me two-fifty for each bunch. I've already spent . . . um . . . what's three times two-fifty? Well, more than five dollars anyway. I like to think what I have is an Ant Memorial. I'm going to have it bronzed. I'm starting on my third batch just as soon as they mail them to me. I'm also thinking about sending away for Auntie Em's Fossil Hunt. That's twenty dollars. Auntie Em says that the Fossil Hunt comes with a pile of dirt, a couple toothbrushes, and twenty authentic fossils guaranteed to be 100 to 550 million years old. But I wanna know how they can tell that they're that old. If they're really 100 million years old I'm sure the date's worn off by now. My neighbor found one of those fossils in her cat box. And she didn't pay anything for it.

You might wonder where these ideas come from, but I really don't know. It's kind of like junk mail; they send it to you even when you move. I should credit my parents with partial responsibility. See, my mother taught psychology and my father taught economics so . . . I lived much of my life in the-

---

6. Marissa "Moose" Minnion holds up a picture from the book. JC
7. An obscure joke: ants milk aphids for their nectar. HMW

ory.[8] (That's one of those intellectual jokes.) Most people don't realize that economists understand supply and demand perfectly. They just don't understand money. That's why my mother always did the taxes. But my father took his economics very much to heart—he would only buy things if they were on sale. My grandmother was like that also. She bought a forklift because it was on sale. I know you think I made that up, but I swear it's true. You don't get like me from a normal family . . . Anyway, it was only $4000, which is a really good price for a forklift. I don't know if you've priced them lately. I think she used it as a second car or something. That way you know you always have a parking space. The best thing my father bought on sale was this player piano. With it came this song called "Basin Street Blues." I will now do my rendition of "Basin Street Blues." I do it as a duet with myself. After many years of not dating I've grown very self-sufficient.

[French horn/voice duet of "Basin Street Blues."]

Barbie Doll Addiction

I get a lot of theories while I eat. I got this theory right after eating my fifteenth Twinkie. I was in a bit of a dither about what to do with the sixteenth—I just hate to separate pairs—when it hit me: people learn drug addiction from Barbie dolls.

Now I know you're saying, "Barbie dolls. [she slaps head] Sheesh. But of course. Why didn't I think of that?"

And all this time everybody thinks we learn drug addiction from MTV and obscene rock lyrics or from homosexual fathers and *Mad* magazine or even from health foods like Hostess Twinkies. But I tell you, it starts even before that. It starts with your first Barbie prom dress. "How can Barbie go to the prom if she doesn't have a dress?" And then you need Ken because "how can she get there if Ken doesn't take her?" And then Ken needs a tux because "Barbie wouldn't be seen with just any old schmuck." You see?

Originally, Barbie dolls were supposed to teach you how to be pretty and grown up. They're supposed to teach you how to wear tight sweaters that don't show your nipples . . . which was a lot easier for Barbie than the rest of us because she didn't have any nipples. I felt inadequate because of Barbie and used to try to paint mine off with white-out.

Barbies were supposed to teach us when to wear gloves and what goes with gold lamé. They were supposed to teach us how to wear plastic high heel shoes

---

8. Here one personality steals material from another. KLL

and especially how to date guys with no genitals. *But all Barbie dolls really teach you is to want more Barbie dolls.*

Like heroin, the more you have the more you want. It doesn't stop with just one doll. You become desperate. After Barbie there's Ken, then you need Skipper and Scooter and Madge the wig doll. And all those stupid wigs. Not to mention Barbie's camper, Barbie's squash court, and Barbie's McDonald's franchise. [pause]

They really have that, you know.

Now this is really stupid because Barbie wouldn't be caught dead cooking a hamburger. It might melt her hairdo. And you think Ken would let her own it? No way! Barbie's too stupid. I had a Barbie campus and it didn't even have any classrooms. All she could do was make foo-foo eyes at Ken in the Campus Sweet Shop. In fact, that's *probably all* she could do with Ken. Ken was much more interested in G.I. Joe. My brother used to dress G.I. Joe up in Barbie's clothes. Cashmere sweater, culottes, and an M16. My brother was an odd kid. But at least it was *something* to do because Barbie is so boring! I'd get all my Barbies out and then stare at them and think, "Now what?" All she ever wants to do is try on clothes. She can't take a bath, she can't go swimming, she's such a prude, she never lets Ken fuck her. Not that Ken would . . .

In fact, the only fun I ever really had with Barbie was when my brother and I would tie her up and let Ken torture her. You know, how come they never had a Barbie dungeon with a little Barbie rack and Barbie manacles? They didn't have anything fun like that. We used to use twist ties for handcuffs and you know, they don't even cut the skin. We even had a Barbie branding iron. It was really handy for identification purposes, like when Barbie had a block party. See, Barbie doll addiction ran rampant in my neighborhood and you know how you can't trust addicts. After a block party you always seemed to have fewer Barbies than you started with. That's because everyone knew that the only thing you can do with Barbies is get more Barbies.

Believe me, I know. I was addicted. It was Barbie hell. I was saved, though. It happened the day the house burned down. See, Barbie had accused Madge the wig doll of being a witch and we were burning her at the stake. Unfortunately the ensuing fire charred a few neighbor children as well. But I got over my addiction. At reform school they don't have Barbie dolls.

Wingy

I have another theory – well, actually, if you don't mind, I'd like to do a little test here. A little research. [She holds up a large white card with the word "Clitoris" carefully written on it in big letters, similar to a flashcard.] How many people know how to pronounce this word?! [There are a few titters in the audience.]

Now how many men actually *know* where it is?

Now how many women *think* the men actually *know* where it is?

See, I have a theory that women are orgasmically frustrated because we don't have a cute, little, perky [she tosses her head] term to describe the most important part of our bodies. How can we say in the heat of passion, "You fucking bastard, yank my" [she holds up card] if you can't even pronounce it? And even if you do know how to pronounce it, who wants to in the middle of sex? It's enough to make you get up and go search for the dictionary. And the thing is, if you don't know how to pronounce it, how are you going to convince men it even exists? They had a hard enough time with the G spot. What are you going to say? Go south? I don't think a compass is going to help you here. And so what does this all lead to? I'll tell you what this leads to!!

[She throws the card down, lifts the French horn to her lips, and plays the beginning of "I Can't Get No Satisfaction." Sometimes it takes the audience a little while to figure out the song because they've never heard it on a French horn before. She yells in the middle of a line, "Feel free to sing along!" She ends by singing "I can't get no! (French horn) I can't get me no! (French horn) That's what I say!"]

And what I say is that we need a new word. A word that doesn't sound like a mouthwash. A word that doesn't sound like a breath mint. A word that you can spell!

And I've got one!

[She flips the card to display a new one with the word "Wingy" written on it in exactly the same fashion. She slowly pans in order to let it sink in. Then, nervously,]

Wingy. That's right. Wingy. Now wait a minute before you say, "Wingy?! What the hell kind of word is that?!" Think a moment. Just try it out. It's bouncy, kind of perky. It kind of rolls off your tongue. [pause]

Occasionally. [pause]

If you're lucky.

It kind of looks like a little wing. I figure it's the female equivalent to "weenie."

Wingy also gives you a whole new vista of slang terms. A lesbian could be a wingy-whipper. A hooker: wingy-to-go. And oral sex could be referred to as "wing around the collar."

Wingy is a very useful term. For example, you can travel with a word like wingy. It's easily translatable. In Germany it would be *Der Vingy*. In France: *La winget*. In New York: [pointing down as if calling a dog] Yo, wingy. In Russian: *Das Vinkovich*. In Pig Latin (which perhaps there's not a lot of call for, but I'll throw it in free anyway): *Ingy-way*. And my personal favorite . . . at a Mexican orgy: *Et chickidas. Donde esta los wingos?*[9]

Moose recounted a time when someone from the audience yelled out, as she stood there with her "Clitoris" placard, "I think you spelled that word wrong!" She said, "Sir, trust me, I wouldn't have written this in twelve-inch letters and stood in front of an audience without first looking it up in a dictionary."

Moose maintained that the whole reason she did this bit was because everyone seems to think that "clitoris" is pronounced "kli•tor'•us." It is not. The acceptable pronunciations are: "klit'•er•iss" or "kly'•ter•iss."

The idea for a stand-up bit about the clitoris came after Moose discovered that the word "cloaca" was only four words away from "clitoris" in the dictionary. Cloaca generally means a sewer. ("Hmmm . . . " Moose is reputed to have said.) After looking this word up in several dictionaries she discovered that in zoology, a cloaca refers to "the cavity into which the intestinal, genital, and urinary tracts open in vertebrates such as fish, reptiles, birds, and some primitive mammals."[10] In other words, a rudimentary vagina. "No wonder 'clitoris' and 'cloaca' are in such close proximity in the dictionary . . . " writes Moose, "their proximity just mirrors life." The definition of "cloaca" which Moose found the most humorous was one that referred to a cloaca as a "receptacle of moral filth."

"And how true that is!" Moose exclaimed at Sam's chemistry Christmas party after explaining this definition to a circle of scientists. Fortunately Sam was amused by this sort of behavior. New York does strange things to people.

---

9. Due to the implied gender, this phrase would only be acceptable at a transsexual orgy. KLL
10. *The American Heritage Dictionary,* Second College Edition, © 1982, 1985 Houghton Mifflin Company. HMW

12
$$- \neq \equiv \neq -$$

(It Was) My Mannequin
(key of E minor)

I was stoned.
It was dark.
It was Washington Park.
So I walked into the Village instead.
I came upon a shop
And decided to stop
Where the men all wear towels on their head.[1]

I looked low,
I looked high,
There was nothing to buy
So I shouldered my way to the door.
But there in the window,
Not just another bimbo,
Was the girl I longed to explore.

It was my mannequin.
(I think I'll call her Mabel.)
She wore a tan afghan.
(Or was it sable?)
I knew she'd be my friend.
Our love would be a fable.
It was my ma-a-a-a-an-annequin.

I asked him how much for her?
Can I get her through mail order?
He clasped his hands and smiled through his eyes.
And then he mumbled, "Hundred"
And suddenly some unsaid
Merry little thoughts materialized.

---

1. Sikhs. HMW

It was my mannequin.
(I think I'll call her Gwen.)
She wore a tan afghan.
(Or was it crinoline?)
She ached for discipline
(She was my Anne Boleyn.)
It was my ma-a-a-a-an-annequin.

I was stoned.
It was hot.
I was at a bus stop
Carrying the girl of my dreams.
Couldn't find a cab,
I had to get to the lab
To synthesize her type and draw schemes.[2]

It was my mannequin.
(I think I'll call her Glenna.)
She wore a tan afghan.
(Or was it burnt sienna?)
Our love would never end.
I'll take her to Vienna.
It was my ma-a-a-a-an-annequin.

I got home.
It was dawn.
I was woebegone.
I knew the law would never spare us.
I was afraid to touch her;
See, I'd determined her structure.
My girl was plaster of paris.

It was my mannequin.
(I think I'll call her Jackie.)
She wore a tan afghan.
(Or was it khaki?)
She was always too thick-skinned
(In the shower she was tacky.)
It was my ma-a-a-a-an-annequin.

---

2. Chemist notation for representing molecular structures. HMW

Miss Yvonne[3]

A friend surreptitiously passes me a baggy of pot in an Italian restaurant in Greenwich Village. Sam and I immediately go and smoke some in Washington Park[4] (one of the advantages of an anarchic New York) and then walk through Greenwich. We walk into this clothing store owned by these Indians (Indian Indians, not American Indians). As I'm idly looking at leather jackets, I hear Sam ask, "How much for that mannequin?"

(I figure he's just playing with the guy.)

The owner says, "Ohmmmmm . . . one hundred dollars."

Sam says, "Moose, we gotta buy a mannequin," like he's discussing buying the evening newspaper.

I look at him at him in mock disgust. "You're fucked up."

"Who do you know that has a mannequin?"

Shaking my head, "You're fucked up."

"How late are you open?" Sam asks the owner.

"Midnight."

"We'll be back."

Sam drags me outside to convince me that buying a mannequin *is* the right thing to do. We get into a discussion with a cop who happens to be walking by. Cops are one of the best things about New York because they've seen it all and they're great conversationalists. Unless you murder someone, they're your friend. (Murder the right someone and you're friends for sure.) New York cops often rove in packs because they're too fat to run away if they see trouble. They don't hassle people like cops do in Los Angeles. For instance, we saw this guy on a bicycle riding alongside a police car. He was yelling in the window, "It's the law, Law. It's the law, Law." He proceeded all the way down the street like this and they just ignored him. New York police allow for individual freedoms.

People smoke pot all the time on the streets of New York and the cops couldn't care less. They know there's too much crime here to worry about recreational drugs. Of course, I can't say anything for the police force's efficiency level. I suppose if I really needed a cop for something I would have a different philosophy. All in all, I would still prefer to deal with the New York police than police from any other city. At least they have a sense of humor even if they are all on the make. In fact, this cop that we're talking to gives us a quick rundown of how many police are involved in a recent shakedown that's just sur-

---

3. This is what Sam and Marissa "Moose" Minnion later named their mannequin. Miss Yvonne is a character on Pee Wee Herman's Saturday morning children's show. JC
4. Washington Square Park. HMW

facing on the news. He shakes his head, "You'll be amazed when the whole story comes out!" (I'm thinking, "No, I won't care.")

Then he jovially asks us why we want a mannequin.

"Because he's fucked up in the head," I say, pointing to Sam.

Sam says, "No, I wanna buy it 'cause even when you're away it'll look like someone's home," thinking this reasoning will appeal to a policeman's sensibilities.

Even though I find Sam's wanting a mannequin uncharacteristic of him (indeed, later everyone will assume that it was my idea), I realize that I like being with someone unpredictable and that I should be the last person to squelch someone else's wacky ideas. So I say okay, but you'll owe me. (I might as well get some sort of benefit out of the agreement.)

We go back and ask the Indians if they'll take Visa. They will.

Sam helps them get the mannequin out of the window. As one of the Sikhs starts lifting her up, he grabs one of her breasts, a natural handhold. Quickly realizing what he's holding and disturbed by it, he shifts his grip to her arm which promptly falls off. Sam and I are in hysterics.

The Indians try to convince us to buy what she's wearing at the reduced cost of fifteen dollars, but I think it's ugly at any price and say no way. However, they won't let us take her out of the store nude. (I think it must be against their religion to allow a mannequin to be transported naked across their threshold.) So we put my full-length coat on her, I wear Sam's jacket, and he has to suffer for art (and he is suffering because it's freezing cold). Her left arm and wig keep falling off as we take her down the street. We are laughing uncontrollably. People yell at us like we're just typical New Yorkers carrying a mannequin and I want to yell, "I'm not from this scumhole!" but I don't.

Sam carries the mannequin to the bus stop and sets her down because she is really heavy. I run and try to get a taxi, but suddenly everyone is trying to get home and there are about fifty people signaling for taxis and only two taxis in all of Greenwich. New York gives one a view of what life will be like when there is less of everything: lettuce, good pizza (whoever said that New York had good pizza anyway?), breathing room, taxis . . . New York is a very competitive society. No one is nice because they're all too busy getting somewhere. (Except for the police. They're happy where they are.) If someone stops to help you, nine times out of ten you'll end up getting robbed. (Don't *ever* let anyone offer to take your bags to a cab when you get off the shuttle bus from the airport!) Actually, there have been days when people have been very nice, but I think that's because they were happy about the Mets. After a week they're back to their snotty attitudes again. You might think I'm making this up, but try living here for a year and then go to California for a few weeks and you'll see what I mean.

Anyway, Sam is waiting there on the bench with the mannequin and this really drunk white guy in a business suit comes up and asks Sam if he can feel up the mannequin. Sam says sure, he doesn't care. This guy keeps asking Sam what the mannequin's name is and Sam says, "I dunno. We just bought her."

Meanwhile, this snazzy little sports car whips up and the driver yells out the window, "I WANT THAT MANNEQUIN! HOW MUCH FOR THAT MANNEQUIN?"

Sam yells, "Hundred and fifty dollars."

"No way! A hundred."

"No way! One twenty-five."

"She's not worth a hundred and twenty-five dollars. Come on! One hundred."

"We just bought her for a hundred."

The driver whips a hundred-dollar bill out of his wallet and waves it out the window. "ONE HUNDRED DOLLARS! HERE IT IS. COLD, HARD CASH."

By this time the guy who was feeling up the mannequin has migrated over to the car and tries to grab for the the hundred dollar bill but is too drunk to do so without falling onto the car, which he does.

"Get your fuckin' paws off my car," the man with the money yells.

I'm actually worried now that Sam is going to sell the mannequin and no one would ever believe that we bought and sold a hundred-dollar mannequin in less than fifteen minutes in Greenwich Village.

"I WANT THAT FUCKIN' MANNEQUIN!" he yells again.

"One twenty-five," Sam shrugs.

The guy floors the car in anger and it leaps into traffic which scares the drunkard so much that he falls back against the mannequin. Sam pushes him off toward the end of the bench. A bus pulls up right then and we get on because it has a stop that's two blocks from our apartment, clear up on the Upper West Side. (That's what they call where we live, though it's really only midway up the island. I call where we live "Soha." [5] This is a New York joke. I actually stole that from a chemist and used it in my comedy act. Chemists don't get mad when you steal their material the way comedians do.)

It is a forty-five-minute party on the bus. (We just kill these two black

---

5. "Soha" is short for "South Harlem"; a take-off of "Soho," which is short for "South of Houston." This is a method New Yorkers have for abbreviating neighborhood locations. HMW

women who howl every time someone comes on the bus and does a double take.) Some people try to ignore the fact that we have a mannequin on the bus—quintessential New Yorkers. Most people, though, ask if we had to pay extra for her in that wise-cracking way like they think they're a comic genius, little realizing that's the first question *everyone* asks. Most people's humor is pretty pedestrian. Anyway, we didn't.

So we come to our stop and have to walk uphill to our apartment. (Sam remembers this better than I do because he was carrying the mannequin.) As we walk into the building, the doorman is panicking because he thinks that Sam is carrying an injured person in his arms. (She is positioned like a model, has no hair and no left arm . . . you don't have to pass many tests to be a doorman.)

After we get her home I paint her nails and nipples (she was made in the pre-nipple era) and let her iron. Sam says when we have kids we'll have to hide her because otherwise they'll grow up thinking that every household has a mannequin and when they go over to their friends' houses they'll say, "So, where's your mannequin?" and then they'll be ostracized. I actually think that Sam wanted to buy the mannequin because there's a good chance that we may end up living in Pennsylvania and he's afraid of becoming part of Middle America.

Thoughts on New York

A dwarf called me a "fuckin' bitch" on the subway today. I suppose she thought I was feeling sorry for her just because I asked her if she wanted to sit down. Actually, I didn't ask her outright, but a seat opened up and, as someone had just stepped on her and she had shrieked very loudly, I waited for her to take it, thinking that she'd prefer not to be stepped on again. She didn't sit down. I asked, "Did you want to sit down?" like I used to ask back in the days when I was polite because I hadn't lived in New York for that long. She yelled, "If I wanted to sit I'd sit . . . fuckin' bitch."

Later that same day a different dwarf (okay, she was a *very short* little old lady) asked which nylon stockings I thought would be long enough for her. She explained that she was very long through the torso and stockings were always too tight. Both pairs she showed me were the same size. She'd been judging the sizes by the pictures on the packages. I explained that this wasn't a very good way to do it. As the stockings were for women five to five feet eight inches tall, I told her I was sure that they would be long enough for her. (I didn't mention that she'd probably have a little excess at the feet. She's gotta be used to that by now.)

I wonder if life gave me two dwarfs today—a bad one and a good one—just so I wouldn't get cocky and think I knew a thing or two about the ways of dwarfs.

Things to remember about NY^2 (a partial list):[6]

1. Chem party—"Are you really a chemist or do you just wear the shirt?" I asked this of a greasy English guy who was wearing a shirt with a molecule on it. He got insulted. I asked if he didn't like people asking him questions—no answer. "Have you ever been to a party before?"—no answer. So I suggested that if he didn't like questions maybe he should turn his shirt inside out. He left.

   Later at same party with Sam and Peter—Sam: "I swear that guy was wearing a different shirt."

2. New York Rule #1: Never wear dresses to the Public Library.[7]

   Men clutch at their privates in New York more than any other place I've ever been.   —New York Public Library, 5/13/86

3. BC and a classmate of his from pilot school drove from Kansas to New York and stayed at our apartment for a couple of days. BC asked if he should take a box of his stuff out of the car. It was his classmate's car. I said, "If you ever want to see it again." I guess BC's friend just heard a female talking and tuned it out. (He was a dick. He said that women are always so glad when he asks them out on dates because they only ever go out once or twice a year. He meant *all* women. I asked him what time zone he was from.) Consequently, BC's friend left everything he owned (stereo, bedding, iron, etc.) in his car, which was parked on 113th Street. The next day—you guessed it—his car had disappeared. BC's friend told the police, "But I locked it." They laughed. The cops said, "Everything you've heard about New York, multiply that by ten." They laughed again.

4. Comedy: I waste so much of my time preparing for those five minutes in which I tell bits and pieces of my life to people who think I made it all up.

---

6. NY^2 was how Moose often wrote "New York, New York." JMVB

7. Observation made after three separate incidents involving men who attempted to look up MM's dress while pretending to look for books on the bottom shelf. Reportedly, Sam commented, "With Moose they hit the jackpot." (MM never wore underwear.) HMW

"Remind me not to let you hold my dick onstage." – Sam's comment after I told him that I bent my French horn key during my act because I was nervous.

I had a wonderful birthday party. There were mostly chemists and comedians there, although more chemists than comedians which I think was a good thing. Too many comedians can ruin a party. Enough chemists think they're comedians anyway.

And wouldn't you know . . . the first day I do stand-up comedy this girl takes me aside and says she wants to talk to me after her act. I think she is going to say how much she likes my material. (This is before I know anything about comedians.) So I wait. She walks up to me after she gets offstage and says, "You're doing one of my jokes. I want you to cut it out." After she goes on for five minutes about how I have to stop doing her material and how she'd done that joke for years and everybody knows it's her joke – and I'm about to cry – she pauses and then says all friendly-like, "So . . . how do you like New York?"

The worst thing is, "her joke" is one of my only three jokes. The one about being Jewish. (She isn't Jewish either.) It's the first joke I ever wrote. I even have a copyright on it because I was crazy when I was younger and used to copyright things because I thought that made them good. But see, you can't get around the fact that everyone's going to think I stole it from her because apparently she's performed around a lot. Tiffily Nevitts . . . ever heard of her? I didn't think so.

I explained the situation to the manager of the Comic Strip because I'm new and don't know the ropes and he said to stop doing the joke but to tell her that I do have the copyright on it and perhaps I can do it other places than New York. (Like what? Alaska? Anyway, we'll see if I ever get to any other places than New York.) He insinuated that perhaps I heard her say the line on the West Coast but he didn't understand that I hate comedians and that I never went to see comedy before I decided to do it. Anyway, I pointed out to him that the wheel was discovered in three different places in the world all around the same time so I think it possible that we both could come up with the same punch line to one snively little joke.[8]

---

8. Some anthropologists, in acknowledging man's pressing desire to be "in," consider the wheel the first fad. KLL

5. Scam where Chinese chem student comes upon woman on 125th Street who says that she just found $18,000 in a paper bag but she needs help to make sure the numbers aren't listed with the bank. Another person walks by, *seemingly uninvolved,* and she says the same thing to him. They all agree to split the money if the money isn't connected to a federal investigation. So the chem student and the other passerby flip a coin to see who goes into bank and who stays out to make sure the woman doesn't leave with the money. It ends up that the chem student goes in and gets $6000 out of the bank and gives it to the woman to hold as a show of good faith. She gives him the numbers of the bills she has in the paper sack and sends him into the bank to check them. The passerby remains with the woman to make sure she won't leave with the $6000. End of story. Oldest scam in the book. How can you not know you should never give $6000 to anyone on 125th Street?

6. Isabel's stories (intern in a New York hospital):

   a. A woman calls 911 to report that she can see a body on the roof of the apartment next to hers. She says she thinks it's either dead or in great need of help. A day later the body is still there. She calls back. "Are you planning to do something about this body?" 911 says indignantly, "You think your dead body is the only dead body in New York?"

   b. A man goes into the hospital with twenty-five pencils stuck up his ass. The hospital X-rays him and cannot determine if they are sharpened. They ask him. He says, "What do you think I am, crazy?"

   c. A husband and wife come to the hospital. He has a cordless vibrator stuck up his ass. It's on. By the time they get to it, it has worked its way up to his intestines and they have to operate and remove part of his bowels in order to turn it off.

7. Peter's stories (chemist friend of Sam's):

   a. There used to be a storefront on 103rd Street where you could go in, walk back to a closed door, knock on the door, say you want "Gold," a small hole in the door opens, you give them ten dollars, they pass you a small brown envelope with a couple of buds in it[9] and, before you take it, they stamp the word "GOLD" on it.

---

9. "Buds" is a descriptive term used for marijuana because it grows in clumps. HMW

b. A white chem student makes a bet with another white chem student that he can go into Morningside Park and eat his lunch at one in the afternoon and not get mugged. Within ten minutes of his being there someone pulls a gun on him and takes all his money. So he figures he might as well continue eating his lunch. Another guy comes up and pulls a gun on him and the chem student says, "Sorry, you're too late. The first guy got everything." Needless to say, he lost the bet.

c. A man jumped in front of a subway train to kill himself, lived but lost his leg, sued the transit system for not having better protection in order to prevent people from jumping in front of trains, and won.

8. Overheard: "You know, you always hear how bad New York is, but everyone's been *really* nice to us."

    —*Really* stupid tourists waiting for the Broadway Local

9. A guy is robbed of everything he owns except, oddly, his camera, which had been sitting out on a table. Two weeks later, realizing that the roll of film is finished, he takes it to be developed. When the film comes back, there are pictures of the robber's behind with the guy's toothbrush stuck in a most unsanitary place. The guy has been using his toothbrush now for over two weeks. (I consider this a public service announcement. If you've been robbed, get your film developed at a twenty-four hour place.)

10. A New York newscaster is hospitalized and off the air for three weeks. It becomes widely known that he is hospitalized because he had a gerbil stuck up his ass. (Everything you've heard is true.) Someone rents a billboard on an expressway and puts up a sign that says, "Save the Gerbils!" (Try putting gerbils in an over-crowded environment and see what they stick up their asses.)

13
$$- \neq \equiv \neq -$$

Childhood

I had two imaginary friends when I was about six: Joan Carsley and Nardie Carnell.[1] Joan wore a black hat with a flower, a dark blue dress, and high-topped black shoes. I don't know when I met her. Nardie wore a magician assistant's outfit: black tights, high-heeled shoes, black tails, and top hat. Joan and I were best friends. Nardie was pretty much a third wheel. We just let her tag along because she wouldn't go away when we told her to. But she knew she wasn't my really best imaginary friend.

Death

Use in will: Just remember, I lived my life exactly like I wanted. I love my family. And please wash my clothes before you give them to relatives.

My body sucked the breath out from under me.

The thing that scares me the most is the fear that I may never count. But by the time I realize that I'll be dead. (Use in section mentioning esoteric fears.)

Anyone who lives in L.A. has at least a few suicidal tendencies.

Consensus

I dreamed I was on a trail that ran along a canal. There were a bunch of other people on it as well. It was part of a traveling game show. All the answers had to do with "keyholes." The question I had to answer was "This book has a rabbit in it. Name the book."

"Of course," I said excitedly, "It's *Alice's Adventures in Wonderland.* That's really easy."

It was the wrong answer. The right answer was *Daniel Boone.*

And everyone said to me disgustedly, "Where does *Alice in Wonderland* have a rabbit and a keyhole??"

---

1. Similarity in names is purely coincidental. JC, NC

The Incredible Game Show Story

First, I want to say that I never meant to be on seven game shows. I don't watch game shows. I don't even watch TV. But it's just one of those twists of fate, those jokes played upon me by the gods. I let life steer me along because it seems a better driver than I.

Second, I'm not particularly good at remembering television lore nor am I knowledgeable about much current trivia. I know trivia along the lines of who authored which children's book or which impressionistic artists were myopic (Degas, I think), but as to who starred on what TV show, which cartoon hero has arms of rubber, or what was the name of George Jetson's dog . . . I confess an ignorance. Consequently, it is a bit strange that I would even get on a game show because the questions tend to be very television-chauvinistic, a self-reflective genre, squaring the importance of TV in the minds of those who watch it. Being on game shows tended to diminish my already nonexistent regard for them. But my curse was that I found I was relatively good at them. For me, game shows were almost too easy to get on. And it seemed foolish not to do them when they were so close at hand[2] and such a great source of income—especially for one who hates work as much as I do. Game shows became a function of my personality, a through line, an easy way to make conversation . . . or become the center of it. (You'd be amazed at how many intelligent people are fascinated by someone who has been on a game show.) And as a study of human nature, game shows allowed me to see the masses in their agitated and resting states.

Because game show contestants generally watch a lot of game shows, I found that the only way for me to do well was to appear on a brand new game show. This way everyone starts from scratch; no one has been able to watch the show for years, boning up on the particular nuances that distinguish one game show from another, the knowledge of which later separates a pro from a novice or, more importantly, a winner from a loser. This explains why I did so poorly on my first game show, "Crosswits"—it was in its third year when I went on, but I had never watched it. The show was based on crossword puzzles: I had never successfully completed one of those either. Not surprisingly, I didn't answer a single question right. However, I went home with an alleged $900 worth of consolation prizes consisting primarily of cheese and bathroom cleaning products.

---

2. The events of this chapter took place in Los Angeles, prior to those in the New York chapter, probably between 1979 and 1984. HMW

You'd think that a person would be happy coming away with anything from a game show. It is certainly more than you started with. But game shows make you feel especially brainless for losing in front of twenty million people, all of whom are shouting at their television sets, "You moron, it's not Princess Caroline, it's Grace Kelly! Princess Caroline was in diapers when they made *Country Girl!*"

My opponent, Lars, a CPA from Geneva, Missouri, promptly won the car on his first word . . . something that happens every – oh – forty or so shows. My celebrities tried to cheer me up. I would have been more cheered had I ever heard of them before. In fact, one of my celebrities didn't even show up so they had to use the girl who usually sits on the car. Her parents were so excited that they flew in from Washington, D.C., to see the show. (She was the one who insisted the answer was Princess Caroline.)

As soon as the taping started my mind departed for some nether world. I'm not sure where it went, but I know it must have had a better time than I did. I was too busy taxing the void my mind left behind with such weighty questions as "What did Darth Vader and Luke Skywalker have in common?"

"Romance?" I tentatively queried.

Everyone laughed, I blushed. Right idea, wrong answer. The correct answer was "The Princess." Now most people might be puzzled by this answer. "Weren't Luke Skywalker and Darth Vader related? Wouldn't that be what they had in common?" you might ask yourself. Ah! You've come to an important realization: just because they're game shows, don't expect them to be right. Indeed, Sam yells at "Jeopardy" regularly. "Tarnish *is* oxidation, you dildos!" (This was when they took a man's points away for what they believed was a wrong answer.)

I learned a lot on that first game show. Primarily I learned about the masses. People will do an awful lot for the chance to win money. They will jump up and down in a very crowded room. They will scream "WE LOVE YOU BRUCE!!" to an extremely bald-headed producer. They will babble ceaselessly on such topics as their families, their jobs, and how many years they've watched a particular game show if they think it will improve their chances to get on. Much later in my game show career I learned that they will also utter such grotesquely American phrases as "BIG BUCKS!! COME ON! BIG BUCKS!!" as if the mere shouting of the words will encourage fate to smile down upon them. This action seems similar to (if not as spiritually pleasing as) the chanting and dancing of the American Indians in an attempt to coax rain from the heavens. If I were fate, chanting and dancing would prove a much more effective supplication than "BIG BUCKS" screamed at the top of some-one's lungs.

Truthfully, I tend to be a bit hyperactive. All my friends know me as uncontrollable; a "game show natural" I've been called, much to my distress. But in a roomful of such "game show naturals," I found them so repugnant, so unquestionably brash as to make me quietly blend into the furnishings, preferring to watch them all act like assholes than to become an active participant. I delight in being different, the anomaly. Even to say that I delight is incorrect. I seem to not know any other way to be. Why do it if someone's done it before? To me, art is setting a pattern and then breaking it for interest. I am the part of the pattern that is broken, that refuses to be part of the pattern. I don't really know why this is, but I suspect it is due to the fact that in my family we knew no peer pressure. You have to have peers for that. I don't mean that as presumptuously as it sounds. As a kid, even though I had friends, I felt distinctly unlike them. Early on I realized that the inside of everyone's house didn't look like our house and, analogously, that everyone's mother didn't act like mine. I grew up with an inconsistent view of life. There wasn't a one-to-one relationship between my behavior and the way my parents treated me. If you are randomly punished you might as well behave randomly. I began to feel unbounded by the rules that everyone else lived by. Indeed, often I would be taken by surprise when someone would say, in effect, "You can't do that!"

"You can't carry your lunch box to school when everyone else is carrying sacks!" The girls in my sixth grade class made this poignantly clear by stealing my lunch box and hiding it in the garbage in the girls' bathroom. Now your first inclination might be to think that I was a bit of a pansy, a priss, that I'd somehow incurred their displeasure through tattling or some other bit of smarmy behavior, but truthfully I think I was just different and this disturbed them. I wouldn't conform. Not out of defiance but out of obliviousness. This obliviousness has resulted in my not caring about the same things that other people do. Things like wearing underwear, getting a good price on a sofa, having my lipstick exactly match what I'm wearing. I worry about things like singing in tune, or my inability to remember people who act like they know me, or my complete lack of rhythm on the tambourine. I especially worry about the fact that I constantly want to get inebriated, even on weekdays.

It's the fact that I *don't* care about the usual things that bothers most people. Things like keeping a job — no doubt why I was fired from the Brentwood Country Club. See, I took a shower in the women's locker room. (I was an employee and employees were supposed to know their place.) No one ever said that it was against the rules to take a shower. But people never make the rules until

I break them. What harm did taking a shower after hours cause? It cost them nothing—they're so cheap, they turn off the hot water at night. My action was a small revolt against pecking orders, cliques, exclusive societies. It was more largely due to the fact that I didn't want to smell during dinner. I will fight political battles if there is some advantage in it for me. Otherwise one becomes a martyr and martyrs don't go out to dinner much.

It is this selective adherence to rules that has created the capricious quality of my life. Many people who know me think I live in a fantasy world, but the fact that it seems to play itself out for me is particularly distressing to them. Primarily they feel anger that I don't approach life like everyone else. By rights I should be unhappy. It just doesn't validate their theory of life:

"If you break the rules, the rules break you."

—Tenth grade English teacher, circa 1972

I haven't found this aphorism to be true. I haven't found rule followers any more contented and rule breakers any more broken. If everyone was so happy why would the phenomenon of game shows exist? Or Las Vegas, or Publisher's Clearinghouse Sweepstakes, or Mary Kay Cosmetics, or any of the crazy get-rich schemes that abound? Why would people be so willing to go on television and act ridiculous in order to have more appliances? Is it that one can never have enough appliances? Or is it that no matter which appliances they get, the manufacturers will always come out with others that do the job just a little bit better and in decorator colors?

I am partially misrepresenting the game show contestants, however; they do go on for more reasons than to gain appliances. Many go on because they are poor actors who know they can sparkle at a game show interview. (They used to never be allowed to admit on the show that they were actors, but I believe this has changed recently.) The second significantly large group is made up of bored housewives who have watched the shows so often that they are tired of answering the questions at home. Then there are the contestants who fill in the statistical cracks: the tourists from Iowa, the cadet in the service, the retired couple, the guy whose neighbor just won $13,000 on "Tic-Tac-Dough" and so he thought he'd try it as well.

Once in the studio, though, a change begins to occur in the contestants. No matter the reasons they are there, suddenly an insatiable appetite for money and merchandise develops. Game shows cultivate this hunger. It reaches epidemic proportions and often culminates in despicable dialogue like, "Well, Tom, I'm here to win all the money I can. I'm going for a year's supply of Squeeze Parkay!" What starts as trivial desire escalates into Dickensian greed.

{ *190* }

Greed is a prime motivator in game show psychology. Most people think they wouldn't succumb so easily to avarice. They underestimate the manipulative power of game shows. From the moment you get there you are conditioned to be greedy; indeed, the contestant coordinators rehearse you to make sure you've gotten it down. They prime the contestants to shout "BIG BUCKS!"; they nod happily as you trade in all the merchandise you've won so far for the chance of winning so much more behind Door Number Three. One is easily persuaded to be as greedy as the network wills.

In order to be greedy you have to know that something exists to want. Therefore, the contestants are presented with all the possible things they can win at the outset in order to start them salivating. The unseen problem with greed is that it leaves a distasteful residue in your mouth. If you lose the prize you feel a buffoon. The game show has set a standard that you failed to meet. The fact that luck is the predominant spring in the game show machine, and real knowledge only a minor cog, is forgotten. Game show losers are always saying, "If only I had said . . . " and continually reliving their little loop of personal hell. Even winning on a game show, if there's more that one could have won (and there always is), is not enough. Game show winners are always saying, "If only I had said . . . "

As a town which has raised greed to an art form, L.A. is the perfect petri dish for the incubation of game shows. This is a town where wealth and poverty commingle, where Rolls Royces drive next to dilapidated 1954 Chevys with broken windows, where trendsetters buy torn sweat shirts in Beverly Hills, seemingly to emulate the bag people who wear torn clothes as a matter of necessity. L.A. is a town where people do become famous overnight and then are just as quickly absorbed into the set of has-been overnight sensations.[3] And occasionally at dinner parties someone bent on trivia will say, "Whatever happened to . . . ?" and invariably someone will know, because L.A. is a town of vultures, fascinated by the decrepit and the bizarre, the bedizened and the jejune, and, most of all, fascinated by the depressing truth that fame is fleeting and most often undeserved. Only a town like L.A. could have spawned game shows: tacky, frivolous, fascinating, a contemporary anthropologist's garbage pile where the most interesting relics of human nature can be examined, categorized, and marveled at. Archaeologists have found previous civilizations' trash

---

3. I knew a guy who played the role of Atlantis in the movie *The Lost Continent*. In his house he had a shrine to himself. One of the newspaper clippings on the wall quoted him as saying, "There I was tanning by the pool and then six months later I was cleaning those very same pools." When I knew him he was dating a witch. (MM)

to be most telling of their cultures. I find our trash to be equally informative. The only difference is, we haven't yet thrown it away.

I didn't have quite this much insight when I started on my game show career. I wasn't so cynical or analytical. I don't hold myself to be all that much different from other contestants. I too have succumbed to greed, have relived my losses, have acted the part of a hysterical contestant (though I *never* shouted "BIG BUCKS, COME ON, BIG BUCKS!"). I assimilate well at times (when it is to my advantage). I try to really lose myself for the moment, whatever the situation, whether it's stand-up comedy or standing in a welfare line. I want to know what living those things feels like. Having an interesting life and learning absolutely nothing from it is like reading *Moby Dick* and saying it's a book about a whale.

Honestly, this is why I do things like game shows, because they're the most excitement that I can achieve on my limited budget. I try to put myself in unusual situations in order to learn about me. I better understand myself the more things that I have reflected off my surface. Besides which, I like attention. I figure it doesn't matter how you get on TV as long as you get on TV.

This philosophy was obviously in effect for my next game show, "SAY 'POW!' " because I wasn't even a contestant, merely one of six on-screen rooters. The show was so low-budget that the consolation prize was six already-opened records by performers that no one wanted to hear (at least not the people who had already opened the records). I was as wild on the show as one could get without being thrown off. As we introduced ourselves on TV, I turned to the "star of the show," and said, very seriously, "I *really* like your tie." (It matched the set.)

Then during commercials I kept offering the other rooters set decorations (fake books, metallic owls, antique-looking maps of the Seven Seas), but when I tried to give them away I found that they were all glued down. The best thing I managed to come away with was a cue card that I found in the garbage. It was from "The Dating Game" and read, "Bachelor #2 is a businessman whose talents range from possessing a black belt in karate to flying and skydiving." I hung it in my bathroom. They had another card which I really wanted, but they were still using it. It said, "Your fly is down."

After two of anything, the third determines a sequence, a possible winning hand, a literary choice (readin', writin,' and 'rithmetic; lions and tigers and bears; chocolate, vanilla, and strawberry). You've demonstrated that it is more than coincidence, more than a simple deal of the cards, more than fate. With the third game show, I was committed. I knew after three that there would be four, five, as many as I was allowed. I look for motifs, mirrors, structures to help me live my structureless life. I know, I know, I just went on and on about how I'm oblivious to rules, but frankly, sometimes I'm full of shit. I need board games as much as the rest of us. I need little squares to count, a roll of the dice to determine my progress. It was this need to create a pattern that brought me to my third game show. Okay, so I went on "Love Connection." Is that a crime? People who say "I've never watched 'Love Connection' " say it as if they're saying "I've never done drugs." Or "I've never raped and pillaged." Speaking of raping and pillaging, "Love Connection" strives for both.

Let me walk you through a "Love Connection" date, a date so awful that it could only be relived through the therapy of stand-up comedy:

. . . And then there's dating. I've tried everything: personals, computer dating. Even "Love Connection." Twice. Do you get that here?[4] It's a game show. See, I was kind of bored in L.A. and I don't like to work a lot. I view game shows as welfare for the hyperactive . . . a group of which I consider myself a member. Anyway, in the "Love Connection" office they show you videotapes of three guys, they give you seventy-five dollars to go out with one of them, you go out, and then you both come on the show and talk about your date. Then the audience gets to vote if you should go out again or with someone else. Just to give you an idea of my range of choices, one of my potential dates looked a lot like Charles Manson. He said that he loved to eat pet fish at parties, that it just killed his friends. The second guy was an expert bowler. [pause] I didn't pick them. I picked my date because he used the word "vapid" in a sentence. [pause] I really like that word. The day of our date he called me at work and left simple rhyming messages like, "Tonight's the night and I'm Mr. Right."

I think he was a poet.

These phone calls made me very nervous because he seemed to think that we were going to have sex or something. And I just didn't think seventy-five dollars was worth it.

When we met, the first thing that he said was, "Hi, I'm Lemuel Spevin, Thespian." What he should have said was, "Hi, I'm Lemuel Spevin, out-of-work aspiring actor," but that would have been too many syllables. I wanted to say, "Hi, I'm Marissa Minnion, Astrophysicist." [pause] That's short for someone who looks into deep space.

I figured that the only way to get through this date was to get completely drunk. Okay . . . so I fell asleep in my salad—or at least that's what Lemuel

---

4. A subtle joke aimed at New Yorkers because they feel they get everything there. (This was performed at the Comic Strip in New York.) JC

said. I don't really remember. I *do* remember throwing up, however . . . [hesitantly] on his shoes. I didn't mean to. I mean, he was holding me up, I figured he could have moved his feet. I was so drunk he had to sign my Visa slip. That was right about the time he started using an English accent. I guess from the stress and all.[5]

So anyway, we go on the show and I, being compulsively intimate, admit that I threw up on him. Then the audience votes and they vote *that we go out again!* He even wanted to go out again. (He said he wanted to make it through the entrée.)

But I said to Chuck Woolery . . . I said, "Can I say no??" (You know— [sigh] I just hate to throw up.)

Anyway, a month later, I notice the Visa slip on my floor. (That's where I file things . . . on the floor.) And you know what? HE ACTUALLY SIGNED IT LEMUEL SPEVIN, THESPIAN!

[pause]

I didn't know if you'd believe me, so I made xerox copies.

(Could you pass these around please? And don't try to charge anything on this. This number was several Visas ago. I wouldn't want you to get arrested or anything. But feel free to take these home. See, I figure, if you're like me . . . well, I just love souvenirs.)

Though this is the end of Moose's comedic monologue, it wasn't the end of her 'Love Connection' experience. She continues in her memoirs:

A few weeks later "Love Connection" called me up and wanted me to go out on another date and then come back on the show. I think it's because the producer likes strife; it makes him feel a bit better about his own marriage. (He also kind of liked me. He would put his arm around my shoulder and tell me about his days on "The Mike Douglas Show.")

I was given the choice of three more men. I picked Steve Floyd because he had two first names. Why not? He said in his videotaped interview that he thought he looked a lot like Al Pacino—which he did if you can imagine Al Pacino with the delivery of Mickey Mouse.

Steve Floyd called up several times before our date, never giving his name. I thought they were obscene phone calls and hung up. When he finally admitted that he was my Love Connection, I knew that this date was going to be similar to the last, but I didn't want to seem impossible to please . . . so I sent him

---

5. Lemuel Spevin wasn't English. JC

on a treasure hunt to find me. (I figured the less time I spent with him the less likely I would be to throw up—I'm very practical.)

I took my résumé picture and cut it into pieces. To my forehead I attached the clue:

> This is the brain
> That thought up this scheme . . .
> ("Not much brain," he mutters)
> And so it might seem . . .
> But if you follow the clues
> (Assuming you're wise)
> The next bit of puzzle
> Resides with the eyes.
>
> This place houses books
> Whose topics all vary
> ("Of course, since it rhymes,
> She means the library . . .
> So where the fuck is it?")
>
> It's very simple,
> But I'll draw a map.
> Just look on the door
> And don't be a sap.

I gave this to Tuesday with the instructions to keep him busy for a few minutes while I dashed out the back door and over to the library. (I was afraid of people taking my clues down if they were in public view for very long.)

Steve found my eyes taped to the door of the library with this clue:

> Mar Vista Bowl—
> What a fun place at night.
> If you want the nose . . .
> Third ball from the right.

Steve Floyd got to Mar Vista Bowl and made a big production number there about how he was on a treasure hunt for a television game show and he apparently got all the bowlers to help look for the clue. Because none of them could find it (even with my explicit instructions—I mean, "third ball from the right" suggests to me that if you go to the right and count back three—Bingo!), he called up Tuesday, who of course had no idea where the clue was, and she told me later that in the background she heard, "Wait! We think we found it over here!" People just love to get involved in crazy television pranks. Especially bowlers.

The next clue, which included my nose and was attached to the bowling ball, read:

> This is the last
> So now you can sigh
> A sigh of relief
> And straighten your tie
> (Or your teeth if you prefer,
> But it'll take longer.)
>
> The rest of the picture
> (He sends up a cheer)
> Is found on a horse
> At the Santa Monica Pier.
>
> I'd give you more clues
> But unless you're a clown (Marissa!)
> The only horses there
> Are on a _____-____-_____.

And there I was, waiting on the pier next to the Santa Monica merry-go-round with a bottle of champagne, two wine glasses, and these three transients who had joined me. They were quite nice, but I had to explain that I couldn't give them any champagne because I was saving it for a TV show date.

They'd heard of TV.

Steve drove up in this flashy white car and bounced out to greet me. Later on "Love Connection" he said he felt as if he were rescuing a damsel in distress.

I thanked him.

The rest of the date was pretty uninteresting except that we went jacuzziing and Steve expressly told me that I couldn't mention it on "Love Connection." He said he "might run for public office someday." God knows, they always dredge up all those old game shows and play them for the constituents.

Now, the best thing about "Love Connection" is that they get me to looking all glamorous and then they just let me talk. The music starts up; the host, Chuck Woolery, says in a rolling California lilt, "Meet Marissa Minnion from Los Angeles, California. She paints eggs for a living and says she may never settle down." I walk in, sit down on their magenta-and-salmon heart-motifed set, and Chuck says, "You say that you think you'll never settle down. Why is that?"

"Well, men seem to have a hard time with my personality. They seem to think it's not really me. Younger men at least. Older men like me a lot. In fact older men and me are like this": I cross my fingers on nationwide TV so that the country can see what older men and me are like.

"How old?"

"Do you really want to know?" I laugh. He nods. "Well, about sixty or seventy . . . " I reveal hedgingly. "I think perhaps I threaten younger men. See, I have a lot of theories. Younger men have a hard time with theories."

"You seem very open," Chuck observes.

"I'm compulsively intimate," I nod.

"What does that mean—'compulsively intimate'?"

"It means that I'll tell anyone everything about myself. I just spread all my cards out on the table and . . . "

"They just pick whichever one that suits their hand," he finishes for me.

"Yeah . . . suuure . . . " I say agreeably, if a little bemused. (He's trying to move me along, but I don't get the hint.)

Chuck laughs. Time to show the audience my choices (a meat cutter, a man with a moustache that belongs on a much larger face, and Steve Floyd) and to introduce Steve.

Steve tells him about my treasure hunt. I have to explain. Steve mentions that I was on another date earlier that evening. I say that I'm pretty busy. Steve tells him about dinner. Chuck says, "And then what happened?"

I say haphazardly, "And then we went jacuzziing in a—oh." (I pause and bite my bottom lip with a look like I just remembered leaving the bathtub faucet on.) "I wasn't supposed to say that." The audience laughs.

"Perhaps we should ask Steve what happened," says Chuck, also laughing.

"Yeah, that's a good idea. Let's ask Steve." I nod. Steve looks annoyed.

"Well, then we went dancing—"

"Right, dancing!" I echo.

Chuck looks at me and starts laughing again.

"Maybe it's time to see who the audience voted for."

They voted for the meat cutter.

After the audience voted, Chuck Woolery told me that if I wanted to go out with the meat cutter they would pay for it. Thinking that I'd had my fill of "Love Connection" dates, I said no. Then Chuck asked me, "What kind of man do you like?"

"Shy and quirky. Kind of like Lewis Carroll."

"Who is that?" he asked.

"He wrote *Alice in Wonderland.*"

After we got off the air the producer said gruffly, "No one will understand a girl who wants to date a dead author."

Needless to say, Steve was upset. I apologized back in the green room. I told him I just got nervous and said the first thing that came to my mind. Steve said that since I had used the word "Jacuzzi," a brand name, he was told that they would cut it from the show.

"Shit," I thought to myself.

Steve Floyd called me the day the show aired and told me that he had called the producer numerous times to find out if they were going to cut the Jacuzzi reference. (No doubt as many times as he called me to make sure I wouldn't mention it.) They wouldn't tell him. Not surprisingly, when the show came on television, you could hear "Jacuzzi" plain as day. I know you're thinking I was awfully mean to the poor guy but believe me, I'm thinking of the American Public. I've saved the country from a fate worse than a Love Connection.

It was my fifth game show, "Fantasy," when I hit it big, and I hadn't even wanted to go on it. Tuesday talked me into it. (She'd seen the show; the premise was to make your fantasy come true. They would reunite a mother and son who hadn't seen each other for years, or let someone stand in a booth of flying money and grab as much as they could, or throw a TV out of a van for someone to catch.) Tuesday thought of a great fantasy for me – singing "Basin Street Blues" on "Late Night with David Letterman." We thought this plausible because Letterman and "Fantasy" were on the same network. Okay, we were stupid. I said it would happen again.

Armed with this fantasy and my sense of game show etiquette, I felt rather well equipped. But fate was to see me even more so. In Hollywood, the night before the game show interview, as we were leaning over the trunk of a Mercedes, we managed to get robbed at gunpoint by a man in a Members Only jacket. We being Tuesday, myself, and Raymond, a friend of Tuesday's who happened to be living in Dee Wallace's house (the mom in the movie *E.T.* – it was her Mercedes). Raymond and Tuesday were auditioning for an improv group in Hollywood; I was along for the ride. We walked out onto Las Palmas Boulevard and Raymond told us (in that Charles Nelson Reilly way of his) that a friend had sent him a mock care package, but there were a lot of things in it that he didn't really need and would we like some? He had just done a commercial and was doing well financially; we, as unemployed actresses, weren't doing anything financially.

So we were leaning over the back of this Mercedes – basically I figure that it's all Dee Wallace's fault: if she had owned a Volkswagen we would never have been robbed—saying, "Oh, I'll take the Lite Peaches. I'll take the granola bars," when a man came up with a gun and said, "I'll take all your money."

We laughed.

"This isn't a joke. Give me your money."

We gave it to him. It was not unlike a business transaction. Then he made us turn around and walk up the sidewalk.

Breaking into a run once we saw him turn the corner, we dashed into a neighboring apartment building just as all these people were leaving. Hysterically we yelled, "Don't go out there! There's a man with a gun! We were just robbed! Can you help us?!" Our words tumbled out of our mouths in disarray.

With barely a look to us, every one of them walked past.

The inner city is amazing in its disregard for human life. Living there one becomes callous. The sheer number of people makes the odds better for all. The fact that we were robbed almost ensured that, for the moment at least, the rest of them were safe. Or this is what they believed. But the odds have no memory. Each roll of the dice carries the same chances.

Everyone having left the foyer, I knocked on all the doors until a shriveled German woman opened hers a few inches. Raymond was outside watching to make sure the man didn't return and Tuesday was, as she later termed herself, "A Walking Convulsion." The German woman, realizing that I wanted something, tried to close the door on me.

"Lady. I have to use your phone," I said in my most authoritative voice as I pushed myself into the room. Realizing that I was stronger than she, the woman gave up. Tuesday followed. The German woman locked and chained the door. Tuesday immediately got claustrophobia and tried to unlock the door. They had a verbal scuffle, neither of them understanding the other, and the German woman finally let her out and relocked the door. As I was trying to talk on the phone to the police, the German woman proceeded to tell me her life story as a sort of guilty confession. She felt badly that she didn't do the Christian thing in attempting to close the door on me. Now, not only did I have to deal with the fact that I'd just been robbed, I also had to absolve this woman from guilt by listening to an incomprehensible story about someone hitting her on the head a week ago. (Or perhaps it was someone hitting her husband many years ago . . . who knows?) But I told her that I understood, that she certainly helped us out, and that, no, Los Angeles sure wasn't what it was twenty years ago.

Finally I escaped.

Finally the police came. If you think being robbed is depressing, wait till you have to stand around and be questioned for an hour by apathetic policemen.

And yet, I couldn't blame them. In this town, unless you're murdered, there's just not a lot they can do. And then they only bury you.

We offered the policemen granola bars to show we were on their side. (At least Raymond and I did. Tuesday was incoherent.) I think that made them like us because they became slightly less gruff.

While we all stood there and they made a report, a guy ran up yelling, "My car's just been stolen!!" Like clockwork both policemen turned to him, looked at him for an instant, then turned back to their report and continued writing. It was something you'd see on "Car 54." [6]

"Aren't you going to do something?" Raymond asked indignantly. Most unwillingly, one of them followed the guy to where his car wasn't. In less than two minutes he returned alone and started to finish his report.

"What happened?" Raymond asked.

"Guy didn't know his license plate number," the policeman shrugged. "Nothin' I can do for him . . . "

And thus you have a shrewd observation from one of the amazing minds that work to fight crime in the bustling metropolis that is L.A.

The next day, before the game show interview, Tuesday and I went to check all the bushes, garbage bins, and waste piles in the area. The police suggested we do this as a mugger will usually want to get rid of incriminating evidence as soon as possible. Little did we know that the area where we were robbed, near Santa Monica and Sunset, is prime hooker territory. As we were walking the street (not, however, the usual way that's done), a guy behind us did a loud stage whisper, "Careful girls, the police are really out today." I turned around and yelled loudly, "We aren't what you think we are!"

"Yeah, right . . . " he muttered.

It's actually not surprising that we were mistaken for hookers. Some of the girls we saw were beautiful: peaches and cream complexions, rich olive tans, young, thin. I doubt that Tuesday and I would have gotten top dollar. Besides, we hadn't really lost enough money to consider it.

Raymond lost the most, about two hundred dollars (he had just cashed a residual check); Tuesday lost about fifteen dollars and all her keys, which she had to get remade. As it turns out, this young babysitter found my wallet. It had my phone number in it. When I came to get my wallet I found that it still had forty dollars in it. I didn't even know I had that much. See, I hide money in my wallet between my credit cards. This has worked successfully twice now

---

6. "Car 54, Where Are You?" was a TV comedy about policemen. I never saw it, but I know that Herman Munster was in it before he was Herman Munster. NC

so I pass it on to you. I tried to give this girl a reward, but she was so sweet she wouldn't take anything. There really are some decent people in Los Angeles. It's too bad that you have to get robbed to meet them.

Such was my frame of mind when Tuesday and I showed up for the game show interview at NBC. We sat there nervously with twenty-five other nervous applicants. The contestant coordinators entered spewing their usual repertoire of semi-funny jokes which all the potential contestants laugh at uproariously. I find that everyone around TV tends to cultivate a television persona whether or not you ever see them on screen. One could almost attribute it to a virus of the personality: easily spread, not debilitating, but something you certainly would be better off without.

We were issued cards to fill out. (I was careful not to touch their hands in case this is how the virus is transferred.) There was no place to put down your fantasy. I pondered. Eventually I wrote it down several times on the three by five card, altering some of the questions to make them fit my fantasy. We handed the cards in. As I recall, mine was a bit of a mess. Then each person had to stand up, introduce themselves, say where they were from, and speak on one of five topics, none having to do with their fantasy. The topics were:

1. The best day of my life was when _____ .
2. My most embarrassing moment was_____ .
3. My Pet Peeve is_____ .
4. If I could change one part of my body, it would be _____ .
5. I like game shows because _____ .

(I think one of the contestant coordinators used to teach Public Speaking in junior high.) Though the choices were pretty grim, we all tried to look peppy because game show people are quick to pick up on dissatisfaction. Anyone who displays signs of being anything short of continually ecstatic is eighty-sixed at the first cut.

I chose the ever-popular: My Pet Peeve is "People who rob people." I explained that we had just been robbed the night before and told them the story. I mentioned that this was the third time I'd been robbed and then told both of those stories as well. I could tell that the other people in the room were a little concerned that I was getting so much attention. (Many people move to L.A. solely for attention, so you can understand a slight consternation on their part.) At one point in my story, however, this apparently bilingual woman said approvingly, "Ah! *Très* good!" L.A. is nothing if not culturally enriched.

One of the contestant coordinators (the one with the most severe degeneration of personality) was so concerned about our robbery that he walked us out to the parking lot so that we wouldn't get robbed two days in a row. I think he may have wanted a longer look at Tuesday's breasts.

The attention was all very exciting and I felt somehow that I would get on the show, but I really didn't think about it much. What I did think about was, why wait for the game show to fulfill my fantasy since they didn't seem particularly interested in it anyway? Why not just write straight to David Letterman?

So I did.

I wrote him forty-two letters.

I began my blizzard of correspondence by explaining that I would be out in his area singing "Basin Street Blues" for a friend's wedding and it would be really convenient for me to just stop by and do it on his show. I know it sounds incredibly stupid to think that the letter would even be read, but I figure if you stab in the dark long enough, eventually you hit something. And I've written a lot of people. Quentin Crisp. Hal Prince. Mr. Sheik of Arabia. I even wrote Elvis Presley once asking for a French horn. He was buying cars for strangers, why not French horns? Ultimately, I like to write and my various clerical jobs provide me with a great deal of excess time. You have to sit there anyway. Writing is a drug for my mind. And you can't smell it like pot. I became addicted to writing letters because I had my own office with a postage meter in it. Free postage is like an intoxicant to me.

I wrote Paul Shaffer and sent him the music to "Basin Street Blues." I wrote David Letterman's mother. I even sent David Letterman a potato that I carved my name and phone number into. I didn't wrap it or anything. I just slapped the postage on the potato and sent it that way. I'd sent a potato like this to my old boyfriend, Justin, and he got it! (I figure it makes a postman's day.) The note taped to the potato read:

> Mr. Postman:
> Please make sure that this potato gets delivered to David Letterman as he is going to let me sing on his show if he receives this. Help a poor starving creative individual. Be a pal! Do it for Christmas![7]
> Thank you,
> Moose Minnion

I also sent him a yam (just in case he didn't get the potato). It read:

> Mr. Postman:
> You could make a drab, downtrodden secretary feel completely elated if you

---

7. The potato was sent in February. HMW

would be so good as to see that David Letterman gets this yam. See, he promised to let me sing on his show if he gets this. I'm going to sing "Basin Street Blues." Know it? *Good song!* Watch in May. Thanks ever so much.
Moose Minnion

All Tuesday could say when I told her that I'd sent Letterman a potato and a yam was, "And I can't believe you weren't even stoned."

I wrote the Head of Shoe Shine. I wrote all the writers on the show and sent them a list of prizes that they could choose from if they got me on the show. One of the prizes was Tuesday. (She owed me a few favors—like the time I retrieved her diaphragm out of the garbage after Clay threw it away. She'd left it on the dining room table one too many times.) I described her as a cross between Dolly Parton and Marilyn Monroe with a little Harpo Marx thrown in. I kind of hoped, in writing so indiscriminately, that my name would be bantered about the hallways . . . Chalk my naiveté up to youthful exuberance.

A month passed and I got called up to be on the "Pick a Trip" portion of "Fantasy." (The contestant coordinator briefly explained to me that I would have the chance to win a trip.) The night before the taping, Tuesday, Clay, and I were out at one of these gimmicky promo deals that abound in L.A. This one was an "Actor's Raffle," organized in an attempt to depict the plight of the performer. Restaurant and nightclub owners were invited to a landmark Hollywood club in order to watch various artists perform and then bid for talent. Someone bid two dollars and that was it for the night. The crazy lady who dreamed up the idea somehow convinced Channel 13 that it was newsworthy and they had a camera crew down there. There are so many news teams in L.A. looking for interesting stories that they'll show up at a mall where someone who used to be on "Love of Life"[8] ten years ago is opening a tanning salon. This is what I meant about moving to L.A. for attention. There are too many cameras there and nothing to put in front of them.

As we were watching this forlorn display by the dregs of Los Angeles, I casually said that I was going to win a trip to Greece.

"That's ridiculous," Tuesday said. "They never go to Greece." (She'd watched "Fantasy" before . . . or did I mention that?) "They go to Las Vegas or Hawaii or maybe New York. Try to win a trip to New York." (She had a love interest there. Tuesday tended to have love interests wherever she'd been.)

But they don't have unspoiled beaches in New York, they don't have whitewashed windmills, they don't have the Acropolis. (Though certainly New York has its own ruins.)

---

8. A long-running daytime soap opera—MM's mother's favorite. HMW

It's the day of the show. I go to the NBC studios in Burbank and the other three girls are already there. I barely remember them now. Typical game show material. A couple of them start talking about how we could cheat. They can't figure out a system. So I help them.

"Look, we could do it this way: we alphabetize our names and when we get on stage, we each silently alphabetize the trips. Then we pick the trip whose rank corresponds to the rank of our name. Alice picks Arizona, say," I explain.

"I don't want to go to Arizona."

"They *won't* have Arizona—"

"But what if they have some place I don't want to go to?"

"Never mind," I say, shaking my head.

The other girls are still trying to figure it out. I realize that under pressure they will never be able to do it. Anyway, I don't care; I know I am going to Greece.

We are bustled from the large contestant waiting room through a labyrinth of stairways and hallways to a room where we are given instructions on proper television etiquette and especially on how to reveal our "Pick a Trip" cards.

The game show mom explains: "There will be four podiums which you will stand behind; whoever goes first will go to the far right podium. On the podium will be four cards, each with a trip printed on it. Say you pick the card which reads 'Go to the Moon.' " She holds up a card that says "Go to the Moon" on it.

"Now, there won't be any trips to the moon out there . . . " She pauses, so we laugh. You have to be quick about that sort of thing.

"I have to say 'the moon' because we have a lawyer here," she introduces the lawyer, "and a person from Fair Practices," whom she also introduces, "and they're here to make sure I don't reveal any trips to you. I don't know what the trips are, but I can't even accidentally say the names. They promised there won't be any to the moon however." We laugh again before she pauses.

"Now, when Peter Marshall says 'Pick A Trip!' I want you all to pick up your choice and hold it right here." She lays the card directly above her breasts. "Then when Peter says 'Reveal!' simply flip the card over like this." She demonstrates. "DO NOT reveal the card until he comes to you personally. The cards will be revealed one at a time. Now I want you to practice this a few times." We practice until our breasts hurt from spinning the cards into them.

"Remember, the placement of the card is very important so that the audience at home can see what trip you picked when you reveal it. Got it? Right here." She pats the card lying on her ample bosom. By the time we get onstage she must have shown us this a thousand times. It interests me that holding these cards over our breasts is so important, especially when Peter Marshall says a word like "Reveal!" and suddenly across the country everyone is staring at a girl's breasts nicely framed by the words "Trip to Aruba."

Two of the girls picked Aruba. I'll never understand that. Perhaps because I still don't really know where it is. Okay, let's both learn:

Aruba (a roo'ba), *n.* an island in the Netherlands Antilles, in the SE West Indies off the NW coast of Venezuela. Pop. 53,199 (1960) 69 sq. miles.[9]

God knows why they picked it, maybe because both of their names began with A and they were still trying to alphabetize, but thank God for that because it left above my breasts—you guessed it—"Greek Cruise."

I'm not doing a good job of explaining this game am I? See, if you pick the same trip as someone else then you don't get it. So the choices were Aruba, Mexico, Palm Springs, and Greece. Two girls picked Aruba, one picked Mexico, I picked Greece. After the first three girls had "revealed," I, as the fourth girl, held the moment for dramatic tension as they had suggested the fourth girl do, my eyes huge, my mouth ready to scream, and, finally able to reveal my card, I went absolutely wild: yelling, hugging Peter Marshall, nearly falling off the stage in my hyperactive but utterly sincere way.

Okay, so I *am* game show material. I told you, I assimilate well.

They whisked us away. You've probably realized at this point that the girl who picked Mexico must have won as well and I've neglected to tell you. Well, she was a bit of a pissant.

Because it was so close to Christmas, they had a special treat for us: a complete make-over from Clairol plus a $250 dress, $35 earrings, and $75 shoes. I told them, "Go ahead, dye my hair any color." They like to hear that kind of thing.

While we were in the midst of our beauty transformation, the Clairol people had a little tiff with the hairdressers. This very foppish man and his abysmally stupid assistant had five hours to dye our hair. It took them four hours and forty-five minutes. And all they did were highlights. They used this process called cellophaning that I hear is supposed to be horrible for your hair where they wrap it all up in tin foil and try to convince you that it's gonna look great.

The girl that won Mexico kept whining, "Oooh, I don't think I like this color." I saw her much later at an audition. I asked her how she liked Mexico. "Oooh, I didn't care much for Mexico," she sniffed. "The hotel was right on

---

9. *Random House College Dictionary,* Laurence Urdang, editor in chief, © 1968 by Random House, Inc. (MM)

the beach. There was sand everywhere. And there's so many Mexicans down there."

"Imagine that," I said.

The makeup artist, a dapper, reedy sophisticate, the type of man who would use a term like "*moderne*" with a hyphen, very quietly let his superiority be known by saying snide things under his breath and posing disdainfully with his brushes. He liked me, though, and I shouldn't say mean things about him because he fixed up my hair in the remaining fifteen minutes after the hair coloring people left. (Time was of the essence because we had to go show the audience the results. One of those "Before and After" things.)

The makeup artist was leaving for Paris that night and right before he left he finally divulged to me alone that he was the private hairdresser for Pia Zadora.

Oddly enough, I ended up looking like a cross between Victoria Principal and Kristy McNichol.

It wasn't until six hours after I won the cruise that I finally got to call Tuesday and tell her, "I told you so."

When I came home that night Tuesday didn't even recognize me. To celebrate my good fortune, we went to Carlos and Charlie's on Sunset and told everyone that we were going to Greece. (Tuesday was my best friend so of course I had to take her. My mother thought I was going to take her because, after all, she was my mother—just the kind of romantic trip you would take your mother on. Several other friends and relatives were hoping or wondering if I would ask them. It's a very ticklish situation, winning a trip for two. An easy way to piss a lot of people off.) At Carlos and Charlie's we also told everyone that we were going to be in a movie. (Tuesday met this crazy guy at that stupid 'Actor's Raffle' who said he was going to put us in his movie, but we didn't know at this time that he had been exposed to Agent Orange and had many grandiose schemes such as owning a helicopter port, studying for the bar exam, peddling Louis XIV furniture, and more, all of which he began to relate to me one evening on the phone when, beginning to get skeptical of Tuesday's discerning ability, I finally demanded, "Tuesday. Let me speak to him." Sadly, as he was blathering inanities to me on the phone about the rights of 'copter pilots, I shook my head at Tuesday, letting her know that we weren't going to be in a movie, at least any movie that he dreamed of.) However, at Carlos and Charlie's, still blissful in our ignorance, we knew, having been in L.A. less than five months, that we were destined for fame. And so we paid the extra thirty dollars required to go upstairs to the private club because what's money when you're going to be famous in a few months? Unfortunately, paying the

{ 206 }

thirty dollars didn't give us the privilege of sitting down and so we stood uncomfortably in our uncomfortable but becoming high heels. There were a great many Latino men there which, Tuesday intelligently pointed out much later, we should have deduced from the use of the name Carlos in Carlos and Charlie's. I mention this only because they can be oh-so-very forward. One Latino man even put his tongue in my mouth for which I slapped him, but I suppose he thought he had the right since he gave us a place to sit. L.A. continues to thrive on an exchange of commodities.

Knowing that I wasn't going to appear on "David Letterman" purely through my fantasies, syndicated or otherwise, I continued to write letter after letter to the show. I would bring them home and read them to Clay and Tuesday during dinner. It became a social event. (We were somewhat starved for social events.)

I had written the Letterman show about my winning a Greek cruise (I tried to keep them up-to-date on my life), but I became a bit concerned that my letters were ending up in someone's garbage. So, anxious for some kind of response, I wrote the ticket people and said, "I would like to get tickets for 'David Letterman' the week of May 18–24. Also, I will be appearing on the show, will you please find out when." Within a few weeks, the talent coordinator CALLED ME UP! She wanted to know why I thought I was going to be on the show. The ticket people, in their confusion, had called her to find out when I would be appearing. You see, I understand clerical minds: they're easily intimidated. The talent coordinator wanted to know what kind of credentials I had. Of course I didn't have credentials, other than the fact that I'm nuts. I mean, I've done things, but I knew the things that I'd done wouldn't carry any weight with her. I was still an unknown. But I knew I was funny. Everyone laughs when I say things. Even people that don't know me. What else is an audience but people who don't know you? Just once I wanted someone to go beyond their bourgeois upbringing. To be daring. To use their imagination. I thought that the mere fact that I had gotten them to call me was proof enough that I should go on their show. She didn't see it that way.

In desperation I blurted out, "Look, my grandmother bought a forklift because it was on sale." (When in doubt, bring up the forklift.) This made her laugh, against her will, and she agreed that I could send a tape of me singing "Basin Street Blues," and they would look at it.

Then I got this GREAT idea! I would go to the Comedy Store,[10] I would tell them about getting robbed, about winning the Greek cruise, about the

---

10. A comedy club in L.A. on the Sunset strip. JC

"David Letterman" show calling me up, I would sing "Basin Street Blues" with my French horn, and THEN I would pass out postcards for them to mail in asking David to be a pal and put me on the show. It went really well the one time I did it, but people thought it was a routine; they didn't know I was serious. And I didn't know then that you have to do stand-up comedy more than once to get noticed.

Dear Talent Coordinators:

    You've simply got to let Marissa Minnion sing "Basin Street Blues" on "David Letterman's Late Night." I just saw her at _____ and she was:

    __ Great
    __ Hysterical
    __ Froward, but funny (Froward: Habitually disobedient)
    __ All of the above
    __ I asked her to marry me (Optional)

    She sings a mean "Basin Street Blues." You would be doing America a disservice not to put her on. And besides, Paul Shaffer probably has the music all arranged as she already sent it to him.
    Give the kid a break.

Sincerely, _____ _____
             (Sign your name)   (Home Town Optional)

P.S. You know, her grandmother bought a forklift because it was on sale.

After such a good response from her first postcard, Moose began making up more cards just to hand to people at bars and in the supermarket.

Dear Talent Coordinators:

I met Marissa Minnion in a bar and she just handed me this card and told me to mail it in.

I forget why; I was too drunk.

But I liked her, so what the hell . . .

_____
(Just sign X if you forget your name)

```
Dear Talent Coordinators:

I met a Miss Marissa Minnion in the frozen foods section of Alpha
Beta and she sang me a snippet of a song -- I believe the title
was "Basin Street Blues" and she was hoping to sing it on "The
David Letterman Show." I thought it sounded like a long shot, but
I told her that I would send this card in if it would help her
cause.

I always send the underprivileged to camp. It amounts to the same
thing.

Sincerely,

_____
```

When Tuesday and I went to Greece I took along the two varieties of post-cards that I had printed especially for the cruise in order to mail them to the talent coordinators. (I knew Greek postage would lend credibility to my story.)

```
Dear Talent Coordinators:

I met Ms. Minnion on a cruise around the Greek Islands and was
suitably impressed.

I found her charming and refreshing. I even had the pleasure of
hearing her sing.

You would do well to make use of her talents while you can
because it is only a matter of time before someone else does.


Yours truly,_____
Yearly Income: (Optional)       $50,000-100,000 __
                               $100,000-200,000 __
                             $200,000-1,000,000 __
               I find figures frightfully decadent. __
```

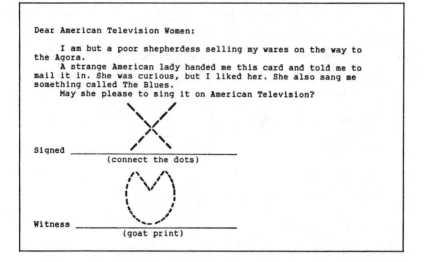

```
Dear American Television Women:

     I am but a poor shepherdess selling my wares on the way to
the Agora.
     A strange American lady handed me this card and told me to
mail it in. She was curious, but I liked her. She also sang me
something called The Blues.
     May she please to sing it on American Television?



Signed _____
              (connect the dots)




Witness _____
              (goat print)
```

But something about being in Greece made me question my need to get on "David Letterman." Greece made me come back to my senses. History does that to me. I see my life more as a continuum. I see my behavior more clearly. I saw myself pushing—a vision I didn't like. Everyone in L.A. is pushing. Pushing for fame, for agents, for phone calls. It leaves you feeling off balance. You expend a lot of energy in trying not to topple over, trying not to succumb to the gravity of your situation while knowing that the only thing which keeps you upright is your delusions. L.A. is a tangle of mass delusions, the result of pushing hard but budging nothing. In one's unrequited desire for fame, one goes just a little bit mad, making up excuses that rewrite reality. Many people live this way for years. They die waiting for the phone, positive that the next call will be the one. I only wasted a bit of my youth. Which is okay, because that's when you have time to waste. I nearly decided to waste it in Greece. But something (probably the fear that the next person in line would become famous) made me come home. It's hard to know if I would have been better off or worse staying in Greece.[11]

When I returned from Greece, via New York, I called the "Late Night" talent coordinators, thinking maybe we could have lunch. (Greece didn't make me give up my obsession entirely.)

---

11. If they don't have Chinese chicken salads in Greece, I would say better. NC

"How was Greece?" they asked, quite friendly-like. However, we didn't go to lunch.

Later I wrote them asking permission to sue David Letterman so that we could go on "People's Court"[12] and I could complete my game show genre. See, Randy, my drug-addict neighbor, took three Quaaludes, fell down the steps at the Oar House, sued, and went to the Bahamas. I figure some sue, some do game shows. "People's Court" is an exciting synthesis of both worlds. Obviously someone agreed with me because less than a year later Johnny Carson sued David Letterman and had Judge Wapner preside. But then again, if the wheel could be discovered in three places in the world at the same time . . .

---

12. A show that takes actual court cases and films them for television. No matter what Judge Wapner's judgment is, everyone wins money. This is why you often see a daughter suing a mother or friends suing friends. There's not a lot of risk involved. JC

14

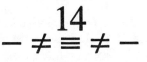

Greece

The discovery of the wheel, an obvious motif for Moose, did not happen in Greece. However, they do use wheels there. It's not clear if this was the attraction. Whatever the reason, Greece had always harbored a mystique for Moose. She had had Greece on the brain since she was ten years old. She attributed winning the Greek cruise to this obsession.

My whole being has been devoted to eventually running away to Greece. I make baklava and drink ouzo; I read all I can about travel in Greece, novels about Greeks, Greek plays; I write about Greece constantly and talk about it incessantly. I set the stage (dramatic Greek metaphor) for going there and then I do something extraordinary and whamo, there you have it. "Greek Cruise" it says in front of me and I have no doubt that I am going, no doubt that I will soon be lying naked on crystalline beaches bordering cerulean waters.

Is it positive thinking? Is it the Fairies? Is it some distant culture cultivating us the way we cultivate penicillin? Perhaps the next level of consciousness, the same distance above us as we are above one-celled organisms, seeks to breed, to nourish the positive, the life sustaining, as well as silence or stymie that which is not. This consciousness has power over us in the way that we have power over cancer. We can sometimes arrest its growth, but so far we cannot wholly overpower it. Could some entity be doing the same to us? I ask again, could there be not one God, but rather a collective number of gods? A large strata of higher powers? Maybe the Greeks weren't so wrong after all. See, I am Greek at heart. I'm sure one of my lives was lived there. I must have been Aristophanes; I would have written something called *The Frogs* also. Irreverence is something one never loses no matter how many lives one lives.

In fact, in Chicago, almost a year before she went on "Fantasy," she had written these words in quiet desperation:

And as I sit here typing, my mind is adrift in the Aegean. I will get there. I will. And soon. I've made a deal with myself. By my twenty-fifth birthday

I will either be on my way to doing my musical or on my way to Greece . . . or else.[1]

Two months before her twenty-fifth birthday, Moose won the Greek cruise.

It was an adventure from the moment Tuesday and I stepped on the plane. Within seconds a Greek steward with very strong body odor introduced himself to us as "The Prince of Greece."

Right.

He said he would bring us a surprise. He came back with an unopened bottle of Scotch. I hate Scotch. It wasn't a cute little bottle of airplane Scotch either, it was a fifth and it still had corrugated cardboard around it.

"Where did you get this?" Tuesday asked.

"Hide it!" he ordered. I guess princes are used to people minding them. "When they show the movie I will come back and we will drink it together." I could hardly wait. His lack of deodorant was overpowering.

Meanwhile, Tuesday, never satisfied unless she could have all the men in the vicinity frothing at the mouth, struck up a conversation with the cute Greek boy behind us. I changed seats with him so they could sit together and began talking to a Danish couple. I also offered my fellow passengers swigs of Scotch seeing as how I was on vacation and had no cares in the world. The Prince returned and was so put out that Tuesday was flirting with someone else that he grabbed the now half-empty bottle from the cute Greek boy and tramped down the aisle. I wondered if this was a sign of things to come.

We landed in Athens on a wonderfully arid afternoon. The air was dry but soft on the skin. The sun felt like it was coaxing the melanin to the surface. I was dazed by the sunlight, by the Greek chatter, by the fact that I was actually there. I was overwhelmed that I finally got my heart's desire (or at least one of them). We took a taxi to Omonia Square, found a cheap hotel that wasn't too squalid, and promptly fell asleep. I woke up first and left Tuesday with the last bit of sunlight falling across her pyrite hair. I love, upon arriving somewhere new and different, to go out alone, especially at dusk because there's a surge, an urgency, a bustling to accomplish everything before darkness falls. If a day were a year, dusk would be Indian Summer. They both have a kind of amber light splayed across buildings and trees. There's a feeling of battening down the hatches, the women calling in the children for dinner, the men having one last ouzo before they leave the camaraderie of an all-male gathering. It's

---

1. Letter to her friend Larkin Hring dated 4/10/82. HMW

the fun time of the day. Most of the arduous work is done. Dinner is approaching. Life waxes lazily poetic.

I bought a cheap pair of cloth shoes for walking. I bought some postcards and stamps. I felt the need to buy something much more than the need to have the things I bought. Mostly I wanted to try out my Greek money.

As much as I love Greece, Athens is quite an ugly city. The buildings are so many varying shades of dun. There is too much traffic and not enough vegetation. Yet it has a pace, a beat, an insistence that I miss. Greece is in my blood.

I returned to rouse Tuesday for dinner. We went down to one of the abundant Greek cafés and ordered a simple meal of salad, bread, Greek olives, retsina. We were ogled throughout our meal. However, it wasn't scary or insulting the way we were watched. It was more out of curiosity. I think Tuesday's hair was of prime interest. Or perhaps it was her breasts. (They often vied with each other, unbeknownst to them, for masculine attention.)

Greece is a very male country. The women that are seen are most often old, dressed all in black, waiting beside the road, following their donkeys with sticks, hanging out the wash. On the islands the only young women one sees are tourists. And yet, despite the predominance of men, I never once worried for my safety. Rape is practically nonexistent. (Though I did have a tense moment once on Corfu when my moped ran out of gas and a man, huge in every direction, offered me a liter. There was a gas strike at the time and I was kilometers from any town. He gleefully took me to his old, beat-up automobile and, patting me all the way, siphoned some gas into my moped. As I was attempting to kick-start the moped, he got down on his knees and began kissing my thigh. Even when the moped had started and I was moving across his yard trying to avoid the goats, he loped along with me, rubbing my leg and shouting endearments in Greek.)

Tuesday and I had a couple of days in Athens before our cruise, so I decided that we should rent a car. Tuesday thought I was crazy.

"Have you seen the way they drive?"

"We live in L.A. It'll be good practice."

We settled on going to Corinth. It was closer than Delphi and these were the only two places on the mainland I'd ever heard of besides Athens. (I always base my decisions on such a foundation of rational thought.) Unfortunately, as it was some Greek holiday, everyone had decided to take the only road that went south out of town (the direction we were going), so it was hours before we saw anything besides scrawny trees, barren rock, and cars flowing ahead of and behind us. Corinth was very interesting once we got there, however. One of the most curious things about Corinth, and this is true of much of

Greece, was the abundance of broken bits of carved stone, so common that one often found, when looking down, that one had been treading upon broken statuary. It seemed somehow sacrilegious, as if one were walking upon history itself.

Traipsing through Corinthian ruins, we immediately found ourselves accompanied by a self-appointed guide named Christos. (Try to find a Greek male not named Christos, Stratos, Dimitri, or Nikkos and you'll be wasting your time.) He was nice, but seemed to fancy me. I like it better when they fancy Tuesday. He insisted upon driving my car. (His didn't work. We never found out why.) He said that driving in Greece was very difficult. I disagreed.

"Not as long as you follow two simple rules: always drive with the white line underneath the car. And if you want to change lanes you needn't look back or even signal; merely honk your horn several times, floor the gas, and go. How hard is that?"

He took my keys. And, being a girl, I let him. I don't remember now where he took us so it must not have made much of an impression. Some beach café where they had very oily tyropita (cheese pie). He wanted to show off to all of his friends that he was in the company of American girls. Can you blame him? Getting rid of him proved harder than finding him, especially since I had given him the name of our hotel.

We returned to Athens to rest, ignored the phone calls of our newfound friend, and then went out to the Plaka. The Plaka is a great sort of open market-walkway set at the base of a hill and gently rising with it. There are restaurants and bars and little shops, all very touristy but still pretty nice because it was May and not many tourists had arrived yet.

We were cajoled into entering one bar with the promise of free drinks. The atmosphere was so lecherous and red-lit and the men so overpowering that we left. Not, however, before we told the story of my winning a Greek cruise. We asked how to say this in Greek. One man offered to write it down for us. I gave him my little journal. He wrote it down and made us practice it several times. Innocent girls we, their smiles didn't strike us as at all suspicious. At least not until the next day when, in a bank, we affably showed the teller the words on the page; her face flushed, she stuttered, and refused to tell us what it said. I sensed a *faux pas* in the air. Not surprisingly, the inscription didn't mention anything about cruises or game shows. We never did find out what it really meant, but I think that with a few deft American words we could have captured the sentiment.

The next bar we went into was much more sophisticated and classy. And it was here that a famous Greek soccer player (famous for Greece; I later saw his picture on a calendar) decided he had the hots for me (or at least some free time) and sent his interpreter/friend, Spiros, over to make introductions. I talked much more to his interpreter than I ever did to the soccer star because the soccer star was constantly being barraged for autographs (coupled with the fact that he spoke no English). He had another friend there as well, Stratos, and they all decided to take us to an even more fashionable bar.

This new bar was downstairs through a seedy little door, but once inside you could tell that everyone was exceedingly chic. I tried to order ouzo and the interpreter looked at me with some distaste and said that they didn't serve that here. So I settled for a gin and tonic. Rather than asking us to dance, the soccer player, Nikkos, suggested that Tuesday and I dance. Together. It seemed a bit funny, but I'm game for anything. Later, as we sat there making small talk, I noticed Tuesday up to her usual tricks. She started playing with Nikkos's knee and giving him the eye. I mentally shrugged to myself and decided I didn't really care. The men resolved, after heated discussion (they sounded like they were arguing but that's just the way Greeks discuss), to go to Stratos's house by the ocean. So we piled into Nikkos's sports car. Nikkos and Spiros tried to make Tuesday sit in the back by herself while I squeezed in front between the two of them. (Stratos had a car of his own.) Well, needless to say, this didn't sit too well with Tuesday. She made a brilliant strategic move and, at the last minute, jumped into Stratos's car. This infuriated Nikkos because he wanted all the American women in his car. Tuesday had the art of playing hard to get down to a science . . . chemistry, I think.

Nikkos and Stratos began hurling Greek epithets out the car windows at each other as they barreled along this deserted stretch of Greek road, the scenery sliding away like a train gathering speed. The moon was the only source of light. Scary, invigorating, intoxicating, this was one of those moments that you want to hold onto with both hands. It wasn't by far the best time of my life—I wasn't even sure I was having that much fun—but I knew I'd never have an experience like it again.

Moments have poignance for me due to the mere fact that, like snowflakes, no two are alike. It is at these times that I sense my life playing out in front of me, like a knitted sweater which, as I wear it, unravels slowly before my eyes and I have no way of stopping it. The more exciting the moment, the faster it unravels.

I suddenly remembered the story of *The Moonspinners*,[2] a Walt Disney

---

2. A novel by Mary Stewart set in Greece. HMW

movie with Haley Mills. When I was ten years old the story captivated me and made me long for Greece.

"Have you ever heard of that legend?" I asked Spiros, the interpreter, "about the Moonspinners? These three women who spin the moon until it's full and then unravel it so that they can start spinning all over again?" I had in my imagination a picture of three Greek women dressed in black, working their spinning wheels, a thin strand of cold, white moonlight streaming up toward the heavens.

Spiros looked at me as if I were an American tourist.

"There's no such legend." He discussed it with Nikkos. Nikkos grunted a few times. Spiros returned, "No, there is no such legend. You hear this in America?"

"It's in a movie called *The Moonspinners.*"

"Then it is an American legend," he shrugged dismissively.

I looked out the window down our thread of road as the trees whipped by, scanning the horizon for a thin shred of unspun moonlight. I try not to believe in magic, in legends, in the innumerable mysteries that fill the unknown, but my heart or my head or the nerves along my spine won't let me completely disbelieve. I ache for things beyond our comprehension. I want magic because it makes the tedium of life much less tedious. It fills my mind with pictures of crimson and gold. Of beings with wings that sit on toadstools. Of time warps and magic lamp posts and dreaming other people's dreams. I lived my childhood reading magic books. It was the only way to get through it. And ultimately, just because there aren't fairies doesn't mean I can't believe in them. Sometimes believing in things seems to make them come true.

We pulled into a long gravel drive that led to a silent house silhouetted against the dark blue sky. Stratos's house was a beachy sort of house, spartanly furnished, with a large deck looking out through the trees toward the ocean. After getting out of the car I walked quickly up to the far end of the deck, needing to feel distance from the others. Needing to claim my hold on Greece, to package it well for storage in my head. Needing to feel as if I were the only person in the world standing on a deck looking out at the ocean, at the moon, at the handsome, intellectual Greek ghosts that my eyes begged to see, begged to come rescue me from the banal men that peopled my life. After a few minutes I suddenly noticed Stratos, the friend who had absconded with Tuesday, tucked away in the dark, watching me and the ocean. He was casually leaning against the house in that careless, somewhat arrogant way that Greek men have. Out of politeness, and a little loneliness, I struck up a conversation. It was the sort of conversation that uses many more words than it does ideas.

A conversation about Greece and weather. I may have even asked him about *The Moonspinners*. (When I get on an idea I don't let go.) After five or ten minutes I realized that Tuesday, Nikkos, and Spiros were nowhere to be seen. I asked Stratos where they were. He said something in Greek and made a gesture with his hands as if to say they had disappeared. I think he was suggesting it was pointless to search. A few minutes later I heard moans and panting.

Not only was it pointless to search, it was pointless as well to be depressed. Over what? The fact that Tuesday was having sex with one or perhaps two Greek men that we had met only two hours before? It wasn't a situation that I yearned for myself. But still I was depressed. I felt somehow that this had been planned, perhaps weeks in advance; yet how silly. It couldn't have been . . . could it? It wasn't planned in any decisive way, though perhaps if I had placed before you all the clues, all the pieces of our personalities, if I had given an equation such that, if Tuesday and I were to be in a Greek bar together and a Greek soccer player and his interpreter and his friend were to meet us, and if we were to drive to a deserted house on the Aegean, this is how you would guess it would turn out. I myself was just a bit slow on the uptake. A bit clumsy at piecing together the clues. Well, I was in a foreign country and I hadn't the instinct for men that Tuesday had. I think Stratos, though quicker at surmising the situation, was a bit disappointed as well. After all, Tuesday had elected to ride in his car. He couldn't have known that it was a chess move, a decoy, a play to incite passion.

Stratos was very nice. We acknowledged, through no words, the scene inside. We smiled wisely but resignedly. He raised his eyes inquiringly to me, but didn't press. Silently, he put a slight offer in the air that blew away due to my negligence. I didn't want to go to bed just to go to bed. Just to know that I had really had a Greek adventure. If that was all that adventure amounted to, I could have stayed in L.A.

I began feeling a bit irritated with Tuesday. Not that this situation was such a big deal, but it was typical of all situations. I tire easily of a woman who thinks herself such a shell that she must always have a man to fill her, both metaphorically and in the usual way. Tuesday would tell you who she was dating and how they were in bed before she would tell you how she was herself.

One-night stands tended to be Tuesday's major source of affection—no, that's not true. She had boyfriends, and for longish durations, but she couldn't seem to kick the habit of surprise sex. I never put her down for it, and indeed, always listened with interest to her stories—the one about the guy whose Mafioso father told her to stop calling his son so Tuesday insisted that we go put a note on the windshield of the son's car at eleven p.m. and then it rained all night; the magician with the dog; the weight lifter who bit her; the chainsaw juggler from Venice Beach who later hosted "The Late Show"; the Yugoslavian hairdresser she gave oral sex to so he'd perm my hair. It was a capricious life-style that suited her well. She had the kind of fast personality that agreed with noncommittal sex. She was blonde, buxom, always on a diet, and this was just a form of dietetic love, a kind of "Romance Lite."

Having stoked my irritation up to the level of disdain, I finally went inside. Stratos had gone in a few minutes before, knowing that all was clear because Nikkos had left the house quickly, walking out to the trees, his shadow becoming obscured by theirs. It was a memorable night due primarily to the shadows and the silence. And to the strands of cool blue moonlight that entangled us.

I walked through a dark room, my face purposefully devoid of expression. I saw Tuesday sitting on a short stool in the white-washed hallway. She was crying. I immediately forgot my irritation. It's easy to be mad at someone for having a good time. When they follow their childish desires and get hurt you can't punish them more. I kept asking her in whispers what happened. Suddenly Nikkos loomed in the hallway. It was clear that we were now leaving so Tuesday refused to explain anything. It was a silent car ride back. So silent that it has washed away from my brain.

The next day I managed to drag it out of Tuesday. Apparently she and Nikkos started having sex together. (Which was really exciting, she added.) Then in the middle of it the interpreter entered the room (thinking perhaps that some translation needed to be done?). Nikkos argued with the interpreter briefly and then left. But who's to say he wasn't saying, "Go ahead . . . " in that characteristically aggressive Greek way? Or perhaps Spiros was reminding Nikkos of the perquisites that come with the job of translating for a Greek soccer star. Maybe his contract says that he gets every fifth girl or something. In any case, Tuesday was left there with Spiros who, instead of fucking her the normal way, took his penis out and started masturbating on her breasts. (As Sam aptly put it later, "You mean he jised all over her tits?" His vocabulary is primarily composed of words like "jised" [third person singular past indicative of "jism"].)

Spiros did indeed jis on Tuesday's tits and then left the room. Tuesday mopped herself up all the while cursing Greek men.

After we discussed what happened, Tuesday suggested that perhaps I was the "good girl" that they were initially attracted to and Tuesday represented the "attainable, sexual girl." Possibly. But I think this takes away any responsibility on Tuesday's part. I was less bothered by losing a male's interest than I was by gaining an awareness that men would always come first with Tuesday. And maybe I feared I was no different. My pride was a little wounded, but what did I really care about some vain soccer player who didn't even speak my language? I cared much more about having the truth thrust in my face: women have a hard time befriending women.

And yet I tried to remember that Tuesday is from Bozeman, Montana, and sometimes feels very nervous about being out of her element. She had changed her name and dyed her hair in order to become someone worldly and irresistible, but though it might have changed the way people looked at her, it hadn't changed her at all. In Greece she constantly drew attention to her sweet, young Americanness. Sometimes this was wonderful: we were given roses in a bank. Men continually flocked to us. As I told the story later, "They all thought she was Marilyn Monroe. And I was Marilyn's friend." She was like a doll to them, or a cream puff, or a sprite. Yet her little girl act could also threaten people, and not unintentionally. She only knew who she was if other women didn't like her. Sometimes she could be such a personification of all that is shallow, cheap, and pink about America. Yet she wasn't really any of those things . . . Well, she did wear a lot of pink, but it was almost out of a sense of humor. She was complex. Sometimes she seemed a spoof of herself—purposefully.

You could have a really good time with Tuesday. She was game for almost anything (obviously). One night we danced, drank ouzo, and smoked Turkish cigars until four a.m. in the lobby of this closed hotel with four young Greek men and this old Greek grandfather who ran the hotel. He kept pouring us drinks from his tiny bar hidden behind the front desk and we danced to new wave European music that for a year afterward played itself over and over in my head.

The last night before the cruise we walked up to the bottom of the Acropolis accompanied by a fast talking, not unattractive man from Sherman Oaks, California, who somewhat voluntarily joined us. We let him, seeing no reason to shun his company; he seemed a little lonely and we welcomed, momentarily, the familiarity of someone from our own country.

The three of us wound our way through narrow passages that almost entered people's homes but twisted cleverly before we were forced to open their front doors, that took us past lively restaurants with strings of small, thick light bulbs hanging off their awnings and Greek men dancing impressively for the few tourists there were. Below the Acropolis we sat on a rock wall and made thin American conversation which at any other time would have felt stilted, but here, overlooking Athens, was all we, still overwhelmed by the fact that we were actually in Greece, could handle. On the way back down we left him at one of the lively restaurants, all of us sensing the end of a moment, as a writer senses the end of a paragraph.

You can never really leave the United States; there are too many American tourists around to remind you of it. At least in the countries where game shows send you.

I was in a foreign country; I wanted to be with foreigners. What's the point in going to Europe and talking to Americans? I could have stayed home to do that. What I wanted was to experience "real life." Not a lot of people know what that is. They need known quantities, backyards, nine-to-five jobs. They think that is real life. But it's not. It's merely existing. Real life is more than just existing; it is taking calculated risks and reaping unexpected pleasures. It is a form of gambling. You don't find real life in Westwood[3] stores that sell magnetized rubber tacos for your refrigerator. You find real life by finding real people, by traveling, by conversing with bums, by learning how to sign for the deaf, by square dancing or reading or playing an instrument or joining a nudist camp or a million other things that force you to react spontaneously, to be, not as others have always perceived you, but suddenly fresh, suddenly undefined by the past. When a stranger asks you your name, tell him "Felicia" or "Trevor" or "Scout," just to see how it feels to be someone else. You may already do this to strange men who try to pick you up in bars. Once at Merlin McFly's[4] this obnoxious cab driver asked me my name and I said, "Micky." He thought I said "Vicky" and began to call me that. Tuesday came back from the bathroom and absentmindedly addressed me as Marissa. The cab driver frowned and leaned forward, "I thought you said your name was Vicky."

"Vicky, Micky, Marissa . . . I was an only child, my mother wanted more children."

I admit that in pursuing real life you may find more than you bargained for. I often end up caring about people I will probably never see again: people who contributed something to my life, to my humor, to my pursuit of truth; people who, though somewhat inebriated, valiantly tried to explain the concept of "*schmoozen*" to me as our cruise ship lunged port and starboard. (I wasn't necessarily playing dumb, they were just trying to demonstrate the finer nuances of the word.) In this case, the people happened to be German. In my admittedly limited experience, I've found that many Germans have a good sense of humor. But that's logical. The Germans of my generation probably have the most need of laughter.

---

3. An area in L.A. where UCLA is found. JMVB
4. Restaurant/bar in Santa Monica, CA. HMW

German Toymakers in Greece

There were two of them—German toymakers that is—but I only had an affair with one. Stephen and Klaus, two hearty, robust German lads, full of good humor, both a bit daft. I call them German toymakers but they actually owned two separate toy-making companies. They were convivial competitors. It was on the third day of the cruise when it happened: as we came back on the boat from the twenty minutes allotted at Patmos, Klaus asked if I wanted to drink some coffee with him. Sure, anything to get away from the planned activity. The activities of the day were all set forth on a handout, gaily decorated with nautical emblems, embellished with quaint Greek phrases like, "How much does that cost?" and delivered to each room every morning. Having been on a cruise ship once before, I realized that the planned activities, and the whole ship as well, were just past mediocre (the wrong way). For one thing, the toilets kept falling apart. Someone at breakfast jokingly mentioned this peculiarity and I exclaimed, "Yours too?" They were seemingly made from plastic do-it-yourself kits. All the parts stuck together by means of protruding pieces that fit into little holes and grooves—unfortunately not particularly well. Every time you wanted to go to the bathroom you had to put the toilet back together. I could deal with rebuilding the bathroom furnishings, but the fact that the swimming pool was never filled with water did annoy me a little. And the one time it was, the smoke stack suddenly belched forth cinders that burned tiny holes in people's clothing and singed parts of their skin. I was burnt above my navel and on my arm.

Incensed and in pain, I went to complain to the tall, big-boned Activities Coordinator, the cruise's spokeswoman. She saw herself as the mother of the ship and all the passengers as her children. She was the kind of woman who spoke her commas. Her lips, rather than a part of her face, were a separate limb. I imagine she could have eaten fried chicken without ever having to redo her lipstick. When I showed her where I was burned she cooed and clucked and acted appropriately horrified. She said, in her queer accent that I was never able to place, that something would surely be done, and oh, this has never, ever happened before, you must believe me, I am so, so very, sorry.

Being of a suspicious mind, I went back later and looked at the *undersides* of the deck chair pads. Sure enough, there were charred holes where a previous volcano of little charcoal bits must have landed during some other tourists' Greek cruise. But when one gets everything free how can one complain and really do the complaint justice? It seemed, in fact, that no one on board had actually paid full price; they were either travel agents or members of the New

York Press Club or entrepreneurs who sold these trips to game shows or finaglers finagling various other legitimate scams. Even Stephen and Klaus hadn't paid full fare.

My opting to miss out on the planned activities was a tactical maneuver because the events were worse than the toilets and singed flesh combined. Costume Night was an example of such moronity. The Activities Coordinator told us (somehow sounding, in that big-lipped way of hers, like Dan Ackroyd doing Julia Child) that materials would be provided to make costumes, and indeed they were if you can make a costume out of three sheets of stained crepe paper, an orange and black tutu that would fit a child of six, a paper crown, three or four belts without buckles, and a bunch of blue stars with glitter falling off. The costume party wasn't as dismal as the costumes, however. Someone did wonders with toilet paper and ketchup and came as a mummy, as good a use of European toilet paper as I have found. A few men came in their wives' clothing (always good for a laugh) and the rest wore their bed clothes and came as Greeks (naturally). It was a threadbare showing, but high spirits abounded — the quality of the costumes improving the more the spirits abounded.

Klaus came back to my deck chair to announce that they were out of coffee and were now serving soup. In his indefatigable way he shrugged, "Soup's good too," and handed me some. We smiled at each other, acknowledging a shared philosophy. I don't remember our first in a series of conversations, but I know it wasn't about the weather. I think we laughed at this couple on the ship who were on their honeymoon. Klaus had seen the husband eyeing me across the room and and I confirmed that he had put his hand on my leg when he sat down next to me on the deck chairs. He was newly married but kept finding moments to corner me and, unused to this type of flirtation and not sure what import to give it, I was embarrassed by his obvious gestures. Which isn't to say that I wasn't flattered. I was used to Tuesday getting all the attention and kept thinking that he must have mistaken me for her, though my breasts just weren't large enough for me to believe this. I suppose I was in my element and it showed. I was thin and tan and in Greece. I had never been happier. Happiness is an aphrodisiac. People are drawn to happy people, especially if they feel a lack in themselves. I always feel so odd at times like these because I like attention but hate anyone viewing me as competition. I found myself alone with his wife and her girlfriend one afternoon and I told them stories about my relatives, which made them laugh and realize I was no threat. And I wasn't. I had way too much personality for the likes of her husband.

Klaus and I discussed their relationship in depth and then all relationships.

{ 223 }

How to deal equitably with people. We had a similar outlook. Considering that I spoke no German and he very little English, our conversations were challenging. Often we were reduced to grammar school English, but this was good because we were both forced to reformulate our ideas. We couldn't use pet expressions, facile explanations, or pre-thought proofs to make a point; we had to break our thoughts down to the building blocks of language. We had to define each complex word with words known to first graders.

Though Klaus was very religious (the only book that he had read and re-read in his adult life was the Bible) and I have always been an atheist, we had arrived at the same philosophies about life, the same code of behavior, the same questions of morality and responses to them. And religion, oddly enough, never got in our way, as it does with many people, because Klaus felt no need to convert others. Without really being aware of it, we began spending all of our time together. This annoyed Tuesday as she was used to having all the boyfriends herself and wasn't enormously happy about being left alone. We didn't leave her completely alone though . . . there was still Stephen and also Miriam, a travel agent from Chile whom we had met, not to mention a whole boatload of people, including a very cute Israeli drummer that Tuesday had set her cap for.[5] Still, Tuesday was unsettled about my time away from her and my attention to Klaus.

Klaus told me from the start that he was married and had two daughters. "*Schmoozen*" with me was all right, but we could go no further. He explained kindly that if he had sex with me he would not be able to look his wife in the eyes; sex was what he reserved for his wife, his unspoken marital promise to her. I accepted this easily at first; we both did. Originally he had been more interested in me than I in him. Klaus was nice, but not what I thought of as my type. He was a big guy, as many Germans are. Nice looking, though not really handsome. But he had a grin that could make you like him instantly. Just thinking of him now, many years later, makes me smile. We began to feel a passion, as two people often do who think the same, and our early, facile agreements about fidelity put us to a very difficult test. We passed, not admirably, but we did pass. There was a desperate moment of desire and hot breath in Klaus's tiny cabin, but something, some thin strand of ethics or decency or truth, prevented us from that small, quick act of such eternal import. It wasn't that having sex was so much more wrong than what we were doing, but it was the turning point for Klaus of his fidelity. And I, respecting him, had to accept his self-imposed rules, whether he thought they came from himself or from God. I know that

---

5. Expression of MM's grandmother. HMW

if we had had sex we would have thought much less of each other and, consequently, have thought much less of all our philosophical debate because we would have demonstrated ourselves as shams. There are no two ways about it: self-sacrifice will always make you feel a better person. Yet, at the height of passion, feeling a better person seems attainable in a different fashion. Self-sacrifice is rarely on one's mind.

During one of our conversations I told Klaus all about my mother. I tried to paint a picture for him, tried to explain the nuances of my mother's behavior. (First I had to explain the word "nuance.") I wanted to hate my mother, but intellectually I couldn't let myself succumb to such a base emotion; if I did I would be no better than she. (Even as I write this, a little voice sounds off in my head, "Who are you to think you're better than your mother?!") I try to forgive her. ("For what?" the voice cries.) I try to understand a little of what her life must have been like. I told Klaus about the time she threw me to the floor and started pulling out my hair. I got lost in the thought. Where had I been when she went crazy? Was I standing in the . . . no, of course, I was in the bedroom . . . It was my closing cast party and I was finally relaxing. My musical had been well received.[6] I'd made some money. And now it was over. It was so nice to feel no pressure again. To not have everyone clamoring for explanations or motivations or where were we going to get a motorcycle helmet from.

It was the summer of 1980. I was sitting in my bedroom smoking pot with Prudence (the friend I had driven to Montana with) and my cousin Darlene. I was laughing. That's what began it . . .

She threw open the door. We all jumped. That familiar dread shot through my veins. She talked in a voice close to hell, low and accusatory.

"What do you girls think you're doing? Just what the hell do you think you're doing!?" Her voice began to rise. "I'm out there working my fingers to the bone while you're in here doing drugs. I should call the police. You're just drug addicts. I've raised a drug addict. And now she and her slutty, drug addict friends—" she began pulling Darlene by the arm "and her slutty, drug addict cousin think they can shit all over my house and shit all over me. Darlene, you're a tramp. I don't want to ever see you again in my house. After I let you stay here and go to school, this is how you repay me. You'll never amount to anything. You'll just sleep around and be the miserable person you always

---

6. *Life is a Low-Budget Musical,* written by Marissa "Moose" Minnion in 1979. It was performed in her hometown by a cast she had assembled. She also directed and starred in it. JC

were. And Prudence—" Prudence had already risen and was collecting her things to leave. She was crying.

"Mrs. Minnion, I'm really sorry. I should have known—"

"Prudence, shut up. You had me taken in for awhile. But you're a conniving bitch just like the rest of them. Get out of my house! All of you get out of my house!!"

The fifteen guests in the other room began to realize that something odd was happening. They started putting their drinks down and thinking that maybe it was time to leave. My mother, the gracious host, came out to say good-bye.

"I'm really sorry it had to end like this and I want you to know that I'm not mad at any of you—" she whipped her head toward me and her other personality yelled again in that voice from hell, "IT'S THAT SLUT OF A DAUGHTER THAT'S RESPONSIBLE! YOU CAN BLAME HER FOR THIS." Then she turned her head back and individually addressed people as they quickly made for the door. "Carl, I'm really sorry that you have to go. I want you to know that you're welcome here any time—IF IT WEREN'T FOR THAT BITCH IN THERE—" She turned back to Carl and shook his hand. Carl left quickly.

Her head turned again. "Marissa, get all your belongings and get out of here. You'd better take everything, because I'm going to destroy anything you leave. I don't want your trash in my house."

So I began trying to collect twenty-two years' worth of belongings in ten minutes, knowing that I would have to leave most of it and hoping that she wouldn't find the boxes in the garage with my name on them until she calmed down. Prudence kept trying to hug me and I said, "Please don't. If anyone shows kindness to me it will just make her angrier. I don't want her to hit you." Theresa, my fifteen-year-old sister, kept crying and I told her it was going to be all right. "Just go to your room and close the door and it will all blow over like it always does. I love you, Theresa." I hugged her quickly as we both kept crying and then I pushed her to her room.

"Marissa! Get the hell out here!" my mother yelled. I went, knowing that she didn't want me to leave. What she wanted was a human voodoo doll, some-one that she could abuse in order to exorcise the spirit that tormented her. I closed my eyes praying that this was a nightmare, that life would not always be so hard. Why did things have to happen like this? I knew why, though it didn't make the situation any easier. My mother was jealous. She was jealous that I had starred in a musical that I had written. That I had gone on TV (admittedly they were just local shows desperate for news), that I had an audience, basically that I had more attention than she. Here was her chance to be in the limelight. Here was "Rose's Turn," only she wasn't singing.[7] My mother raised me to be someone that most parents would have been proud of and then hated me for it.

"You think you can walk all over me. You think you're so much better than your father and me! We scrimped and saved to put you through school and this is how you show your thanks!" She began slapping my face. I ducked and then she shoved me to the floor and began putting her fingers in my hair and pulling with some result.

"You think you're too good for junior college!!" (This was always a sore point with her.)[8] She had me down on the floor and was punching me as I curled under her in an attempt to protect myself.

"You fucking cunt!" I yelled. Though it was muffled by the floor, she heard it.

"What did you call me?!" Enraged by my words, she became incredibly strong, as people are in times of great passion and high adrenaline. She was kicking me and hitting me and I was trying to push her off, but it was impossible. Many people were still there, but nobody moved. Everyone was stunned.

Immersed in all this hate, I suddenly felt a calmness come upon me, as if I were in a dream, watching this scene being enacted by someone else. I'd never called someone a "cunt" before. I've always thought it a cute word, a word for vigorous sex, but in this context it was bait. I realized that by calling her names I was just inciting her further. And I didn't want to call her names. I didn't want to hate her. I knew that somewhere in her mind she wanted me to get mad and lash back; she wanted me to go crazy also and I wasn't willing to do it. Suddenly I had the crux of the world before me: what does one who works for logic and reason do when confronted by blind and seething rage? I knew that fighting her ran counter to everything I'd ever believed in, that if I succumbed to retaliation I would be just like her. And in becoming her, I would go crazy. I remember thinking that I had to be the adult. I had to be clever. And fortunately, before I had to be too clever, my father pulled her off.

There are so many crazy, extraneous details to this story. I had bought a bottle of good Scotch to give my parents as a present for all their help. My mother found it in my room and accused me of drinking it on the sly. It was unopened.

---

7. "Rose's Turn" is the denouement, the penultimate song in the musical *Gypsy*, which portrays the life of Gypsy Rose Lee. Rose was the stage mother who pushed her daughters to perform. At the end of the musical Rose pathetically takes the stage to finally do what she'd only done through her daughters vicariously. JC
8. MM's parents both taught at junior college. HMW

I said uncomprehendingly, "I don't even like Scotch." They knew that. They'd been drinking Scotch for years and I always told them that it tasted like something you'd kill termites with. I hadn't lived at home in some time and I'd forgotten that my parents lived by different rules than other people. I wasn't innocent before being proved guilty. Rational thought had no foothold here.

My mother also accused me of letting Theresa's friend Bawahini get drunk. Bawahini was quite capable of getting drunk on her own. She was born in America but her parents were from India. She was soon to be the bride in a prearranged marriage; this most likely accounted for her wild behavior. She had gotten so drunk at the cast party that she had thrown up all over our patio. Though she was supposed to spend the night at our house because her parents were away, my parents, in anger, took her home and left her there, not even watching to see if she got in the door. When Bawahini's mother came home the next day she was scared to death because the front door was wide open and Bawahini was passed out on her bed with her legs spread and the hem of her dress thrown over her head. Her mother thought she had been raped and called the police. Bawahini came to and told her she'd merely been to a good party.

It had been a good party. But now I wished I'd never even heard of musical comedy. I wished I'd broken both arms before I ever learned to write. My upbringing conditioned me to give up, to give in, in fact, to do what my parents abhorred most: drugs. Drugs make it easy to dream of what you will never accomplish. They take away desire, move it to another hemisphere. I learned acquiescence early in life. Every time I wanted something badly I was thwarted. My parents would make promises they would never keep. They would make us do chores for an allowance and then decide that we didn't deserve an allowance. (This used to enrage me so much that I would draw pictures of my parents and then stab them with pencils; I would write incantations willing them to die; I was the only person I knew who actually *wanted* to go to boarding school.) I realized that the only power I had was indifference. I wouldn't be drawn by their carrot, their tidbit hung before me. They could make me do something, but they couldn't make me care. It is a practiced art, not caring. It is turning all bodily functions off. Or at least believing that you have. It is relaxing, feeling everything drop downward. It is one step before catatonia. It is acquired complacence. It is living death. And it is freedom.

Indifference takes practice, however, and after a year of college and living away from home I'd forgotten how, forgotten the need. I should have just left their house amidst my mother's raving, but I hadn't the presence of mind. She had too hypnotic a hold on me. Raising children is like having them under your spell. I was in a trance. I listened patiently as she accused me of more things

I knew I hadn't done. It was almost two hours after her initial outburst, but she wasn't through with me yet. I was exhausted and still she railed on. Tears were streaming down my face. I was so tired. I wanted to be from a normal family. My childhood welled before me. I wanted to cry for all the times I had been misrepresented, misunderstood, mistaken for a punching bag. I remembered the time my mother broke a yardstick on me. The time when I was nine when she pulled some of my hair out, and, brushing my hair the next day, wondered aloud why I was going bald. There was the time when she grabbed the wheel away from my father and was going to drive us all into the concrete wall of the freeway. I remember her keeping, under the car seat, a piece of wire cable that telephone linemen use, five-eighths of an inch in diameter, ready to "beat you to a pulp" for the slightest infraction. If you ask her, she'll deny it, but my memory has scars. And the psychological torment, done so well because she had a master's in psychology. My life left me drained. I stopped having emotion because there was no more to have.

Near the end of the second hour, I finally cracked. All I remember is whirling around the living room screaming things at the top of my lungs. I felt like I wasn't in my body. My father grabbed me and just held me. I suppose it was all he could do. My mother said disgustedly to me, "Oh, you're so theatrical." I don't believe I ever hated her more than I did at that moment.

Finally growing tired, my mother went into the other room to regroup. My father, throwing caution to the wind, let us escape. Prudence and I quickly walked down the street toward my cousin Darlene's apartment, a mile and a half away. I had on my nicest dress and a pair of tennis shoes. I was lugging a heavy suitcase in which I had tried to cram everything I owned. We walked painfully slowly, stopping often to rest, going from nowhere to nowhere. I kept thinking I was waiting for Godot. Why is it you always understand literature better after your parents throw you out of the house?

We made it to Darlene's and finally got to bed at four in the morning. Prudence left the next day and Darlene and I relaxed by the pool. That night Darlene, Theresa (who had managed to get away from home by saying she was going to a friend's house), my brother Paul, Darlene's boyfriend, several of his brothers and sisters, and I all played the board game "Family Feud." We didn't realize at the time how ironic it was.[9]

---

9. "Family Feud"—a TV game show consisting of two teams of families who compete with each other by trying to finish a phrase with a particular word, a word that most of the people polled across the country also came up with. For example, the board might display " _____ food." The

I was paranoid while we played, thinking that my mother would come hunt me down. My paranoia was only a few hours too early. The next morning at 7:30, my mother called to say that I'd better come get the rest of my stuff or it would be destroyed. (She'd found the boxes in the garage.) Then she hung up. As I hurriedly got dressed, I dreaded the scene that I knew was to come. It came sooner than I expected. My parents showed up at my cousin's house and demanded that we let them in. Darlene refused. My mother yelled (at eight o'clock on a Sunday morning) that she was going to kill Darlene. So Darlene called the police. My parents left. The police came. I told them everything, about my musical, about the pot, about my mother, everything. They were very nice. They said, "All we want to do is to help you get your stuff."

"Okay, but don't let her see you. Let me just see if I can get it without her getting all upset. If she sees the police, she'll go crazy."

They promised that they would stay out of sight unless she did something violent. They dropped me off half a block away and I walked to my parents' front door and rang the bell. My mother came to the door in all her reined-in fury.

"How did you get here?" she demanded.

"I walked."

"How are you going to take this stuff?" She loved having me in a bind.

"I guess I'll put it on the street and then carry it to Darlene's."

She slapped me.

"You're such a goddamn ungrateful—" she tried to slap me again and suddenly the police were there. She went crazy.

"You called the police! How dare you call the police!"

"I didn't call them."

"Who called them?!"

Calmly the curly-headed policeman said, "We're just here to see that your daughter gets her stuff and then we'll go."

"Don't call her my daughter! She's not my daughter! She's an ungrateful brat!"

"We just want to get her belongings."

"Do you know what she did! You should haul her off to jail. Do you have any idea what she did?" They nodded but she didn't notice. "She was smoking

---

sister on one team would say "Chinese food!" and the board would register that seventy-five percent of the people polled also said "Chinese food" and then her family would all yell "Good answer, good answer!" and pat her on the back. Basically a game which encourages mediocrity. JC

marijuana! In my house! Go ahead, haul her off to jail!! Why don't you?!" She was now screaming so loudly that the neighbors came out of their houses.

"We know what she did," the curly-headed officer said easily. "She told us. We just want to get her belongings."

"She told you?!" That really made her angry because I had taken the wind out of her sails. She thought for sure she'd gotten me there.

"You all smoke marijuana, don't you!! You all shoot up drugs. No wonder you won't take her away. You're on her side."

The other policeman spoke up. "We're not on anyone's side, ma'am, we just want to get whatever belongs to Marissa."

"Halden, they're on drugs. I don't have to speak to policemen on drugs, do I?!" She noticed the neighbors watching and yelled to them, "What the hell are you looking at! Get back in your house!"

She started to break down. She told the policemen, "You don't understand. You don't have ungrateful kids that you did their whole goddamn musical for; I sent out all the mailings, I got the whole audience. You're men." She said this with incredible disgust in her voice. "You don't know what it's like. We're rebuilding our cabin and now the dishwasher's broken again . . . " On and on she continued about every facet of her life. I started crying as I leaned my forehead against the front porch post. I thought, now everyone's going to see that my mother's nuts.

"I know how it is," the other policemen said. "I've got kids of my own."

"No you don't!!" she yelled, all fired up. (Nobody knew the trouble she'd seen.) "You don't know shit!"

The curly-headed policeman said again, "Look, we just want to get your daughter's stuff; now are you going to let us or are we going to have to get a warrant?"

My father, who had been looming in the entryway, said, "Zoe, let's let Marissa get her stuff and get them out of here. I'll drive it over."

My mother looked at him with intense hatred and then stormed to their room, slamming the door.

My father moved aside so that I could come in. I said nothing to him. I found him pathetic. All my life he had been cowed. When they fought he would always say, "I'm just nothing, Zoe. I'm a bastard. I don't deserve you."

And she would say, "Well you're right about that," laughing sadistically at the irony.

They had one fight. And they fought it constantly. My mother played the aggressor and my father always cried. I didn't know anyone else whose father cried. I knew that men were supposed to be able to cry, but his tears disgusted me. I would sit in my room and move my lips to their words, knowing what followed next, making a mockery of their fight, knowing when my father would beg my mother not to kick him out.

"Oh, please, Zoe. I won't ever do it again. I'm just no good. Please don't make me go," he would sob convulsively.

But occasionally he would have to go, for a day, never two. They needed each other in a perverted, little way. My therapist said not to be fooled by my father's passivity, however. Often the passive one can be the controller. They know the things to do that drive the manic one crazy. It's hard to say who controlled whom. I see my parents like a machine that's built of two necessary components, grinding away at each other until they both break down for good.

I gathered my belongings while the police and my father watched. As I took the boxes out to the driveway my mother emerged and, without warning, threw a box of mine down the driveway. My father got hold of her and coaxed her back into the house. When he came back out he said that he would drive my stuff to Darlene's. I would rather have gone with the police, but he insisted. As soon as all my stuff was in the car my mother came out and yelled, "What the hell do you think you're doing?!"

"Now, Zoe, I'm just going to take this stuff over for her. How can you expect her to get it there herself? You wanted her stuff out of the house . . . " His voice quavered with fear and emotion.

"If you leave, don't expect to come back."

"Now, Zoe."

"You're not coming back in this house," and she slammed the door, locking it.

We went to Darlene's and the cops followed us. They talked to my father for a while, but I didn't listen. Apparently, they all went back to my parents' house. I think they wanted to suggest counseling for my mother. Hah! The police didn't know my mother very well. I heard later that things got ugly. My father ended up trying to punch one of the cops and they almost took him off in handcuffs. The police got them both to promise to go see a counselor and they did, but only because they had to get something signed by the counselor or else go to jail. My mother yelled at the counselor, who was our family doctor, because he started talking about his kids and she said she didn't want to hear about his goddamn kids. So he let them go.

I went to my therapist a lot during this time. And I wrote. Writing helped. It always helps. It consoles. Writing makes me think there's more of me than me. It is my force field. My privacy. My magic fairy ring. I am protected. I needn't waste my time on "sniveling individuals and trivial minds."[10]

Writing keeps me from laughing in quiet places. It is my time line, the supplement to my life. I write so that the people who never met me can catch me in paperback.

I attempt to perceive my life in as much a literary sense as possible. Alcohol helps as well. A little wine just to give me enough fuzz, enough blur to be mesmerized by my mundane life. It helps, and yet why do I still feel this tremendous outpouring? I want the world to see the world through my eyes.

I am a vanguard. And even my thoughts walk before me. They surpass me, merely use my body as a vehicle. I am as the ink, the pen, the paper. My neurons are manipulated by thought, by intelligence far beyond my own. As soon as I stop to think, to use my brain, I am prodded on. It is not my duty to think. My thinking ceases the flow of thought. I must "unthink" in order to have thought. And yet "I," the concrete matter which is my brain upon which this ephemeral but higher level of thinking rests, become more intelligent. I learn, become learned. It is a synergistic exchange. To think the most, I must think the least. I must let thought itself take over, to breed. And, as with higher entities, procreation is a private matter. I leave it to itself.

But afterward I feel dazed. Spent. Used. Sated.

Thought can be quite sexual. Especially when it is all you have. But ah, when you also have sex, true, good sex, thought is even more intense. And I wonder, will there ever be one, ones, who understand, embrace, corroborate my mental fumblings? Who revel in thought for its pureness, its untainted state, untested by reality? Who cares for tests? Not I. Tests are only random samplings, attempts to substantiate reality when no one reality exists. And yet I know that tests are a pitiful necessity. They keep us in line. But I have no wish to be kept in line. Say you test a hundred people for the meaning of a word. No one knows it. Yet if the word is used in context, if its meaning is sidled in, then of what use was the test? Since all words are arbitrary anyway, since they were created for our purposes, does it really matter if such a word exists as long as the general concept is clear? If people didn't begin to use nonexistent words we would have no existent words to distinguish the nonexistent ones from.

You see, this is important to me because I am an impressionistic thinker: the whole concept is there, just a bit blurry, a bit hazy, with the verb before

---

10. MM, in her fall letter of 1982 to Larkin Hring, wrote, "If you quote things then it's not like you really said them." HMW

the noun or no verbs at all and then six strung together. Most people don't appreciate the telling, just the imparting of knowledge. Not that I should necessarily be appreciated—just tolerated. I'll even allow them to feel a bit superior. I don't just march to a different drummer, I march to a very bad French horn.

I believe that I am an impressionistic thinker because I have so many different rooms in my brain, two-dimensional rooms: dark chambers, crypts, nooks, crannies, niches, alcoves, hollow cavities, all housing hallowed thought. Rooms filled with numbers, theories, origami, and musicals; religion, atheism, ambivalence, and confusion; Montana and irony, eggs and marmalade; fisticuffs, figured bass, and iambic pentameter; rooms I only enter when I'm stoned; rooms that produce art; rooms with large dictionaries; rooms w/vu; rooms without enough oxygen, which causes me to be very bilious and consequently believe that I am the only one truly conscious of the world spinning; rooms with self-confidence; rooms with piercing fear; little rooms, holes really, under the stairway where I sit with trepidation; oubliettes lined with Gothic mysteries which I read on the sly; rooms with baked brie and ballroom dancing, with Poland Chinas and other porcine beasts, with sleight-of-hand and cloven foot, with saunas, Jacuzzis, the John Paul Getty Museum; trendy rooms with neon, poetry, drum solos, and sushi; rooms with contemplation, dim lights, and imperfect perfect pitch; rooms with the "muchness of [too] muchness"; rooms with excess sensory stimulation; and mostly rooms larger than my whole head, rooms that turn my mind inside out and become the universe.

And this, this very specific room where I continually battle my crazy mother, I enter hedgingly, unwillingly but unfailingly. Accidentally I plunge, headfirst and, sprawled upon the floor, I try to stand and am knocked down. Was what I did really that bad? I never know. She raised us to never know. To never know if she was going to hit or caress us.

My father accuses me of being addicted to drugs. He says that L.A. is a bad influence. And that my therapist is making me crazy. They don't recognize that they have simply lost power over me. I am an adult now.

It seems so long since I've been pent up in this room, paced the floor, stared at the gray walls, read the morose graffiti, kicked the used Kleenex on the floor. Nothing's changed since I was last here—when was that? March? At least I've let three months go by before I stumbled in here, dazed, bloated, alcohol on my breath, forbidden food on my lips, a victim once more. Again writing the same morose graffiti, cleverly penned at times, but saying nothing new.

I wish I could just instantly combust. I don't want to go through the effort of dying, I just want to be dead. I tried to kill myself. I tried cutting my right wrist. I just don't have sharp enough knives. I got them from a game show. My whole life is somewhat of a spoof.

I always say that Monopoly wouldn't be much fun if all the squares were blank, but suddenly I remember that I've never much cared for Monopoly. For one thing, Paul always won. (And look at his life now . . . so much for success at games predicting success in life.[11]) I never liked games, especially those which emulate life. I now realize that this doesn't bode well for my liking life either as was recently brought to my attention by the fact that I started cutting my wrist. Killing oneself is ritual. And I hadn't any pot, having decided that I absolutely must stop smoking it because it hurts my throat so much, but pot has always been my escape valve, my very precise destruction that requires a certain detachment, a certain following of set patterns, certain utensils. Killing oneself has these same requirements. To be able to stick a knife into one's skin requires a mind that has drugged itself, but not with external opiates. The mind can create its own euphoria in order to alleviate the pain it feels or imagines it feels. And once one starts cutting it becomes easier. If I try to kill myself again it will be that much simpler having already had a dress rehearsal. I wasn't so much going to kill myself as feel what it was like if I decided to.

Mostly I'm just tired. I haven't any interest in life if it continues to be so difficult. I admit, I'm a baby. Why do it if it's not fun? That's always been my philosophy. I just can't get myself excited enough to live. I never learned to rejoice in merely waking up in the morning or going to work or watching TV. I also fear that the pattern is too strong; my history, genetic or environmental or both, is insidiously weaving itself, kudzu-like, around my brain. I try so hard to shake it, to rip it out, twist out of its grasp, but I'm beginning to wonder if it's even worth the effort. I'm beginning to suspect that the outcome was set all along. After three and a half years of therapy I feel no further along. I did feel so, but I think it was an illusion. I've never tried to kill myself before. I just can't see a way out. Death wells up at every turn.

This bleak image of my mother keeps coming back to me, the time when she was sadly putting away her suitcase in the hall closet. She had packed it

---

11. Paul was kinda lost. For example, he had this theory about the number three describing the universe: "You know, there's zero, one, and negative one; positive, negative, and null; lepton, meson, and baryon; the stone, the paper, and the scissors—"

"Wait, Paul," I said, "that's a game."

"I *know*," he said impatiently, "but the stone loves the scissors."

"No, the stone *breaks* the scissors," I corrected him in a sisterly fashion.

"No the stone *loves* the scissors because the scissors make the stone feel powerful and that's why people mate." (MM)

to leave, to run away from a life of two kids and a husband and not really a whole lot else. She is crying as I watch her, defeated; my five-year-old brain trying simply to make sense of her desperation, my thirty-one years of acquired wisdom now looking back and realizing that she had accepted her fate of eternal hell right there in Pasadena. Our family moved, but hell followed along. It's hard to escape hell when they've packaged it along with one's software.

I've painted my mother as the evil character, but only because of the power she had over me. She was no more evil than I; she was just very unhappy with her life. I remember her recalling a time in her childhood when an uncle boasted that he could pin a glass of water to the wall. It was a family gathering and cousins, aunts, and uncles filled the room.

"Oh hell, I've dropped the pin," he said impatiently. He motioned to my mother, "Sis, come over here and pick this up."

("I didn't even have a real name," my mother sighed in the telling.)

Dutifully she bent down to pick up the pin and, without warning, her uncle poured the water on her head.

What can a kid really do around adults who are assholes? Another in that situation might have become the clown or kicked the uncle, but my mother just took it all in and seethed. To this day I believe that my mother has a fascination for water. Angry because a neighbor refused to remove his car from a driveway they shared, she sprayed him with a hose and told him to "cool off." One time in a trailer park she was mad at the neighboring trailer for making noise and threw a cupful of water at them which landed directly in my face—I was sleeping in the car in front of our trailer. I rolled over and sighed. I hated her being so weird, but I was grateful when it wasn't directed at me. I didn't even mind the water. The punishment was rarely as bad as the vengeance. When I told my aunt my water theory she said that my mother admitted to her that she's always having dreams about water. And my aunt's daughter, Olive, chimed in indignantly, "She threw a drink at me once." My brother Paul said that she also sprayed his bridesmaid. (Not at the wedding; he never had a wedding. My mother didn't think that he was old enough and called up all the guests and told them it was canceled—my brother was twenty-five.) Paul said she sprayed this girl with the hose for a full minute. Now I cannot honestly comprehend someone allowing themselves to be squirted by my mother for a full minute. I think the bridesmaid should have had the wits to know that you don't get near my mother when she has a live hose.

Like my grandmother, my mother was forever trying to correct wrongs that had been instigated by people long dead. There is no satisfaction in that. I think it only makes you more miserable. I sense myself continuing the pattern. But

I'm just a bit braver than my mother. I won't accept a life that I hate. I will leave. My life is better than hers, but my descent into oblivion seems just as powerful. I would not, at this time, lay bets on which side will win.

I admit, there is solace in desperation. I am proof that one can know exactly what one is doing and still succumb against better judgment. Intellectually I see so clearly why I am this way, how my childhood laid the groundwork for self-punishment, what I must do to stop my masochism . . . yet do I stop? If one as clear-headed as I (though with muddy emotions) still cannot seem to change, what hope have those poor souls who've grown up in the ghetto or a war zone or in a more hellish existence than I can even imagine? If they haven't an awareness of their form, how can they hope to change their content? And I, aware as I am of my makeup, of my container, will I be able to alter my contents? Or will I break the vessel and scatter that within, leaving only random pieces of myself here on these pages? I do not know and the question only interests me in a detached, literary sense. I suppose I should care, but if I do kill myself I will be just another story which is only a little bit more than what I am now. Killing oneself for a bit of fame . . . I am that silly, I confess.

"Marissa?" Klaus's voice suddenly brought me back. I shook my head slightly. I had forgotten where I was.

I looked at Klaus and frowned sadly. How could I possibly explain all that? And why should I? Because of my constant need to use the world as my therapist? Yes, but it's more than that. In my sharing of such stories, not only do I understand things better, but others do as well. Others have a glimmer of a life unknown to them. I explained to Klaus that if people have been hurt by me it is because they were trying to control me, to get something from me. If my mother has been disappointed by me it is because she wanted to live through me to the point of funneling her personality through my body. The reason that the pot upset her so much was not that it was a drug—she had tried pot before (she'd even given my brother back an ounce that she found in his sock drawer and told him to keep it somewhere else)—but rather, her anger stemmed from our having been close through my whole musical: I had relied on her to help me; she had thrown cast party after cast party, sent mailing after mailing, forced my father to build the set and my sister to be stage manager, and because of all this she saw herself as closer than my closest friend—she saw herself as me. And suddenly here I was, fracturing this vision.

I am a mirror for people's projections of themselves: they see me stupid because they find no sense in theorizing; they see me cruel because I won't be possessed by them; they see me hurtful because they've given me power to hurt them. This book is, in effect, a defense of my life, a tying of loose ends, a forum for everything I've ever done to come together and create a complex montage that gives credence to my existence, that finally yields a logic, a reason for my mind, for my having lived. It's nothing more than any-one else would want.

More than a defense of my life, however, I want to make a defense for all lives, for every human being that one comes into contact with, not just those people starving in other countries. We must care as much for the person stand-ing next to us as we do for those who are suddenly designated as "People to Save." Recently we have seen a rash of crusades to stop starvation. One could say it's about time. Or one could say it's about money. The only way we can save other countries, other people, is if it becomes a fad: if a rock band donates their concert proceeds, if all these big celebrities get together and their record-ing session makes *People* magazine, then saving people's lives becomes big business. I know, I know, I sound the complete cynic, and if commercialism is the only way to prevent people from starving then the method should go un-challenged. And yet nothing should go unchallenged. Do not misunderstand me. I am not suggesting that all these benefit concerts should not have been done. I am saying that it is a sad fact of our era that we need MTV to awaken people to human suffering.

This argument started with my friend Colin. He played the humanitarian well until it came to his personal life. He made eloquent speeches about the starving Ethiopians and then, as I ventured an opinion, he told me flatly that I didn't know what I was talking about. (Like he knew starving Ethiopians.) Decency starts with the person next to you. It's a small but important step. Starving is quite far removed from rudeness and yet they are both multiples of that same insecure indifference which, the larger it gets, the more evil and powerful it becomes.

Being decent to people is not painful and in fact, once one starts, it can feel pretty good. If being decent made me feel absolutely terrible I probably wouldn't do it. I admit there is a pay-off – that is the practicality of life. But after practicing reasonableness for so long, it becomes a habit. One doesn't need to be rewarded every single time. Just like those rats that continue to push the bar even when they don't get food,[12] I don't always require someone to match my

---

12. Intermittent reward theory—rats given food every time they press a bar will stop pressing the bar the first time they do not get food. Rats given food intermittently will continue pressing the bar even when they do not get food because they have been conditioned to receive food, not every time, but eventually. KLL

kindness with kindness. Not retaliating has become too strong in me. I refuse to be merely a reaction. It gets down to pride, really.

See, I want to demonstrate that my philosophy is not a religious, fanatical, Katherine Coleman[13] kind of thing—rather, it is eminently practical. It is weights and measures, cause and effect. It is math. Higher Math.

And here we have the principal theory that Moose was trying to promote throughout her short life: the Arithmetic of Reason, Social Algebra, the Vector of Decorum. What she was really saying is that everything we know is a system . . . even human rights.

We must have a system in order to conceptualize, in order to discriminate, in order to have pattern recognition. Structure is the foundation to understanding, form, the vessel of content; so everything, in effect, is math.

She quotes again the Life Science Library volume on mathematics:

"[Math] . . . can apply to our world and universe because . . . [it was] designed . . . to apply to every possible world and universe that might be imagined along logical lines. . . . [Math] reaches into a realm of such ultimate sophistication that the truth or non-truth of any given premise no longer matters. What does matter . . . is that the premise be correctly reasoned to its conclusion."[14]

So math is fantasy, but a very specific fantasy. It is "What if . . . then . . . " Math is giving entities a one-to-one correlation with a meaningful label and then forming patterns which are consequently meaningful. But we apply the meaning. That is math. Nature only gave us the stones, we counted them and gave them a purpose; we gave them *our* purpose.

There is old math, new math, algebra, and calculus; there is topology, physics, logic—all of them forms of math; there is math of a very elevated nature, such as Einstein's Special Theory of Relativity, and then there is what I've termed "Higher Math," because it deals with human beings, and that should be considered the highest of all. Higher Math is human decency, analytical goodness, all the benefits of religion without the guilt, without hell, without phoniness, dogma, or pretension.

Religion was invented to keep people in line; it's when the platitudes become

---

13. Katherine Coleman was an evangelist who smiled a lot. HMW
14. *Mathematics,* David Bergamini and the Editors of Time-Life Books, © 1969 Time, Inc. (MM)

hackneyed, the "Hail Marys" become glib, and the ritual seems only pomp and circumstance that the dogma must be discarded and we must remember again what it means to be human.

Klaus saw the Bible as still the most important book that existed. Perhaps it is, in terms of a code of behavior for people who feel more secure in having right and wrong spelled out for them. But when a book like that becomes so old that the examples are no longer applicable for today's sense of ethics, where do we turn for help? Who can really get behind "Do not covet thy neighbor's wife"? Especially if one has a neighbor whose wife needs a little coveting because he sits watching TV and drinking beer every day. The Bible is like trying to navigate by the stars in a world that uses satellites and navigational computers to travel: you can still cross the ocean, but you cannot be too choosy about where you end up or how long it takes.

I realize that I tread on dangerous ground when I get into morals and ethics because I'm probably better at comedy. (My life is certainly more funny than it is moral.) But I've tried so hard to be good all my life, to finally please my parents I guess, that striving to be good remains in my life even if my parents do not. Forgive me my moment of conversion. Blot it out of your mind if you wish. I really haven't any more answers than the next guy, I just think I do and I'm long-winded.

Klaus found me long-winded, but he liked that about me. We liked that about each other. We had lots of opinions. We seized every moment for conversation as we felt our time together drawing to a close. When our cruise took us to Istanbul for two days of sight-seeing, I went on the German tour. "I find it interesting to 'do' one country in the language of another," I explained to Tuesday, who was frustrated by my leaving her to her own devices. She was afraid of being sold into the white slave trade and grew very upset when I refused to change my mind. I told her she could come with us, that Klaus would translate all the really good tour jokes, but her powerlessness over me angered her and, instead of coming with Klaus, Stephen, and me on the German tour, she threatened to move out of the apartment we shared when we returned home to L.A. She thought this would change my mind, but I merely decided that if Tuesday could scream in Istanbul like she'd been screaming in our cabin, then she had enough balls to fend for herself and maybe, if captured, would even like white slavery.

I want to clarify that Tuesday means well, but when she feels cornered by things foreign she tends to cower behind behavior that she has seen on "All My Children." She uses tactics that have become second nature to her: brittle repartee, laughter disproportionate to the joke just told, a continual quest for men, sharp put-downs of people who don't fit her qualifications for "cool." Something about Tuesday bothered Klaus. He said, searching for the right words, "I have never met someone so . . . wrong." He frowned, not satisfied at his ineloquent and bald way of putting his feelings. I tried to explain that she was insecure and young, as she was, but I wonder if Tuesday will always be young, young in a self-involved way. And if one day she will suddenly turn old, suddenly become soulless as she realizes that the things she has always treasured do not become a woman no longer able to play the pert, young thing. (Long, bubble-gum pink acrylic nails seem somehow anachronistic on wrinkled, arthritic hands.) Those who live for the superficial, ephemeral values of the culture will one day find that all they have left are several ceramic Pierrot masks on their wall, Dexatrim in their cupboard, and too many Michael Jackson records.

I don't want to paint an incorrect portrait of Tuesday. I want to make her a complete person, list things to weigh on her positive side. However, if I list them now it will only appear to be a pathetic attempt at being fair. And one doesn't write to be fair. One writes to be accurate.

I saw Tuesday recently. She called me to meet for dinner. She always calls me. I never call her. She always asks me excitedly about my book. I answer hedgingly, knowing that if she knew the bent it is taking she would never talk to me again. How can I have such duplicity? Should I hurt her now or later? Should I take out every reference to her and be untrue to myself? Or untrue to her? And where does this fit into my scheme of decency to others? Have I just shown myself to be a fraud? And if not, how then do I justify it?

I don't.

I just present life honestly; I don't hide my vested interest, my hurt at her dealings with me or her choosing shallow, Hollywood values over true friendship. And now I'm polite when we meet; I try to be interested in her current boyfriend, or her mini-hoopskirt (the latest in fashion), or the short film her comedy team is shooting for the Playboy Channel, but I'm not really interested because I'm partly jealous and partly disgusted. I want to be in her position but I don't want to be her. And I believe that one is not possible without the other.

I took Tuesday to Greece because she was my best friend. But "best friend" is a term easily used until tested. I had to be on the other side of the world to find this out. I had to be in Istanbul.

Istanbul is a dark, twisted city. Men, wiry and suspicious, overrun the streets and hang in the shadows. Women are kept wrapped in robes, cloistered indoors. Istanbul is a place I long to go back to because it is unlike any other place I have been. As Greece is light and airy, Turkey is dim and laden with fear. But it is fascinating.

The five of us (two German toymakers, two American innocents and a travel agent from Chile) disembarked the night we arrived and walked just a few streets away from our ship. We weren't on a tour. (The "Nightlife in Istanbul" tour was to start in an hour. All of us were going on that. It was the German tour the next day that Tuesday wanted me to forgo.) We had decided that we wanted to see the "real" Istanbul first before the tour started, but we weren't prepared for the squalid sights we saw just steps from our ship. We were overcome by the darkness, by the poverty. Tuesday remarked later that there were a lot of shops that sold lights: ornate chandeliers, gas lanterns, anything to illuminate the sordid darkness. Soldiers were everywhere with loaded rifles. One felt suffocated by the lack of freedom. We tried to walk down a street that had two boards crossed in the middle of the entrance. We thought they signified some type of construction work in progress. Men lined the street, many of them hunched and deformed. They reminded me of rats, the kind of rats that are so well camoflauged that it takes you a few seconds to realize how very many of them there are. One of the men, as we started walking past the crossed boards, made this loud, rapid clicking noise with his tongue, effectively stopping our progress. Klaus managed to understand from a man who spoke pidgin German that this was the street of the prostitutes and women were not allowed. They eyed us with suspicious curiosity. I felt myself get goosebumps. After this disturbing encounter we all returned to the boat and decided to wait for the "Nightlife in Istanbul" tour because the foreignness of the country scared us.

The next day, on the German tour, Klaus, Stephen, and I saw mosque after mosque and rug store after rug store where beautiful rugs were flung before us, unrolled by a quick snap of the wrist and then piled on top of each other. We were offered ouzo or beer or Turkish tea while we watched this demonstration, this dance of the rugs, and the rug sellers spoke the language of the tourists, fluent German for the Germans—until they discovered that I was American and spoke no German. Confusion cluttered the rug sellers' faces and Klaus was amused by their incomprehension. The Germans all made German jokes about *schmoozen* and soon it was time to leave. Next we were taken to a museum with huge emeralds and other enormous jewels, but we barely had time to see them as our tour guides prodded us on. Anyway, I was more interested in the children, dressed all in black, on a school field trip. They were even more quickly trooped through the museum, each having to keep close hold on the child in front of them. They said hello to me in English and I said hello back. I told them my name and I learned from their teacher, who spoke

English, "*Neel sis stenis*," which means "How do you do?" I tried to learn all the children's names, but there were too many and they shouted them out to me too fast, vying for attention.

Ten minutes later, in another part of the museum, a little boy yelled "Mareesa" and soon all the children were yelling "Mareesa, Mareesa," and asking me about America. The Germans, not having seen me talking to the children, thought it was amazing that they all knew my name. Klaus smiled. I was touched. This is why I travel. To have strange children shout my name in a cramped museum. To realize that even in a dark, forboding country, children still act like children, their minds unclouded by their country's pervasive control. Seconds later, however, I turned my head and saw children just a few years older doing a military goose step and practicing war with sticks for guns. A chill ran over me and I realized that if you don't get to people while they're young, it is soon too late to civilize them, too late to instill the type of etiquette that will ensure the humanity of our species. It is places like Istanbul that make me wonder if my silly little beliefs in the logic of human rights will ever make a difference to a desperate and insecure world.

It isn't evil that permeates the world; don't for a second think that it is. I don't believe in evil. I call it by its real name: fear. It is fear that makes men fight wars, the rich hold tight to their money, the oppressors control the oppressed. To call it evil renders it immutable; to call it fear allows us to see it undisguised, to perceive a solution. A solution that will be a long time in coming, but a solution nonetheless.

Perhaps you argue, "Fear is too simple an answer. It's more complex than that."

I agree it's complex, but the root is still fear, insecurity, needing to dictate truth to others in order to trust that it is truth ourselves. Those who are afraid that there isn't any meaning will fight to the death to prove that there is. And if that isn't fear, I don't know what is.

It is this insecurity that makes religious groups solicit door-to-door, that creates fads, that forces everyone to be like everyone else. We are social creatures. Our decisions are made as a group. We think this makes the decision correct. But it only makes it happen.

Theory of Consensus

(To be illustrated on fingers.)

If there were only five people in the world and four of them believed in killing and one didn't, there would soon be no one left to believe in anything. Now if only one of them believed in killing and four didn't, they'd lock the one up, and all die of natural causes. Therefore, the absolute morality of killing is irrelevant because it has little bearing on whether or not people want to kill. If they do want to kill they will justify it and make it moral. *Life isn't run by morals but by consensus.*

Klaus called me *"Blint Huneken,"* which he said means "lovely blind chicken." In Germany they have an expression which says, "Even a blind chicken can sometimes find food." I think he called me this because, without any real guidance (parents, religion, Girl Scouts, whatever), I have managed to stumble upon a preferable system of living. It's harder to live one's life by trial and error and yet, one discovers the truths and untruths for oneself and occasionally ventures into areas as of yet uncharted. Those realms where neither God nor alcohol nor pop psychology nor anything but one's brute intelligence (what I think of as highly evolved gut reaction) and the desire to survive can see one through. And once one is through, a clarity, sometimes even a philosophy descends. It's almost as if one has to be willing to forgo sight in order to eventually see. Because although it may seem that there is light, we are really all in the dark. We operate blindly and, blindly, think we can see. But, as I have said before, when you stab in the dark long enough, every now and then you hit something. And every now and then I find food.

It is here that Moose Minnion's narrative dissipates into unraveled ends of disparate stories. She was in the process of weaving these very memoirs together when her cataclysmic imbibition of the oil of a Brazil nut (*Bertholletia excelsa*) sent her off into a comatose, twilight world from where the doctors have little hope of her return. All of us have tried, some more than others, to piece together her life through her writing, as well as through interviews with friends and associates. Would that we had had her to guide us, but at least her prose is crafted so as to carefully preserve her personality. In the death-defying words of Moose Minnion:

If you can't see the movie—read the book.

Happily, there is now a book to read.

Epilogue

In the midst of preparing this manuscript for publication, we received a joyous phone call informing us that Marissa "Moose" Minnion has come out of her coma and rejoined the living.

We feared she wouldn't approve of this book, yet, not having even read it in its final form, she gave us the go-ahead to publish it anyway. Her last words, as she boarded the plane to Greece (where she is to recuperate), were, "Mail it to me!"

Alas, we don't have her address.